Blue
Winnetka
Skies

Ron MacLean

Swank Books • Boston

Cover art by Karin Weiner, used by permission of the artist
Cover design by Kroner Design, Somerville, MA (www.kronerdesign.com)

Printed in the United States

LIBRARY OF CONGRESS
CATALOGING- IN- PUBLICATION DATA
Ron MacLean, 1958
    Blue Winnetka Skies / Ron MacLean. – 1ˢᵗ American ed.
        ISBN 0-9744288-1-7

Swank Books
P.O. Box 447
Jamaica Plain, MA 02130

"There's a world of trouble
tryin' to take its turn,
I can hear it shaking underground."

–   Gillian Welch

1.

They drove through the night, following Interstate 10 across the border into California. The Winnebago moved gracefully and they kept the speed down, stopping only occasionally to add some food item to their stockpile – something one or the other of them decided, as soon as they thought of it, that they couldn't live without.

"Tapioca pudding," he'd say. "Those little plastic cups." And they'd visit supermarkets, combing aisles of as many stores as it took until they'd find it. This was their job. To take care of each other. To keep darkness from closing in.

Cole stretched. He watched the highway slide by through his own pale reflection in the windshield. Deep-set green eyes. Soft mouth.

"Let's sing cowboy songs," Joanna said. She sat behind the huge steering wheel with a kind of glee. Swiveled in her seat. She loved to drive, even when she was too tired to do so safely.

A canopy of stars stretched above them. The road to Blythe spread straight to the horizon. It hadn't rained in days, felt like it would never rain again.

A smile ripened on Cole's face. He examined himself in the glass. Squared his jaw. Sang softly.

"As I walked out on the streets of Laredo
as I walked out in Laredo one day."

He couldn't remember when he'd slept last. It seemed important that they keep moving. That they stay awake as long as they could. Fortify against the crash they both knew would come.

Joanna scooched forward on the seat. Sipped from a bottle of Coke. "Not that one," she said. "The other one."

They'd bought those flexible straws that bend at the top. She had one with a red stripe.

Cole made his lips into a thin line. He couldn't decide if he looked rugged now, or if the dimness of his image in the glass simply allowed that illusion.

Joanna sang,

> "Oh give me land
> lots of land
> under starry skies above.
> Don't fence me in."

"I have a confession," she said. She had small, strong hands. "Don't hate me."

"Don't worry." Cole was happy to listen. To drift. Open his eyes occasionally on desert night. Wide open country. "Shoot."

She took a deep breath. "My favorite version is Sinatra's. It's got this great horn arrangement. He recorded it during the war."

Through the enormous windshield Joanna could see stars, make out the tops of foothills. She felt herself, the two of them, soaring above the desert. She felt twenty, though she knew she no longer looked it. Neither of them did. Traces of gray in hair. Faces faintly lined.

"World War Two, I think," she said. "Does Sinatra go back that far?"

No wind. No clouds.

She sang,

> "Let me roam
> through the wide
> open country that I love.
> Don't fence me in."

She rubbed the back of her neck. Black hair, traces of faded magenta along with the gray. "But maybe it wasn't Sinatra at all. You know how that happens sometimes? You make it a certain way in your head?"

Cole spun in his seat. A full 180 degrees. He was glad they'd opted for the Winnebago. The subtle interior touches that make a mobile house a home.

2

He wished the radio worked, although there was something nice about the quiet, the fact that it wasn't a choice, just something you had to accept, like a flat tire, or a flat Coke, or eight miles to the gallon. It allowed time to simply occupy the space of being together. It gave their conversation room to float in and out, to surprise each other, to be pleased at the simple sound of a human voice.

She sang,

> "I want to ride to the ridge where the west commences
> gaze at the moon until I lose my senses
> I don't like hobbles and I can't stand fences.
> Don't fence me in."

Cole raised and lowered the armrest. Delighted in the convergence of movement and their cocoon-like world.

Refuge and protection, wherever they may go.

A harp-shaped marquee.

The letters W-I-N-N-E-T-K-A spelled out in fading, lime sherbet-colored script across the top.

Below, more modest in both size and type style, DRIVE-IN.

Add an Indian princess, buckskin-clad, brightly colored beads, outlined and belted in long-neglected neon. Braided hair, bright smile, a drum major's baton. You can still imagine the light, the colors – deep orange, fiery red. How the baton, glowing yellow, would fly up into the night, twirl in a neat neon circle, and land safely in her hand, every time.

The blacktop is cracked. A rusted spotlight planted inches above the ground. In better days the fixture, no doubt shrouded by bushes, shined its light on marquee and princess, green and aqua blue, crimson and sepia – a wonder.

Now, dust encroaches, drifts unabated across the entrance. Through the abandoned refreshment stand. Between the undulating rows where once cars would maneuver in search of the perfect view. Where poles with long-neglected speakers jut like hitching posts in a Western town whose gunfights still echo, where you sense that if you could listen clearly enough, tune your ear to the proper frequency, you'd discover miracles.

They stopped at places they'd read about and wanted to see. The Natchez Trace, the Badlands, the Black Hills of South Dakota. They etched an erratic line across the country, gleaning edible treasures from small-town markets, choosing destinations based on the sound of a name – Hoxie, Arkansas; Alamogordo, New Mexico. They moved west not by design but by implicit consent, thinking of foods they wanted to gather, putting miles, vast sections of the country, between themselves and what lurked behind them. The midwest as a buffer zone.

"You haven't gotten any smarter with age."

Joanna behind the wheel. East of Indio. The Mojave around them, all expanse and shadows.

Cole wore his sunglasses, despite the darkness. California made sense to him. It was where you went for a new start. "What did you expect?" he said.

"Never mind." Her right foot tingled, half asleep. She tapped it on the floor. Wiggled her toes. The Winnebago slowed noticeably. "I expected you might be smarter is all."

As sensation returned to her foot, she pressed the accelerator again. She had no use for automatic pilot. She relished contact with the pedals, her foot and the vehicle's speed.

"I thought it would be different out here," Cole said.

"It is. Look around you." Headlights cut a swath of road and dust. She could feel the hills in the distance. "Think like you're seeing it for the first time. Like it's only just been discovered."

Cole pushed the sunglasses on top of his head. Straw-colored hair extended in a braid between his shoulder blades. He craned his neck to see the broadest possible stretch of night sky. "I mean, I thought I'd *feel* different out here."

"You will," she said. "You're tired is all."

4

Their faces dim reflections on the windshield, imposed on the night desert.

"How about you," he said. "Do you feel different?"

She fumbled in the tray between the seats. "I'll tell you how I feel," she said. "I feel like having a Mallo Cup." Her fingers found one. She rearranged herself in the seat. Leaned forward. Shook away sleepiness.

He wondered if she hurt any less. She had a runaway teenage son. She had broken a heart in Pennsylvania. But Joanna was the queen of bob and weave. Joanna always knew the location of the nearest exit.

They passed a green highway sign. *Indio 46. Los Angeles 183.*

"Almost the end of the road," he said.

She turned to scowl at him. Red-rimmed eyes. The sweet taste of chocolate and coconut. "Don't be unpleasant," she said. "I thought you were going to be different out here."

He smiled. Spoke to her reflection. "I'm trying."

Interstate 10 stretched straight west, as if it would never end.

"Try harder." She pressed her foot on the accelerator. The Winnebago surged forward. "Have a Mallo Cup."

Ten movie screens. Wooden frames and giant whitewashed panels. Shrouded skeletons that loom over this still-quiet corner of the valley. Define this dusty stretch of real estate. A dozen acres, circumscribed by beech trees and live oak, by gently rolling foothills. Odd how the land lies undeveloped. No housing. No mall.

You get the sense that if you were to drive along a row and pull into a parking space and turn on an old toaster-shaped speaker, you might hear a radio report, frozen in time, that would recount the fall of this place, that would unfold the tragedy lurking beneath the dust.

You can hear the voice, a confident echo of years, a conjurer's tone carrying magic.

Like the movies themselves, beaming mystery and hope into the desert.

Ten screens.

Showing nightly.

Words of promise that whispered enchantment into countless valley nights. Nights where something like alchemy would waft from the screen, wend through the wide streets, stir the languid fronds of palm trees, wedge through cracks of windows and doors that were never fully closed because there was nothing to fully close against, bump against the Santa Susana Mountains. A valley flooded with hope and possibility.

Numinous.

"Houston, we have liftoff." She used her TV announcer voice. Squirmed in her seat. Her ass numb from sitting so long. The Winnebago swerved a bit and she adjusted, frowned, opted for prolonged wiggling in her captain's chair. She tapped her left foot.

"Pull over," Cole said. "You're making me crazy. I'll drive."

"No." Joanna grinned. Sunlight through the windshield. "I'm having fun."

They moved north on the 101 Freeway, deep into the valley. Sky brilliant blue. Mountains crisp and clear, as if there were no smog, as if there never had been. Even the freeway wide open.

A dusty Mazda pickup rattled in front, now behind them.

She caught his eye. "Doesn't it feel as if we could just take off?"

She liked driving fast enough to create the illusion that they were airborne, a flying bus, a steel dirigible defying gravity. But the truth was anything beyond sixty and she started feeling anxious on the turns.

Balboa Boulevard. Reseda. Tarzana. Beyond the freeway, the houses became less densely packed. Joanna kept her left hand on the wheel. Made her right into a fist and punched Cole hard, on the arm.

Out of the blue.

"Ow. What was that for?"

"For being a guy. For getting into a pissing contest. For not being smart enough to walk away clean."

The road bent to the left. Four lanes. Clear sailing.

"They stole my livelihood," he said. He paused to let the weight of this sink in. His arm throbbed.

They watched the road, felt the comforting rhythm of wheels beneath them. They'd bought matching sunglasses at a drugstore in Tombstone, Arizona. Aviator glasses that hugged their cheekbones. Wrapped close against temples.

Cole tipped his head back, flopped his braid back and forth. "Peanuts?" he asked, handing her one of the small bags the airlines give away. He'd found a convenience store on the highway in Banning that sold them. He'd bought two boxes, 64 bags each.

She took a bag and smiled. Untouchable behind her shades. Sixteen-ounce glass bottle of Coke in the cup holder. They'd stocked up on those, too. Three cases from an IGA outside of Eloy.

They had enough to get started. That was all they asked.

"I had no choice," he said. "I did what I had to do."

SCREEN FOUR

Three men on horseback – dust-colored men on dust-colored horses in a dust-colored country. The horses side-by-side, impatient. The men gaze into the distance, as if trying to pick up a trail – vagabond, outlaw, the vapor of some lost thing. The horses ready to give chase. Heads twitching. Nostrils flaring. The men stare. Hands rest on the pommels of dust-colored saddles.

Square-jawed. Tight-lipped. Leathered skin on faces etched by trouble. A knife scar down one cheek. Crow's feet carved deep around wary eyes. A nose slightly bent from breaking. On such faces, age is both impossible to determine and irrelevant. They ooze confidence: if they have survived this frontier, they will not be beaten. Whatever comes, they will fight it, bite it, shoot it down.

The men on the flanks keep the one in the center in sight, deferring to him.

The camera pans the countryside, mesquite and sagebrush and unrelenting sun, the light of late afternoon casting a golden glow across the valley, all the way into Mexico.

"Mighty pretty country," says the man in the center. He sits a little taller in his saddle than his companions. His jaw that much more square.

"How far you reckon we got to go?" says the man on the left. He is the smallest, the most talkative.

A hawk soars overhead.

The man in the center grabs the reins of his horse. Spurs the animal forward. "Far as it takes."

"Cut!" A squat man dressed all in black appears before the riders. Soft fingers rubbing the bristles of buzz-cut hair. He pats the horses. His face red.

"God dammit, Duke. You're a cowboy. You speak grudgingly when you speak at all. You don't admire the fucking landscape."

Duke looks out across the valley. "Couldn't help it," he says.

The director scratches the back of his neck.

"Fine," he says. "Mistakes happen. Let's try it again."

Postcard: Tombstone, Arizona.

"There are no tombstones," Joanna said, surveying the long main street, hands on blue-jeaned hips. Wooden buildings, scrubbed and painted, white red brown. Old style carved wood signs. The blond-wood boardwalk, spotless, creaked under their feet. Not even a stray gum wrapper. Every shop, regardless of its purpose – Boot Hill Drugs, Tombstone Camera, even Big Nose Kate's Saloon – sold souvenirs.

"If this is Tombstone, shouldn't there be tombstones?"

He shook his head. Squinted. Sunshine so stark it seemed manufactured. They wandered Fremont Street, skeptical, curious. "You want tombstones, we'll find tombstones." Strolled among the shops of this real-life theme park, craving the aura of ancient gunplay.

They were often mistaken for siblings, when they weren't taken for lovers. Same gray-green eyes, same laconic stride. Same lanky build.

Behind them, American sun beat down on the streets of Tombstone. They reveled in its warmth. She had no desire ever again to feel cold.

"But first," he said, "I'd like a sarsaparilla."

"Get me one," she said. She lit a cigarette, tossed the match.

Cole wandered into McLaury's General Store. Joanna found a bench – blond wood, like the boardwalk – and sat down. She leaned her head back. Smoked. Of the two of them, she was better able to put aside larger concerns and enjoy the moment. It was a skill she needed more and more. Empty her mind. Revel in the aura of the Old West. The scrape of boots on wood.

A family walked by. Mother, father, two daughters, the girls sporting suede vests festooned with bright plastic beads, *Tombstone* scrawled in script in yellow thread.

Joanna ground out her cigarette. Lit another. Where the hell was Cole?

He returned moments later, all smiles. Pulled two aluminum cans from behind his back. "Abracadabra." He handed one to Joanna, popped open the other and drank.

They slid to the other end of the bench to stay in the sun.

"We're running out of country," he said. "What are we gonna do?" He wore a red t-shirt. Rumpled khakis.

"I want to watch cowboy movies," she said. "How about you?"

"I'm serious," he said.

She set the can next to her on the bench. "So am I. Panavision. The real West."

"Fine. Then what?"

"You mean life insurance? Homeowners?" She sighed. "You're getting like that. I hate it when you get like that." She put her arms behind her head and stretched. Smoke burned in her chest.

Across the street beckoned Big Nose Kate's. Whitewashed sign. Swinging doors. Honky-tonk piano.

"So what's your idea?" he said.

"How'd you know I had an idea?"

"You always have an idea."

She cast a hand in front of her. "Our own vast desert landscape. A little unwanted corner of the world."

"I will not live in South Dakota," he said.

"We need supplies," she said. "Ring Dings. Mallo Cups. Doritos. Nutty Buddies. Those little orange peanut butter crackers. Lots of Coke. Bologna."

"Bologna?"

"Bologna. For sandwiches."

"Anything else?"

"I want to take up golf," she said. "I want to have recreational sex with a variety of young women."

He leaned forward. Sunshine and sleepiness conspired to make his eyes small, distant. "Okay, you don't want to talk about it right now. That's fine."

"I want to see tombstones," she said. "I want to see them re-enact a gunfight."

They visited the O.K. Corral.

Tour the site where Wyatt Earp, "Doc" Holliday, Virgil and Morgan Earp fought the Clantons and McLaurys. See live gunfight re-enactments.

"Earp," said Joanna.

The site was essentially a vacant lot, tucked between Frye's Photo Studio and the Harwood House. They sat on wooden bleachers and ate popcorn from a paper bag. Elderly couples in sweatshirts and jeans. Families, children eager for a taste of the Wild West. Cowboys. Outlaws.

Boothill Gunslingers re-enact the West's Most Famous Showdown. Daily at 12, 2, 4, 6.

They caught the day's first show.

"High noon," Joanna said.

They'd bought matching sunglasses at Boot Hill Drugs.

"When Doc Holliday and Wyatt Earp went looking for the Clantons that October afternoon," the announcer said, "it was only a question of time before bullets flew." The announcer wore a white shirt, a vest, a big brown Stetson.

A dozen wooden rows, half-filled. It reminded Cole of high-school basketball. Little League baseball.

A sign posted by the entrance – Clanton Ranch, Home of the Notorious Clanton Gang – gave one rendering of events. Under a drawing of the shoot-out, it told how "the Earps and Doc Holliday murdered Billy Clanton and Frank McLaury on Oct. 26, 1881."

The announcer told a different story.

"When Earp saves rogue gambler Holliday from mob violence," the announcer said, "the two team up to rid the West of the lawless Clanton gang."

Joanna munched popcorn.

"So much for history," Cole said.

Applause from the audience. The Wyatt Earp and Doc Holliday characters moved onto the set. Long black coats. String ties. Earp had bushy gray hair and a handlebar mustache. Holliday short, clean-shaven.

Cole watched through lenses that darkened greens and browns, electrified reds and blues. "Which version you think is true?"

Virgil and Morgan Earp walked on-stage.

"Both," she said. "Neither."

The bleachers creaked as spectators leaned forward.

Four men emerged. Thick white trail coats. A casual air. Two stage right, two stage left.

"My money's on the Earps," Joanna said.

Cole munched popcorn.

A child called, "Look out."

It was over in seconds. Frank McLaury dead from a shot to the stomach, Tom felled by Holliday's shotgun. Billy Clanton dying from chest wounds. Morgan and Virgil writhed wounded in the dirt. Smoke rising from pistols. Sulfur heavy in the air.

Cheers from the crowd. Jovial laughter.

Cole smiled. "Cool," he said. Through his sunglasses the blood almost glowed.

A few people got up to leave.

In the row below them, a boy stood and pumped his fist in the air. The father smiled, a hand on the boy's shoulder. Cole gave them a thumbs up as they left. He had been a parent himself once. There had been a wife, Corinne. A girl, Rebecca. A family, delivered whole. But that was a long time ago.

"God bless them," Joanna said. Sun beat down on her head. She felt giddy. Heat and dry air. "It's not easy to create a believable illusion."

Cole flipped through the program. Saw an ad for Boot Hill Graveyard. Nudged Joanna. "Here we go," he said. "Next stop, tombstones."

Joanna needed to leave, and it was her day to talk with Cole, so she got into the Corolla and drove to Boston.

"Jo. What are you doing here?" The narrow doorway of Cole's building made it a cramped welcome.

Every Tuesday since college, they talked. No matter where they were, what they were doing. Twenty years. Extraordinary fidelity. Except for the year after her divorce. And the past several months. Since Anthony left.

"You going to invite me in?" Joanna stood on his doorstep with a suitcase and a peanut butter jar filled with human hair. He hadn't seen her in almost a year. She had lost weight. All skin and sinew. Streaks of magenta in short black hair. Her eyes scanned him, the hallway behind him, the sidewalk. Constant motion.

"I broke a heart," she said. "It's time to light out for the territories."

Inside, they sipped vodka from frozen glasses and held hands.

The peanut butter jar on the table before them, a white mailing label with words in green capital letters: "DIANA'S HAIR – THE LONG PIECES."

Cole nodded. He was willing to accept this. You couldn't push Joanna for details. "You're going to carry it around with you?"

"Penance," she said.

She planned to stay overnight. No longer. She couldn't keep still. In the heat of his South End condo. On the roof deck, pacing. Stormy eyes.

"I'm not doing well," she said, urgent. And then, "I don't want to talk about it."

She said, "It's time to light out for the territories."

But she didn't. Not right away.

She cooked instead. Cornish hens, stuffed grape leaves, roasted vegetables.

She listened to Cole's story and told him his time as programming guru at Z-Tech was over. To act before he was acted upon.

She thought they should take off together. "You and me," she said. "Huck and Jim. Butch and Sundance. Fear and loathing."

"Let's face it," she said. "Warren hates what you represent. The writing's on the wall. You should be the one to make the move."

Her theories were plausible. Things he had considered himself.

Joanna paced the living room while she talked, and she talked fast. "Think about it," she said. "On one side, a methodical campaign to make you miserable. Cost/benefit analysis. Project approval cycles. And time sheets, Cole. Time sheets. He puts the screws to R&D, experimentation. It doesn't take a genius to see this is a problem." She paced, hard angles around furniture. "More important, even if you swallow and see the project through, they dump you. This is fact. We have documentation." She confined her steps to a strip of floor alongside the coffee table, peanut butter jar at its center like a talisman. "On the other side we have Cole, armed with information, and the question – given what Cole knows, what will he do?" She stopped for a moment, faced him. All eyes and nervous energy.

"We'll take off," she said. "Poof. Gone."

He loved her ability to believe this. To make him believe this. The force of will. The promise that if you don't like something, you can erase it.

"You make it sound possible, Jo."

"It is possible," she said. "It's a big country. Most people are not willing to really turn their backs. To walk away and not even sneak a glance. It's the looking back that kills you."

There was truth in that. He'd seen Joanna walk away from at least two past lives. Her son Anthony the only common link. Now here she was again. But Cole was different. He needed grounding. Consistency. "You'll turn your back on me. You'll move on."

Joanna was evangelical. Locking onto an idea. "No," she said. "We'll stick together." Her body exuded confidence. It charged the air. "You and me. The open road. We see something we like, we stop." She slapped the palm of one hand with the back of the other. "We make it happen."

Her eyes shone. "How many people get this chance, Cole?"

SCREEN FOUR

The director, black t-shirt, black jeans, black stubble of hair streaked with gray, black-and-gray goatee, stands with his back to the valley. Encouraging his actors. Kirk, looking off toward Mexico, watching the fading light. Mitch squatting at the dirt, intent. Duke hands on hips, anxious to get on with it. Basalt stone a dark veneer on the sandy soil.

"I want the landscape to be the star in this shot, as much as you all," the director is saying. He loves this valley. Scouted locations for two weeks, mindful of every plant, every nuance of light. "I want the valley stretching endlessly before you, the vastness of the work that lies ahead. The physicality of the horses. Let that speak for us." He looks behind him, surveys the changing light. "We need to shoot this. Duke, I want to try ending it with your first line. Leave that second line unspoken. Let it be understood from the sweat and dust."

"Wait a minute," says Duke. "Which first line?"

"The one about the landscape. It's in."

He turns his back on the actors. He claps his hands. "Let's do it," he says. "Horses." Over his shoulder, he says, "Ride them hard, boys. Like you mean it."

Postcard: Lordsburg, New Mexico.

Gassed up. Looking for a diner. Cole at the wheel. Two-lane highway. Dusty shoulder. Eyes darting from road to rearview mirror. He saw something he didn't like, swerved left at the last minute onto a side street.

"We were on this road before," Joanna said. "There was nothing here." She cocked a thumb behind her. "Closer to the Interstate."

He adjusted the mirror. Stared into it.

"What are you doing?"

Cole's eyes riveted. "Panicking."

She looked behind them. A police car, framed in the back window, maybe a hundred yards back. "Ask them where to eat."

He tried to maintain a balance. Drive slow enough not to appear panicked, fast enough to create some distance. He used to pretend sometimes with Rebecca, Corinne's daughter – his daughter, for a time – they'd be driving and he'd pretend they were being chased. An excuse to drive fast, a little wild. Rebecca was thirteen now. Would he know her? He turned right at the last minute, past a Union 76 gas station. A quick left. Seeking the shelter of narrow streets. Tall buildings. A supermarket with trucks parked in back. Somewhere to hide.

Not in Lordsburg. Flat. Occasional stores. Strip malls.

The police car paused at the gas station, turned down the road they were on.

"Shit," he said.

"Maybe you should stop driving like someone with a guilty conscience."

Video Stop. *Chez Luis* Hair Styling.

"I've got to shake them."

"What do you expect," she said. "You're driving a Winnebago in erratic circles in a small New Mexico town."

He looked at her. In the mirror. Back to the road. He began to feel dizzy.

"Listen to me," she said. "Take a deep breath. Keep driving."

Blue light flashed around them. Reflected off the windshield, the roof of the cab.

The police car closed on them.

Cole began to sweat. "Fuck. What now?"

"Don't be stupid," Joanna said. "Pull over."

Cole hesitated. Even with sunglasses on, he squinted from the glare off the pavement. Two narrow lanes. A warehouse set back from the road. A Denny's up ahead. He eased the wheel to the right. Tapped the brake. The police car stopped behind them. Cole's eyes on the mirror.

Joanna heard a door shut. "We stopped for gas," she said. "We're looking for the Interstate. Got a little confused."

She watched his face. His shallow breathing.

"You told me you'd done nothing illegal."

He shot her a quick glance. "I never used the word illegal. I said nothing *wrong*."

"Good morning." The officer stood at the driver's side window. Sand-colored uniform. Silver nameplate. "License and registration, please." Thin mustache. Thick arms.

Joanna fished the registration from the glove box. Cole pulled out his wallet. Concentrated on not shaking.

The Winnebago rode high enough that Cole handed the items down to the officer. "Is there a problem?" He tried to keep hostility from his voice. The way police always make you feel like a child.

The officer took the documents. Blue light bounced around them.

"Wait here, please," he said. Walked back to the patrol car.

Cole rolled his eyes. Leaned his head back against the seat. "Shit."

"Is there something I should know about?" Joanna asked.

"The law isn't clear," Cole said. "A court could decide either way."

16

She rubbed her hair, greasy from days without washing. Rested one foot on the dash. Untied, then retied her shoelace. "You took it with you, didn't you."

The road empty and quiet. Two blocks ahead, it ended in a T at a busier street where traffic flowed contentedly. They could see a ramp reaching up to the Interstate.

Cole didn't say a word.

Behind them, the car door shut.

"Boys and their penises," Joanna said. "How fucked are we?"

Cole watched the mirror. "It's hard to say."

"Would you mind stepping out of the vehicle, Mr. Newton?" A squared-off stance. A refusal to look up at Cole.

Cole opened the door, stepped onto the road. The heat dizzying.

Joanna began to climb out.

"Wait there please, ma'am."

Here we go, Cole thought. He had no idea how to behave in a showdown. He didn't feel properly dressed. He faced the officer. Squinting. A ringing in his ears. Holding his breath without wanting to. He saw himself, twin reflections in the officer's sunglasses. He lifted his chin.

"Temporary registration." The officer held it. "You just buy this rig?" A man who liked his beer. A body still strong from high school football. Cole could feel the man's eyes searching his face.

"Yeah." Cole concentrated on not lowering his gaze. Looking just past the officer. Swallowing fear. "Traded her car in Tennessee."

Piercing sun. Cars in the distance.

"You know you have a brake light out?"

Breathing room, or a taunt? He'd never had much luck reading the intentions of law enforcement personnel. *Proceed with caution*. "No," Cole said. "I didn't."

The officer nodded.

Cole impatient. A growing feeling of *if we're going to have a crisis, let's get on with it*. He imagined himself – the new Cole – lunging for the officer's gun. Grab his nightstick and knock him cold.

In the cab of the Winnebago, Joanna hummed a tune.

"Here's the problem," the officer said.

"Problem?" Cole said. He heard his voice waver.

"I've got a suspicious nature. Tennessee plates. Mass license. Handwritten bill of sale. Peculiar driving. And my computer's down, so I can't check you out."

Cole's knees felt weak.

The officer shook his head slowly. "I don't like it," he said.

"No," Cole managed. "I guess not."

"If my computer were working, would it tell me anything interesting about you?"

Cole wished he could see the man's eyes. He willed his knees not to shake. His voice steady. "No, sir," he said. "I don't believe it would."

A car rolled past. Some big Ford. A wave of heat from the engine. Cole concentrated on breathing.

The officer nodded. "Well," he said. Handed back license and registration. Inscrutable. "Guess we'll send you on your way. You take care."

"You bet."

Then handed Cole a moving violation. "And be a little more careful."

"Yes, sir." A long exhale. *Fucker.*

Cole waited until the officer reached his patrol car, then melted slowly into the driver's seat.

"Nice and easy," Joanna said.

Cole handed her the registration. She popped it back into the glove box.

"All is well," she said.

Cole eased the motor home back onto the road. Headed for the on ramp to 10 West.

"Asshole," he said. "They always have to bust your balls." He turned onto the ramp.

Joanna rested her arm on the seat back. Her body turned to face Cole. "We'll just get back on the road," she said, that soothing tone. "Find somewhere else to eat."

Cole took a deep breath. Gripped the steering wheel tighter to keep his hands from shaking.

The miles slipped behind them.

18

Interstate 10. The Christopher Columbus Transcontinental Highway. They passed a green sign. Exit 11.

She did curls with a dumbbell they kept on the floor of the passenger seat. "I think you pissed your pants back there," she said. "You want to tell me what's going on?"

Cole flushed. "Lack of sleep," he said. "An inflated sense of my own importance in the world."

She held the weight still. Her arm extended. "Yo," she said. "This is me, remember?"

He had to piss, but he wasn't about to tell her. He crossed his legs. "Legally, it's a gray area." His eyes followed the broken white line that marked the lane. "It'll be fine."

"Look at me when you say that."

He looked at her. "I did what I had to do."

"No," she said. "You had to leave. You didn't have to steal the code."

"I didn't steal it," he said. "I created it. It's mine."

They moved west at sixty miles an hour.

"You'll never survive prison," she said.

"Fuck that," he said. His bladder hurt. "Don't even joke about that."

She wiggled his ponytail. "You'd be dessert. Everyone's candy boy. They'd slice you just for fun."

Cole would never have believed everything could blow apart so quickly.

"If you look at my work in the short run, my style appears wasteful," Cole said. His living room felt smaller with Joanna there, penned between the table and the wet bar, worrying a line into the floor. She was electric. A storm front moving in off the coast.

Cole on the couch.

"All the best ideas we generated were happy accident, experiments that happened outside the scope of projects, a tangent someone followed. That takes a kind of trust in your developers." Joanna raised a hand to stop him, but Cole kept talking. "A belief that the best things happen outside the boundaries."

Warren lived by the bottom line. Make a projection and stick with it. Every project justifies its cost.

She rested a hand on the bar. Behind her, a series of photographs, a shrine to a young Rebecca. "We're not debating the value of your work style. We're looking at a situation. Where you can leave on your own, pick the moment, or you can be forced out. This is the question. How badly you want to finish this project. How you choose the moment." Back and forth, along a strip of carpet. Her eyes fixed on some point in the air between them.

"I want to finish. This is years of work. A defining moment."

The project: an electronic commerce engine for KBC Corporation, owner of Valu-Mart department stores, Valu-Rite pharmacies, and Kidman's catalog clothing sales. In developing the engine, Cole had found a window into a next-generation encryption package, one that would speed e-commerce transactions even while making them more secure. He wanted the satisfaction. He wanted the acclaim. He wanted time to imagine himself somewhere else.

"I've taken precautions," he said.

Joanna's hands moved as she paced. As if she were speaking. She reached the end of the table near him and hovered. A high-pressure system. Neck muscles strained. She swallowed.

"I don't want to see you get burned," she said.

Warren had assigned an arbitrary internal launch date. As if it were a matter of plugging in numbers. An allotted amount of effort for a predictable result.

It's time we bring some discipline to this. Our clients have been complaining.

Show me, Cole had said. And Warren had shot him a patronizing smile and walked away.

Cole found himself doing things he never thought he'd do. Cracking Warren's e-mail password had been simple – a child's birth date, obtained from the personnel files. Cole had it within an hour. He wanted information. He wanted control. Deliver the project before he left.

Golden parachute him, but get him out.

E-mail from Warren to the new C.O.O., Tolman. Cole found a series of messages painting him as weak, the beneficiary of an indulgent system. A plan, approved by Tolman, to force him out once he delivered the encryption project.

That was when Cole began to keep the real project files at home, and put an older, critically flawed version, on the Z-Tech network.

"Fuck them," Joanna said, fingers splayed on the table. "Walk away." She stood inches from him. She radiated heat. She had an uncanny ability to put troubles behind her. Swallow them like smoke.

"We were pioneers," he told her later, in the Winnebago. Talking through the windshield, into the night sky. Speaking to the barest reflection of himself in the glass, to the world slipping behind him, to Joanna driving. The occasional road sign. *Laramie 98.* "Exploring the frontier. Marking out territory. As long as we could roam, it was possible to do amazing things."

SCREEN FOUR

A panorama, a desert valley, unfolds before the camera. A crisp blue sky. Sweetbush and desert holly, spiky yucca, the occasional dormant ocotillo rising up awkwardly out of the valley floor, bathed in the golden light of late afternoon.

The camera moves in, zoom on sweetbush-not-yet-tumbleweeds, until the sky disappears and the very rocks and dirt are ennobled. Past granite boulders, skirting sandstone cliffs, the camera tracks the land, mountains hazy in the distance.

A sound, faint at first, then pounding like the beating heart of the valley. Hooves. Up the crest of a ridge; the camera arrives at the same time as the horses, snorting, foaming. Reined in. A tight shot. Leather reins. Teeth. Neck muscles straining. The angry neigh of an animal just beginning to feel its power.

Three horses glistening with the sweat of a hard ride. Panting, catching at breath, as if oxygen lived just ahead of them. Just out of reach.

Three men squinting into sun, clothes and faces covered with dust. Long shadows cast on the desert floor. The man in the center taller in the saddle, a bit forward of his companions. The man on the right wipes a forearm across his face. Even now, no more than an hour before sundown, the valley bakes.

Snorting from the horses. Shuffling of feet. They are eager to run. Steady breathing from the men.

The man on the right, the smallest, the most talkative, opens his mouth, but it is a few seconds before words come out.

"How far you reckon we got to go?"

The man on the left, hands now resting on the pommel of his saddle, looks over. His answer unspoken.

The man in the center retrieves a canteen, sips at water. Wipes his mouth with the back of a hand. Before he spurs the horse on, he takes in the landscape whose pallet is already changing, the gold fading to a gentler brown, soft greens emerging. He holds the reins in his hands. Shakes his head.

"Mighty pretty country," he says, and they ride on.

Postcard: Cheyenne, Wyoming.

They wandered the narrow aisles of Happy Jack's Dollar Store, looking at Rubbermaid products, dingy blue and tan and white containers to keep things sealed up tight. Dusty boxes of Glad trash bags, faded cans of insect repellent. Shelves half-full. Air musty. Thirty-year-old pop songs droned from a radio somewhere.

"Look at this," Joanna said, hoisting a can of Raid off a sparsely populated shelf. A thick film of dust covered it like a veil. She blew on it, sending a few clumps into the air. Most stayed on the can. "Must have been here since 1956." She replaced the can, moved further down the aisle. "What are we doing here, anyway." No air in there. No room.

Cole followed behind her. "You wanted to."

A lone cashier guarded the front, a tall, bleached blonde with thirty extra pounds. She could have been 35 or 50. The only other customer looked as if the store had been built around him. John Deere cap, day's growth of beard, royal blue shirt and suspenders, well into his sixties, he stood at a bargain table holding a can of Brasso and reading the label through a pair of black half-frame glasses.

"It's disgusting," Joanna said. She stopped to show Cole the dark residue of grime that clung to the tips of her fingers. "No wonder this town's in such sad shape," she said, raising her voice so the cashier would hear her. "No wonder Wal-Mart is spreading like cancer. You can't expect to be a vibrant American town if you don't offer people a quality shopping experience."

The cashier showed no sign of having heard. She nodded her head vaguely to the sounds of the radio. Penned behind an L-shaped counter at the front window. The Brasso man looked at them over the tops of his glasses.

Cole pulled up beside Joanna. Spoke into her ear. "I appreciate your disappointment, Jo. But this is the West. People carry guns."

She pushed him away. Glared at the cashier. Willed the woman to acknowledge her. Nothing.

"Do me a favor," Cole said to her. "Let's not piss people off."

Cheyenne had been nothing like they'd hoped for. Main Street with franchises of national stores, a few small local shops. JC Penney. ValuMart. Kiwanis signs. Nothing to suggest a rich western heritage. They picnicked in a municipal park, sat at a wooden table in the grass and ate fluffernutter sandwiches. Joanna had been restless. Impatient.

Now she stalked the dingy aisles, Cole at her heels.

She stopped short. He bumped her.

"Christ," she said. "I can't move without you on my ass."

"I just think"

"Don't," she said. "Don't think."

She spun back toward the Raid, grabbed the fingerprint-smeared can and walked toward the counter. Blood beat against her temples.

Cole groaned. His footsteps behind her.

A display of motor oil, yellowed cans in a pyramid.

The cashier stared out the window.

"Excuse me," Joanna called. No movement. No response.

The Brasso man's eyes followed her – them.

Joanna reached the counter, thrust the can at the woman. "Excuse me." She kept her voice just below a yell. Balled her free hand.

Cole in her ear. "This is a bad idea, Jo."

She swatted at him. Leaned across the counter, forcing eye contact. "I picked this up off the shelf. Look at it. How can you expect someone to buy this?" Joanna held the can out, her arms fully extended. Jaw clenched.

The cashier stared at Joanna for a long moment. Held her gaze. Neither of them looked at the can.

"If you don't like the way it looks," the woman said finally, her words measured. Cheeks flushed. "You don't have to buy it."

Joanna hovered inches from the woman's face. Her legs pressed against the formica. She smelled body powder. Peppermint. She hated peppermint. "I'd like to know how you expect to sell this. Why you don't clean things off."

The woman turned her back. Glanced at a newspaper she had on a shelf beside the register.

Joanna stepped around the counter. Grabbed the woman's arm. Spun her around. "I'm *talking* to you." The can clattered to the floor.

"Stop it, Jo." Cole lunged around the counter, took Joanna by the arms. Shoulder to shoulder, the three of them.

The woman, eyes wide, pulled back. No room. "You get out," she said. Her breath on Joanna's neck. She swung an arm out hard. Part push, part punch. "You get out now."

Joanna's heart raced.

Cole at her elbow. "I'm sorry," he said to the woman. "She's not herself. She lost her son recently."

"*Fuck you.*" Joanna spat at him. Adrenaline. Peppermint. She drove her hands against Cole's chest. He rocked back and she leaned in to cover the distance. She stared, breathed on him, and he stared back. She struggled to keep her hands at her sides. Fists clenched so tight her palms hurt.

"You don't *do* that to a person." The cashier's fierce voice. "I don't know where you think you are."

Joanna looked back at her, leaned against the counter. She wanted to hurt someone. She wanted to be outdoors.

Cole touched her elbow. She flinched, took a deep breath.

"Come on," Cole said. A step back.

He reached for her again, slowly, and this time she let him take her elbow.

Room to breathe.

He walked her outside, and she let him. The cashier did not move. Did not take her eyes from them.

Cole didn't let go until he'd led her a block away. The muscles in Joanna's body clenched.

Neither of them spoke all the way to the motor home.

Back on the road. Interstate 80, just west of Laramie. Joanna finished a Three Musketeers bar, hummed "Red River Valley."

Cole at the wheel.

Joanna stopped humming. She folded the candy wrapper into an isosceles triangle. Unfolded it. Tossed it on the floor. "Okay. I was out of line back there."

Cole let out a long breath. "God, Jo," he said. "Sometimes." He sounded as if he were addressing a child.

"The place was a shithole." She grabbed a rubber ball from the floor. It had the face of a seal. "At least have the decency to listen to a customer. A little respect."

"Come on, Jo. It's not about that."

She showed him her fingers, stained from the can. "Look at this. This is shit. Her attitude was shit."

"My sternum's bruised. You want to talk about what's really bugging you?"

"*No. I don't.*" A knot of rage. She squeezed the ball. Watched the road. Sunshine. Blue sky. She wished he were a radio she could turn off. A speaker she could smash. "How's the wife and kid, Cole? Talk to Rebecca lately?" Her fingers dug into the ball until it was no bigger than a clam. She kept the words coming. Kept her voice sharp. "It's the little things, isn't it. The way you wish you could pick her up after school and take her for ice cream because she got a hundred on her spelling test. Help her study her times tables. Tell me, Cole, do you miss her? How does it *feel*, Cole?"

She squeezed and released the rubber ball.

Cole silent beside her. Hands on the wheel. Eyes hidden.

She stared out the windshield.

"Drop it," she said. "It's over. Want a candy bar?"

Cole shook his head.

A blue highway sign – gas, food, lodging.

"You shouldn't have made that crack about Anthony."

"I apologize."

Joanna nodded. Propped her bare feet on the dash. "I haven't lost him. I know where he is. I talk to him."

She started to hum again. Stopped. For the first time, she felt claustrophobic in the motor home. Anxiety encroaching, the push of an incoming tide. Resist. Reinforce. Take refuge in the truth: she does not know where he is, what he has been doing. The road yawned before them.

"Fuck," she said. She yearned for curves, hills, anything.

"Forget it," he said.

Later. Dusk. All color drained from the sky. Cole pulled on the headlights. The great plains in silhouette.

"You know why cowboy songs are so sad?" she said. Wan. Worn.

"No," Cole said. "Tell me."

"Out there at night, prairie stretched around you, sitting at the campfire. You're alone under this gaping expanse of world. You can't help feeling that the way you spend your days is just a distraction to keep you from thinking about the way things really are, which is you there, alone, the empty night."

Cole kept his eyes on the road, straight and flat.

"That's where the songs come from," she said. "Whatever the words might be." Toes curled on the dash. Lips pursed.

26

She was still. Receded. She was the ghosted image in the glass, what lingered in the space where Joanna used to be.

A sign at the side of the road read "Rawlins 80 Rock Springs 162."

The last straw had been a hyperlink headline that almost escaped Cole's attention.

> ValuMart to launch online store with next generation encryption

He had to look at it twice to be sure it wasn't his imagination. Check the URL to be sure it wasn't a practical joke.

"I fucked up," he told Joanna over dinner. "I lost it."

Roast chicken stuffed with rosemary. Rice pilaf. Fiddleheads. Chardonnay. Joanna fidgeting. "Tell me."

So he did.

– Warren, how did NewsNet end up promoting this launch?

– I had Hope send them a press release.

He told Joanna how he had shouted at Warren and hung up the phone. How he should have left it there, and he knew it, even as he dialed Hope's extension.

"How bad?" Joanna licked chicken from her fingers.

"Very."

"Expletives?"

"Several."

"Ouch," Joanna said. "What are you going to do?"

"Quit." A course of action that had existed in embryonic form for weeks had developed a pulse. A heartbeat. "It's time to light out for the territories."

Joanna stopped fidgeting. "You sure?"

"Sure." How could he be sure. It didn't seem the kind of situation where certainty was possible. There were simply things that had to be done.

He stood. Grabbed the phone. Punched a number. Ate a bite of chicken. "Hope? It's Cole. I know it's late. This is important."

He chewed. "I want you to know how badly you've fucked this project. This company." His face red. He fought to stay rational. "No, you listen. I'm sorry. I just want to ask you something. No. Listen. Please. Z-Tech used to mean something." A breath. "Listen to me. People did good work. *It mattered.* I don't expect anything from Warren – he's not human – but you, Hope. You were there. What happened, Hope? Hope? *Fuck!*"

He threw the phone to the floor. Rubbed the back of his neck. His voice quiet. "It was a reasonable question."

Joanna poured wine into her glass.

He chewed chicken. Speared a fiddlehead with his fork. "I hope I can still get a deal."

Joanna spoke without moving. "They want you out. They'll deal." She sipped chardonnay. Watched his face. "What about the project?"

He'd already considered that. Already decided. A shrug. "Fuck it." He tapped his temple. "They can't take what's up here."

Twelve hours later, he was ushered out of Z-Tech, monitored while he cleaned out his desk. He had expected suspicion – that his abrupt resignation would arouse doubt, his plea of burnout be manifest as melodrama. But no.

A chasm of emptiness inside. An almost giddy rush of freedom.

"It's a very attractive package, Cole," he heard Tolman's voice saying.

The deal was this: a year's severance – full salary – plus a bonus for signing a non-compete. Cole held the bonus check in his hand. He had to agree not to work in application design for two years. A lifetime.

"Take some time off," Tolman had said. "Recharge the batteries."

Ten years of his life ending in a day, a whirlwind.

Hard to stand there, smile and nod. Even if he didn't intend to keep the agreement.

That night, they were on the road.

"You know," Joanna had said, behind the wheel of her Toyota, even before they crossed the 495 belt, "I love my Corolla, but if we're going to do this, we ought to do it in style."

SCREEN ONE

The old Sheriff sits in a straight-backed wood chair, dressed only in a gray union suit. Hands cuffed behind him. Thick mustache. Jowly face. Sleep in his eyes. Angry that they've roused him. That they've shown up in his town. In his dining room.

"There's a towel in the drawer that you can use to gag me," he says.

Two outlaws. A man and a woman. The man stands beside the window. Peeks out through the curtains. The first traces of morning light nibble at the horizon. He's nervous. This wasn't his idea.

The woman kneels beside the Sheriff, her old friend, her mentor. "We're going to start over." The room lit only by a hurricane lamp.

"Start over." The Sheriff almost spits out the words. "What makes you think anyone would let you start over?"

The woman stares at the floor boards.

"They're just gonna let you wander off in the sunset. You'll leave them alone, so they should do the same for you. After all that's happened. That's what you're thinking?"

"It's possible," she says. She pushes a pearl-colored hat back on her head. "It's an idea."

The Sheriff shakes his head in disgust. "You're two-bit outlaws," he says. "You're done for. Your time is past."

The man watches out the window, his body hidden. Looking for horses, for the telltale puffs of dust that will tell them they need to keep running.

"I never met a soul more affable than you," he says to her, and to him, "you're the best I've ever seen, but you're still two-bit outlaws. You're gonna die bloody. The only thing you can do is choose where."

*

"There should be two distinct types of sexual relationships."

Joanna behind the wheel. Somewhere in South Dakota. The great moonscape of the Badlands behind them, air conditioning on high, bright midday sun on the vast American highway. Cole swiveled in his seat. Sipped a Coke. In one part of his brain, Willie Nelson sang "Don't Fence Me In."

"Are you listening?" Joanna asked. Gray wraparound sunglasses gave her a teenage aura.

"Two types of relationships," Cole said.

"Exactly. The ones where you're committed – the deep, lasting, let's-work-things-out kind, and the purely recreational, for release, with both parties clear on what it is."

"We're talking about Diana here."

Joanna nodded. She loved the feel of the big steering wheel in her hands. The sense that she was driving the whole world. "I made a mistake. She was too young to appreciate the distinction."

"She's an undergraduate, Jo. She's what, twenty-two?"

The Winnebago swallowed highway. Entire chunks of country left behind them, rapidly reducing the amount of space between them and the end of the road.

"What can I say. She's young. She'll get over it."

Cole held the peanut butter jar, long brown strands of hair inside. There was sadness in Joanna's voice. Cole tried to picture her living in Carlisle, Pennsylvania. In all the years he's known her, Joanna has never been good at conforming. She has paid a price. In moments like this, it was possible to feel the weight of what Joanna carried with her. When it leaked through a crack in the wall she'd constructed and altered the density of the air, the pounds per square inch of pressure on the skin.

"I stopped for pizza," she said. "Carlisle looked like a quaint college town." Her eyes burned. Road-weary. "And there she was. Sweet. Open. I pounced."

Cole swiveled in his seat. The part of his brain that played music had switched to "Blue Shadows on the Trail," a gently swaying rhythm like a horse cantering.

30

"Maybe I did her a favor." Hands on the wheel. Road slipping away. "She's not a dyke – she's checking out girls. A college thing. Maybe now she'll find a nice man."

Cole looked askance at her. The weight of the air had become uncomfortable.

"Okay, that's bullshit. I broke her heart."

"And the plaintive wail from the distance
comes a-driftin' on the evening breeze"

Cole realized that the song in his head was coming out his mouth. He didn't know when that had begun. He didn't know how – from where – he knew the song. He caught Joanna's eye. He shrugged. Swayed to the rhythm.

"You ever think," he said, "how it shouldn't be so easy to walk away? Most people our age have ties. Commitments. They would be missed." He hummed a few notes.

"You can't think that way, Cole."

He hummed. His brow furrowed, then unfurrowed.

Joanna's lips curled into a smile as he sang.

"Soon the dawn will come,
and you'll be on your way
but until the darkness sheds its veil,
there'll be blue shadows on the trail."

They were on their way to California, though they did not know it yet.

"Did I get us a deal, or what?"

Interstate 40. Rockwood, Tennessee. Driving rain. Thick drops bounced off the highway.

Joanna held the Winnebago steering wheel tight. After the cramped Corolla, the cab felt expansive.

Cole held a snow dome, a large white theater. Roman columns. "We made a good choice."

The windshield wipers seemed eight feet tall. Joanna checked the speedometer. Flicked the lights on and off. "I'd say I was brilliant."

The salesman, a slight twang, a step behind in his awareness of evolving gender roles. Had questioned Joanna's ability to handle the Winnebago.

Cole had watched her eyes flash.

She turned, hands on hips. "What exactly are you saying?"

"I meant no offense, ma'am." Thinning hair. Helpless smile. "It's just that it's a heavy vehicle, and if you've got no experience with them."

An outdoor lot, a grass field at the side of State Route 116. Ned's Motor Home Sales. They'd torn the ad from the Yellow Pages, followed two-lane roads under a thickening sky. Ned tried to backpedal, but he wasn't near fast enough.

"You might want to consider a smaller model, is all."

She jerked a thumb at Cole. "I'm stronger than he is." Eyes locked on Ned, that grin that might be amusement, anger, or a combustible mix. "I can beat him arm wrestling." She rolled up a sleeve. "Wanna try me?"

Ned looked to Cole for help. A distant rumble of thunder. Cole smiled. "She's small, but powerful."

When Ned threw out a price, Joanna scowled. Gave him her profile. "That's a sucker's price." How far could she press her advantage. "I've seen the same model, three thousand less."

In the end, Ned met her halfway, and doubled the trade-in on the Corolla. To celebrate, they drove to Dollywood as the skies opened.

Now, on the road, Cole shook the snow dome, watched plastic flakes settle on a miniature Parton Palace.

"Let's sing cowboy songs," she said.

"I don't know any cowboy songs," he said. "Do you know any cowboy songs?"

"I don't know," she said. "I'm not sure. She fingered the dashboard dials. Shook rainwater from her hair. "The only one I know I know is 'Don't Fence Me In'." She hummed three or four bars. "At least I think it's a cowboy song."

They took their time.

He wanted to see the Rio Grande and she took him.

Socorro, just outside El Paso, he stood at the riverbank and looked out over the brown water across the border into Cuidad Juárez, all narrow streets and low stucco buildings, and he tried to ignore the stockade fence, to squint and picture the land as it had once been, open country, a frontier.

Hikes in Saguaro National Monument.

Shooting pool in Agua Prieta. A cantina just across the border. Dark wood. Dim light from ceiling fixtures. They drank Tecaté from blood-red cans and played nine-ball, badly.

"So you're a fugitive." She rested her cue on the floor, held it near the top, while he lined up a shot at the five.

"Not technically." He drove the orange ball toward a corner pocket but it caromed off the cushion.

"Yeah, I know. The law isn't clear."

"They won't come after me," he said.

"You left them a copy."

"I left them a deeply flawed copy."

She missed on the five in the far corner. It bumped the nine, and the nine rolled in. "Shit." She slapped a dollar on the table.

"So you think they don't know you have it."

"They can't know I have it."

"Unless you use it."

He grinned. "Unless I use it."

Joanna racked the balls. Glared at him. Mexican pop songs played from a stereo behind the bar. "Don't be stupid," she said. "I will not visit you in jail."

They drove to the edge of the country and looked off.

Sunset Boulevard runs into Pacific Coast Highway just north of Santa Monica, and if you go straight across PCH you find yourself in a municipal parking lot, six rows of white lines painted on faded blacktop, and if you pull to the west edge of the parking lot you encounter a steel cable which, along with a narrow stretch of beach, is then all that stands between you and the Pacific Ocean.

Joanna nudged the Winnebago forward until its nose rested against the cable. Turned off the engine.

She stared out at the water. Breakers. White foam. The tang of salt in the air.

A man, white shorts, shirt open to the breeze, strolled the beach, sandals dangling from his fingers. The digital clock on the dashboard read 4:49 am.

"Here we are," Cole grinned. "America."

Joanna swiveled to face him. "America," she said, amused.

"The West. Where it all begins. Can you feel it?"

Waves on the shore. She felt cramped in the cab. "I need to stretch my legs," she said. "Let's walk."

He opened his door. "I'll catch up. I need to see a man about a horse."

She walked on wet sand, just beyond the waterline. Smooth shore. No rocks. A weight in her forearms. An ache in the knees. The miles had taken a toll. She felt old and hard and empty. She flashed on Anthony as a baby, riding on her chest in a Snuggli while she combed Wells Beach for starfish, sea shells, called out the names as she lifted them from the sand – mussel, scallop. Placed his tiny fingers on the ridged surfaces so he could feel and remember.

Cole's footsteps behind her. "I just want you to know I've marked my territory."

She laughed, eyes on the horizon. "I'm happy for you."

He fell into step beside her.

"We're free, Jo. We're brand new." His tired eyes big as moons. "We have no history, no limitations. Who have you always wanted to be, the Jo you couldn't get to because of the one people knew?" In the distance, a pier. The silhouette of hills. "I'm going to wear a black hat. A badass grin." His smile was a child's – exuberant, infectious. He didn't seem to notice she wasn't playing. "I'm going to saddle up and ride hard. Let the sun bake my skin, sleep under the stars. I will cotton no boundaries." He raised his eyebrows to mark the verb. He was all teeth and grin. "I'm going to ride to the ridge where the west commences. Gaze at the moon until I lose my senses. I'm going to learn what hobbles are and then I'm going to hate them."

"You really believe we can start over?"

"I do," he said. "You're living proof."

She stopped. Looked out at the ocean.

"What's wrong?"

Fading stars. A warm breeze. "He's out there somewhere." She stared, intent, as if she might see Anthony among the waves, floating.

Cole was not prepared for gravity. Not interested. He was all but on horseback. "Fuck. Not now." He hadn't meant to speak the thought, but there it was. He tried to think of something kind. He put his hand on her shoulder. "He's sixteen, Jo."

She pulled away. "He's my son."

Cole watched with her, the foam of waves, the incoming tide. A shape. He made it an arm. Anthony's arm. He tried to give the image flesh. So they could effect a rescue. So he could show her she wouldn't. "You're here, Jo. Don't look back."

A wet wind. Joanna felt salt against her face. She wiggled her fingers. Watched the muscles ripple in her forearm. Stiffened her voice. "I carried him inside me," she said. "Still do. Always will."

Dawn edged the horizon. "That's other people, Jo. Not you. You can walk away from anything."

Water swirled at her feet. Seeped into her running shoes.

He hovered behind her, near enough that his shirt brushed against her back.

She could feel his breath on her neck, his words in her belly. She wrapped her arms around herself. Goose-pimpled.

They stood there. They did not move.

The sky slowly brightened. California coast stretched before them like possibility.

They had come across the country and stood at its edge. They had a motor home filled with snack foods. They had each other.

They slept in the Winnebago. In the parking lot, with the nose of the motor home nudging the steel cable. They pulled the curtains closed and slept through the morning and most of the afternoon.

2.

The beach would never do. They were in agreement on that.

"Too crowded," Cole said.

"Too many cheerful people," Joanna said. She munched SmartFood popcorn from a bag between the seats. "We need solitude."

"Space to rebuild."

They watched the sun set over the Pacific. They had paid their three dollars to park. They had not moved back from the edge.

The valley was Joanna's idea.

"Smog," Cole said. "Congestion. Strip malls."

"We'll go north. We'll find a place. An untouched corner."

"This is Los Angeles," he said. "There are no untouched corners."

She opened her mouth to speak, found no words. Snappy retorts tasted sour on her tongue.

"We need a break," she said softly. "We need to chill."

She recalled a theater. Multiple screens. Ornate marquee. "I know this drive-in. I brought Anthony to California, after the divorce. He was thirteen. We did the amusement park tour of the Southland. Disney and Six Flags. Universal Studios and Raging Waters." They'd stumbled upon this theater, sat in their rental car with the windows open and watched Sharon Stone play a gunslinger in *The Quick and the Dead*. "Bunch of screens," she said. "Those little speakers."

"Where?"

"In the valley. We'll find it."

Santa Ana winds warm the night air, toss a tumbleweed across the abandoned lot. The distant sound of cars. Stars reaching deep into the beyond. The wind stirs the leaves of the few scattered trees. Rustles the spiky branches of a creosote bush. Rattles the corrugated aluminum fence where bolts have rusted and broken loose. The tumbleweed scrapes off the fence, rolls toward the stuccoed refreshment stand, padlocked against the night, the lizards, the encroachment of vandals. Skips lightly over dust and grass, bounces off one metal speaker pole, and another, careening like a cartoon drunk. A speaker dangles from thick black wire like something in need of rescue. A banana moon hangs in a sky so distant it seems part of another galaxy. The Santa Anas blow in fits and starts, gusting, waning, never fully stopping, the tumbleweed slows and almost rests before it's caught up again. Over a rise where cars once parked. Caroms off a pole, grazes the dangling speaker, and spins crazily along. Then a sound, unlike those the wind has stirred. The rumbling of a truck on the distant freeway, the metallic scrape of speaker against pole, or the crackling of amplified sound, a trace of an old cowboy song released on the breeze.

The enigma of arrival. How a place can be both there and gone. A marquee. A padlocked refreshment stand. Joanna had almost missed it. The darkened entrance. Weeds sprouting through cracked blacktop. But she saw the screens. Anchored to wood frames. Staring back at them. Skeletons. Carcasses.

"This is the place?" Cole sees nothing in every direction he looks. Dust and weeds and long-abandoned speaker poles. Ten giant screens, surrounding it all, enclosing it. Windows to nowhere.

"Must have shut down the night after you two were here."

Joanna drove in over cracked pavement and weeds. A tall wooden fence lined the way to a carport with overhang, a ticket booth long abandoned, aqua blue.

She could almost feel Anthony beside her, almost see his smile out of the corner of her eye, his teenage amusement-not-excitement at the adventure, the humor – a Western at a southern California drive-in.

"Kind of its own country," Cole says.

Rows of speaker poles fan out in five directions, toward five screens, from a central area with playground – swings, a slide – and a concrete outhouse.

Joanna guides the Winnebago along one lane, the ground humped on either side, the speaker poles shadowy creatures, keeping vigil.

"Well," she says. "We can camp here for free."

They need sleep. A place to rest.

She steers the motor home to the end of the lane, pulls up alongside a speaker pole three rows from the front, faces a gaping screen. Shifts into park. "What do you think?" she says.

Cole looks out into the night. At the wide white screen. "Too eerie," he says. "Too close."

She follows the dirt road that leads in front of that screen, to a gap between two sets of rows.

She backs the vehicle in.

"How about this?"

Out the windshield, speaker poles fan in five directions. Three screens, at a friendly distance, look harmless. Amusing.

Cole nods.

Joanna turns off the engine. A good night's sleep has only made her crave more.

"Peaceful," he says. It seems to him a good place to start, a landscape entirely new.

They sleep soundly. They half expect to wake to a hum of activity. Construction of a shopping mall. Instead, the chirp of morning birds. The occasional sound of a distant car. Sunlight bathes the motor home. A window of brilliant blue. Joanna watches the sky and waits for Cole to wake.

They take their breakfast outside. Set up lawn chairs in front of the vehicle, one by each headlight. Tombstone sunglasses.

"There's something spooky about this in the daytime," he says. Three screens yawn above a corrugated tin fence a hundred yards distant. A cluster of oaks beyond. Speaker poles in neat rows, an orchard of stunted trees. Cole eats a raspberry frozen fruit bar. To their left, across the packed dirt road, loom wood frame supports, a giant X of two-by-fours, the back side of a screen. Giant white rectangles scattered in the distance.

"This is it," she says. "A little unclaimed corner of California." Ahead of them, a slide and an old metal swing set, animal-shaped swings hovering a foot above the ground. Rest rooms, a squat concrete building with peeling aquamarine paint. "Wide open spaces. Our own desert hideaway." She peels the pink, marshmallow-coconut shell off a Hostess Sno-Ball and swallows it whole.

"Those things will kill you," he says. He has his eye on the old refreshment stand, perched between the two star-shaped clusters of parking spaces. "You two get popcorn there?" He nods toward the building.

"Yeah," she says. "Probably."

He wonders how she'll do here with the ghosts of her son. The ongoing hurt. How, even with Anthony settled in Colorado – a room, a job – he doesn't want to see Joanna. Or talk to her. Afraid she'll be mad. That she'll try to convince him to come home.

Cole is transfixed by the color, the fading paint. It reminds him of Mexico, where he's never been. "I like it," he says. It feels good to sit somewhere outside, somewhere that might become home. "I want to set up shop. Get to work."

A sideways glance. "Remember," she says, "we're starting over."

A bite of juice bar. The frozen fruit stings his teeth. "I remember."

She watches him. Eats the creme-filled cupcake.

"How about we move over there," he says, "by the side of the road. We could see trouble coming."

Joanna licks crumbs from her fingers. "Tell you what," she says. "You be in charge of location."

SCREEN SIX

A man in a gray suit and bowler hat stands before a small crowd. A small wooden table before him. Magnolia tree behind. Night falling on a dusty street in an old West town. Across the street, the saloon does a brisk business. Piano music and laughter.

The man paces before his listeners. His voice smooth and urgent.

"Skepticism is our stock in trade," he says. "It is hard currency in this great nation. Which of us has not had the experience of being hoodwinked, my friends – buying into something only to find out that it was an illusion, or worse, a deception." He pauses. His body in profile to the audience, his head turned to face them. "We've been stung by so many false claims we prefer not to believe anything. Our trust betrayed so often, in so many ways, that it's more prudent – less painful – not to give it."

"This world is filled with frauds – mountebanks and charlatans. Our leaders are discredited, our products don't perform as advertised, our institutions invariably disappoint us. You have to protect what you know and believe. Certainty – conviction – these are precious commodities. Hard to come by. Reality is slippery. What is it, how do you hold it? Is it what you see? What you can hold in your hand? Is it what fits the things you know to be true? Our world changes daily, our lives altered irrevocably by abstractions, the working of forces we cannot see or touch. Pollutants poison our atmosphere. Toxins collect in clouds, fall with the rain. We engineer the foods we grow, doctor the milk we drink, rewrite our histories, twisting the tales to trumpet our own agendas. All of it moving so fast we can't keep pace with the questions, let alone formulate answers. What is real? It's no wonder our children are confused. Enraged. We can't guide them. We can only scratch our heads. A town dying of cancer from chemicals spilled in its soil a generation ago. Who is to blame? Where do you take your anger?"

On a shelf set into the front of the table sits a glass. He pours into it from a carton with Paul Newman's face on it.

"What brings me here tonight? Nothing short of a miracle. I know. The very word makes your throat dry with distrust. It is this skepticism I appeal to, ladies and gentlemen. For what intelligent man could stand here claiming miracles and expect to be believed?"

The man reaches under the table again, this time removes a brown bottle from a cardboard box and sets it on the table top.

"And yet here I am. Placing in front of you this bottle and laying claim to the word miracle. Why? Because these eyes have seen the stricken walk, the dead rise up and take breath, the hopeless and broken-hearted find cause to continue.

"Ladies and gentlemen, Dr. Bell's Elixir sounds pathetic. A cruel joke. A degrading exercise that belittles our problems. We dare not believe in the possibility of a leader with integrity, let alone this. But I'll challenge you with the very outlandishness of the claims. Listen. A cure for AIDS. Yes, you heard me. Reversal of the greenhouse effect. Significant. Yes. But these things are just the beginning. Because I'm talking about something deeper." He pauses. Touches a finger beneath his eye. "Discernment. Clarity of vision.

"If I had not witnessed the stunning effects of this elixir, if I could not claim first-hand experience of these miracles, I would not have the courage to stand here and play the fool.

"But I ask you, does there not come a point at which we must follow the wild hope and, despite all evidence, believe in possibility. Because the not believing will cost us our very lives."

There is a commotion, a bustling in the audience as the crowd surges into one mass of uncertain intention.

"Please, ladies and gentlemen. No pushing. There's plenty for everyone."

An outdoor cookfire. Dusk falls on Winnetka. Joanna sits in a beach chair with a tall tumbler of Newman's Own Lemonade, watching Cole stir a pot of hot dogs and baked beans.

"Wow." Joanna's legs stretch in front of her. "This is going to take some getting used to."

Cole is transformed. Gone is the ponytail. Inch-long hair now flat against his head. The contours of his skull visible. It gives him an air of seriousness. Determination.

He grins. "It's the new me."

"I applaud you." Joanna sips lemonade. Her calf and thigh muscles ache. "I may not recognize you, but I applaud you."

"Eight bucks. Roy's Barber Shop." The new Cole squats at the fire. Western sky streaked purple and orange. " 'Lose it all,' I told them. 'Short enough so I can't comb it.' I didn't look until the job was done.'" Head high, shoulders back. Proud of his bravery. "I hardly knew myself."

The fire crackles. A ring of stones surround the blaze.

"This is great," he says.

"See? I told you."

The cookpot suspends from a hammered iron arc anchored by granite. It had been Joanna's idea. Her design and construction.

They'd gone to the beach every day for a week. Bought brightly colored bathing suits and drove down the coast highway. Malibu. Topanga. Santa Monica. They collected sunscreen. He worked his way down from SPF 60 to SPF 30. The right degree of protection mattered. Heavy coverage on the nose. The tips of the ears.

Joanna laughed at him. "Relax," she said. Waves crashed at Zuma. Matching beach chairs. "You haven't fried yet."

"Because I'm obsessed." They went to the beach in the mornings. Will Rogers State Park for hikes in the afternoons. He dug his toes in the sand. Watched the tide come in, the water edge closer with each wave. "I'm not sure I can do this much longer."

"Too decadent?"

"It's my delicate skin." More and more, he was preoccupied with thoughts of command strings.

"What do you want to do?"

He grinned. "Watch cowboy movies."

They bought a television with built-in VCR. An armload of Westerns. A giant bag of popcorn. They lay on their beds and watched Paul Newman and Robert Redford rob banks, then try to go straight. Butch and Sundance loading pistols, their last, futile stand. Pushing their bullet-ridden bodies out into the courtyard where scores of Bolivian soldiers waited to gun them down. Cole paused the tape.

"You think they knew it was over?"

"No way." Joanna munched popcorn. "Look at those faces. They were riding out of there."

They watched John Wayne on a cattle drive. Cowhands gathered around a cookfire, beside the chuck wagon, eating beans from tin plates.

Now here they are. Plastic camping plates substitute for tin. The smell of woodsmoke. The gurgle of beans. Cole has to admit it feels good. "When you're right, you're right."

"We should get a guitar," Joanna says. "Do you know how to play guitar?"

Cole shakes his head. His short hair a shade darker, sand-colored.

She sips lemonade. Rubs her thigh. "I ran this morning."

"Yeah?" He tastes beans from the cooking spoon. Not done yet. "I didn't hear you go."

"You were already up and out." She sets her glass on the ground. "Early appointment with the barber?"

Wood smoke drifts past her. Cole pokes at the fire with a stick. The sky becomes muted as the light fades.

"You dove in, didn't you?"

He stirs the pot, lets steam escape. There was something deeply satisfying about reading through the code. It filled him. Gave a recognizable shape to his day.

"Asshole."

The bottom edge of the sun slips below the foothills.

"So what if I finish it. Doesn't mean I'm going to *do* anything with it."

"Meet the new Cole," she says. "Same as the old Cole."

"I can't just walk away."

"Sure you can. That was the whole idea." Beans flavored with molasses. The fire crackles, pops. "Remember?"

"Don't worry," he says.

"I'm not worried. I'm angry." She lights a cigarette. "We had a deal. A fresh start. No looking back."

"I'm here, aren't I?"

"I don't know. I was talking about more than a haircut and a change of scenery."

"We can't all reinvent ourselves every other week."

Teeth on her lower lip. She smiles. "A little imagination, Cole. It's all I'm asking for." The hum of crickets. "Don't fuck this up."

He stirs the beans. Scrapes the spoon along the bottom to raise the crust.

Her eyes small. She smokes. Watches the sky fade.

Joanna stretches her hamstrings. One foot on the ground, one on the third rung of the thick metal ladder that leads up to the slide. She bends toward her raised foot until she can feel the pull. Sun well into its morning climb. Joanna will stretch and run. It is a habit she hopes to re-establish. A physical sensation she misses. She needs a regimen of exercise. Needs to engage and exhaust her body to keep her mind from working overtime.

She extends, touches her nose to the knee of her raised leg. Feels the muscle respond. Beside her, a row of swings hang from a metal frame, the swings some indistinguishable sea mammal – dolphin, porpoise, shark. She stretches first her right leg, then her left, and then she does 20 push-ups in the dirt and grass where the rows from five of the movie screens converge. She does the push-ups slowly, the weight of her body in her arms, the sun in her pores. Then she shakes out arms and legs, bounces on the balls of her feet, and runs.

She runs down Winnetka Avenue, along Devonshire, Moorpark, Buena Vista. She runs past houses – pink and beige and white stucco, Spanish tile. Entire blocks of California apartment buildings, two-story structures with glass doors opening onto courtyards with pools, the buildings all called Something Palms or Malibu Something, or Pacific Rest, which sounds to her like a funeral home, the way it has always bothered her when flight attendants say "or wherever your final destination may be." Joanna does not want to think in terms of final destination. Joanna wants to sweat. To experience fatigue.

When her mind is working overtime, she sees pictures. Pictures of Anthony leaving. Anthony struggling with homework – say, eighth grade math – herself poised in a doorway. When to enter that room. When to let him find his way. Pictures of a golf course in Oregon.

She runs harder through Chatsworth. Bungalow-style houses with thick, coarse lawns. The kind of grass that stands up to a desert climate. Her feet bounce off the pavement. She can feel the impact up her calves. Breathing hard but strong. The thing she most marvels at about California is how the curbstones are so neat – sharp angles untouched by time or temperature, street addresses stenciled on the side. It bothers her, this neatness. A vaguely insulting investment of material resources. She is lithe when she runs, her body almost weightless. She is damp in a sport bra and shorts. She is in motion.

She does not know where Anthony is or what he is doing. She reminds herself of this. She cannot control the possibilities that run through her head.

She pulls up at the corner of Devonshire and Topanga Canyon, a small park. Her heart pounds against her rib cage. Deep clutching breaths. Sweat. She wipes her brow. She walks in large circles.

She cannot arrive at answers, cannot locate her son and so to play it out, water the seeds of possibility planted in her mind, is simply a form of torture. But as soon as she stops running, her mind goes to work.

She does twenty push-ups on arms that feel like rubber. She runs down Topanga Canyon to the reservoir, runs fast and light around the valley's water supply, a sumptuous lake amid hills of yellow-brown grass. Her body happy. Her mind content. She remembers stories of drought a few years back – how folks in Fresno Sacramento Salinas had to ration drinking water while those in Los Angeles hosed down driveways. She's never before understood water as a commodity.

She will run around the reservoir, wind back through Chatsworth, up Winnetka to the drive-in. She will grab the metal pole from the swing set and swing herself around it, the finish line, the place where two days ago she nearly cut open her hand on a jagged area of the pole. She had taken a hammer and pounded the gouged metal back in place, at first to make it safer, and then because the pounding itself, in rhythm with her pounding heart, her rubbery exhausted arms, felt good. She discovered tears on her cheeks when she finished, tears that lingered while she wrapped duct tape around the wound. She is making a place for herself. She is learning strategies for survival in the desert.

Cole sits on the floor of the refreshment stand. Stained linoleum. Trace odors from years of butter flavoring, salt. Coca-Cola at his side. Peanuts in his fist. He pops them into his mouth two at a time. Stares at the computer screen. In some ways, it is as if he never left Z-Tech. The concentration. The focus on solving a problem, the need to see beyond it, the tinkering with half-lines of code, breaking an obstacle down into its smallest bits, isolating it in order to get past it.

```
if (rsa_private_decrypt(session_key_int, session_key_int,
        sensitive_data.server_key->rsa) <= 0)
```

In some ways, of course, it is entirely different. California sun through the window. Long afternoon breaks when the heat is at its peak; sometimes a siesta, sometimes a walk, through the woods behind the movie screens of the far cluster, or into the foothills beyond the driveway. The Honda generator that hums behind the building, his source of power. He has cleaned this new work space, scrubbed the walls counters floor until it is drab, not dirty. Joanna has encouraged him to walk. To learn the plant life. She is teaching him yoga. Simple starting positions. The dog. The candlestick. He has watched her do the turtle, body bent in half, arms extended underneath, and yearned for that degree of flexibility.

"Start small," she has told him. "You'll get there."

And he is.

The biggest difference is working alone. He misses the simple camaraderie of hallway conversation. You could drown in this work.

When he had imagined this life, when Joanna had conjured this vision of a new start, it loomed as an adventure. Cole had not foreseen days stretching endlessly before him. Free time as a curse. It had not occurred to him that a new life could mean a life empty even of those things he'd had before.

```
for (i = 0; i < 256; i++) rand[i] = arc4random();
```

He walks the path of shrouded language past the point where he led Z-Tech astray, the place that stymied him for weeks. Grins at the thought of all the false trails their new programmer would go down before arriving at a solution, the hard work still to be done. He wonders who they would hire to replace him. Some kid willing to work 16-hour days to prove himself. To try – in vain – to hit Warren's launch date, only a month away.

```
RAND_seed(rand, sizeof(rand));
      /* Demote the private keys to public keys. */
      u_char *session_id2 = NULL;
```

The difficulty in writing an encryption system for electronic commerce is to make it complicated enough to assure adequate security, but simple enough to allow fast transaction processing, so that potential customers don't lose patience, or doubt the system's integrity. The more secure an encryption key, the longer it takes to process, yet that very delay tends to make inexperienced users distrustful. As if the longer the transaction takes, the greater the likelihood that some clunky machine is malfunctioning, their credit card information broadcast in cyberspace.

The greater the number of variables involved, the greater the risk that any one of them could be an avenue for a security break – a weak link – thus the need for a longer key. But a longer key – a string of integers that could run 250, 300 characters – takes longer to process and plays into consumers' fears that the Internet is an enormous, unpredictable cipher – an anarchic alternate universe where thieves prowl undetected. And it was Cole's – and

Z-Tech's – job to quell those fears. The version Cole had left Z-Tech was an early iteration, complex but slow, which also failed on certain browsers. Z-Tech would discover the problem quickly, but there was no quick way around it.

He was counting on Z-Tech to attack the problem from the browser end first. It was the logical thing. And yet it was a red herring. Cole had discovered that the solution lay elsewhere. Like a bad chemical mix, something in the 128-bit key version that he'd left triggered a reaction whose results emerged in one spot, whose roots were in quite another. Even when Z-Tech's developers determined that it wasn't a browser problem, it could take them weeks to trace the real cause. Longer still to find a solution. He had stumbled upon it one day, through sheer frustration deciding to add to the length of the key, creating a 132-bit algorithm and determining to make it as fast as the 128-bit version. For reasons that defied logic, it worked.

Sun bakes the small building. By midafternoon, he is forced outside. To a beach chair in the shade of the motor home. So he works hard in the mornings. Starts early.

The application of time and energy. Cole's skill and experience versus a kid's ambition and drive. The more Cole works, the more he wrestles stubborn sequences that yield so slowly, the more he wishes he had the boundless energy of youth, the unbridled confidence that he could make any problem knuckle under through sheer force of will. He begins to wonder if he can do this. And if he can, can he do it before Z-Tech.

The Winnebago has two beds, side-by-side, that are more like benches – narrow, not long enough – so that he has to sleep curled up, or with his feet hanging off, and she fits just snug, head gently touching at one end, feet resting against the board at the other. They lie in bed and talk. They like to imagine they are cowhands in a bunkhouse, or sheriff's deputies protecting a town under siege.

"Remember in *Rio Bravo*, how John Wayne and his deputies bunk at the jail before the big showdown with Claude Akins' brother?"

"Is that where Dean Martin and Ricky Nelson sing that duet?" He pulls a blanket over him, even though it is warm. His feet stick out from the covers, off the end of the bed. He wiggles his toes. Pictures Dean and Ricky, enlisted as deputies to help protect the town against a ruthless cattle baron.

"Yeah." She tucks her hands behind her head, her fingers interlaced. "And Dean is trying to prove – mostly to himself – that he's no longer a worthless drunk – that he can be counted on."

"And they've sent the Duke off to the hotel to make nice with Angie Dickinson, and they're all feeling pretty good about being together, like they're untouchable."

"Which is how you know trouble is coming." Her bed has a window, and out the window she can see stars, a sliver of moon. "And even Walter Brennan sings, remember?"

They laugh at the thought, though neither of them can remember the song that Walter Brennan sings.

"It's right after he has that great moment where the pressure's starting to get to him – he's been alone protecting the prisoner, listening for any sound that might be a hint of the trouble he knows will come – but no one will acknowledge him. The Duke is focused on keeping Dino from going on another bender. And Walter Brennan says, 'I guess you have to be a barfly to get any attention around here.' And he grabs the bottle and says, 'I might as well start now.'"

Cole conjures the movie in his mind. Casts himself as the Ricky Nelson character, the reluctant deputy Colorado, mysterious and untamed like the land. A drifter, good with a gun. The law isn't what matters to him. It's the adventure. The chance to show what he can do. Cole tries out Joanna as Dino, the experienced one, savvy but erratic.

They sleep side by side. Dappled in moonlight. The space between their beds small enough that, if they reach out in the night, they can touch.

*

She runs in the mornings. Showers. Smokes. Eats an enormous breakfast on her beach chair in the sun. In the afternoon, she makes excursions. Travels through the valley, to learn its contours, to understand its shape. She searches out antique stores and junk yards, browses shelves rows aisles of salvaged objects.

On one of her excursions, she finds a western wear shop in Reseda. Buys herself a pearl-colored Stetson. The hat sits huge on her small head – it's a 7-1/4 and she's not – she has to tip it back until the brim touches her spine, and even then it threatens to cover her eyes, but it's the only one the color of sun-whitened stone. A thin band of brown leather. She picks out presents for Cole. A buckskin vest. A black hat. She sees it and can't resist. She is not angry. He lacks experience in new starts. He doesn't understand the working of invisible forces; the immutable laws of nature. She is disappointed, but she has the strength to show him.

"Would you cut the tags off," she asks the sales clerk, an ancient man with black framed glasses, a plaid flannel shirt and bolo tie. "I'm not sure we have scissors at home."

The man looks at her out of the corner of his eye, but nods and does as she asks. The store smells of dusty wood. He bags the purchases.

"I'll wear that hat," she says, taking hers. She hums "Red River Valley" without realizing she is doing it.

She stopped because she spotted a junk yard – Max's Salvage. Parked a few doors down, the first available string of two parking spaces. The western wear shop was right there.

She carries Cole's hat and vest in a paper bag through the entrance to the junk yard. A driveway.

Sun high in a faded blue sky.

A dog she cannot see barks twice, deep-voiced.

Along a cyclone fence, a row of ceramic bird baths, lopsided and uneven. Refrigerators and stoves, many with doors missing, interspersed with lawn ornaments – jockeys, flamingoes, hoboes. A door to a small office, empty. A tangle of abandoned cars and car parts.

50

She wanders past the bird baths, finds a steam radiator, cast iron, a set of fireplace tools beside it. The radiator has begun to rust.

The dog barks again. She looks around and sees a blond German shepherd turn the corner, eye her. One more bark. Half-hearted. Enough to let her know he's trouble when he wants to be.

"King." A man's voice. "Shut up." The man – old stooped body, big square bald head, large gray eyes, skin so pale it's nearly translucent – has emerged next to the dog. "That's King. He's a good dog, most times. He's miserable when it rains." A small smile on a slightly sour face. Loose rayon shirt. Gray plaid pants. He looks like a retired town clerk.

"You Max?" She runs her hand along the radiator.

"I am."

She pushes the hat back off her eyes.

"You don't look much like a junk yard owner."

"You don't look much like a cowboy."

She grins. "How much you want for these?" She has one hand on the radiator, the other on the fireplace tools.

"Which one?"

"Either," she says. "Both."

"What's it for?"

She has an idea forming. A relic from her Catholic past. "That affect the price?"

He scratches his head. "I don't suppose. Call it fifteen each, twenty-five for the whole deal."

Penance. Absolution. The bliss of forgetting.

King barks at someone – something – on the street. This time, the sound of a dog that means business. "I'll take the radiator."

Inside the small office, she hands Max fifteen dollars. He has donned a pair of Latex gloves. Puts the money in the drawer of an old cash register. He wears a hearing aid tucked behind his right ear. "I thank you," he says. "I'll help you out with it."

She thinks he must be in his seventies. She thinks about what types of metal can be pounded into different shapes. She wonders why this man wears Latex gloves. She will add the radiator to a small collection of metal objects she is accumulating.

An hour later, she steers the Winnebago through the cracked driveway and into the lot. Row after row of poles with attached speakers. It looks like a farm, its crop some strange, heavy gray fruit. A squat building set in the middle of it all, paint peeling.

She has the hats, the buckskin vest and two sheriff's badges she bought at Pic 'N' Save on the way home.

She finds him in the building, the old refreshment stand, sitting on the floor, knees pulled up before him, notebook computer on his lap.

A small room, walls painted robin's egg blue, floor of white linoleum squares veined with gray. A Formica counter holds a Coca-Cola fountain unit. Cole leans against the counter, under the Coke sign.

"Hey." She is surprised at how easily she has adapted to this short-haired Cole. How she already has trouble remembering him with his ponytail.

The air is close. The faint smell of old popcorn.

He smiles. "Nice hat."

"Bought you one." She hands him the bag.

He grins. Pulls out first the hat, then the vest. Fingers its soft leather. "Thanks." He slips the vest on over his t-shirt, a giveaway from a computer graphics trade show. Holds the hat in his hands. "Black."

"They were all out of badass grins. See if it fits."

He tries it on. A little loose, but okay. "Is it me?"

She raises her eyebrows. "We'll find out."

He sets the hat low over his eyes.

"Wait," she says. "There's more." She produces the sheriff's badges out of her jeans pocket.

"Raise your right hand," she says. "Do you promise to uphold the law of this town?"

"Depends," he says. "Which law?"

"The only law. The law of the frontier. No looking back."

A smile. "I promise."

She pins one badge on his vest. Hands him the other. "Now you."

He holds the badge with both hands, as if it were a sacrament. "Do you promise to stick this out?" He pauses. "To love and cherish, for richer or poorer, in sickness and in health."

"Shut up," she says. "I promise to be a good Sheriff."

He pins the badge to her shirt. "Close enough."

They are untouchable.

She takes his hand. "Let's take a turn around the town."

Of the hundreds of lines of code Cole has written, pasted from project files, tested and tweaked until they are everything he wants them to be, there is one phrase, one small sequence, that stymies him. It is a tiny part of the whole, yet without it the application is useless.

```
for (i = 0; i < options.num_host_key_files; i++) {
buffer_append(&b, "\0", 1);
```

Cole sits on the smooth linoleum of what used to be a refreshment stand. Legs stretched before him. Computer on his lap. This is the part of the job Cole has always liked best. Isolate a problem and peck away at it. There are a finite number of possible solutions. It is simply a matter of having the patience, the willingness to remain focused, to spin a tight web of possibilities and then execute them.

A fly explores the small room where somehow the smell of grease lingers after all these months. These years. Cole will type in a command string and let its implications play out. Then he'll adjust it, changing a character here, a number there. Correcting the order of the pieces. He has the discipline to make this work.

```
MD5_Final(session_key + 16, &md);
memset(buf, 0, bytes);
```

Cole misses the telephone. The escape route from isolation, from hammering through a problem alone. The instant connection. A casual call to Andrew, or Olga, or Lou, former colleagues. The ebb and flow of shared business, the easy bleed into occasional social time – *let's go for a drink, how was your weekend.* The loose network of fellow professionals. Enough to feel that you have a life. Now there is no context. Now there is a phone line, but no phone. A data line – a concession – in Joanna's name.

Cole's vision of the West is companionable, not solitary. It is the buddy movie. The easy banter of Butch and Sundance. The casual camaraderie of Duke and his pals in *Tall in the Saddle*, or *Santa Fe Stampede*. It is Cole and Joanna riding together on the open plain. Not Cole alone all day in a small room, where he is prone to fear and loneliness.

He munches a sugar cone. He found a box of them in a cabinet, along with loads of napkins and an enormous package of paper cups. Artifacts. He'd trusted that sugar cones would have an indefinite shelf life.

He presses the delete key four times. He scans the command string, looking back a few lines, working by feel, searching for a combination that satisfies. This is the pure thing. The essence. Creating what has not been before.

```
i = sia_ses_init(&entity, argc, argv, NULL
*sy = 2 * FRUSTDIM/viewport[WID];
```

It is a revelation to Cole how much his life has been built around work. Corinne would find it funny, that Cole could be still – again – surprised by this. He thinks about calling Corinne. But Corinne does not want to talk to Cole. This is long established. Besides, to call Corinne was to open himself up to a litany of all the ways he'd failed. Of all that he wasn't.

The fly lights again on the grill, on the cash register, an early LCD display model. A no-pest strip hangs from the ceiling, outdated, useless. Cole doesn't mind the fly. It's an element. It can be incorporated. Cole has the skill. Cole has the discipline, but he wonders does he have the time.

```
if (0 == debug_flag) { debug_flag = 1;
```

"Fuck." Not working. He stops typing. Takes the computer off his lap. Deep breaths. A change in focus. He attempts a yoga position. The dog.

Hands and feet flat on the floor, ass in the air, he tries to make with his body a right angle. It is a basic position. It doesn't look hard. "Straight lines," Joanna has told him. "It's all in the breathing." Somehow, invariably, Cole ends up doing a strange form of push-up. He is dispirited at how little progress he's made. He cannot even conceive of creating a straight line through breathing. He abandons yoga, picks up the computer.

```
else if (options.log_level < SYSLOG_LEVEL_DEBUG3) {
```

If this is a race, it is a marathon. Long, slow hills that exhaust the muscles, that breed doubt and cultivate despair. A fortnight on a single phrase that shows no signs of surrender. And for what? To know that he saw it through. To win, even if only he will ever know it. But he could lose. Passed in the home stretch, outkicked by younger, stronger legs. But Cole will not be outrun.

As he attacks the code, as he executes possibilities, he pictures himself roaming through Z-Tech's encryption undetected, treacherous. The mysterious man in the black hat. It is a vision that he could make real. Because there is a back door, and Cole has the key.

SCREEN EIGHT

A sound stage, made up to look like a city street, Upper East Side, Manhattan. A score of people milling about – cowboy, motorcycle cop, indian chief, construction worker. A handful of jeans-clad young men and women scurry about them, adjusting costumes, checking hair. A goateed man dressed in black paces in the foreground, paper coffee cup in hand, muscles permanently tensed. The director, Yvon.

"The cop needs more rouge," he shouts to no one in particular. "We're not as young as we used to be." A thin red-haired woman hurries offstage, returns a moment later and tends to the officer's face.

"Music cued?" asks Yvon. Salt-and-pepper buzzcut hair.

"Got it," says the redhead, patting the now-rouged officer on the arm.

The half-dozen costume-clad men begin to prowl, like cats. Taking deep breaths. Shaking shoulders forward and back. Puffing chests.

"Places, everyone." The director walks from band member to band member, determined dissatisfaction on his face.

"Wardrobe," he shouts. Bodies scurry. The red-haired assistant moves into the background, hoping to lose herself. A short, dainty man with a ponytail sidles over to Yvon, makes his face into a question.

The director sets down his coffee cup. Stands before the Indian chief, a tall black man. A teenage boy in flannel shirt and jeans fusses with a headdress, barely able to reach the chief's head. "Stop," Yvon says, but the boy doesn't seem to hear him. Yvon turns to the wardrobe man.

"Tell him to stop," he says. "I want the longer one." He pushes away the hands of the boy who is still trying to make the wrong feathers right.

"He can't dance in the long one," the shorter man says.

"He'll have to," says the director. "I want the long one."

A pulsing disco beat kicks in, loud enough to shake the floor.

"Turn that shit off," he yells. "We're not ready." He yanks the headdress from the Indian chief, thrusts it at the flannel-shirted boy. "The long one. Now." He stalks the set, eyes electric.

The construction worker, who has been ready for half an hour, kicks at the faux curbstone. "Let's get this *going.*"

"Two minutes," Yvon says. "We're rolling in two minutes. I promise." He forces a smile. "Look pretty now." Turns to the red-haired assistant. "Where's my coffee?"

She gathers the objects. She makes it her task to collect, to devote her considerable energy to the accumulation of shrapnel, of flotsam – machine parts, rusted-out iron husks, bits of broken glass. From these she will construct a shrine, a prayer for healing, an offering to keep the victims alive. She tells herself that she cannot be sure, reminds herself that the reason she is here is to avoid being sure. To keep alive the possibility that it is not, in fact, true what she believes to have happened.

It begins with the drive shaft from a totaled Range Rover, and a pair of suspension springs from a semi-truck. She knows that she wants gentler shapes – hard objects don't easily take on gentle shapes, and she likes that, too. She needs to do something physical, something to keep her mind focused, her heart hopeful.

She goes to the hardware store. Finds thick cotton working gloves. Iron pry bars in assorted sizes. A variety of hammers – sledge, claw, ball peen, even a tack hammer, just in case.

There are calluses. She loses more weight. She comes to love the feeling of bathing in sweat. As if she is shedding something.

She bangs at the drive shaft until it becomes rounded, softly curved. It is a sort of miracle to her. Inspires her. She stands it on end, plants it in the ground, in a remote corner of the drive-in lot, by a stand of jacaranda near the path to the wash. She wants privacy. She digs with her hands, with the shaft itself, scraping away dirt and rock. Her muscles quiver. She plants it a foot deep, packs earth and rock around until it will not be moved. A saguaro made of rusting steel.

She visits Max. She is particular about what she gathers – an oven door with a tempered glass window, its white porcelain finish intact – because she has time, because this is not about quantity. The suspension springs, in fact, she discards..

She sits with Max on the little bench inside the Airstream trailer behind his office. They drink coffee thick with cream and talk about his grandson, Nolan, who is allergic to the world – environmental allergies threaten to immobilize him every time he steps outside.

Max, eighty, ran an auto body shop for thirty years which has evolved into this junk yard. Max has learned a new language – multiple chemical sensitivity, anaphylactic shock – a new perspective. Max's rough hands handle metal all day – rust and dirt – but they don Latex gloves for dealing with the public.

"My son gets mad at me. Wants me to grow old graciously," Max says. He moved to Los Angeles the same year the Dodgers did, and for the same reasons. "Hell with that."

They talk about Joanna's project.

"The springs didn't work," she tells him. "As I stretched them out, they lost form. They cracked." They watch out the window, where King wanders the yard in the heat. She wonders if the hot pavement hurts the dog's paws. "They just weren't right."

"People are amazed at what you can do with metal," Max says. He sips coffee rich with cream. She makes it strong. "You ever do any welding? I could fix you up with an arc welder."

"I don't think so," she says. She can't picture herself in a welder's helmet out in the heat. She sweats enough as it is. "That's more than I want to get into." She sips coffee. "I want to do a ring of glass – the bottoms of bottles, jagged bits, set into concrete. Framed in iron."

Max has not asked her why she is doing this, and she has not offered to tell.

Some days as she works she listens to the radio, a small portable that never locks in to a station, so there's always a trace of static, the echo of another program. Other days she works quietly, listens to birds, the distant sound of cars, amazed that anywhere in southern California cars could sound distant. She returns to the Winnebago for lunch – a bologna sandwich, a glass of milk and a couple of Yodels, or a peanut butter and jelly sandwich and corn chips – and to see Cole, to remind one another that they are not alone.

"You should try it with potato chips," she says, munching a peanut-butter-and-honey-and-Ruffles sandwich.

Sunlight through the window. A plastic daisy in a glass on the table. She talks and chews. "How come you don't wear your hat? Don't you like it?"

The black cowboy hat sits on a shelf at the foot of Cole's bed. "I'll wear it. It's hot is all."

"No one said it would be easy under the black hat. Just remember, candy boy. You made this choice."

He sips from a bottle of Yoo Hoo. "I solved a subroutine this morning," he says. "Thanks for asking."

She has told him only that she is messing around with sculpture, that it is a hobby she's investigating. A way to spend her days. She feels guilty – hypocritical – to tell him more. She tells herself she is moving forward, not looking back. That he is the one dragging the past with him, weighing them both down.

After lunch, she returns to work. She whistles. Sometimes she whistles entire songs, sometimes she will break into singing. She works with jagged bits of metal, shards of glass. Her gloves, the thick cotton gloves from the hardware store in Reseda, are brown and torn – shredded in places. She cuts her fingers, scrapes her forearms. She hardly notices. She listens to the radio. She whistles. She sings. "Red River Valley" is her current favorite.

"From this valley they say you are going"

She remembers a music store, a black metal rack of sheet music. She can picture the music to Red River Valley on that rack in that store. A red cover, black-and-white drawing of a man in a cowboy hat, bandanna tied around his neck. She doesn't know if this is a true memory, or one she invented, but she likes to sing the song.

"I will miss your bright eyes and sweet smile"

She loves to work with the sledgehammer, and brought home a large piece of scrap metal – a car door – just to be able to pound at it.

"I'll remember the Red River Valley"

She does not know the extent of the injuries. Does not know the condition of the victims.

She does not tell Cole the significance of what she is doing.

One of her favorite salvage items is an industrial fan, enormous blades in a square casing. She set it at the side of her work area, where its blades spin idly in the breeze. She views her sculpture as an act of prayer.

She does not know the condition of the victims. Does not know if they have remained alive. If they will remain alive. Does not know where her son is or how to reach him.

Does not know – has protected herself from knowing – does not know if her son is responsible.

SCREEN FIVE

A black-and-white scene, a domestic scene, a living room. Contemporary Colonial. June wrings her hands. Ward walks through the front door, carrying a briefcase.

"Honey, I'm home."

He sees her pacing. Kisses her forehead.

"What's wrong, dear?"

Framed photographs on end tables. Cork coasters in a neat stack.

June's face etched with worry. "It's the boys. I'm afraid they're in some trouble."

Ward smiles. Relief washes over him. "Ah, the boys. What have they done now?"

She shoots him a reproving glare. "This is serious, Ward."

"Let's take a turn around the town."

She has decided she wants to tell him. To come clean about Anthony. Share her suspicion.

She wears her Stetson. Tombstone sunglasses. She finds him in the refreshment stand, huddled over his computer.

"Now?"

"Yeah." She has run six miles. Tried to read. Walked. Smoked. She does not feel the euphoria of one who has made a clean break.

She waits. Fidgets. Suppresses an urge to storm the computer, smash the mother board. "I won't stay for the showdown."

He flushes. Presses save. "Isn't gonna be a showdown."

"There's always a showdown."

He shuts down the computer. She helps herself to peanuts.

They walk, down one lane, up another. The hat slips over her eyes. She pushes it back.

"A fresh start," she says. "That's why people come west."

It takes him a minute to disconnect himself from the virtual and plug into Winnetka. She knows this.

"Brits came to America to escape. Americans came west to escape. You don't seem to grasp the pattern."

He runs a hand through his hair. Seems surprised to find so little. "Escape is fine. A noble tradition. But it's also about opportunity. Wealth. Power. How one group gets rich, writes laws to make sure they stay that way. Close off opportunity. Hire guns to shoot anyone who argues. That's the West, too."

"You're missing the point."

"Point is, maybe only the outlaws stayed true to what led everyone out here. They didn't cause the problems. They just found themselves on the wrong side of someone else's rules."

There isn't a cloud in the sky.

"And maybe they were opportunists, into thievin' and killin'." It's like talking to Anthony. "You want to be an outlaw, be an outlaw. But don't paint it pure. Have the balls to see it for what it is."

He pauses at one of the speaker poles. Fiddles with the volume knob. "'Scuse *me*. I thought we were talking. Having fun."

A shadow passes overhead. A red-tailed hawk sails skyward, talons clutched around limp prey – an antelope squirrel, or kangaroo mouse.

"I want to talk to you," she says.

"So talk."

Joanna scrapes her feet, her hiking boots, through the dust. "I'm not good at this."

They are surrounded by movie screens. The screens are in remarkably good shape. There are no gouges, no cracks, no spray-painted graffiti.

She lights a cigarette. Scowls.

"Part of the reason I married Ben, that I agreed to get pregnant, was that I thought he was the grounded one, the one with a clue about how to parent. That whatever I could contribute would be a bonus. Turned out he was into the idea of a baby, not the real thing."

A lizard wanders across the rise between rows. She has heard that if you grab a lizard by the tail, the tail will come off and the animal will escape.

They walk side by side. Stride for stride.

"I remember coming home, Anthony was three months old. I'd just started back to work. Ben kept him for the day. I could hear Anthony screaming from the time I reached the sidewalk. Ben had the headphones on, poring over texts. Eight, nine hours the baby hadn't been fed or changed." She smokes. "I knew then I would raise Anthony myself. That he would only get what I could give him."

Joanna's feet moving forward. Eyes on the horizon.

"He's a smart kid, Jo. A good kid. You did fine."

There's no way to ease into this. They reach the end of a row, and turn.

"So what happens if you call him? Arrange it with Sean?"

She doesn't know how to begin. Can't find words.

Sun beats down on them. Sunglasses are a necessity here, and she is grateful for their protection. Their cover.

They walk in the shadow of a movie screen. For the first time, she is afraid of them.

He hears it sometimes in the day, while he sits on the stained linoleum in the old refreshment stand, computer on his lap. The pounding of horses' hooves. The approach of riders. Feels the constriction of his throat that tells him the posse is closing in. That he should abandon his work. Run. He can tell himself there is no logic to experiencing these things. That they are the physical and psychological manifestations of fear. He can tell himself that he is safe. Can list for himself the reasons why Z-Tech will not pursue him, would never prosecute. And most of the time he believes them. Bases his actions upon them. But in the times when fear takes over, logic is worthless. Muscles clench in his stomach and back.

On the days when it gets bad, he takes time out from coding to peruse the Internet – News.com and deeper, C-net, the Hackers Home Page – looking for news of computer crime arrests and prosecutions. The pictures of hackers in handcuffs. The headlines. He particularly is drawn to the charges, a perverse fascination with the minutiae of legal definitions – how companies manage to prove they've been violated, to give a name to the silent, invisible intrusions into their financial affairs. Not burglary. Not trespassing, or grand theft. Wire fraud. Unauthorized access to a computer system. They don't sound like real crimes. It is hard to imagine the arrests. The manhunts. Yet the record is there.

Fifteen days to launch.

They cannot know what he has. Unless he reveals himself. He has recited this mantra in his head. And it has calmed him. Until now. Because there is a back door into the Z-Tech system, and Cole has considered using it. To monitor their progress. To assure himself victory. A door – a string of code that, when keyed in, bypasses security – that he created in a moment of anger, that would drop him into his rival's work. To monitor it. Or change it. Cole has the key, the bit of code, in a file on his hard drive, scrawled for backup on a business card in his wallet. He'd wanted to leave knowing they were vulnerable, that he could hack them anytime. He never thought he'd use it.

He flexes his fingers. Practices breathing. His yoga positions. The fish.

He sets aside the computer, lays on his back on the floor, extends his body. He visualizes that he is tall, that his muscles are not clenched. He breathes. Arches his back, his shoulders, cranes his neck. Reaches with his arms, his hands, underneath his body as far as he can. Under his ass. Claws to stretch further, like Joanna showed him – see, she'd said, smiling, breathing, calm, a twenty-year smoker, fingertips reaching halfway to her knees – but his back muscles rebel. Spasm. He grits his teeth and scrapes at the linoleum with his fingers. *Stretch. Relax.* Except for being on the floor, this is the position he'd be in if he were handcuffed. *Fuck.*

Against his better judgment, he tries the turtle. Folds his body forward on the floor, pushes his arms under his legs. His torso resists. It takes patience. Enough with patience. He forces his face toward the floor. His arms behind him. Something flares in his back. He is frozen. Pretzelled. Nose against knees. Ass on linoleum. He imagines being stuck here, Joanna finding him immobilized, a heap on the hard floor. A muscle flutters. Hot pain. He manages to untangle himself. Pushes to a sitting position. Scoots across the floor until he can lean against the counter. Breathes deep and slow, like she taught him, until the muscle he's strained relaxes some and he can get back to work.

He reads about an arrest in San Jose. The computer system of a southern California company had been breached. The perpetrator, a 22-year-old whiz, had called the company – and a number of others – to offer high-priced security services. When told he was not needed, he threatened to shut down the company's system. The owner hung up, considered it a crank call. Fifteen minutes later, every monitor in the company went blank.

Cole smiles. The strained back muscle flutters, a dull pain.

On some level, the young man's transgression is just a step beyond a childhood prank. A game to test skill and wits. But a high-tech crime specialist traced the suspect through phone records. Waited. Patient. Depending on what he found when he seized the hard drives, he might not even have a case for unlawful computer entry. Two weeks later, with carefully worded search warrants, the detective had made the arrest. His work a careful manipulation of language to describe what could reasonably be found, a sifting of law to attach that data to a crime. Computer searches and seizures are legally complex. Cole could take heart in that. But what he notices is that the arrest was made. The conviction earned.

But Cole is not interested in theft, or destruction, only in hindering progress. Anonymity would be key. He'd have to plant himself on a public machine. He is just speculating. But he can't stop himself from reading this stuff. Can't stop thinking about Z-Tech's back door. Can't tune out the sound of approaching horses.

When it gets this bad, he forces himself to turn off the computer. To go looking for Joanna. To call it a day. The muscle seizes in his back when he stands and he grabs the counter, clings, bends until the pain fades. Straightens gradually, almost completely. He crosses the compound, small steps, in search of comfort.

This day he finds her in her beach chair, in the shade of the motor home, sipping lemonade. Empty seat beside her. "What the hell happened to you?"

He scowls. Surely he's not so stooped. He's made the effort. *Homo almost erectus.* Good yoga breathing. "Pulled something."

Tombstone sunglasses. A smirk.

He drops his body into the empty chair.

"It's no wonder you pulled something," she says. "Sitting on that floor all day. You should get out more."

Exterior. Day. One of those red Coca-Cola signs you see on low-rent variety stores, places that sell soda and chips and lottery tickets, or overpriced suntan lotion and sunglasses if they're near the beach. Once in a while, they house a discovery, like coffee milk shakes. The signs always have a white bar at the top where the store can have its name stenciled in black letters. This one's at the corner of Beverly and Alameda in Los Angeles, on the outskirts of Little Tokyo. And the sign, above where it says *enjoy Coca-Cola* in white letters on a red background, says The Atomic Café.

It's exactly what Cole had hoped to find. He rode the RTD bus to Little Tokyo, wondering what year Internet Café made it as a yellow pages category. Stepped off into a wave of heat, walked down Alameda to Beverly, and smiled when he saw the sign. It reminded him of a place in Gloucester, Massachusetts, a variety store with gas pumps out front, at a bend in Route 127 near Pigeon Cove where he and his high school friends would skip school on hot days to swim, then stop on the way back, put some gas in Tom Skinner's Ford Falcon, and get milk shakes.

Best coffee milk shakes Cole has ever had came from Willow Rest. He knows it's an exaggerated memory. That we wax nostalgic not so much for the thing itself, but for the freedom we had to enjoy it.

Cole sought out the Atomic Café hoping for an anonymous modem hookup, and found much more. Scrambled eggs and home fries, chrome and red vinyl, a counter, a series of tables, a half-dozen semi-circular booths with multimedia PCs and G4 Macs. And Victoria. It was a little slice of heaven, and Cole quickly became a regular.

She was conversant with truant officers. Knew most of them by name. Armonk an affluent suburb, not the kind of town where truancy is a problem. And it's not as if Anthony was slow. He played the saxophone. Could sight read music intuitively. Sat with a sketchbook in class, drawing caricatures of his classmates. Had developed a pretty fair style by tenth grade. Taught himself to play guitar. His yearnings were to write jazz. To paint. To live simply, grow his own food. In many ways, he had a mature understanding of what his yearnings would require of him. He just couldn't make himself bend, do all he needed to do before they would allow him to go there.

"If I know what I want," he said, "what difference does it make how old I am?"

"Societies," she said, "are set up to serve *most* people. There are always other people. The trick for the other people," she told him, "is to find a way through without being crushed."

"What does that *mean*, Mom?"

"It means you need to finish high school."

The guitar – electric, a Les Paul – he bought with money he earned delivering newspapers – the *Times-Union* – at 5:30 a.m. She drove. That was her contribution. To pilot the Escort wagon through the sleepy streets while the sun came up. The late winter days were the worst. Damp cold. Slush. Dawn arriving without brightness. The occasional jogger.

66

"Ten points, mom," he'd say, goading her to drive through puddles, to splash them.

Or, "Sun's up earlier today. You can feel Spring coming."

He was the optimist of the pair.

On the crowded streets, she'd drop him at one end, and he'd run from house to house, zigzag across the pavement, drop the morning's news on porches, on concrete steps. She'd drive to the end of the block, put the car in neutral and watch him draw closer, his image moving in and out of the rear view mirror.

He got them both up every morning. Shook her alert enough to drive. Made coffee and breakfast when they got home. She taught him to make the coffee strong, so it would stand up to cream. At first, he made cereal. Frozen waffles. As he got older, he embraced the job. Grew into it. Fresh-fruit pancakes. Eggs over easy. Home fries.

She didn't fault the teachers or the school system. Everyone tried. Lenient boundaries. Alternate homework assignments.

She had chosen places to live based on the school districts. Bethesda, Maryland. Armonk, New York.

"We're going to work with him," Anthony's sixth grade teacher, in Bethesda, had told her. "We can make accommodations. But the bottom line is he's got to get it done."

The experimental school within the high school, in Armonk, they'd had high hopes for. She'd told him to hang on, gut it out through eighth grade then he'd do fine in the experimental school, called Murray Road because of its location. But it was too late. He'd lost trust, didn't believe school had anything he wanted. When he did do the book report it was on the Anarchist's Cookbook; and although it was clear to her that this was a cry of frustration, a gesture that could be laughed off in recognition of how hard he found this, his teacher wasn't feeling *that* experimental.

Armonk schools even had a psychologist, who was understanding, up to a point. "There are scores of children who don't fit," the psychologist said. He and Anthony had great conversations. They liked one another. "But the fact is that to survive in this culture, in this society, everyone needs to find a way to adapt – a place where they're willing to accommodate themselves. Socialization is, after all, a large part of what school is about."

It would have been different if he'd been defiant. She might have forced the issue. But they talked. To a great extent, they were together on it. He understood the consequences.

"I can't do it, Mom. I've tried."

And, "Why mold myself into someone I don't want to be?"

And, "I'm willing to live outside this culture."

"You can't know what that means," she told him. "What it requires of you. You're too young. You have to bend."

"Why? You don't."

By then, Joanna was dating women. By then, they had lived for a year in Costa Rica, where Joanna had baked bread at a restaurant and taught Anthony on her own. By then she had spent a summer living in Tahoe with a new girlfriend, who didn't last.

They sat at the kitchen table. Huddled over coffee.

"You don't do anything the normal way," Anthony said. "You take off when you want to."

The anger was natural – he was ten when she and Ben divorced. Any boy would respond that way. It was later, when Ben and Anthony would start weekend visitations with shouting matches, when his father finally ended all visits and banished him from the house he'd rented – it was then, four years later, that the Anarchist Cookbook thing started. A friend at school gave it to him. A cry for attention, for boundaries. She couldn't take it seriously. Didn't take it away. Why fuel the anger. Why give it a locus.

"I know you're angry, Anthony," she said over a breakfast of scrambled eggs and Canadian bacon – he'd kept the paper route, remained diligent with it, saved the money he'd earned. Gotten them out of bed every morning for four years. "You've got a lot to be angry about."

He sat with her. Sipped coffee. Ate rye toast.

A couple of fist fights at school. A conversation or two about constructing explosives. The infamous book report.

"I told her I knew how to build a pipe bomb. Listed the ingredients. Recited the steps."

"*Anthony.*" A part of her wanted to laugh. Another part of her wanted to flip a switch that would force him to conform.

"Relax, Mom. Just wanted to see if she was paying attention."

And that was as far as it went. Then he was into illustrations of plants. Precise scientific drawings, genus neatly labeled in block letters beneath each picture. She told him he had to stay in school until he was sixteen. Even after she had become convinced that, for him, there might be a better way.

"This isn't about me anymore," she would tell him, driving the white Escort station wagon, a stack of *Times-Unions* on the bench seat between them. "There are laws. People who will enforce them. It's not a choice you're allowed to make. Not until you're sixteen."

"*Why?*"

"I can't explain why. What I know is that it's hard to live outside society. You should stay connected. At least until you're old enough to fully understand the life you're choosing. The consequences."

So they dealt with truant officers and guidance counselors and school psychologists. They stayed close, and she was proud of that. They got him through. Until his fifteenth birthday. And then he left. Stayed with Sean for a while, in Boulder. And hard as that was, she could live with it.

Now he is out there. Somewhere. She thinks she knows where he is. But she hopes with all her heart that she is wrong.

SCREEN TWO

Wide shot of a golf course, early morning. Looking out from the clubhouse – the green-and-white striped awning intrudes at the top of the frame – onto the first tee. It's a straight-ahead par four, 330 yards, the ground sloping down to a fairway lined with oaks and red maples, a creek running across just before the apron to the green. On the left side of the frame, beside the tee, a row of electric golf carts stand neatly aligned, sparkling, ready for action.

There is the chirp of sparrows, the rattle and clink of clubs, the clack of spikes on pavement.

The camera pans left, to the carts. Twenty, maybe thirty, clean, white-roofed, cartoon-like, scorecard clips on steering wheels, E-Z-Go in silver letters on a red rectangle on the front. Sky postcard blue, grass almost eerie green. The camera joyfully slides along the row of carts. The sound of footsteps, the rattle of clubs, lingers. The camera slides back to reveal a man in a greenskeeper's uniform walking toward the vehicles. He has the languid pace of someone just starting his day. Behind him a man in yellow cardigan and gray slacks hops onto the seat of a cart whose rear compartment is filled with buckets of red-striped driving range balls.

The greenskeeper plops into the driver's seat, the second in the row of carts. Turns the key. There is an explosion, a ball of bright orange flame. Flying fiberglass.

Fade to black.

Exterior. Atomic Café. Cole parks a faded red VW Squareback in front of the café's picture window, grabs his memo book and roll of quarters. Santa Ana winds blow hot already – the day will be a scorcher. Cole pumps the meter full and goes inside. He'd bought the Squareback the week before. Paid $1500 cash to a kid in Laurel Canyon, a teenager who lived to surf, who loved the car but needed to either sell it or find a job. Cole had always wanted a Squareback.

Cole pushes open the door to a blast of air conditioning. A kind of country-western tune flows from the juke box. He is alone in the café, except for the young woman who works there.

"Hey, Victoria." He waves to her and parks himself in the booth that faces the picture window.

Victoria sits behind the counter reading a paperback. "Hey," she says. "What's up?" Chiseled features. Black hair falls loose around her shoulders. Graceful but rough around the edges – a Degas ballerina from the Granite State. She wears a dozen earrings in her right ear. "You're back."

"Of course I'm back." Cole logs on to the computer and chooses Virtual Reality Soccer from the games menu.

The café got busy at night, Victoria had told him. Became something of a hot spot. But it was quiet during the day. Especially in the mornings. She likes it that way. So does he.

Other times he's been in, there've been a few stragglers at the counter, drinking coffee and reading the *Times*, or *Daily Variety*. Today, he has the place to himself.

"So what can I get you?" Victoria sits on a ledge next to the grill, sandaled feet on the counter. Lime green t-shirt and jeans.

If he is honest with himself, she is part of the reason he comes back.

"Tall juice," he says. "When you get a chance."

He opens the memo book. Checks his notes.

She hops down from her perch. "With ice, right?"

"I'm flattered." He is cultivating an environment. Establishing a presence.

"Don't be."

He comes to the Atomic Café to play VR Soccer. He is restaging the World Cup in elaborate matches where he battles the computer, always taking the underdog – his Sweden against the computer's Brazil, his United States against the machine's Italy. He records the results in his wire-bound memo book, meticulously logging game scores and individual player statistics.

She delivers a tall glass filled with fresh-squeezed orange juice and crushed ice.

"Thanks," he says. "A boy needs his vitamins."

Victoria smiles.

He also comes to the Atomic Café to hack into the Z-Tech network. To use a public modem to connect to the Internet. To access the beta test version of the encryption through the exposed back door and prowl its corridors.

He sips juice. Makes notes in his memo book. There is a section for soccer, and a section for sabotage. He feels like a schoolboy. He has learned that Z-Tech will launch a placeholder version of the encryption system on Warren's target date. They will plan to replace it with the enhanced version – the version Cole is competing against – 30 days later.

Victoria wipes down the adjacent booth. She watches him make entries in the notebook.

"You're an odd guy." She lingers beside him, elbow on the booth back.

He laughs. Glances at the page to be sure he's not revealing something. "What's odd?"

"I don't mean in a bad way. You seem nice and all. Not dangerous." A truck rumbles east on Beverly. "Just the notebook. The game. Something a kid would do." Hands on hips, she watches him a moment, then moves behind the counter. Picks up her book.

This is Cole's third visit to the Café, to Z-Tech. On his first visit, his fingers had hesitated. He couldn't be sure if his key would work, or where it would take him. He'd fiddled with games – Galactic Bloodshed, Flight Simulator, VR Soccer – until he had the rhythm of the place, a confidence that no one cared what he was up to. Then he had taken the card from his wallet. Established the modem connection. Entered the URL for Z-Tech's development server and keyed in his back-door password.

He didn't feel like a hacker. It didn't feel like trespassing.

But his finger had hovered over the Enter key. Then, a rush of adrenalin as code filled the screen. He'd looked around, furtive. A couple grayhairs at the counter hunched over tabloids. Victoria making coffee. He felt his face flush. Fingers on the keyboard arrows, he scanned the code to see how far his rival had come.

Surprise.

This file was familiar. Fully familiar. It was Cole's old file – the one he'd left them – now functional. The new code nowhere to be found. Good news, bad news. If a repaired version of Cole's old file was in beta, that meant Z-Tech would be launching with it. Which meant the new guy's code was not ready. Would not be ready. So Cole could not monitor his rival's work. But Cole had time. To perfect his program. To develop a plan of attack. Because Z-Tech would have acknowledged to KBC that this launch version was only an interim solution, a functional application which they'd promise to replace with the full package – encryption's Holy Grail – soon.

Cole had sipped orange juice. Chewed ice. *How soon?* He pictured Warren, mouth pinched, eyes tight, having to break this to KBC. He pictured the team meeting afterward. *How soon?* Two months was reasonable. Warren would give them one.

Victoria wipes down the empty counter. He has come to trust her presence, to view her as good luck. She makes him think of his distant daughter, of how he hopes Rebecca will turn out – personable, self-assured. He sips his juice.

She's watching him. "So I'm curious."

"Yeah?" Voice wary.

"What is it with you?"

His eyes go from monitor to book to woman. From the menu in his brain he selects *jovial.* "I'm a reclusive billionaire," he says. "An eccentric."

"Nope," she says. She tucks the cloth in her pocket. Looks out the window. "You're not the type."

On the juke box, a woman's voice sings a country ballad, a recording that sounds remote, evocative, as if it was made in a tunnel.

"What type am I?"

"You're the type that's hiding something," she says. A wide grin.

He feels himself flush.

She moves to the booth across from him. Leans her back against the table. She lowers her head, raises her eyebrows as if to see inside him more clearly. "Or hiding from something."

He tells himself it's play. They are having fun. "Yeah," he says. Mouth dry. "That's me."

"Might be you've left behind your life, walked out on it, like in one of those stories where the guy goes for a walk and comes back 20 or 30 years later and no one recognizes him."

He sips juice. Chews ice. *Is this a normal conversation. Is this how people talk.* "Why not a billionaire?"

She has a big smile, the kind that transforms a whole face. "You don't have that billionaire feel." Head cocked to one side. "Maybe you're on the lam from trouble back east. You owe money to someone you can't pay and you're afraid they're going to find you, but you figure you've got time." She speaks as if she's recounting a movie plot. Or inventing one. His ears burn just a little. "Oh, yeah. And there's a wife and kids in there somewhere, a family you can't see now because, of course," she makes a little gesture with her hands, "you're on the lam."

She wipes mock sweat from her forehead. "So how'd I do?"

The burning has moved from his ears to his stomach. He is grinning. He fears the grin is too big, the grin of a man with something to hide. He suspects that if this were a detective movie and she were the detective, she'd know she had something. But she's not a detective. He's a cliché. They are having fun.

"Not bad," he says. "It's trouble back east. I'm a hit man for the mob – and an inveterate gambler – and I'm into Manny the loan shark for six large and I've missed payments and he's sending his guys and I've got to duck them because these hands" – he holds up his hands for inspection before her – "I'm like a surgeon, you see, these hands are my life."

"Wait," she says. She leans out across the aisle between them. Arms folded across her chest. "If you were a hit man, why would you run? Wouldn't you just kill them?"

He shakes his head. Firmer ground. "That's not how it works. Protocol."

"Ahh."

There's an eerie quality to the music. Like it's the house band for a country-western bar on some unknown planet.

"Okay," he says. "My turn."

She nods. "Shoot."

"You're nineteen years old. From the suburbs – north Jersey. Your parents – both avid Jets fans – divorced when you were eleven and you bounced back and forth between them ever since. You hate football. To this day you never wear green and white together. You struggled through high school – not that you weren't smart, but all that trouble, it was a distraction. You quit college after a year to move west, write songs, join a band. You work here, struggling to make ends meet until you can live your dream. You pierced your ear as a way to feel the pain of the divorce and express your frustration."

She thrusts her hands into jeans pockets. "You're close."

"So tell me."

"Twenty-four. Graduated UCLA last year. Double major, business and English, thank you very much. My parents have been married twenty-seven years, we get along so great it's boring." She fingers her left earlobe. "I first pierced my ear when I was ten. I get a new hole every year on my birthday. A good year goes in the right ear. Otherwise, the left."

He does a quick count. Three bad years. "You're twenty-four. What do you know about bad years?"

She fingers the earrings on her left ear one by one. A silver stud. "Twelve. My little brother bit me so hard he drew blood. Week before my birthday." A small silver loop. "Fourteen." Another. "Fifteen. No explanation necessary."

Pedal steel guitar through the speakers. Victoria looks back toward the counter. "I need to make coffee."

He gestures toward the computer monitor. "Cuba and Spain are waiting. If the players stand around too long, they pull muscles." He watches her walk away. Turns his attention to the computer, where he can move freely between soccer and sabotage. He is into the first round of the World Cup. Cuba v. Spain. He is exploring possibilities. Cataloguing opportunities. How to be a disruptive presence. He connects to the Internet. Enters the URL for the Z-Tech server:

http://ztest0052mercury/beta/index

Three items:
- Project Mercury – Beta
- KBC Commerce Engine
- Bug List – updated 7/23

He scans the bug list – the usual stuff. A certain quantity or price that malfunctions. Bad interface with a particular browser version. They'll be testing, running hypothetical transactions in every conceivable combination to ferret out glitches before going live. Cole has choices.

From where he sits, at a booth looking out the window of the Atomic Café, he can wreak several kinds of havoc. And so his job, while he sips juice and sets up the soccer match, is to consider what kinds of havoc he most wants to wreak.

He could disable the system right now, mangle the beta code so badly that Z-Tech could not launch. He could create new bugs faster than they could fix them, or undo the fixes once done. But, satisfying as these might be, they would disrupt Z-Tech only internally. And risk exposing Cole. Better to wait. To let the stakes grow bigger, the consequences more public.

At launch.

If there are problems with the system at launch, Cole reasons, if there are botched transactions or failed functions, Z-Tech will be thrown into a panic fixing those. It would damage their reputation. And stall development of the revised system. At launch, Cole could manipulate transactions, doctor accounts, re-route or alter purchases.

Launch is the time to begin. Then he will give himself a fortnight. And then he must be out.

SCREEN EIGHT

A dozen or so people milling about a sound stage designed to look like an Upper East Side street block. Brownstones, wrought iron, trash cans. The look and feel of summer. Yvon, the black-clad, goateed director, prowls the set. Pops a handful of antacids. Tosses an empty coffee cup. A vein raised on his forehead. Assistants bustle around him, adjust costumes – soldier, construction worker, Indian chief.

A harried assistant director appears center stage. Worried-thin, she casts quick glances around the room. Yvon disappears.

"Okay, people. How we doing?" Pallid complexion. Wispy hair. "Camera?"

A voice from offstage. "Ready."

She takes the slate, chalks the words, *Village People 2000, Go West.*

The actors converge center stage. Biker. Cop. The soundstage is heated to mimic the oppressive air of Manhattan in August. Production assistants drift into the background.

Yvon reappears, fresh cup in hand.

"No, no." He waves an arm at the scene. "Am I hallucinating here?" He approaches the Indian. Touches the feather headdress. "Did I or did I not ask for the long one? Who here has decided they can fuck with me?" The Indian rolls his eyes. "Where's that kid?"

The pallid A.D. shrugs.

Yvon takes the slate from her, tosses it onto a chair. Sips coffee. The vein on his forehead pulses. "Go count the olives in the enchiladas or something."

Midnight. The garment district. Olympic and San Pedro. Cole and Joanna comfortably numb. They've been alternating shots of tequila and espresso since dinner. Joanna parks the Squareback and they walk up San Pedro Street. Ghosted warehouses. Distant traffic on the Harbor Freeway.

Joanna cocks her head at a nondescript building. A concrete rectangle. "This is it."

Cole tries the door. Locked.

"Not that way," she says. An alley leads around behind. "This."

Joanna has a slight buzzing in her head. The feeling that she is a spectator in her own life. There are nights when she can drink tequila like water, never get drunk. Never get beyond this slightly distanced feeling.

The hum of street lights. Beige stucco either side. A moonlit alley.

"You having fun?"

Cole unusually colorful in lime-colored t-shirt and khakis. "I am."

They had a leisurely dinner at La Fogata in Van Nuys, played miniature golf in Sherman Oaks, walked along Seal Beach. Now she has convinced him to check out a club she's been visiting.

Joanna boosts herself onto a loading dock platform. "Here we go."

"How did you find this place?"

"Someone told me."

In through a fire door to a dim hallway. A throbbing pulse of bass from above.

Into a freight elevator. The old kind with iron doors that open vertically. With canvas handles and wood plank floors and the steel cage that rides up to the second floor, where the music is.

They push open the doors on a driving techno beat and a room not much larger than the elevator. White-painted brick. A thin sculpture in the middle of the floor. Papier-mâché arms, sheathed in black evening gloves and set off with pearls, reach elegantly up from a four-legged base, Windex-blue. A handful of people, only one of whom notices the elevator's arrival. A young woman, hair the length and texture of a troll's – so black it shines – she's looking for someone not them.

"I'm a sucker for shiny black hair," he whispers to Joanna. His anxiety palpable. This has not been his scene for a long time.

Joanna follows the music down a short, angular hallway into a room only slightly larger than the first, and more crowded. A dimly lit DJ sways. Headphones on, she's in her own world.

"Voilà," Joanna says, her body catching the beat. "Nirvana."

Her eyes scan the room, filled with women all shapes all sizes.

"You didn't tell me this was a lesbian club," Cole says, leaning into her.

"It isn't," she says. "Not strictly speaking." She spies out a man in the crowd, shaved head, oval glasses. Points him out. "See?"

In college, she and Cole would dance at dyke bars so she wouldn't get hassled.

"Besides, you like women, I like women."

Cole speaks into her ear. "If I'd known no one here would be after my body, I wouldn't have gone to such trouble grooming."

Joanna pokes his ribs. "Shut up and dance."

She lets the beat enter her body. They slide into a loose cluster of dancers. Sprinkled in among a predominantly twenty-something goth crowd are a few older faces. A dowdy librarian type, long dark hair streaked with gray. A lumpy hippy in a loose tye-died dress. Many faces Joanna has seen before. More of the papier-mâché arm sculptures – kiwi green, safety orange, cadmium yellow. Cole wanders off toward the bar. Joanna closes her eyes. A guilty twinge of relief. A female voice in her ear.

"I was hoping you'd be here."

Eyes open. A pixie. Black hair. Soft eyes that suggest an Asian lineage. A face younger than her years.

"Emily." Joanna smiles. She did not realize until this moment that she had hoped to encounter Emily. That she planned to sleep with her. Bass and drums pulse through speakers. Shake the floor. Joanna leans into Emily. Loses herself in the music. The sea of dancers, stretching back to the distant bar and beyond, doubled in the mirror behind. Light and sound and glorious motion.

Cole is at work on his second margarita when he notices a woman standing beside him. Rail-thin. Stubble of hair on a shaved head. Black band tattooed around her right bicep. Slim silver ring in her nose.

"Hey," she says. "You look familiar. You in a band?"

Lights from the dance floor pulse in the mirror behind the bar. Reflected bodies in motion.

Cole shakes his head. " 'Fraid not."

The woman leans back against the bar. Studies him. "Where do you live?"

He's turned on by the proximity of a woman with a shaved head. He feels contemporary. "North of Reseda."

"My boyfriend Honey lives in Reseda. He's a DJ. You know him?"

"Nope." He stares at her skull. The contours. The black fuzz. "Honey? That's his name?"

"Yeah," she says. "He's half Egyptian."

"I see."

The woman extends her hand. "I'm Morgan."

"Cole." They shake.

"I'm sure I know you from somewhere."

"People often think I'm someone else."

"Oooh," she says. "Sorry."

On the speakers, a song he knows from the radio. The Chemical Brothers. An impulse. "Can I rub your head?"

"No."

"Hmm." Thundering drums. "Buy you a drink?"

"Sure." Morgan raises a slender arm, calls out to the bartender. She wears a black vest, no shirt. Cole finds himself watching her move. "Cosmopolitan." The bartender slides away.

Cole places a ten-dollar bill on the counter. The woman with troll hair stands across the bar. Her eyes still searching. They land on him, then flit away.

"This DJ sucks," Morgan says. "Honey's much better."

Cole feels pressure against his leg. Something thrust into his pants pocket. Car keys. He turns. Joanna, a woman behind her. The woman is young. A buoyancy that once radiated from a younger Jo.

"Hey," Joanna says in his ear. "We're going to smoke a cigarette. I'll meet you home."

A tap on his shoulder. Morgan. "I know," she says. "Ever been to Greece?"

Morgan's drink has appeared. His ten dollars gone.

"Nope."

A nudge at his leg.

"You okay to drive?" Joanna asks.

He nods. Driving won't be a problem. Finding the car might be.

Joanna leans into his ear. "Nice hair," she says. "But don't try to go home with her. The dykes won't like it." She moves away, then leans back toward him. "I didn't plan on this," she says. Then she's gone. Until she said it, Cole hadn't considered the possibility. He turns his attention back to Morgan, who's sipping her Cosmopolitan.

"Girlfriend?" she asks.

"Roommate," he says.

She nods, as if that explains everything.

*

The more time Cole spends in his new office, the former refreshment stand, the more insensitive he becomes to the odors, the traces of its former life that linger, infused into the cracked linoleum, absorbed into the paint on the walls. Salty grease, sugar syrup, the not-quite-rightness of butter flavoring. Only after he leaves at the end of a long day of coding can he smell it on his clothes. Joanna catches it, on his clothes when he returns, on her occasional visits to watch the master programmer at work. "It's unhealthy," she says. "You spend too much time in this little room by yourself."

And it's true. He does. But it's what the project demands – a painstaking process of trial and error, balance and counterbalance, where even his best efforts can be thwarted by a bad chemical mix, the interface of particular hardware with his software creating a problem that wouldn't exist if run on another machine. It requires patience. There is no substitute for long hours spent developing the algorithm, testing it in various configurations, identifying which piece among the hundred involved derailed the transaction.

She sits on the counter chewing Mallo Cups while he runs sub-routines. She has just returned from wherever she spent the night. Dark lines under her eyes. Tousled hair. Cole works to remain immersed in the minutiae, the sub-strata, dug down through layer upon layer until his focus can hone on the finest grains, until he can analyze the interaction of those infinitesimal pieces invisible to the untrained eye. It is part of what he loves about the work, how strangely difficult it is to scramble data so that no statistical hooks remain, no toeholds which can be clawed out to extract information. And to do that as simply as possible, so that the entire transaction – a world of numbers – happens in seconds. Unnoticed. It is also a way to keep Joanna from seeing that he misses her.

"Cryptography is a black art, even to most computer geeks," he tells her. A tequila fog lingers in his head. A sour sediment in his stomach. "Even a simple e-mail travels a complex, unpredictable path." He wears his bemused smile. "Bounces from computer to computer, never going the same way twice, each route determined on the fly based on network traffic, on the random decisions of routing computers. An e-mail message from Sherman Oaks to Tarzana might travel through Singapore, or Paris."

"Whatever," Joanna says, hands raised as if in defense.

Cole has always been a puzzle solver. "Encryption software isn't like ordinary software," he tells her. "If there's a small flaw in ordinary software, it may mean that a spell checker wouldn't catch a certain mistake – or a sequence of characters may lock up the keyboard. With encryption software, the smallest flaw can push the doors wide open, to let anyone who knows what they're doing – who knows what's there for the taking – walk right in."

He's drawn by the possibility of perfection, tens of thousands of keystrokes operating without a glitch. And the race to deliver. Each obstacle an enemy. He challenges himself to find weaknesses, fuels himself with whatever anger he needs to keep going.

"So let me get this straight," she says. "All these hours. All this work. You're going to finish it and walk away."

Cole feels himself flush. "Sure," he tells her. It is unmapped country, and he is a pioneer. "Why not?"

She munches a Mallo Cup. Raises an eyebrow.

"I just want to know I can do it."

She has that tired look she gets in the afternoons. Miles of running. Hours of pounding steel.

"There are so many ways someone can break in. Sniffers, a bad digital signature. Hacking into root privileges. It's fascinating. Because it all comes down to a compromise between security and convenience. You could easily create a system that was, for all practical purposes, uncrackable, but no one would have the patience to use it."

Joanna yawns. "Fascinating," she says. She crumples her third Mallo Cup wrapper. "If I'd known you were going to be stupid I'd never have done this."

The heat. The undetectable-to-Cole's-nose odors. The lack of air. This is not the place to be hungover.

"What's that mean?"

"I don't know what it means." She throws the wrapper to the floor. "It means I'm tired. It means I don't want to know about this." Her runner's feet dangle in the air. "Maybe you should consider a different hobby," she says. "Gardening. Chasing women."

"Maybe you should try getting some sleep."

Joanna makes a little O with her mouth. "I see," she says. "Artist at work." She hops down off the counter. She has spent much of her adult life ping-ponging around the East Coast. Now the West. The miles are beginning to show. "Guess I'll have a nap."

Nights are the most dangerous. In the time when the world grows quiet and sleep begins to pull at her, that's when she is susceptible. That's when she thinks about Anthony, and fears for him. When she thinks about all she could have done differently. This is what she thinks about – as she drives, as she runs, as she watches the stars. This is when – and why – she starts to sing.

"Let's take a turn around the town."

Joanna stands over him, white hat on, tin star pinned to her burgundy silk shirt. In her hand, the buckskin vest.

Cole silent. Immobile. Asleep in a lawn chair in front of the motor home. Stars twinkle overhead. A half-moon sky.

Joanna shifts her feet. Hands on hips. She resists the urge to kick him awake. His haircut is what used to be called a regular boy's haircut. She wonders if Cole is what could be considered a regular boy. She is thinking about conformity. About the price you pay – the price your children pay – when you don't.

A song of crickets. Somewhere, a frog. She should let him sleep. But she has no sympathy for the reason he is tired. She kicks at the chair. "Come on," she says. "Please." He has a cowlick, hair whorled at the top of his head. Beyond Cole, she sees trees. Gentle slopes. Winnetka at rest.

On bad days, she can take it as far back as preschool, to interactions with a teacher she referred to as the Crayon Nazi. She was the parent of a child who would not color inside the lines. She taught him a phrase at four years old, they'd practice in the car, Anthony upset by the teacher's criticism of his pictures.

"Two words," Joanna would say. "Here's what you tell her: artistic license."

Stopped at a traffic light on Delaware Ave. Anthony in her rearview mirror, studying the world.

"Try it," she'd say, a playful smile.

"Artistic license." And they'd laugh together.

Ridiculous to ascribe meaning to this. Yet on bad days, she can't help herself.

A jackrabbit hustles into the bushes. A flash of gray. Everyone – everything – looks solemn in half-moon light.

She puts a hand out to rouse him. Fingers on his shoulder. How anyone sleeping looks like a child. How she cannot separate Cole from the work he is doing from her own failure to leave her fears behind.

"What?" Eyes open.

Fuck it. As soon as his eyes open, as soon as they make contact with hers, she knows she cannot talk to him. Doesn't want to. Cole is complicated. Joanna wants easy. She pulls her hand away. Fishes in her pocket for the car keys. "You'll fuck up your back again," she says. "Go to bed."

He has a post office box, and an elaborate system for receiving the monthly checks from his former employer. The checks are large – $10,000 large – and the agreement is he will continue to receive them each month for one year, assuming he does not become active in application design.

The checks are generated in Boston. They are direct deposited to a bank in Lexington, Kentucky, to an account Cole created for his college friend Bo Wilson. Bo is an artisan, a former application designer who developed a successful speech recognition technology and bought his way out of Silicon Alley. He now makes and sells pottery in Berea. He handcrafts bowls, paints them meticulously, drinks tea with his wife, and watches his daughter grow. Cole has visited them, the little brick house on a large plot of land. The tree swing. The whitewashed garage where Bo does his pottery. The pink bicycle that daughter Molly rides around the back yard. The odd horse, Rambler, that lives next door, so wary of human contact that when it sees someone coming, it walks slowly backward toward the barn until its tail touches the weathered wood; the horse that Molly tries to coerce to the barbed wire, but succeeds only in early spring, when the daisies bloom in the drainage near the fence. Cole thinks of all this the first of every month, when the checks are deposited in Lexington, where Bo will wait an agreed-upon three days, write a check, and mail it to a post office box in Key West.

In Key West, Alan will receive Bo's check. Alan lives on a houseboat, having cashed out his share in a software group that built an Internet commerce application. Two years into the venture, they'd jumped at an offer from a conglomerate. Now Alan lives on a houseboat, fishes, cultivates cooking skills, and builds a wine cellar.

Every year for Cole's birthday, Alan sends him a bottle of wine. Every year it is Cole's favorite birthday present. They all went to college together – University of Vermont – and have remained friends.

Alan deposits the checks in Key West, waits three days, and sends certified bank checks to a post office box in Ventura, where Cole collects them.

It's not only that he needs the money. It's the principle. And it's a way of knowing, each time the check comes, that they are not on to him.

It's an elaborate system for receiving the checks. But Cole believes in triangulation. He has a similar, somewhat less elaborate system for sending checks, which he also does every month. To his ex-wife Corinne, half-French, half-Dutch, fully exasperated with Cole. He had been effectively absent for so many years, his style not conducive to family living. There would be weeks where he simply didn't show up, immersed in a project – Cole you missed a soccer game, Cole you missed the recital, Cole it's Rebecca's *birthday* – then blam, instantly available for a few days, a week, and Corinne, and Rebecca, finally gave up.

*

SCREEN THREE

Grainy black-and-white, a lone outlaw perched on a rock, beside a split-rail fence. Horse tethered. A guitar picks softly in the background.

CUT TO

Scrub oak beside a dusty trail, a rider in the distance, coming closer. He's unshaven. His horse is black. A harmonica joins the guitar.

CUT TO

A third man, a rider, silhouetted atop the crest of a hill. He spurs his horse forward, meets up with the unshaven man on the dusty road. Their horses fall into step, side by side. They reach a fork. There's a rock. A split-rail fence. A lone outlaw stands, brushes dirt from his pants. Mounts his horse. Three men, three horses. Black hats, black vests, determined faces. They ride together. Silent. Inscrutable.

The three bad guys ride toward town as Tex Ritter sings.

Do not forsake me oh my darling
on this our wedding day

CUT TO

The quiet street of a western town. Storefronts, saloon, good honest people going about their business.

The three outlaws ride slowly into town.

If I'm a man I must be brave
and I must face the deadly killers
or lay a coward – a yellow coward –
or lay a coward in my grave.

As the riders pass, a Mexican woman wearing a shawl steps into the street. Crucifix around her neck, worry on her face. With her right hand she blesses herself, the sign of the cross.

Every sound structure has more than one entrance. Any builder will tell you this. Doors. Windows. Fire escapes. Granting visitors access to different areas. Means of egress in emergencies.

Brings a building up to code. It's only natural that Cole would have included a back door. He's a reputable builder. He wants to make the structure accessible. This door, this series of keyboard characters – numbers and letters – will soon open a door to a world of financial information. Hundreds of transactions. Thousands of dollars a day. From a national department store chain. A sporting goods manufacturer. A catalog-based clothing retailer. All clients of his former employer. All vulnerable to the door that he built. All unaware of their vulnerability.

Each day that Cole comes to the Atomic Café, after he banters with Victoria and conducts a World Cup match, he accesses the development server and enters the back door. A silent intruder.

The bug list is shrinking, the launch a week away.

Victoria sits at the counter, thick book in hand. Her hair in those thin braids. Cole struggles to remember what they're called – corn rows?

"Hey, Vic," he calls. "What'cha reading?"

She looks over the pages at him. "Food book," she says. "Recipes and all."

He wants to ask if that's what they're called – corn rows – but instead he asks, "Expanding the menu?" He feels clever. Flirtatious.

Four students eat pancakes in another booth.

She doesn't look up. "Something like that," she says.

Cole tests possibilities. Downloads files and runs sample transactions. Testing the level of satisfaction. The degree of disruption. He stands at the threshold. How will he enter. What will he infect. The possibilities range in his mind from the most subtle, eroding Z-Tech's credibility and the confidence of its client companies, to the single dramatic act that would bring it all down at once.

Through this door, he can flood the system with false orders and shut it down minutes after launch. He could disable the calculation function, so the system could not compute the total price of any order. Every transaction a failure. The drama, the publicity are appealing. But such grand gestures are easily traceable.

Through this door, he can access individual transactions, the records of purchases in progress. He could freeze a single minute of a day – 10:42 am, 3:19 PM – and hold all those transactions in electronic limbo. Customers would see their orders as confirmed, but the store would not receive them directly. Cole would, in a file created for the purpose. He could review the captured transactions at his leisure. Change an order, increase the quantity so a customer gets four yellow blouses instead of the one she wanted, or so that the unit price charged is $64 instead of the $42 listed. Change the shipping address so that the order goes out but doesn't arrive. He could arrange so that snow skis are sent out when water skis were ordered. He could have the purchase charged to someone else's Visa card. Charge the skis to the woman who ordered the yellow blouses, the blouses to the man who ordered water skis. He could invent entirely false charges on any of the credit card numbers in any of the systems relying on Z-Tech for secure electronic commerce. Then send the orders through.

This is the subtle approach. Word would leak out that companies handling e-commerce through Z-Tech are dissatisfied. A slow poisoning. Z-Tech unable to find a bug in the system. KBC companies get queasy about e-commerce. Gun shy. And Cole sits behind it all, invisible.

The students have left the café. Victoria wipes down the booth. Braids flop back and forth. The hair is shaved from the base of her skull.

"Hey, Vic," he calls.

She turns to him. She looks tired. "What do you need?"

"Cool hair," he says. "Isn't it a pain to do it that way?"

"Yeah," she says. She holds one of the braids. "I don't sleep much."

He will search for herbal remedies. He has come to depend on her. The sound of her voice. A dose of Victoria, three or four times a week.

Cole taps at the keyboard. Plays with a number here, a command there. He could create code that only derails transactions with an order quantity of three. That miscalculates sales tax for orders between \$40 and \$50. He could change his tactic every few days.

If he keeps his acts small and frequent, the problems will be nearly impossible to find and fix. Z-Tech would look for bugs – systematic glitches. They'd pull all programmers – even the one working on the upgrade – to stop the bleeding. Damage control.

He'd be done and out before they'd look for him. It would take a few days for KBC to register the complaints: failed and flawed transactions, erroneous credit card numbers. Customers receiving shipments they never ordered. Another week before Z-Tech put together the crippled system they'd inherited with the ongoing problems as anything more than evidence that their launch had been premature. Before they entertained even the possibility of sabotage.

Cole feels dangerous. He tests the possibility of sending 44 pairs of sandals to Ernst Prinz in Redlands, California. Runs it through the system to make sure the change is clean. When he gets to the confirmation screen, he cancels the order. For now, it is enough to know what he is capable of.

SCREEN TWO

The rumble of a steam engine idling. A train looms in the foreground on the right of the screen. The vastness of the West looms behind and beyond it.

A woman, pearl-colored hat, bandanna-covered face, pistol in hand, confronts the freight car.

"You don't want to get blown up again, do you?" Her voice exasperated. "Open the door."

A man, her partner, jumps to the ground from the roof of the car. Buckskin vest. Bandanna across his face. "What's going on? We don't have all day."

Coal dust on his shirt and vest. Frustration in his voice. Hands on hips, he glares at her.

"I work for the Union Pacific Railroad –" comes a voice from inside.

"Are they paying you enough to get killed over?" She shouts. Waves her gun in the air.

"We don't have time for this," he says. "Blow the door."

"Fine." She lights a fuse, backs away. "Don't say I didn't warn you," she calls.

The man and the woman step away from the train, down a small incline as the long fuse burns toward the dynamite stuck into the door handle.

A bang like sledgehammer on rock. They are into the car in seconds. They will get the money and get out.

A mousy man with thinning gray hair and a nervous manner picks himself up off the floor. "Now listen. If I've got to be robbed there's no one I'd rather have rob me than you two, but I work for the Union Pacific Railroad –"

"Would you shut up, Walter!" The man interrupts.

She looks at the safe. It's brand new, thick steel sides and door. Two combination locks, each with separate handles.

"Oh, Walter." She gestures at the tiny fortress. Waves her gun hand in disgust. "What'd you have to go and do that for?"

Walter's face turns red. He looks at the ground. His head shakes slowly from side to side. "It's just that the last one you got into so easily, and it's not my money."

"That's the *point.*" The man's voice an explosion. He wipes a hand across his face, leaves a black smear on his cheek. "It's not your money, Walter."

"Yes, but I work for the–"

"Get dynamite," he says. An angry glare at Walter. "A *lot* of it."

She hops down out of the car, and a moment later hoists herself back in with five sticks of dynamite.

He sets the explosion. Kicks a money bag aside.

"Take cover," the man spits at Walter. At the woman.

"You don't have to get cranky," she says. "He's just doing his job."

They cower in a corner of the freight car, beside a filing cabinet. The fuse sizzles. An explosion turns the screen bright white. Bodies fly past. Scraps of wood float to the ground.

The camera follows one scrap to the dirt, where the man is the first to rise. Then the woman. Then Walter. Dust-covered. Woozy.

"Think you used enough dynamite?" she asks.

The freight car is decimated. Only the chassis remains, with the shell of the safe atop it. The man, hands on hips. Chewing his lower lip. Something drifts in the air behind him.

The camera pulls back to reveal a sky full of cash, paper money raining toward the desert floor.

She finds Max in a dark corner of the junk yard. Late afternoon. He flings items from a set of metal shelves. Kitchen gadgets, tools hurtle to the ground.

King stands beside his master, barking. Head lowered. Front paws planted.

"Max." She shades her eyes against the sun.

An egg beater flies past. A toaster oven.

She has to dodge a door knob. "Max!"

He stands. Turns to her. "God dammit. Don't sneak up on me." Max never quite stands straight – the upper part of his body lists a few degrees to the left, a back problem that never gets any better, but only rarely gets worse. Max wears a hearing aid. A clear plastic tube tucks behind his right ear.

"What are you doing?"

He scratches his bald head. "Looking for something." Two shelves cleared, he starts on a third.

"Winning lottery ticket?"

"Toaster." Disgust in his voice. He launches a vacuum cleaner attachment. A section of heating duct.

"A toaster."

"Someone came in looking for one of those vintage toasters, the bullet-shaped ones from the '50s."

"Why would someone come here for that?"

"I don't know. They did. And I have one."

"Max, it could be anywhere."

"It was on these goddamn shelves!" Red-faced. Huffing. "I put it here. I know I did."

King barks twice.

"Maybe you sold it."

"It was here last week." He picks an old crank-handle meat grinder off the shelf. Hurls it to the ground.

"Maybe you sold it after."

"I didn't sell it!"

"Maybe you forgot."

A monkey wrench crashes to the ground. Two pairs of vise grips. The shelves are empty. "*Maybe you* —" Max puts his hands on his hips. Curses under his breath. "What are you doing here, anyway?"

"Came by to say hi."

He surveys the mess on the ground. Steps around some of the junk, walks a small circle. The hearing aid emits a slight whine as he turns.

"Max, you can't keep track of everything. It's just a toaster."

"Why don't you go home?"

"I don't want to."

Deep breaths. A sheepish smile. He squints at her. Kicks at the meat grinder. "Alright, alright." Watches King watch him. "Why'nt you stay for supper, since you're here. Help me clean up this mess."

Joanna smiles, nods.

"I'm no great shakes in the kitchen, but the food won't kill you."

After they restock the shelves, they have dinner in Max's Airstream, where he keeps a small kitchen setup, an easy chair, a cot. King laps water from a metal bowl that slides around the floor as he drinks.

"In theory, I'm gracious about my decline. In practice, I goddamn hate it. Starting to forget things. Scares the hell out of me." He takes a package of hot dogs from the refrigerator. Digs out a fry pan. "The other day, I couldn't remember who it was hit that home run to win the Series for the Dodgers, back in '88."

Joanna folds her arms across her chest. "You're right, Max. You are slipping. Time for the home. I'll drive you."

Max fries hot dogs in vegetable oil.

Joanna's stomach sours. "I can't eat any more hot dogs. You got anything else?"

Max looks at her a long moment. "There's always cottage cheese and pineapple."

She steels herself. "I guess I could do that."

"I'm joking. There's cold cuts. Make yourself a sandwich."

King barks, full voice.

"King, shut up." Max reaches into a box of dog biscuits. Throws one on the floor. "Have a cookie." He turns the hot dogs with a fork.

Joanna makes a sandwich – ham, smoked turkey.

"I've got this headache," he says. He splits a hot dog, slaps it on a thick slice of rye bread. She sets out plates for them. A high-pitched buzz coming from his ear as Max sits down.

King whines.

"God dammit, King. Enough."

"Max, your hearing aid's acting up."

Max scowls. Pulls it off. "Damn thing." He scoops hot dogs into King's bowl. Puts another on a slab of bread for himself.

They sit at a small wood table with their sandwiches and iced tea. The thick smell of grease in the air.

"What are you doing here, Jo? What do you want with me?"

"I'm your best customer. I like to visit you."

Max chews, swallows. Grumpy-voiced. "Gibson. It was Kirk Gibson hit that home run."

Joanna laughs.

"Get to be my age, there's no time for bullshit. People think, an old fart, he's got nothing to do all day but sit around and shoot the breeze. But what I see is how short a time I have left." He sips a glass of iced tea. "Concentrate on the things that matter. Like Nolan."

King's plastic dish scrapes the base of the wall as he eats.

"How'd it happen with Nolan?"

"Don't know. Doctor says his mother may have had some toxic exposure. Could be as simple as bad air in the building where she worked. Carpeting treated with resins that never cured. Pressboard furniture saturated with formaldehyde." Growing anger in Max's voice.

"I'm sorry," Joanna says.

"The smallest things. The simplest. Didn't harm her, but Nolan was born vulnerable." Max runs a hand over his skull. "Sixty-some thousand toxic chemicals out there," he says. "It's a fucking crime."

Sunlight angles through the small window.

Max waves a hand in the air. "Enough." His eyes small, red. "Nolan's a good kid. We're lucky to have him."

"I think he's probably lucky to have you, too."

"Yeah. It's easy being a grandparent. Don't ask my son if he feels so lucky." A laugh, loud and clipped. "You have a boy."

"I do." A pang. Heartburn. "He's on his own now."

A picture flashes in her mind. Anthony beside her in a movie theater, age seven or eight, eating popcorn. They'd go to matinees to escape the summer heat.

"Good kid?"

"Yeah," she says. She tries not to let her voice falter. "He's got some stuff to figure out, but he's a good kid."

A dim light burns in the trailer window, casting a soft trapezoid glow on the ground. From a distance, the Winnebago appears as a toy abandoned in some suburban back yard. A full moon leaks silvery light on Winnetka, its softly undulating rows of dirt and grass, and a hot wind blows an ice cream wrapper, yellow and white, stained with traces of chocolate, across the open field. All is quiet on the home front. Inside the trailer, Cole sings and tells himself he isn't waiting for Joanna to come home.

94

Happy trails to you, until we meet again.
Happy trails to you, keep smiling until then.

Sometimes he feels as if they have boarded different trains headed in different directions. In his mind he holds a picture of him and Joanna, hands clasped in solidarity. A fortnight ago, when she'd first started leaving, when he'd first felt the distance. The way she could erase it in a moment.

Cole sat in a beach chair in the shade of the motor home. Snapped the ends from green beans. Dropped them in a tin saucepan. The pan he'd bought at Valu-Mart in Cheyenne, for the sound it would make as he dropped in the beans. Now, it sounded hollow. Joanna sat on the steps, smoking a cigarette. Picked tobacco from her tongue.

"What is it?" she asked.

He snapped beans. Dropped them in the pan.

"You're sullen." Her smoke drifted toward him.

"You're bored," he said. "You're going to leave."

"No," she said. She smoked. Flicked ash onto the dirt.

"Emily's recreational, Cole." Her elbows rested on her knees. Her body leaned forward into the space between them. "But even if she wasn't."

Cole set the pan in his lap. Looked across his shoulder at her. "It's not that," he said. A breeze riffed across the landscape. "I'm counting on you is all."

Joanna squatted before him. Heat shimmered up from undulating rows of movie speakers. The poles seemed to waver. "I'm not leaving."

She rubbed her palms together. Raised a hand to her mouth. Spit into it. "Come on," she said. Reached out to Cole. "Spit shake. We're in this together," she said. "No matter what."

Just like that, she was back.

He spit into his hand. Clasped Joanna's.

Now, he holds the memory of that handshake, and wiggles his toes in bed.

Who cares about the clouds when we're together
just sing a song that tells of happy weather.
Happy trails to you 'til we meet again.

Out in the drive-in the wind carries a trace of his voice, row after row, until it fades into the screens. Clouds slide across the night sky, obscure the moon. The wind picks up, swirls the ice cream wrapper, drags a tumbleweed along for a ride. Even with the shrouded moon, the screens glow with a hint of silver. If Cole were out here, he might see a flicker cross those screens, almost like lightning; he might see a hint of motion in a back row, near the darkened refreshment stand, a glimmer of light that seems to ricochet from the screen, enough to make him scratch his head and check the sky for storm clouds, enough to make him think that, for a split second, he could have seen a dun-colored circle of rope, looping and twirling in the air.

Interior. Wells Fargo Bank, Sherman Oaks branch. Day. A handful of customers in line along a guide rope. Cole waits, check in hand, to make a deposit. Bounces on the balls of his feet. Hums a tune in his head. Ten thousand dollars. He wants to dance a two-step with a teller. The fact that the check has come, that Z-Tech is paying him while he undermines them. A toddler plays with the rope while the mother waits her turn.

Cole has come from Ventura, where he picked up his check, bought a smoothie at a little storefront – Fresh Start Fruit and Produce, pictures of carrots and strawberries – then sat in traffic on the 101 South. Crawled back to LA County. Yearning for third gear. He'd spent the morning at the Atomic Café. Where Victoria had the day off. Where Cole had settled on a launch day disruption tactic. Where Cameroon bested the Ivory Coast to set up a quarterfinal showdown with surprising Finland.

The bank branch reminds him of a school assembly hall. High ceilings. Fluorescent lights. Heavy blue curtains. The tellers sit behind a high counter, dark wood. Each time he comes, they grow more beautiful. He wants to hand people cash. Hurl money into the air, declare a holiday. He is next in line. The toddler tries in vain to climb the counter while her mother completes a transaction. Three surveillance cameras watch everything. Cole stares into one. He has his deposit slip filled out. Check in hand.

"Sir. May I help you, sir?" A teller waves him over. She is luminous. She has tall hair piled in a bun. She is too young for such hair, but Cole forgives her. Maybe he'll tip her a twenty. "Hi, Lupe." He reads her name from the brown plate. He tries to do it subtly. "Nice to see you." He comes here once a month, but wants to be a regular, one of the gang. Lupe has a role in his triumph, and he wants her to know he appreciates it. She smiles vaguely.

Cole slides the check and deposit slip beneath the window. Lupe types on a keyboard. On the wall behind her, the Wells Fargo logo. Stagecoach. Horses. A frown crosses her face. A blush. She looks at Cole a long second, then back at the screen.

She presses a button beneath the counter. "Just a moment," she says. Her eyes meet Cole's, then flit away.

Cole has seen tellers push these buttons. In movies. When the bank is being robbed. Cole is not robbing the bank. He is depositing a check. He has asked for cash back.

"My manager's on his way," Lupe says. "Sorry for the delay."

Two security guards hover, one at each entrance. The one nearest Cole, a burly man with a red face and crew cut, shifts his hands, tucks thumbs inside his belt. Cole interprets this as an aggressive act. *Fuck you,* he thinks. I'm depositing a check. He looks for hidden earphones. He begins to sweat. Hasn't anyone told Lupe that buns are strictly for women over 60?

Cole takes deep breaths. *Z-Tech has stopped payment. Issued an APB.* He watches the guard out the corner of his eye. Envisions how he will create a diversion, make a run. He imagines the manager on the phone, listening. *Stolen highly sensitive material. Detain.*

How could Lupe do this to him?

"Good afternoon, sir." The manager has appeared at the window. Gleaming white shirt. Red hair. Blue tie. Give him a paper hat, he could manage a burger joint.

Cole nods. Unable to speak. He envisions using the toddler and the mother as interference. Sees himself running. Serpentine.

"I'm sorry to keep you," the manager says.

In his periphery, Cole watches the security guard for signs of action. A hint that would tell him to flee.

The check sits on the desk in front of the teller's hand. Cole considers grabbing it and finding another bank. He tells himself this is an administrative snafu. Within the normal range of business. That Lupe would not betray him.

"Let me explain." The manager is short. Lupe, on her stool, with her bun, towers over him.

Cole does not want to hear explanations. He wants to escape. His breathing is shallow and rapid. He cannot move his feet.

"We've lost some signature cards. A filing error." The manager slides a white card across the counter. "If you could just fill out a new one. And let me confirm your ID." He smiles. "I apologize for the inconvenience."

Adrenaline pumping. The words register. The smile duplicitous. *It's a trick.* Cole looks to Lupe for the truth, but Lupe's face reveals nothing. She has betrayed him. He squeezes the pen so his hand shakes less. Tries to slow his breathing. His peripheral vision has gone black. He cannot read his own signature. Fuck it. He can play it cool. He hands over the signed card along with his license.

Ready to run.

The room is fluid. The walls, the floor undulate.

The manager examines the license, the card. Holds the card closer. Farther away. Looks beyond Cole. To the door. Shakes his head.

"I'm going to have to ask you to do another," he says. He shows Cole the signature card. There are no recognizable letters. "It's for your own protection."

Cole forces a smile. *Bullshit.* He listens for doors opening. Guns being drawn. The woman with the toddler gathers her papers, ready to leave. Cole will take a deep breath. He will count to ten. Then he will run like hell, and hope the mother and child will screen him.

He scrawls a signature, shoves the card back at the manager. *One, two, three...*

"Thank you for your patience, Mr. Newton. Lupe will take care of you now."

An ordinary afternoon at the bank. Lupe hands him a receipt, lays out a row of twenties.

"Thanks," she says. "Have a nice day."

Dizzy, Cole gathers his cash and crosses the lobby. His vision a narrow tunnel to the entrance. He nearly tramples the toddler. Mutters an apology. Makes his steps slow, deliberate. He nods to the security guard, and steps out into a Los Angeles afternoon. Deep breaths. He will learn to be cool. To banish fear.

SCREEN SIX

The bride, her dress and hat all lace and bows, stands at the window, looking down at the street. Anguished expression. Sun-baked dirt, hitching posts on either side, a row of buildings eerily quiet. Somewhere down there, her new husband awaits the noon train, awaits the killer.

She has told him she'll be on that train, with or without him, headed for the new life they are supposed to begin. She stands beside the window, stares down through the gap between lace curtain and window frame.

The camera cuts to the empty street. The train tracks. The bride at the window. The picture of beauty and innocence.

A clock ticks in the background. It's twenty minutes to noon.

Cole sits cross-legged on a flat rock at the crest of a small hill. From this vantage point, he can see the road leading into the drive-in. He can see the refreshment stand. He has a full view of four movie screens. He has a book in his lap. *Desert Flora and Fauna.* He has found miracles in this valley. A brittle agave, scrawny stalk rising as tall as he. Sharp green leaves that hug the ground. Hearty brittlebush, its leaves gray-green and rubbery. Daisy-like flowers blooming after a rain, then faded the next day.

He wants to learn his environment. The day is nearly silent. The distant hum of cars. He gauges from the angle and heat of the sun that it is late morning. Joanna has gone to see Max. Has taken the Squareback. Cole marvels at how rarely a cloud would sully the sky. At the unbroken blue. The sun heats him from above, the rock from below, radiating warmth through his walking shorts. His pasty-white Anglo-Saxon skin finally toughening to a sun-baked brown.

Car wheels on the dirt. Cole's Tombstone-shaded eyes flash to the entrance. A Chevrolet Nova, gray. The muscles in his back constrict. Maybe the Squareback broke down. He is conspicuous on his rock. The Nova moves slowly, first toward the refreshment stand, then angling right, toward Cole. It is not Joanna. He tries to decide if it's trouble. The windshield reflects sunlight and sky. The car stops a respectful distance away. He interprets this as a positive sign.

A woman gets out. Closes the door. She's small. Round sunglasses. Black hair.

"Hey," she says.

Cole nods. He closes his book. He makes no other move.

She walks toward him. "Joanna around?"

Cole shakes his head.

The woman takes off her sunglasses. Shields her eyes with her free hand. "Cole, right? We met a couple weeks ago. I'm Emily."

He smiles through a sour taste in his mouth. "She's not here," he says. "She's out."

Emily is maybe ten feet away, slightly below him, sun in her face. Tie-dye t-shirt. Jeans. "Hmm," she says. She squints up at him. "She was supposed to call a couple days ago. I wanted to make sure she's okay."

"She's okay," he says. "She's with a friend." He realizes he likes the teasing implication of that, and lets it hang.

"I see." Emily's face young, open. She holds her sunglasses in her right hand. The skin of her fingertips raw. A biter. He wonders if she needs Joanna to reinforce her sense of self. He's tempted to tell her to forget about Joanna. That she's out of her league. He's tempted to show her the jar of human hair, as if it were definitive proof of something untouchable about Joanna.

Emily waits.

"That's new, isn't it?" She gestures toward him.

Cole shifts the book in his hands. He does not want to know her. Does not want to learn what Joanna sees in her. "Huh?"

Emily rubs her cheek. Her chin. Points to him. "The beard."

"It's an experiment," he says. He's been growing a beard for a week. Since it has stopped itching, he's forgotten about it.

She looks around her, down across the undulating rows that define this landscape, and for a moment the oddity of the situation strikes him, where he's living, how isolated they are.

"Nice place you've got." Emily grins. He can't interpret whether it's an effort at shared humor or whether the joke's on him.

An uncertain smile. "It's home."

Emily shades her eyes again with her hand.

"How'd you find us?" Tension in his back.

Emily nods, as if she realizes this is the question Cole has been burning to ask. "Joanna told me you all were living at a drive-in. There aren't that many in the Valley." She puts her sunglasses back on. Her face no longer seems vulnerable. "I'm sorry if I intruded."

Cole flinches. Starts to say something, then doesn't.

"Tell Joanna I said hello." Half-statement. Half-question. Emily drifts slowly down the hill.

Cole opens his mouth, but he has nothing he's willing to say. Instead he feels his face, the little strip of skin on either side of his mouth where his mustache and beard should connect, the place where whiskers had failed to grow the last time, nearly ten years ago, where they are failing to grow again. It infuriates him that he cannot produce hair in that place, that his beard could be thwarted by such a simple-seeming problem.

Exterior. Beverly Boulevard. Day. Cole pulls into his parking spot in front of the Atomic Café, plunks his eight quarters into the parking meter, arms himself with his memo book and prepares to do battle against the soccer gods.

Victoria, behind the counter, consolidates two half-empty pots of coffee. She turns as she hears the door shut.

"Juice," she calls. "What's up?" Heavy-lidded eyes. Corn row braids.

"Queen Victoria," he says. "Good morning." He produces a sprig of yellow wildflowers from behind his back. "From my desert hideaway."

She grins. Nods her head in courtly fashion. "Thank you. They're lovely." Produces a short glass, adds an inch of water. In go the flowers. "You keeping a step ahead of the thugs?"

An Asian man, slicked-back hair, blue Armani suit, sips coffee, reads the Wall Street Journal at a stool. His eyes quietly follow the interaction.

Cole raps a fist on the counter. Jangly with adrenaline. It's a big day. "So far, so good."

Victoria notices the man's attention. Nods toward Cole. "He's on the lam from loan sharks back east," she says. "Don't tell anyone. We kind of like him."

The man, unsure whether to acknowledge that he's been caught eavesdropping, meets her eye. He smiles at Cole and returns to the newspaper.

Cole heads for a cyber booth. Amazed at his own confidence. An aura of invincibility. A young couple, early twenties, chows on corned beef hash, engrossed in the food and each other.

On the juke box, Violent Femmes sing "Country Death Song."

Victoria appears beside him, a tall orange juice, one hand behind her back. "The usual," she says. The other hand emerges. A scone on a plate.

"What's this?"

"A present."

"You don't serve scones."

"That's right. My latest experiment from home. Ginger-peach. You're my guinea pig."

"Thanks." He pokes it with a forefinger.

"You don't play with it," she says. "You eat it."

He tastes it. An explosion of flavor. "It's delicious. Marry me." She laughs.

"No?" He takes a bite. Looks admiringly at her. Undiluted essence of twenty-four-year-old. The sheer unabashed confidence. The belief that anything is possible. There is nothing more attractive. "How about we go bowling sometime. For real."

She blushes. Red blotches on her cheeks. "That's sweet, but I've got a boyfriend."

He thinks about telling her he's not trying to move on her. That it was just a moment. "I understand. I'm crushed, but I'll live." Munches the scone. "What's the boyfriend's story?"

"It's sad. He's in cooking school –"

"That is sad."

"In New York, smart ass. We're going to open an inn."

The man at the counter has finished his coffee. He places a bill next to the check.

"Need change?" Victoria calls.

He looks at her. At the pair of them. Shakes his head. And then he's out the door. Cole's eyes follow the man down the sidewalk. *Who is he?*

Cole has fired up VR Soccer and prepared a second round match, Sweden against Czechoslovakia.

"How goes the World Cup?" Victoria leans against the back of the adjoining booth, watches the screen.

"Finland has advanced to the quarter finals." It's no wonder she thinks he's odd.

"Go Finland." She folds her arms across her chest. "When I was a kid – third grade, I think – I told everyone in school I was from Finland. That we only came to the U.S. because my Dad got transferred in his job." She laughs. "I guess I wanted to sound exotic."

He smiles. He will give his all for Finland.

This is the day of the provisional launch. The day Z-Tech will expose its weaknesses, the day Cole will begin to exploit them. A misplaced digit in the purchase total of a few transactions. An overcharge here and there. Enough to annoy a customer. To start a ripple.

"Newton Cole," Victoria says.

"Yup." The players on screen line up to begin the match. The crowd cheers. He will not start the game just yet.

"It's not your real name, is it?"

She unnerves him. It is as if she knows everything and is mocking his anxiety. It is as if she is a 24-year-old waitress enjoying the company of a regular customer. What to make of her. She has surely noticed times when the screen does not display soccer.

He had inverted his name for her. He'd always wanted an alias. He flashes his exaggerated grin. "I'm afraid it is." Newton Cole. Cole Newton.

She nods. Eyes him. There are forces transpiring. "Okay, Juice," she says. "If you say so." She pushes herself away from the booth. "Go Finland," she says.

Today, soccer will wait. Today he will dial in first and make his move. He leaves the players poised. Dials up the Web connection. Enters the back door. He can watch transactions happen. The speed of commerce. Valu-Mart Department Stores. Business is slow. Twenty or thirty orders. He picks out a few names. Wehner, Patrick. Brown, Jennifer. Botts, Ruth. A few keystrokes. A blazer goes from seventy-five dollars to two hundred seventy-five. Twill pants from sixty-two to sixty-eight. Slippage in the decimal makes the price of socks $42.00 per pair instead of $4.20. And then he's out. It's as if it never happened. It's as if he has spent the morning re-staging the World Cup. He clicks start.

The players release. The crowd cheers. The game has begun.

3.

Joanna had called Sean, who owns a coffee shop in downtown Boulder. A co-worker from her Towson days. They'd jointly run a building materials cooperative in Baltimore, and Sean had been more of a father to Anthony than Ben ever was. Anthony had ended up working for Sean when he first moved west.

"Hey," Sean had said. "What's up?"

"You see the news today?"

"No. Why?"

"Never mind," she said. "Is Anthony okay?"

"Last time I talked to him," Sean said, his voice guarded. "It's been a couple weeks. What's going on?"

"You haven't seen or talked with him for a couple weeks?"

A pause at the other end of the line.

"He's not here. You knew this. He moved a couple weeks ago. What's wrong?"

"Moved? You mean like to a different street?"

"He was going to Seattle."

She bit her lip. The fear in her stomach expanded.

"He told me he'd talked with you about it. He told me he'd call when he got there."

She reminded herself there was no rational reason to believe that what she was thinking was true. That her 16-year-old son had built a pipe bomb, carted it to a golf course in the wee hours of the morning, and wired it to the ignition of an E-Z-Go golf cart.

"He didn't tell you, I take it. You haven't heard from him."

"No. What about that job. He was doing well – cooking breakfast at that Inn?"

"Rooming house. Yeah. Far as I knew he liked it. We'd talk a couple times a week. This came out of the blue. I just assumed from what he said that he'd talked it all through with you. So I left it alone. Is something wrong?"

She shook her head. "I just wanted to talk to him."

"I'm worried now. I didn't know he hadn't called you."

"It's okay. I'm having one of my worry-about-Anthony days. He's fine. He'll call."

A long, straight stretch of two-lane highway. A world mostly sky. Sun a white dot, remote in a wash of electric blue. A car cuts through the landscape, bisecting the stripe of road. Saab 9-3 convertible. Black. Steam hisses from the grill. The car pulls onto the shoulder. The door opens and a figure emerges. Sandy hair slicked back. Dark glasses. White linen shirt. Shoulders a little hunched. Neck a touch stiff.

A hawk soars overhead.

William St. Martin lifts open the hood. Steam billows up and out. He waves a hand at it. Uses a handkerchief to wipe his brow. Mutters to himself. "Forty grand you'd think it wouldn't overheat every other day." With the handkerchief, he eases loose the radiator cap. Turns his face away. A burst of steam and the cap pops into his hand. A truck zooms past in the northbound lane. The car shakes in its wake. St. Martin wipes the grillwork, leans against it, arms folded. He stares at the strip of road leading south.

"Nothing to do but wait," he tells himself. He reaches into the front seat, retrieves a video game. An aquamarine plastic fish. "Might as well do some fishing."

He leans back against the car as the engine cools behind him. He presses the cast button and makes a quick forward motion with the game. Watches a digital worm sink toward shadowy bass. He's in the San Marcos Pass, on Route 156 somewhere between Gilroy and Santa Nella. The Santa Claras slope gently around him and a scorching sun burns down from above.

He's in no hurry. He has caught the scent.

Cole and Joanna on a camping trip. Joshua Tree National Park, the southeast edge of the Mojave Desert. So many shades of brown. They hike mostly in silence. Blazing sun in a vast sky. Cole likes the idea that everything they need they carry with them. Tent. Sleeping pads. Food. Water. He likes the way the weight of the backpack presses him to earth, adds substance to his step. He is out to cover ground, to lose himself in the thrill of movement. The blissful thoughtlessness of not standing still.

They climb a small rise. Loose dirt and shifting stone make the way slippery. They stand at the crest, looking out over a plain sprinkled with gnome-like Joshua trees, awash in a yellow blur of tiny flowers.

"Brittlebush," Cole says. He measures his breathing. Soaks in the heat. He wears a baseball cap the same color as the Mojave sand. Flecks of gray evident in his close-cropped beard.

"It's beautiful." Joanna, hands on hips. Breathing steady. Cole marvels at her physical resilience. She has lost weight in the desert, like a second skin, to emerge streamlined. Her step light on the land.

Cole has been reading about the flora and fauna.

Joanna pulls a plastic water bottle from a pocket on the side of her pack. Takes three short sips, and offers it to Cole. He takes a single long drink. Their movements the only sound. When he's finished, she replaces the bottle, and they walk on.

There's a peace in their rhythm. A deep satisfaction in their matched pace. It is a balm to Cole, who had suggested this trip.

"How about it?" he had said. "A couple of days away."

"I like it," Joanna said. "A vacation from camping in the desert by camping in the desert."

"It's supposed to be magnificent," he said. "Besides, it's a chance to break up the routine. Do something together." And, unsaid but on his mind, to prove that avoiding each other isn't the only way for them to get along.

So they came to Joshua Tree. Merged in the preparations. The measurement of drinking water. The shared experience of physical exertion. A landscape to discover.

They come to a stand of Jerusalem thorn, a fragile-looking tree with olive-hued wood and bright yellow needles, whose presence in this desert seems a miracle. Smiles. The joy of discovery.

The path narrows gradually, indiscernibly, until they cling to rock with their fingers, search out toe holds.

"Here," Joanna says. She leads the way. Indicates with her left foot – her trailing foot – the spot for Cole to land. He watches. Follows.

He sets his right foot on a narrow sandstone slab. Shifts his weight slowly. "You think astronauts still drink Tang?"

Joanna works her way along the rock. "Huh?"

"Tang. The orange breakfast drink. Went into space with all the Apollo astronauts. Ungodly stuff."

Side by side. Faces toward rock. Backpacks hanging over the edge. When Joanna turns to him, there's a smear of dirt below her right eye. A smile on her lips. "You're a strange person, Cole."

"Not strange. Complicated."

"You wish."

Down into an oasis, where a single palm tree testifies to the occasional presence of water. They squat in the shade of the cliff and sip from a plastic bottle. Mid-afternoon sun coaxes out the red in the gently sloping rock across the wash.

"This is great." Cole drinks, hands Joanna the bottle.

Joanna pours water on her hands, rubs the back of her neck. "Amazing. There's a whole world outside that little room you live in."

Cole stifles a comeback jab.

Here in the basin, the Joshua trees are sparse. Coppery creosote dominates, hugs the ground.

"It's not like that." Cole leans against a boulder, rests his hands on his stomach. "It's like diving into another universe, where you experience everything on a molecular level. You look close enough at some tiny detail, it opens into a world."

Joanna looks at him out the corner of her eye. "Some people choose to *live* in a world."

"I go out."

"The mystery café." Joanna lights a cigarette. A whip-tailed lizard scoots between rocks. "How is your little waitress?"

He swallows. He won't take the bait. "That's your thing, Jo. I go there to use the computers." A sip of water.

She leans forward. A light of recognition in her eyes. "You're up to something."

"What do you mean?"

The Joshua trees sprinkled on the far hillside have the odd posture of human figures. Unbalanced. A branch stuck out at random. A gawkiness of stance.

"Why do you need those computers?"

"Internet connection. Keep up."

"Bullshit. You're up to something. What is it?" Smoke curls in the air. "The truth, Cole."

Hot sun. A gentle breeze. He tosses a pebble. "Keeping tabs on the competition. Making sure they don't move too fast."

"Translate."

He runs his tongue around the inside of his mouth. It's no use. "I've influenced a few transactions."

She puffs on her cigarette. Swallows the smoke. "Influenced. That's a nice word." She rests an arm on the rock between them. Starts to say something. Doesn't. Stares out at the desert.

Cole watches the Joshua trees. Part of the reason he likes them is their awkward look –they're not really trees, they only aspire to be trees.

Joanna smokes.

"I'm careful. A few small changes and I'm out. Untraceable."

A yucca moth flits among the rocks, never quite landing.

Joanna disappears behind her sunglasses. "Don't even talk to me," she says.

Cole had bought a tent. Sleeping pads. Backpacks. He had hoped to get her input, but she wasn't around much, so he made the preparations a sort of gift.

Joanna laughed when she saw it all. "Why don't we just take the Winnebago?"

"We need to do this right," Cole said.

In the end, Joanna bought into it. Balancing the weight of the packs. Appreciating the tent's engineering. "Six pounds," Cole said. "Including poles. One person can set it in five minutes."

Joanna sets the tent while Cole digs out firewood. Two logs. Precious cargo. She's turned quiet. They've brought tamales. A container of rice. Brownies.

Muscles burn after the eight-hour hike. Heat dissipates with the sun. The air cools. Evening primrose open, vermilion buds burst into bright yellow flowers. The crisp smell of desert chicory.

A mesquite tree, three trunks splayed out from a gnarled base, greedy roots wrapped around withered bur sage which the mesquite has choked out. There is water to sustain only so much life.

Cole stretches. Heat from his shoulder muscles travels down his arms. They eat rice from the shared container with plastic spoons. Four tamales each. Juice boxes. Plums. "I love gorging after a hike."

Joanna leans back against a warm rock. They've camped in the shade of a boulder, on its east side to cut the wind. The sunset-colored tent behind them.

A scattering of creosote. A solitary Joshua. Desert dandelions.

"Anything else you have planned," Joanna says. "Armed robbery? Murder?"

Cole licks cheese and cornmeal from his fingers. Food has never tasted so good. "Nope."

She nods slowly. Chews her last tamale.

He sucks the last bit from the container of apple-raspberry juice. "A little mischief," he says. "Nothing serious."

"Whatever." She waves his words away. Her eyes small. "That code of yours'll kill you." She brushes crumbs off her legs. When she looks up, she's miles away. "I'm glad you told me what's going on."

Something hops in the dust at Cole's feet. "Poof," he says. "She's gone."

She shrugs.

"What I do or don't do on the computer has nothing to do with us."

Joanna stares at him.

"What?" he says.

"Nothing."

"What?"

"Emily's right. You need to get a life."

"Fuck Emily."

"I have. I will."

"You tell your *friend* my life is full. I can take care of my own life, thank you."

"That's obvious." Joanna lights a cigarette. Blue smoke into the evening air.

A toad makes its way along the sand, a wary eye on Cole. Rough gray-green skin. Pink-orange spots. Cole tries to hold onto the ways the desert fills him: its warmth, its miracle colors and subtle smells. He tells himself it is progress that they are together. He notices the first traces of stars overhead.

Joanna slides into song.

> *"I'm back in the saddle again*
> *Out where a friend is a friend.*

"Fuck you," Cole interrupts.

"Get over yourself. It's a song." A rich tobacco smell. "I still love you." She leans her head against the rock.

> *Where the longhorn cattle feed*
> *on the lowly gimsun weed,*
> *Back in the saddle again."*

Night falls around them. The sky is boundless. Cole's voice. "What happens when she gets hooked on you?"

Joanna rummages in her backpack. "I won't let her." She pulls out a plastic-wrapped package of brownies.

> *"Where you sleep out every night*
> *and the only law is right*
> *back in the saddle again."*

Peace. It is possible to imagine that it will last. Cole's body blissfully fatigued. Joanna's confident determination.

"Have some dessert," she says.

*

She had brokered building materials in Baltimore. Produced the weather for a cable channel in Connecticut. Survived a suffocating marriage. Nurtured fourth graders in Armonk, New York.

Then Anthony left, and so did Joanna. Quit her job and drove away.

She spent July and August on the road. Up and down the eastern seaboard. The cities of the interior. She'd call Cole one week from Biloxi. The next from Charlotte. Then Akron. Two months of this. A stretch in Cincinnati. Where she dropped out of contact. She'd always wanted to spend time in Cincinnati. Finally, she'd landed in Carlisle, where she taught seventh graders and broke Diana's heart.

There is a way of looking at her life that says she has bounced around a lot. There is another way of looking at it that says she has been extraordinarily stationary for long periods. Seven years in Towson. Almost five in Armonk. Either way you look at her life – and she has looked at it, studied it, both ways – there is a history of leavings.

Baltimore.

"I'm not coming back," she'd told Sean. Drove up in her ten-year-old Datsun 510, packed with everything she wanted to keep, including ten-year-old Anthony. Once the divorce was final. "I need to hit the road."

Sean had tried to talk her out of it. It was spring. It seemed hasty. Impulsive. "Take some time," he said. This was the way her actions often appeared. When in fact, she had considered – agonized – for weeks. "Take a month. Clear your head. We've got a good gig here."

She shook her head. She could feel hair flopping back and forth. "I need to clear out," she said. "Mexico. South America. A year."

"Ben is okay with this?"

"I've made certain concessions," she said. "Longer vacations. A summer when we get back."

Buds on the trees. The promise of sunshine. Sean had leaned on the car door.

"Is this the best thing for Anthony?"

A rise of anger. As if she hadn't considered that. "It's not the worst thing for him," she said. "He'll learn Spanish."

She sold the car for parts in Laredo. They rode a bus across the border. She sent postcards from Puntaremas. She taught Anthony Spanish. The history of the Underground Railroad. She found him a biography of Harriet Tubman.

Burlington.

She'd stayed a year after college, working at a local newspaper. She'd met someone. Hannah. Put her communications degree to work covering city politics, though she knew she could have done better. Even though the relationship didn't work out, it was a good year. She got to know Cole that year – she'd met him only the year before, her last at UVM, his second – and they spent a lot of time together. Dancing. Hiking. Lunches.

"I want to do this," she told Cole. "I'm not ready to settle." She had a job offer – produce TV weather for a station in Connecticut.

It was an amiable break. Everyone – Cole, her father, even Hannah – applauded her decision.

"I didn't realize the weather needed producing." Cole sat on the couch on the porch of the apartment she shared.

"Sure," she said. "All those maps. The way the clouds move. Swirling tropical storms."

This was the one leaving everyone saw as positive – a young woman establishing a life on her own. To Joanna, it wasn't – it isn't, it will never be – categorically different from the others.

Carlisle.

What Cole doesn't know is that it wasn't Diana that drove Jo away. Diana was a factor, a reminder that Jo had caused pain. They ran into each other in town. The Morning Grind. Lancaster Books.

Joanna just wanted to finish out the school year. She liked teaching seventh grade. She was accustomed to kids with troubles.

She taught *The Catcher in the Rye* and thought about Anthony. Imagined his new life in Boulder. Had almost made peace with the idea. He was finally free of school. He would figure things out.

Paulie – *not Paul, Paulie, it's on my birth certificate, you wanna see* – who sat in the front row and snapped gum. Every day.

"Throw it away, Paulie."

He'd walk to the trash can.

"Paulie, how many times have I asked you not to chew gum in class?"

"About a million."

"How many more before you remember?"

A smile. "About a million."

They'd just gotten back to the book when the fire alarm rang.

In the schoolyard, teachers huddled talking. She heard the words bomb scare. She wasn't always privy to conversations. She was a fill-in. Her status provisional.

She heard, "These kids will do anything to avoid a test."

She wondered if Anthony had ever tried this. A way to break up the day.

It was a half hour before they let everyone back into the building.

That night, on the TV news, a report from Oregon. A bomb at a golf course. She called Sean. She got into her car and left. Did not stop until she got to Boston.

In spare moments now, while his computer runs lengthy subroutines, Cole estimates the number of times he's tried to fix this phrase of code. To unstick the program from this point. Fifty? A hundred? A thousand? His memory blurs. The ability to concentrate on specific possibilities is taxed. The steady drip of small glitches can wear away confidence.

The heat gets to him. In the middle of the day, when the sun bakes the roof and old odors creep out from their hiding places. Late afternoon, when the sun slants in through the high windows and he wishes he and Joanna were not so far apart.

114

```
if (st.st_uid != 0 || (st.st_mode & (S_IWGRP|S_IWOTH))
!= 0)
```

It's still stuffy now, though the room is dark, save for the light of the computer screen. Code flits past his eyes. Snatches of it register in his brain. Sometimes he imagines he can make out words, that it is a secret code, a system of symbols with a message for him. He has placed himself in this little room, apart from Joanna. But it is more than that. It is her, and him, habits that have hardened over years. It is perhaps human nature. Programmed codes of behavior.

He is creating a new code. Maybe he will write a code of ethics for a new frontier. What would such a code look like. What sub-routines would connect law with logic, power with justice. What command strings tie people to one another in ways that would last.

```
if (ai->ai_family != AF_INET && ai->ai_family !=
AF_INET6)
```

An empty jar of peanuts beside him.

Time for a walk. Deep breaths. A change in focus. He pushes outside the rickety screen door into moonlight. Waits for his eyes to adjust. Stretches his arms overhead. Twists his torso.

"Well," he says. "Hello, Winnetka."

There's a sound on the breeze. Someone humming. Joanna? He walks behind the refreshment stand. There's an open area, and a cluster of scrub oak, where he never goes.

Back by the trees, a figure – no, a projected image – twirling a lasso. Humming a tune Cole thinks he should recognize.

Cole closes his eyes. Opens them again. The image hovers with no readily visible source. Fully defined, but without substance. A movie without a screen. Cole approaches.

The figure of a man, black shirt, sky-blue piping across the chest and down the arms. Pearl buttons. Beige handkerchief tied smartly about his neck, its loose ends wrap his shoulder in obedient angles. Stocky body in profile, posture erect, gaze fixed on some distant point. One hand cocked jauntily on his hip, resting on a gunbelt. The other twirls the lasso. Smart leather gloves and finely tooled boots stitched in bright yellows, blues, reds. Tall white cowboy hat.

Cole nears him – it – warily. Through the figure – the image – he can see the trees. The ground.

The figure turns. "Howdy," it says. The hand twirling the lasso stops. Catches the rope coiled.

Cole nods. "Hi." Two thoughts occur to him simultaneously. One is that his former company has created this as a way to track him down. The other is that, in all this isolation, his mind has slipped.

"Are you talking to me?" Cole asks the figure.

The image laughs. Sounds distant, as if through a speaker. "No one else around." The man cuts a smart figure, projected like a rainbow on the valley floor. Cole circles at a distance. Wary of his own senses.

"I'm Gene," the figure says.

"Cole."

"Pleased to meet you, Cole."

Cole looks back at the refreshment stand. Around the drive-in. Seeking a projection source. A mirror. A sense of whose practical joke this is. "Where are you coming from?"

Gene furrows his brow. Cocks his head. "Oh, I've been here quite a while now."

Cole shakes his head. Moves in a slow circle around the figure. The image never breaks. Never wavers. "No. I mean who's projecting you. From where."

Gene removes his hat. Scratches his head. Thick, wavy brown hair. A smile both cordial and watchful. "I'm not sure I understand."

"Who are you working for? Who's controlling you?"

"Well, sir. I'm my own man. Always have been."

Cole scans the ground for speakers.

"How long you say you've been here?"

"Long while," Gene says. "I'm retired. I used to make movies."

"I can believe that."

Something about the man – an affability, a genuineness, a level of comfort with his illuminated self – causes Cole to walk lightly.

"You know that you're a holograph. That someone must be projecting your image. That there's a laser, a series of mirrors, that make it possible for me to see you."

Cole circles him, seeing no source of light, no projection.

"I've heard the phrase. I know I'm not the man I once was." He pats his chest. "But I'm still here. And I've picked up some things along the way." Sets the hat back on his head. "I reckon I'm a little smarter now than I used to be. Not quite so headstrong." He chuckles. "Guess that comes with age."

Cole feels a tightness in his chest. Why – how – would Z-Tech have created this – sent this? An intricate surveillance system to monitor his actions? A homing device to keep track of him until someone comes for him? An elaborate staged production, somehow documented, the ultimate, irrefutable evidence to make the case that he is crazy? Not tethered to the same observable reality as those around him. He puts his hands on his hips. Switches the direction of his circular pacing, as if in doing so, he will catch the trick of light that's creating this illusion. Nothing. Just this cowboy movie standing before him, dimensional but not wholly substantial.

"I didn't mean to slight you," Cole finds himself saying. Trying to avoid paranoid thinking. To stay grounded. What are you supposed to do when a holograph shows up and engages you in conversation.

A lizard skitters across the dirt.

What would Joanna make of this. Cole will check it out. Rein in his curiosity. Consider what's going on then decide what to do.

"I should get back to work."

Gene holds the coiled rope loosely. He shuffles his feet. Dust swirls around holographic boots. "What kind of work you do?"

Cole, short of breath. He thinks about how to answer. Is he being recorded. Would this constitute admissible evidence in a court of law.

"I gotta go," he says. He can't keep fear from his voice. Tries to sound casual. Points to the refreshment stand. "Yoga class."

He takes a step back.

"Nice to meet you," Gene says. "Hope to see you again."

Cole offers his hand. An experiment.

The cowboy holograph meets Cole's fingers. They shake. Nothing but air.

"Good firm grip." Gene laughs. "I like that." He turns. Walks back beyond the scrub.

Cole watches the image disappear into darkness, a dim glow like moonlight in its wake.

Interior. Atomic Café. Day.

Victoria attaches a metal cup to the beater of a milk shake machine. Rattle and hum.

Asian man at the counter. Armani suit. Black frame glasses. *Wall Street Journal.*

Cole enters.

Victoria turns. "Hey, Juice. What's shakin'?"

His eyes hurt behind sunglasses. He's wearing the t-shirt and khakis he tried to sleep in. "I am, your majesty."

She looks him over. "You look like hell. What happened? An injury to the Finnish midfielder?"

He shrugs it off. His mind and heart race. He's amped, and exhausted. This cowboy has him worried. Manic. What to make of it. It's a deep breath day in Cole land. "Nothing a tall cranberry won't fix." He manages a smile. "And an upset in the quarterfinals." He lacks the stomach for sabotage today. Today, as yesterday, every order placed with four items will misfire, the second item lost. His eyes survey the room. The Asian guy has been here before. Federal agents don't wear Armani. A couple of construction workers – dusty plaid flannel shirts, jeans. A young woman poring over a textbook.

Victoria pours a chocolate shake into a tall glass. Sets it in front of the Armani man. "There you go." To Cole. "So, who is it today?"

Cole watches the man sip his shake. Could be Z-Tech, a Warren hire sent to ferret out Cole. He tries to picture the man, at Winnetka, in the dead of night, setting up a holograph. Perhaps he's Japanese. The Japanese are crazy for cowboys.

Breathe. Don't be paranoid.

"We've got Cuba against Egypt. A surprise appearance this late in the tournament." The routine helps Cole relax. "Gheith has five goals the first two rounds. He's unstoppable."

The night before had seemed endless. Avoiding Joanna's eyes. Mundane answers to questions about his day. Afraid to admit the possibility that he'd slipped.

Victoria delivers a cranberry juice. "Finland's still alive, right?" She wears a maroon peasant dress over a white t-shirt.

Cole nods. "They're next up. Take on Cameroon. A defensive powerhouse."

"They're gonna win," she says. "I can feel it."

The sunglasses come off. The memo book open. He'd been unable to sleep. Confined on his narrow bed. As if anywhere he moved he faced an obstacle. A wall. A cabinet. A fall. Joanna had read herself to sleep. Lain on her bed and told Cole about how stolen water gave birth to southern California.

Victoria slides behind the counter. Two drawings – crayon, child's artwork – hang from the silver refrigerator doors.

"Nice," Cole calls. "Yours?"

"Cute," she says. "My niece."

Two pastels. A shaggy-hair dog, a sandy-haired boy.

"Charlie the Breakfast Boy and his dog Buster," Victoria says. "From stories I tell her. Charlie's love for breakfast leads him on adventures around the world. Buster's a wheaten terrier. Dumb as a post, but loyal and endearing."

"I like it," Cole says. He pushes the glasses back up the bridge of his nose. "God save the Queen."

A mock bow. "Thank you."

Armani man – milk shake man, been-here-before man – has half an eye on the *Journal*, half on their interaction. Cole is watchful. His sensors are up. His spider sense tingling.

Victoria walks toward his booth.

Cole nods toward the man. Whispers. "What's he after?"

"What do you mean?"

"You know, why he comes here." He keeps an eye on the man, to see if there's an attentiveness.

Victoria stares at him a long moment. "You okay? Really?"

He meets her eye. Clicks himself back into place. A grin. "I haven't slept."

The woman with the textbook waves a hand at Victoria.

"I'll be back," she says.

Cole launches VR Soccer.

He'd taken a walk. Taken a flashlight. Combed the area for evidence of hidden equipment. Traces of the cowboy holograph. Nothing.

Bats. Lizards. Desert squirrel.

On the monitor, he sets up the match. He will play Egypt against the computer's Cuba. He clicks the start button. The players take the field. The crowd cheers in anticipation.

Under a half-moon sky, he'd searched around the refreshment stand. The scrub oak out back. Walked the path that led beyond. Down to a locked gate that bounded the property. He'd examined the physical structure of the building, explored its stucco surface, probed the joints, the fissures, the overhang where wall met roof. On a ladder he pulled from a storage area, he ran his fingers along every seam, combed every crevice for traces of projectors, wires. Confronted the possibility that there really is something wrong with him. That if Z-Tech has created this holograph as a way to push him over the edge, maybe they've won. He returned to his bed. Spent the wee hours staring into the abyss. Come to the conclusion that he'd prefer, as terrifying as it would be, that this were some sort of surveillance. To know that he were being tracked. Hunted. It would be more terrifying to not trust his own mind.

Gheith takes a long pass in full stride, behind the defense. Draws the goalie out of position with a quick move left, a move

Cole has perfected. The joy of a computer opponent – you can exploit the same move again and again. Gheith drives the ball into the right corner of the net, giving Egypt an early first half lead. The players celebrate. The crowd roars.

"Who scored?" Victoria, hand on hip.

"Egypt, one zero."

Seconds to halftime. Cole goes into defense mode. Protect the lead. The players head for the locker room.

"Hey," he says. "Do you believe in magic?"

She sits across from him. "Which, like sawing a woman in half, or voodoo dolls, making things disappear, the chemistry that happens between people, what?"

He considers. "The possibility that there are things that exist – that have some sort of real, physical presence – that shouldn't. That are, according to all the rules we know, not technically possible." He holds up a hand, opens it like a blooming flower. "Conjured."

Her turn to consider. "Sure," she says. "As a possibility. Why?"

He raises a hand. A barrier. "It's enough," he says. "A possibility."

Victoria stares at him a long moment. He fears the strain of the work is taking its toll on him. Becoming visible. But his days are nearly over. His time as intruder nearly complete.

"Hey, Juice," she says, chin in hand, elbow resting on the computer monitor.

He looks up.

"Found this bowling alley in Little Tokyo. Thought of you. Want to go some afternoon next week?"

He starts to flush. Smiles. The idea of bowling in Little Tokyo. The idea of seeing Victoria. "Yeah," he says. "I'd like that."

Her expression turns serious. "Just to be clear," she says. "This is not sex. This is not a date. Remember, I have a boyfriend."

"I understand," he says. "I have a computer."

*

Her sculpture is taking on heft. Substance. Four or five feet in diameter. Taller than she is. Max has given her a small wooden stepladder, its surface splattered with years of paint, which she uses to circumnavigate the structure. A loop-de-loop from a miniature golf course. A lion's head door knocker. A brass candle holder with candle.

She sits beside it, forces herself to sit still and look at it for a few minutes every day before starting. She may or may not turn on the radio. She may or may not begin to sing.

In the course of the past week, she has added two prize pieces. A gate from a wrought iron fence, which she has painstakingly molded, bending its bars over the course of several days, working against them with a pry bar until they crest and fall like the ripple of a newly formed wave. And the tail fin from a 1956 Cadillac. Aqua and chrome. Red and white lights intact. The metal surface veined like an old leaf, like wax paper that's been crumpled and smoothed out again. Veteran of many dents and reshapings, it has a fragile quality. Max had saved it for her.

Max trusts her. Max has let her in.

"Come on," he told Joanna. "I want to show you something."

A dozen bed frames littered the yard, items that weren't there a week ago. Joanna wondered where he got these things. Why.

She followed him behind the trailer, through a garage with no front wall. They reached a metal door that stuck when Max tried to open it. He kicked the bottom. It popped open.

"The inner sanctum," he said. He tugged a string and a light bulb popped on. Shelves and shelves of signs, typography carved in wood, sculpted in wrought iron.

"This is amazing." Joanna touched pieces at random. "Where'd you get all this?"

Max shrugged. "Most of it's stuff I did," he said. "Over the years."

"I had no idea."

"I know." Max surveyed the room. "Not bad, eh?" He rested a hand on a shelf. "I had a friend in the advertising business. A guy I grew up with." The air had a musty feel. "A client of his was starting a restaurant – family steak place. Anyway, he needed a sign, and my friend had this idea that something like a branding iron would be good. He knew this guy who knew his way around metal, around an arc welder." Max smiled. "He also knew the guy would work cheap."

"You could make a fortune on these." Joanna's eyes wide in the dim light.

"Funny how things work out," Max said. "I got paid a fraction of what I could have. My friend thought he was getting away with something. Like I didn't know the value. Truth was, I enjoyed the work, and it was a way to keep in touch with Dave. Now, Dave's long gone, and these signs have paid for Nolan's medical care."

So now she thinks of Max when she manipulates metal.

She works in a sleeveless undershirt. Her muscles have developed tone and shape. She likes the look of her arms. Their utilitarian strength. She could heft the fence gate to the top of the structure without strain.

A breeze stirs the blades of the industrial fan which has become the centerpiece of her discard pile. She has painted cornflowers on each of its blades.

She will work in silence today. She will create distance from the noise in her head. From the circumstances she cannot change. She spreads a plastic tablecloth, red and white checks, and sets the tail fin on it. Opens a tin of polishing compound. Kneels on the plastic cloth, beside the fin, dips a rag into the polish, and rubs the surface gently. She doesn't know how far she'll be able to bring it back. She knows that the veined quality is there to stay, but she wants to make this shine as much as it will. Beside her is a block of old wood, a section from a door, one rusted hinge still dangling. Beside the wood a pile of three-inch iron nails, their heads rough-hewn, square-ish, not at right angles with their bodies. She has probably a hundred of them.

Sun burns off low clouds. Late morning. You can almost watch the cloud cover give way under the sun's intensity. Within a half hour what might appear to the untrained eye to be a gray day emerges into another perfect southern California afternoon. Joanna sometimes misses real clouds.

Lately, she struggles to focus on the work. She tells herself she is engaged in a noble pursuit. As if the work itself could influence healing. But lately she feels as if her work has succeeded only in fencing herself into a small corral, with Anthony pacing the periphery, never far off. So she takes refuge in Emily.

Emily is not dangerous, because Emily is leaving. Emily is raising support to participate in a year-long march. She will walk from Maine to New Orleans. Travel from New Orleans to Senegal. Tracing the route of the old slave trade. She will leave in October, take a bus to Maine and meet up with others. Joanna has trouble imagining that there would be others. And when Emily returns, it may not be to California. So Emily is safe. So Joanna is willing to maybe learn something from Emily as well as sleep with her.

Emily told Joanna about the march during the restless time, in the early hours, after they'd made love.

Joanna lay on her stomach, forearms propping her head and chest off the sheet. "Why?" she asked.

Emily laughed. She lay on her back, knees up, looking at the ceiling. "I've asked myself that a lot," she said. "Because it will change the way I see the world. Because it's an act of hope."

Joanna would not normally find herself attracted to such a person. Would not normally trust such a statement. But this she understands, even if she will admit it to no one.

"Did you know you're closer to my son's age than to mine?" Sunlight bathed Joanna's face.

Emily stretched one leg in the air, then the other. "No," she said. "Am I?"

Joanna felt soft as soon as she said it. "Well," she said. "Not quite." She has begun to question her agility. How much longer she'd be able to dodge and feint before she fell prey to entropy. She rested a hand on Emily's stomach. Traced the outline of her navel. Lingered longer than she intended.

She does not know what she will do when she is finished with her work, or how she will know that she is finished.

She has driven a perfect square into the section of wood door. Eight rows of eight nails. She has rearranged the wrought iron gate, shifted its position and observed it. This is an item she will wait on before she commits. Before assigning its permanent place.

She is polishing the tail fin, restoring a shadow of its former glow. The sun has shifted from over her left shoulder to over her right.

She does not hear Cole's footsteps approach. To her, it is as if he materializes behind her, a magician's trick.

"Hey."

She stands. Faces him. Places her body between him and the sculpture. "Hi."

Even with his Tombstone sunglasses, he cocks his head at an angle against the sun. He's standing like he stands when he needs to talk.

"What's up?"

"You didn't come for lunch."

"Wasn't hungry."

He scrapes the toe of his sneaker against the dirt.

"Something's bugging me," he says. "About this Emily thing."

"Later," she says, tight-lipped.

"Did you tell her where to find us?"

Joanna wipes sweat from her brow. "I may have said the Valley. A drive-in. It's not like I gave her directions."

"Because it's important that you not do that."

She nods. He is trespassing. "You're right. I'm sorry. We'll talk about it later."

Cole appears small. In his body posture, hesitant, she sees herself as a child approaching her older sister's secret clubhouse. "I mean, the whole idea of a hideout is that people not find us." Behind his sunglasses, he could be studying the sculpture. He could be studying her.

She is conscious of avoiding eye contact. Of looking at a patch of sky beyond his left shoulder.

He turns to go. Then a glance back, an afterthought. "It looks good."

She flexes her stomach muscles against a twinge of guilt. Tells herself that she has not pulled away. That he is crossing lines he shouldn't cross.

SCREEN FIVE

The doorbell rings. June moves to answer it. Ward sits on the couch, a bemused smile.

June opens the door on a beaming Eddie. Rail thin, body wound tight.

"What a lovely dress, Mrs. C. Why, every time I see you, you're looking lovelier and more radiant."

June takes in the compliment. Her shoulders relax. "Why thank you, Eddie. Come in. The boys are upstairs."

Eddie bounds up the stairs, two at a time.

June returns to Ward. "You think this is funny."

"No, June. It's just that they're boys. They're bound to get into a few scrapes. What have they done?"

"They've made a mess of their room. People have been injured." June's eyebrows furrow. "I think you should have a talk with them."

The key to a successful encryption system is twofold: security and simplicity. While any system can be hacked given the application of enough time and energy, encryption needs to be good enough to make it impractical – more effort than it's worth – for anyone to hack in. It's the perception of impregnability that companies like Z-Tech are built on. They're working against the public's innate distrust of electronic commerce. But the impression of invincibility by itself is not enough. Simplicity also counts. If purchasing products over the Internet becomes complicated, people won't do it. There are too many other convenient – and time-tested – ways to buy things.

"Easy as pie," Cole says to himself. "Keep it simple." On screen, he checks his work, a series of sub-routines he's built to try to streamline the order confirmation process, to reduce the amount of time it takes to check a purchaser's credit card information.

"Slash star space," Cole mumbles as he types. "Parse arguments, and set up interface between OpenGL and window system."

He's called functions from his old files, his previous design, and created a new set to try to knock five or six seconds off the processing time. It's the kind of change that, if he can pull it off, could be worth six figures.

"There," he says. "Now test."

He waves his hand like a magician over the machine while it initiates the test. He looks at the beads of sweat on the Coca-Cola bottle on the poster.

Time to take a walk while he waits to see how far the process will get before a glitch appears. This work requires patience. Endless testing. But time grows short. As the upgrade date approaches, Z-Tech will throw hungry 22-year-olds at the coding problem until they have it licked.

Out the screen door. A loud squeak. He keeps meaning to oil it, to buy the oil. He reaches for his Tombstone sunglasses. Then stops. Surprised by dusk. He pulls the visor of his baseball cap down over his forehead. The cap is black with white lettering on the front panel that says, "Shop secure. Shop the Internet."

He's out behind the building, his back to the rising moon, when the holograph comes walking over the hill. Six-guns in a holster on his hip. Legs slightly bowed from too much time in the saddle. White hat tall on his head.

He waves to Cole from fifty yards away.

Cole feels his back stiffen. He looks around him for sources of projection. For telltale traces of Asian men in Armani suits. He wants to believe that this is simply Gene come to say hey. He wishes he could.

"Hey, Cole," Gene calls. "Nice to see you."

Cole smiles. Nods. Runs through possibilities in his mind. Who would do this and why. A trace on the cellular phone account. Bo or Alan giving him away. "Evening, Gene." Events have taken a strange turn. "How you feeling?"

"I'm still here," Gene says. He wipes a hand across his brow.

"I guess you are," Cole says to himself. With his eye he traces angles from the holograph to the building, searching for clues. "In a manner of speaking."

"What's that?" Gene says.

Cole waves him off. "Nothing." He kicks at the dirt with his sneaker. "Mind if I ask you a question?"

"Not at all." Despite his poor resolution, Gene fits the landscape. The echoes of a thousand cowboy movies in his dusty clothes. His stance. The way his boots rest on the hard dirt.

"Are you for real?"

Gene removes his hat. Scratches at his head. "Now, son, I don't know how to answer that."

Cole nods, trying to find the answer – the question – he wants.

"When I was a boy, I used to wonder. We all do, I suppose." Gene shifts the hat from his right hand to his left. "I used to wonder if anything had really existed before I was born, or if it was all just a story made up so the world made sense to me." Gene squints. Puts the hat back on his head. "We don't any of us know for dead sure whether we're not all just fragments of each other's imagination." He rests a hand on his holster. "You seem to need to know something about me that I can't tell you," he says. "I am what I am. You need a name for it, you go ahead and give it one."

The tips of Cole's ears burn. He stares at the ground. It seems impossible that this man is a projection. It seems impossible that he isn't. "I didn't mean to offend you."

"You didn't. In my day, we saw the world in black and white. Made decisions easier. Made choices clear. Nowadays, it's clear only that the world's not so simple. But I don't need to tell you what's what."

Gene shimmers in the moonlight. Fiddles self-consciously with his holster.

"What exactly do you do on that computer of yours?"

Cole hesitates. Sympathy teeters with distrust. Could someone have rigged sound and projection into the drive-in speakers? He's suspicious of a two-dimensional image. "Programming. Pretty boring stuff."

"It's beyond me."

"Me too, lately," Cole says, hand on the visor of his cap. Trying hard not to think about what the cowboy's presence means.

"You just keep at it," Gene says. "You'll get there."

What does Gene know? Cole had planned a parting shot from the Atomic. Charge a heap of women's clothing to Warren's corporate card. Perhaps he'll skip it. Perhaps he's done enough. Greed and overconfidence have undone so many outlaws.

Gene walks behind the refreshment stand, off into darkness. "Good luck, son. See you around."

"Yeah," Cole says. "See you around."

SCREEN SEVEN

A suburban kitchen. Gleaming white appliances. Sparkling Formica counters. Everything neatly contained in canisters, boxes, drawers. Sun streams in a window. Homemade curtains, white with orange dingle ball fringe.

A rumbling in the distance. A swinging door bursts open and a tiny covered wagon charges through. Clatters across the bright linoleum. Horses panting. Red and white checkerboard canvas. Camera zooms in to show the driver. White cowboy hat. Black shirt with sky blue piping. Neckerchief arranged just so. Gene Autry cracks the reins. A big grin. Beside him, in brown t- shirt and buckskin vest, black hat and anxious eyes, a man rides shotgun. One hand clinging to the bench seat. Every few seconds looking behind them. They are miniatures in a land of giants.

Pull back. The team careens toward a bowl on the floor in a corner of the room as the swinging door bursts open again and a dog races in, all hair and drool and scrambling legs. A wheaten terrier. Bearing down on the toy wagon. He could smash it with a forepaw. Devour its riders whole. He charges across the tile after it. The driver steers it home, on his face the joy of the chase, the knowledge that it's all a show. The sidekick feverishly shovels dog food into the bowl. The dog skids to a stop, paws thrashing. Instead of attacking the wagon, the giant dog attacks his dinner. The driver smiles. The sidekick leans on the shovel, wipes a forearm across his brow.

A voice-over says, "Chuck Wagon. Dogs just can't wait to get at it."

An outdoor cookfire. Sun slips behind the mountains. Joanna in her green-striped beach chair, sipping a tall tumbler of Newman's Own, while Cole stirs a pot of black bean chili.

"Leave it be," she says. Her legs stretch in front of her. "Come sit." She pats the seat next to her. "I poured you some lemonade."

Cole abandons the spoon in the pot, takes the seat. The last traces of color – pink, purple – drain from the sky. Smoke curls low, hugs the ground, drifts reluctantly from the fire.

"Isn't this great?" Joanna stretches. Lights a cigarette.

Cole leans forward, hands tucked under his chin. Turns his head every few seconds to check on dinner – to have something to do.

"Next time I go into town, I'm going to find us a guitar," she says. She manages to semi-recline in her beach chair – legs extended in front, hands tucked behind her head. She manages to look comfortable. "Nothing fancy. Something we can knock out a few songs on."

The fire defines a circle of light around them.

Cole moves to stir the beans. He wishes sometimes that she would stop talking. The topics he'd like to introduce need transitions. Translations.

Baked beans stew in molasses. Chunks of beef provide ballast. "Did you bring the bread?"

"I forgot. I'll get it." Joanna heads inside.

"Beans are almost ready," Cole calls after her. He half expects the scent of food to attract Gene. He wonders if this holograph can smell. He wonders if he has the courage to tell her. He can just about live with the possibility that the appearance of this insubstantial cowboy means he has lost touch in some fundamental way with reality. He's pretty sure he couldn't live with Joanna confirming it.

130

The Winnebago door slams shut. "Ta Da." Joanna displays a sourdough baguette as if it were a trophy. "Smells great."

Cole dishes up food. Adds a log to the fire.

"Cookie," Joanna says, wiping her mouth with a cloth napkin. "You've outdone yourself."

"Shucks." He scoops a spoonful of beans. He cannot shake the hope that she will find something else in this. Fashion in it something solid.

"Joanna, I've met someone."

"The waitress." She rests her fork on the plate. "I knew you'd fall for her."

"No." Cole shakes his head. "Not like that."

"What then," she says. "Tell me."

"Someone who's living here," he says. "Kind of."

"At the drive-in?" She dips bread in bean juice. "You're being cryptic."

"I'm not sure if he lives at the drive-in. It's kind of odd." Cole can feel his face flush. He's questioning the wisdom of this. Considers backpedaling.

"You look scared," she says. "He's a bully. You want me to beat him up."

"I'm afraid Z-Tech might have sent him to spy."

She gives him a wary look. "What do you know about him?"

"He dresses like a cowboy. His name's Gene."

"Z-Tech sent a dress-up cowboy to spy on you."

Cole is losing courage. "It's like he's from some other time. And he seems to live somewhere around here, but it's not clear where. Or how."

The fire pops and hisses.

"He's not exactly normal," Cole says.

"We live in a trailer at an abandoned drive-in. Talk to me about normal. What makes you think he's spying on you?"

Beef dry in Cole's mouth. He chews. Chooses words carefully. "His form."

"Cole, what are you talking about? Spit it out."

"He's a holograph."

Joanna holds a mouthful of beans. She's not swallowing.

Cole is cliff diving. Bungee jumping. He does not know where – or if – he will land.

Finally, Joanna swallows.

"Okay," she says.

"I need you to tell me I'm not crazy," Cole says.

"You're not crazy."

A spurt of flame as a log collapses into the center of the cookfire.

"I need you to believe me."

"Okay, I believe you."

"I need you to mean it."

She nods. "That's fair." Neither of them is eating. "So tell me about him."

"He doesn't seem to be projected from anywhere. He's free. Self-directed."

"I see."

"I've checked all around for mirrors. For a light source." Cole pours more lemonade from the sweaty carton. Paul Newman's reassuring smile. "Nothing. I found him one day out behind the refreshment stand. Heard him humming. He was fooling with a" – he gestures with his hands, spinning and twirling – "what do you call it, a lasso. We talked."

"You talked?"

Cole nods. "I talked. He talked."

Joanna sets her plate on the ground. Raises her eyebrows. Leans back in her chair. "Whoa." She sets her fork on her plate. "Have you seen him since?"

"Once more. Same place. Right around there anyway." Cole shakes his head. "It's not like I've been working all nighters," he says. "I'm taking care of myself. I take walks."

"Look," she says. "We've made some big changes. The nature of your work is fairly obsessive. It's not out of line for something like this to happen. Don't be embarrassed."

The sky loses its color. Only a trace of purple remains.

"I've seen him twice, Joanna. I'm not hallucinating."

"Okay. How do you explain it?"

"He's a cowboy. His name's Gene. He says he used to make movies."

A smile breaks onto her face.

"Wait a minute," she says. "Back up. Describe. What did he look like? What was he wearing?"

"I don't know. Kind of short. Stocky. Funky boots. Cowboy hat."

"What color?"

"White."

"What else?"

"Dark shirt with a line of stitching around here." Cole points to his chest.

"You mean piping?"

"That's it. Piping. This *trés* dapper neckerchief done just so. Dimples."

Joanna leans forward. "You're telling me you've seen Gene Autry."

"A holograph of Gene Autry," he corrects her.

A sliver of moon emerges above.

"Z-Tech is spying on you by creating a holograph of Gene Autry. The singing cowboy."

"I don't know that they're spying. They may be trying to make me think I'm crazy."

Joanna smiles. A warm breeze. "You need to get out more."

For all the fear Cole had expected to feel, now that Joanna calls him on it, fails so completely to believe him, he finds himself gaining confidence in his perceptions. "He's real. Whatever that means. What I'm telling you exists. What would it take to convince you?"

Joanna sets her plate on the ground. Her smile is a challenge. "Invite him for dinner."

Cole searches the sky for the evening's first stars. Determined to prove himself. To enlist her help in making sense of this. "I'll do that."

SCREEN EIGHT

A television sound stage, well-appointed. A pair of men in padded swivel chairs, comfortably clad in sport coats, sweaters and slacks. Behind them, a projection screen shows an image of a cowboy – big white hat, smiling round face, neckerchief draped neatly over the shoulder. Gene and Roger. Roger and Gene. An American institution.

"Welcome back," says Roger. "Tonight we're taking a look back at some of the oldest Hollywood movie traditions. Our next segment features the original singing cowboy, a man who for more than fifteen years was virtually a studio unto himself. A man who starred in more than fifty films spanning three decades, who did as much as anyone, even John Wayne himself, to define the American Western. His classics include 'Oh Susanna', 'Man of the Frontier', and of course, 'Mule Train'. I'm speaking of Gene Autry, perhaps our first true Western hero."

The camera pulls back to reveal Gene, chin resting on his fingers, shaking his head.

Gene leans forward. He uses his hands when he speaks. "I'm no great fan of the Western to begin with," he says. "It's a genre largely doomed to self-parody."

"How can you claim to be a student of film and not revere the Western," says Roger.

"Sentimental, overblown, and one-dimensional." Gene looks disdainfully at Roger. "May I finish? I'm no great fan of Westerns, though at least with some of the epics – John Ford's 'The Searchers,' Sergio Leone's 'Once Upon a Time in the West' – there's a context to explore interesting themes, the evolution and loss of the American frontier, the impact that has on what is possible in this country." Gene talks with his hands spread wide, his speech moist. "But to lionize someone like Gene Autry." He closes his mouth into a tight line. "These films were diversion. They're hopelessly outdated. The only possible reasons to view them today are to mock them or to exercise a particularly pathetic form of nostalgia."

"Call me pathetic," says Roger. "I like them, and I think there's value in looking at the kind of hero Autry was, and why that character was so embraced."

"Please, Roger. Enlighten us."

Roger's smile is bemused. "As an early Western hero, Autry is an interesting figure. The hero who still believes society can work, that the structures which govern are essentially good and right, tarnished by a few bad apples. That things can be set right."

"And?"

Roger, undaunted. "Consider an early entry in the series. *Man of the Frontier.* Autry becomes a fence rider to help the Red River Valley Company find out who's sabotaging the construction of a bridge. It turns out, of course, that the corrupt local banker, working in cahoots with the project's foreman, is trying to make the job fail so he can foreclose and take it over. So the film is a study in greed and its effects. The slow poisoning of society from within. Autry is the outsider able to bring perspective. To come in and see motives for what they are."

"Motives? Study? It's the most simplistic and formulaic of plot structures."

"I disagree. Autry, in this film and others, prefigures the later, alienated Western heroes – Eastwood, the later Wayne films – and even hard-boiled detective heroes, with this suggestion that any hope of setting things right must come from outside the system. That the forces of power will clamp down to squeeze out honesty, make the truth harder and harder to discover, until eventually, the possibility of truth disappears."

"You're telling me that Gene Autry prefigures the post-war *film noir* antihero?"

"In these Autry films lay the seeds and suggestions for much of the richness that would develop. I'm saying that the yearning for the frontier is one that has never left us, never left our films. It has merely changed form. Space travel. Detective films. Aliens. And that Autry, unlike later heroes, cultivated a softer side. He sang."

"Are you finished?"

"I'm finished."

"When we return, Roger will extol the virtues of Lee Marvin."

*

"I didn't think you even *owned* a tie."

Joanna, hands on hips, inside the trailer door, fresh from a hard day of penance.

"I didn't." Cole adjusts the clip on a bolo. White shirt. "It's a special occasion."

"You *shaved.*"

"He's an old-fashioned kind of guy."

Joanna pours herself a glass of water. "Do we have to play this out?"

Cole has folded out the table and covered it with a pale green cloth.

"I was about to come get you," he says. "He'll be here any minute."

"I'm supposed to get dressed?"

"Do what you want. I'm not your wife."

Joanna flops onto her bed/sofa. "I promise I don't think you're crazy. Now, can we not do this?"

Cole paces. Ignores her. *How does a holograph know what day it is? Will he be visible indoors?* What if, after all, he is just a figment of Cole's imagination?

Joanna dons her cowboy hat. "Fine. what's for dinner?"

"Pho."

"*Faux?*" she says. "How appropriate. Let's eat."

He indicates a brown bag on the counter, stapled shut. "And fresh spring rolls." He can't shake the fear that Gene is an illusion about to come crashing down around him. He tries to sound confident. "We'll eat when our guest gets here."

A voice outside. "Hello. Anybody home?"

Joanna looks at him. "Oh, God."

Muscles loosen that Cole didn't know were tight. He's entering virgin territory.

Cole pushes open the door. Gene in white hat, black shirt, blue piping. Luminescent. The boots have been shined, the neckerchief done with a fancy knot worn in front. He lingers in the doorway, vaporous. In his hands, a bunch of real – tangible – daisies.

"Gene. I'm *so* glad to see you." Cole holds the door open. Gene shows no hesitancy – or difficulty – moving indoors. Cole careful not to bump or block him, concerned that at any moment, Gene could flicker and fade.

"Thanks. I don't get many dinner invites." Inside, he looks more vulnerable somehow. "This must be Joanna."

He extends a hand.

Joanna stares. Stupefied. Looks at Cole, as if for instruction. She pushes the hat back on her head.

"Gene Autry," she says. Her hand moves automatically toward his. Her voice distant. *"How?"*

"Pleasure to meet you," he says, a hint of a drawl.

Joanna has a look on her face that Cole has most often seen on television programs, or in movies – usually following a visit from an alien space ship.

"Come in. Sit down." Cole motions Gene to the makeshift couch. "Want some lemonade?"

"Thanks." Gene sits spraddle-legged on the couch. Leans forward. Forearms on thighs. "Brought you these."

Joanna tentatively takes the daisies. "Thanks. They're beautiful." She sniffs them. Shifts the bouquet from hand to hand. A vague expression, as if she can't remember what it is she wants to remember.

"They're not much, but they are fresh."

Joanna reaches for her water. Seems surprised by the flowers in her hand. Uncertain where they came from. She drops them in the water glass.

Cole pours lemonade, giddy. At this moment, he wouldn't be surprised if Paul Newman leapt off the carton.

"Nice place you got here," Gene says. "A little cozy, but right comfortable." He accepts the lemonade with a nod. Cole's hand lingers under the tumbler a moment in case the transfer won't work.

Joanna's eyes look hypnotically in Gene's direction. Cole has never seen her like this. She sits at the table. Stands up again. Unpacks the food. "It's Pho," she says. "Vietnamese noodle soup."

"Smells great," Gene says. "I can't eat much, but I do enjoy the tastes."

Cole sets out bowls. Preoccupied with logistics. *Does a holograph go to the bathroom.* He enjoys watching Joanna reel and recover, try to play host to an insubstantial image.

Soup. Spring rolls. Lemonade all around.

"Dig in," Joanna says.

She hovers behind Gene, a curious look on her face. She reaches an index finger toward Gene's shoulder, slowly, tentatively down through the air above him. He is hunched over his soup, metal spoon held to holographic mouth. Cole tries to make eye contact with her, to send thought waves – *DON'T DO IT* – but she's mesmerized, her finger approaching black fabric – the image of black fabric – fuzzy at its edge, like a crescent moon on a hazy Autumn night, the finger down toward shoulder, on it, into it, through it. Fabric projected on skin. Cole, frozen, spoon in hand, half expects to see Gene recoil in pain, or pop like a bubble. Instead, he sips soup. Joanna's finger retreats. A puzzled smile blooms. She inspects the finger, and Cole regains the use of his arms.

She leans toward Cole. "This," she whispers, "is a major mindfuck."

Cole puts a finger to his lips.

They watch Gene eat. Cole marvels – *where does it go.*

"Delicious," Gene says. He catches Joanna's glazed eye. "I guess Cole told you I was a little different from what you might expect."

"Yes." She blushes, which makes Cole grin. But the rush of blood seems to lure her out of reverie. "He also told me he thinks you're a spy sent by his former employer."

"Come again?" Gene's face the picture of innocence.

"Never mind," says Cole. His turn to blush.

A mockingbird sings outside the window.

Soup spoons knock against bowls.

"How'd you two come to be out here?" Gene says. "Kind of off the beaten path."

"We needed to get away," Cole says.

Joanna's mouth curls into a sardonic smile. Her eyes alert again. "We came out here to start over. Build a quiet life away from it all."

"Sounds nice," says Gene.

"It is," Joanna says. "Except Kid Crypto here decided to wear a black hat." She gestures toward the foot of Cole's bed, where his hat gathers dust.

Gene pauses, spoon near his mouth. "I don't follow."

"He's a wanted man."

"That's not true."

"An outlaw. It complicates things."

Gene eats with raised eyebrows.

"Hogwash," Cole says through a mouthful of soup. "I'm a man doing a job. Using my skills. I can't help it if people make rules against that."

"Shucks," she drawls, then drops the accent. "You're so full of shit."

Gene, red-faced, concentrates on his soup.

Joanna, one hand on her knee. "Jesse James was just a guy doing his job. Billy the Kid."

"In a way," Cole says. "Yeah."

"Billy the Kid was a murderer. Jesse James was a bank robber."

"They did nothing worse than what the other side did. They broke the law, sure, but the law has always been a tool, a set of rules put in place by the wealthy and powerful to make sure they stayed that way."

Joanna rolls her eyes.

"I'll grant you," Gene holds his spoon in the air, "the law doesn't create a plumb line about what's right."

"I'm not arguing that," Joanna says. The big hat dwarfs her face.

"They were kids," Cole says. "Playing around. They liked the West because there were no rules, no boundaries."

"They liked the West because they could do – and take – what they wanted." Joanna pushes an egg roll around on her plate. "Don't get me wrong. I love the West. I love outlaws. I'm just saying look at it for what it is. Butch Cassidy was a bank robber. You're a cyber thief."

"That code is mine."

"Hacker. Saboteur." She chews a mouthful of egg roll.

"I thought you were on my side."

"I am."

"And I'm doing what's right, even if it's not strictly legal."

"I don't care about the law." She pushes her empty bowl away. "We were supposed to start over."

They are three people having dinner on a summer evening. She slouches in her seat. "Gene, what's the first rule of outlawing?"

Gene ponders. "Never think you're smarter 'n the other fella."

Joanna frowns. "What number is 'never call attention to yourself when you're supposed to be hiding out?' "

A holographic grin. "I think maybe that's number two."

"Thank you. And committing a crime generally calls attention to you." She grabs Cole's hat, sets it on his head. "All I'm saying is, if you're going to wear it, be smart. And be ready to take the consequences."

Cole tosses the hat on the bed. His ears burn.

Gene looks up from his soup. "You two okay?"

"Hell." Joanna puts her arm around Cole's shoulders. "We're fine. I just wish he wasn't so stupid."

"Thanks, darling."

Gene helps himself to another spring roll. Cole marvels at the mystery.

Joanna's mischievous grin. "Gene, where do you put it all?"

He blushes. "Oh, I can't eat but a fraction of what I used to."

The Winnebago is filled with warm food smells. They eat. They talk. Cole stifles the occasional urge to search under the table for a puddle of food. Struggles to take the evening on its own terms.

As the light fades, Gene appears more substantial. He narrows his eyes. "You know, the thing about the frontier was all that space, you could escape the consequences of your actions. Those boys – those outlaws – could do what they wanted, long as there was room to run." Gene slaps a hand at the table. Cole waits for an impact that never comes. "Once that's gone, you've got accountability. Compromise."

Cole drains the dregs from his bowl.

"I'm not saying there weren't some who were different. Like you said Cole, men doing their job. Not worrying which side of the rules."

"Alan Ladd," says Cole, "Shane."

"Yessir," says Gene.

The room has gone gray. Joanna's hand warm on Cole's shoulder.

Gene leans back. Stretches. "It's been a fine meal and a good conversation," he says, "but I don't want to overstay my welcome."

"Nonsense," Cole says. "We still have pie and a movie. Joanna's a huge fan."

"And Cole's never seen one of your movies." She scans the shelf behind her. "Where's the tape?"

Cole grabs it. "*Man of the Frontier*. Do you mind?"

Gene smiles. "I'd be honored. It's been a while."

Later.

"He's no spy." Joanna stretched on her bed. Watching out the window. A rectangle of stars and night sky.

"How do you know?" Cole restful. Eyes open. Body relaxed. The dark safety of their trailer. The sound of Joanna's voice. He could stay like this forever.

"Whatever he is, he's genuine." With the shade pulled up, she can see Orion's belt. "Besides, no company – especially not your former employer – would show that amount of whimsy in a hostile situation."

"There's only one problem." He tucks his hands behind his head. "If he's not a spy, what is he?"

Joanna yawns. "That I don't know." She rubs her eyes. The refrigerator hums. "But I think we should buy him a horse."

"Where do you find a holographic horse?"

"Not a holographic horse. A real one."

"What makes you think he could ride a real horse. Let alone feed and water it."

"He ate real food. Picked real flowers."

"I know. I half expected to find a puddle of soup on the seat when he was done."

They are recognizable to each other in the half light.

"Where do you think it *goes?*"

He smiles. "I'd love to ask him."

"Yeah."

"I doubt he knows. Or even thinks about it."

Joanna watches the stars. "Just for the record," she says, "I never *really* doubted you."

"Bullshit."

"Okay." She laughs. Looks in his direction. His shadow beside her. The mystery of a new thing. "You like the movie?"

"I did. That Smiley Burnette's a trip."

It's peaceful. Just soft moon shadows, and soft voices in the dark.

"So what do you think about the horse?"

"I'm game. If we can find a way to do it without calling all kinds of attention."

She plays connect-the-dots with the stars. A horse. A rider. "I'm sorry for doubting you."

Cole stretches his toes against the ledge. "Hey, I doubted me." Blanket tucked under him, friend by his side. He hums Red River Valley.

Joanna joins in.

Fade to black.

Sandy hair combed straight back. Streaked with gray. Olive skin. Feet up on a large oak desk in a white, Hacienda-style office in Los Gatos, California. Links Pro on one monitor. His late afternoon golf break. On the other monitor, a sniffer program delivered screen shots captured from a suspect's computer, twice a minute over the past 24 hours. St. Martin kept half an eye on the sniffer screen as he prepared to blast out of a sand trap on the seventh hole at Castle Pines. A door opened and closed out in the courtyard. Clogs on the stone walkway. A suite of professional offices – chiropractor, bankruptcy attorney, physical therapist. His shot rolled to within eight feet of the cup. A short putt to save par. Nothing of substance from the sniffer. Instant Messaging with a variety of friends. Web surfing. *Salon*. *The Onion*. Mundane stuff. Waiting for a call from Archer, who was busy recovering files from the suspect's seized hard drive. St. Martin hoped to close the case by day's end. Hard evidence in one form or the other to turn over to the police. Maybe play nine holes – real holes – before dinner.

The telephone pulled him away from his putt. "St. Martin." Linen shirt, pale yellow. Brown slacks.

"William St. Martin?"

Disappointment. Not Archer's voice. "That's me."

"The private investigator?"

"One and the same." He clicked his mouse, sank the putt. Canned cheers.

"This is Warren Pettinger, with Z-Tech. We've got a problem I hope you can solve."

"What sort of problem?"

"We're not sure yet." Fatigue in the man's strained voice. "Our system's been hacked. It goes deep, but we don't know how deep. Our flagship product is corrupted. False transactions. Sabotaged commerce. Bugs and glitches out of nowhere."

St. Martin pulled his feet off the desk. "It's more than a single intrusion?"

"It's ongoing."

"What about the police?"

"We want to pursue it quietly – out of the public eye – until we're sure we can get an arrest."

St. Martin fiddled with the mouse, then turned from the screens to give the call his full attention. "Where you located?"

"Waltham, Massachusetts."

A raised eyebrow. "I'm mostly West Coast. I could give you some names."

"We'd prefer to work with you."

"Okay. Why me?"

"Reputation. Track record."

He consulted his Palm Pilot. "It'll be a few days."

A pause. "When can you come?"

"Friday."

Long pause.

"You might get a faster response locally."

"We'll wait."

"Meantime, trace all passwords – especially new ones. Interview staff – has anyone else had access to their computers. Start a list of disgruntled current or former employees." St. Martin spun back to his computers. The par-5 eighth hole awaited. Nothing of note from the sniffer. This suspect spent his life on IM. "And hope whoever it is loses interest." He checked wind direction, clicked a forefinger on the mouse, and teed off. Long and straight. "Don't worry, we'll get 'em."

SCREEN FIVE

Yvon stands in the living room, hands on hips. A framed counted cross-stitch on the wall shows a cozy house in brown, with red letters spelling Home Sweet Home. A collection of glass animals decorate a table. The furniture is colonial. The carpet plush.

Ward and June sit on the floral pattern couch, looking attentively at Yvon.

"I think what we need is to crank up the intensity a little," says Yvon. "A little urgency. Maybe even desperation."

Ward and June nod and smile.

"Righto," says Ward. White shirt. Thin tie. A wave in his brown hair that gives him a jaunty air.

"Sounds good," says June. Her olive dress casual.

"Work with me here." Yvon sits on the arm of the couch, next to June. He sips coffee from a sky blue mug. "You're worried. This is a whole new realm. A kind of trouble you've never envisioned. Never imagined. I mean, it's not like they've dented the car by riding a bicycle into it. It's not as though they've trampled the neighbor's flowers. Or even glued grandma's dentures in her mouth."

June nods her head. Her face solemn.

"We're talking about a pipe bomb." Yvon puts his hand on June's knee. "Black powder. Metal pipe. Clothespin. Tacks. We're talking about a messy explosion. A deliberate act."

"I understand," she says.

"Good," says the director. He moves to the other end of the couch. Squats on the floor, facing Ward. A basketball coach and his star player. Eye to eye. Ward's face has that confident, ready-for-anything cast. "This requires a firm hand. There are ramifications. Serious forces at work. You didn't see this coming. What parent could?"

Ward's brow furrows, as if he's sympathizing with someone else's plight. "Got it," he says.

"Good, you two." Yvon stands. Puts his hands together. "That's great. Let's try it again."

Joanna sits on the steps in the shade of Max's trailer, patting King. Sipping coffee.

Max has taken a customer into the secret room, the room that pays for Nolan's medical care. The room of signage and sculpture, crafted in wrought iron. Joanna wonders if there is cause for concern.

"Old man going to make a sale?" She rubs behind King's ear. She loves his thick fur. His quietly indifferent manner. "Steak for you tonight, boy."

The dog's ears twitch.

Max emerges around the corner, trailed by a man with an expensive haircut and a grateful smile. Polo shirt buttoned to the top. Slate gray sports jacket. The man has a rectangular block of wood tucked under one arm.

"Thank you, Max," he says. "Good to see you."

"You take care," Max says.

Joanna sips coffee. Hands Max a mug. "So what was that one?"

Max peels off Latex gloves. Tosses them into a trash can. Accepts the mug. "Back in the fifties I did a few prototypes for Wells Fargo Bank. Their logo in wood and iron. One or two even used bronze." He sits beside her on the steps. A sparrow eyes them from atop an old refrigerator.

"Everything okay?"

"No new crisis, if that's what you mean." Max flashes a check. "Boosting the bank account. He's had his eye on that piece."

Joanna digs her hands into the dog's fur. "Steaks tonight, King."

"That's right." Max tucks the check into his shirt pocket. "But you didn't come here to talk about steak. What can I do you for?"

"What do you know about horses, Max?"

Max's bald skull looks like the desert itself – brown and pocked and dry.

"I know the ones I bet on never win. What do you want to know?"

"I want to buy a horse. Where would you go to find one. What would you look for?"

"Stay away from horses, Jo. Good God. You were worried about welding."

"I'm not talking about raising them," Joanna says. King's eyes fall shut. A hot Santa Ana breeze lulls the day. "I want to buy one. As a present."

"A present?" Max scratches at a scaly place on his scalp. "Some present." He sips coffee. "Only thing I know is check the teeth. Don't even know why."

"Come on, Max," she says. "You must know someone." She wonders how Max would react if she told him about Gene.

King moans softly. Rolls onto his side.

"Used to know a guy up in Thousand Oaks. He had a stable. Maybe he could fix you up."

She kisses his cheek. "Thanks, Max. You're a prince."

He smiles. "That's right." Gestures toward the drowsy dog. "He's the King and I'm the prince." He holds the door open so

146

she can follow him in. "I got his name inside." Fishes through a stack of papers in a drawer of an old steel desk. "For your boy?"

"Huh?"

"The horse. A present for your boy?"

Joanna's jaw tightens. "Nah."

Max's hands keep searching the drawer but his eyes are on Joanna. "How is the boy?"

She looks hard at Max. "Could we focus on the horse guy?"

"Sure." Max searches in silence a minute, then retrieves a business card. "Here you go. Here's your man."

She takes the card. "You want me to write it down?"

"No. You bring it back when you're done is all."

"Thanks." She turns to go.

"Jo."

"Yeah?"

"He in trouble?"

Joanna presses her feet against the floor. Fights the pull of the undertow. "He might be."

Max closes the drawer. Leans a hand on the desk. "If he is, and you can help him, do it." His body like the trunk of an old tree – gnarled, strong. "I raised one son. Lost another. Do what you can while you can. Don't carry that around with you the rest of your life." He leans the upper half of his body left, exaggerating his bad posture. "It'll do this to you."

She's torn. Eager to escape, grateful for the friendship. "I gotta go." Halfway through the door, she turns her head. "Max," she says. "You're amazing."

"I should be." He scratches his head. "I've had long enough to get there."

The sun peaks past two in the afternoon. She is learning to submit to the heat, to drink it into her body and adjust the pace of her work, the intensity of her effort, to the conditions of the day.

She has brought the radio with her and listens to an FM station that, at least for today, plays Motown. Smokey Robinson and the Miracles. The Four Tops. Martha and the Vandelas. She is not loyal to one station. She flits from song to song, hungry for what she wants to hear.

She has pounded iron bands into straight, flat lines. Four inches wide. Four-or-so feet long. She has bought a bag of cement. She has gathered glass, the lenslike bottoms of bottles, shards of many colors. She will fashion a mosaic of glass in the cement. She will band it in iron. She will build two more and use them to bound her sculpture.

She sits on the ground, sorting glass, reserving the pieces she likes best. She sings along with the radio.

I've got sunshine on a cloudy day
when it's cold outside, I've got the month of May

Brown and green and clear. The brighter bits are newer, less weathered. Other bits are cloudy, faded in the sun. One piece so fogged it could be sea glass. She loves the variety of them. She imagines that she is a prospector, panning for gold.

I've got so much honey, the bees envy me.
I've got a sweeter song than the birds in the trees.

Her sculpture looms behind her. She imagines it is part of the landscape, sinking roots into the earth, reaching for sustenance.

She sorts the glass, separating piles with her hand to more clearly delineate the one she will use from the one she will not.

The radio station takes a news break. She frowns, too absorbed to get up. Too much enjoying the sun on her back. Then her hands stop. It is as if she can anticipate what is about to be said, as if the knowledge of it begins in her fingers, travels up her arms and through her chest into her head, and reaches her brain at the same time the words from the radio enter her ears.

Seven are dead and sixteen wounded after an
explosion rocked a charity ball in the Seattle
suburb of Bothell, Washington last night.

She looks around, a reflex. To remind herself of where she is. To search for an exit.

Police know of no motive for the blast that
came from a crudely constructed pipe bomb
placed under a table at the Black and Blue
Ball, an annual charity event to benefit the
Muscular Dystrophy Association.

Her chest feels constricted. She breathes in gasps. The heat oppressive.

While there is speculation that this may be
connected to an April bombing at an Oregon
golf course, police officials say that other than
the homemade nature of both explosions, there
is as yet no evidence to suggest the incidents
are the work of the same person.

She is surrounded by glass. Green, white, blue, brown. Fenced in by suspicions. They press against her chest, erupting, insistent. The voice on the radio keeps talking. She squeezes a jagged bottle bottom, balls her fingers around it into a fist, until the pain in her hand equals the pain in her heart and causes a white flash in her head, and she falls back into the dirt.

SCREEN THREE

The sheriff strides down the middle of the dusty street, now deserted. Everyone has either left town or sought refuge from the imminent trouble. Empty buildings. Quiet storefronts. The sheriff stands straight and tall, hand poised at his gun. Hearing only the sound of his own footsteps in the dirt. Squinting into sunlight. Worn hat hot on his head. Crows feet deep around vigilant eyes. Strong, determined chin. In the distance, a train whistle blows.

The camera pans up to the hotel window, where the bride wears an anguished look. A close-up, in profile. High cheekbones.

"I don't care who's right or who's wrong," she says. "There's got to be a better way for people to live."

*

She is still and quiet. Has hardly moved all morning. He has made and drank several cups of coffee. Has cooked scrambled eggs, hoping that the sounds and smells would rouse her. That she would emerge, and tell him what has happened.

He covers her with a wool blanket. Sees that her eyes are open. She is curled in a tight ball on her bed. Outside, the day is in full flower. The heat has begun to penetrate, to bake their small living space.

She does not move. Not even her eyes.

"Does it hurt?"

"It hurts."

Her hand is wrapped in gauze. Blood has seeped through.

He stands beside the bed. "I need to change the dressing. Clean it."

She looks at him, puzzled, then down at her hand.

When she had first heard the news about Oregon, about the golf course on the TV news, something small and sharp had lodged in the lining of her stomach. She had driven to Boston, driven her Toyota and listened to the radio and heard it again, a headline at the top of the news hour on National Public Radio. She'd caught a snippet as she flipped through stations –

> *"a golf course in Oregon. Police have not determined a motive for the bombing, although they suspect it may have some connection to the tournament, which had drawn such technology luminaries as Bill Gates and Paul Allen."*

There had been no reason to believe that Anthony was involved. Thousands of kids worked as caddies. Any number of them became embittered on the people who played the game at exclusive clubs, who often treated their charges as serfs. Anthony was not alone in this. This experience did not translate to violence. And Anthony had been in Boulder, had left Armonk on his fifteenth birthday to go to Boulder, where he'd stayed with Sean. There was no reason to think that Anthony was connected.

She had watched the six o'clock news. Watched the woman in the flame-colored suit recite reports of Federal investigations into campaign finance abuse, looked at footage of the damage wrought by a hurricane in Mississippi. And then the small, sharp fear had begun to scratch at the lining of her stomach.

The female news anchor, short black hair, her face a study in measured seriousness. Projected behind her a map of Oregon, with a little star in the lower left and the words Klamath Falls.

"Police tonight are still searching for clues after a bomb shattered the early morning stillness at Victory Pines Golf Club, where a tournament was slated to begin later in the morning. Speculation has centered around the presence of business leaders Bill Gates and Paul Allen. Police are working to ascertain whether the blast, caused by a crudely manufactured pipe bomb, may have been intended for one or both of these men. Two others – greenskeeper Richard Banks and assistant pro Jonathan Katz – remain in critical condition tonight in a Portland hospital."

SCREEN TEN

The two fugitives – male and female – seated at a café table, in a courtyard, in what is supposed to be turn-of-the-century Bolivia. Plates of overcooked steak and beans before them.

He wipes at the gravy from his beans with a dry flour tortilla. "Well, we've tried going straight," he says. "What now?"

Two horses and a mule rest in the shade across a courtyard of whitewashed adobe.

She pushes the pearl-colored hat back on her head. He wears a black Stetson. A buckskin vest.

"Don't worry," she says. "I'll think of something."

"You keep thinking," he says. "It's what you're good at."

A high-pitched whine cuts the air. His plate explodes. Shards of porcelain, bits of steak scatter.

"Dammit," she says. "Remind me not to eat here again."

They draw six-shooters from worn leather holsters. Take cover behind pillars on either side of their table. Rifle shots explode around them.

"How many you figure there are?" She calls to him.

Steady staccato bursts of gunfire around them. Windows, planters shatter. Bits of adobe fly off in puffs of dust.

"At least three," he says, spinning the chamber of his pistol to make sure it's loaded.

First he, then she emerges, six guns blazing. They fire at an enemy they cannot see, try to get one to show himself so they can mount a defense. They spend their ammunition. Retreat behind posts.

A volley of bullets burst around them.

She shows him her nearly empty ammo belt. "I'm going to need more," she says. "One of us is going to have to get to the mule."

"I'm a better shooter," he says. "I'll cover you."

She swallows. Nods. "I hate this," she says.

"Run fast," he tells her.

She tosses him her gun. He loads each chamber of both. "Okay," he says. "Go."

She runs in stages, moving from post to post, post to wagon, wagon to mule, as he fires to protect her. Bullets raise dust at her feet. She thinks every second that she'll surely be hit, but somehow it doesn't happen. She hides herself between the mule and her horse, lifts three extra ammunition belts from around the pommel. Bullets whiz past, miraculously hitting only air and dirt.

He fires. Loads. Fires. He is patient. Determined.

Cut to outside the building. The clatter of hooves. A line of riders on horseback, a hundred mounted men arriving. Dismounting. Climbing the clay steps to the roof, rifles at the ready.

Back inside the courtyard, she swallows hard. Dust. The musk of horse and mule. The sharp stink of sulfur. She is acutely aware of everything around her.

"We're going straight," she says to the mule. "Why can't they leave us alone?"

She catches his eye. Signals her readiness to return.

He reloads. Breathes deeply. Nods at her.

Then he's out in the open, firing away, and she's got one hand on the pommel of the horse's saddle and the other on that of the mule, and she stirs the animals to movement and they begin to lead her back toward him, across the courtyard in an explosion of gunfire, what must be tens, hundreds of rifles, fireworks bursting without pause and the animals drag her across but then something buckles and the horse falters, down on one knee, and then grunting, over on its side and she hits the dust, rolling not stopping and a flurry of metal sparks the ground around her and she's vaguely aware of the mule and more aware of him whom she can see not more than twenty yards away and coming out to get her.

He tosses her a gun and she catches it at the same moment she catches a bullet in the leg, then one in the shoulder, an eruption of pain. A fire. And she drops to a knee and stands back up, her and him, holding on to each other, firing, wave after wave of bullets raining down at them. Then his movement slows, she has to pull him, and she dives for cover and he's right behind her and they roll to the safety of their alcove to regroup.

Fighting for breath. No time no space to acknowledge pain. The hail of bullets momentarily halted. The silence eerie. Footsteps above them, boots on clay tile. They pull themselves to sitting positions, side-by-side against the wall as the gunfire begins again. They take now two pistols each, reload.

"I've got an idea," she says. "I know where we should go next."

"You mean when we get out of here," he says.

"That's right," she says. "When we ride out of this." She wipes at her forehead. Bites her lip against the pain.

"Okay," he says. Breath heaving. Body beyond pain. "Where?"

"Australia," she says.

Soldiers move down stairs into the courtyard.

"Is that right?" he says.

She nods. "It's got the perfect climate. Clean air. The outback. Better than the desert. Bigger." She spins the cylinders of both pistols. Cocks them in place. "No one would find us."

"I'll think about that," he says. His face a grimace. "You ready?"

She nods.

One horse remains. Across the courtyard, tethered to a rail.

The camera does not reveal whether they realize they have no chance.

"We give it all we're worth until we hit the horse," he says.

"Then we duck down and ride like hell," she says.

They flash each other a smile, hoist their guns, and haul their battered bodies into blazing sunshine.

He sits in his favorite beach chair – blue and white striped nylon webbing, wood arms, three height adjustments for the back, seat set low to the ground. He sits in the shade of the Winnebago and waits for her. Periodically he walks away from the refreshment stand, toward the east end of the lot and the railroad tracks where, for some reason, neither of them ever go. She is there now, and when he gets tired of waiting he gets up and walks over to where he can see her, seated at the end of a railroad tie tossing stones into creosote bushes. Each time he walks over, he thinks about going all the way, about joining her, and each time he goes back to his chair. He can't say how long this has gone on, except that he has moved his chair twice to keep it in the shade.

Hands behind his head. He drinks Newman's Own Lemonade from a blue plastic cup. He trusts Paul Newman's face. He tries to extend his patience. No use.

He ducks inside the Winnebago, grabs the buckskin vest she bought for him, silver star pinned to the breast. Grabs her hat, star pinned to the side.

Heat ripples through the air, so that both she and the railroad tracks waver, as though they are a reflection in some vast pond. She scoops a handful of stones, tosses them one by one at the bush, until her hand is empty. Then she scoops again. The scooping hand is the injured hand. The bandage gray and brown.

He stands beside her a full minute before speaking. She has not looked up. Has not varied from her rhythm of tossing stones.

"It's Anthony?"

Now she stops, slowly, as if she were a wind-up toy whose spring had wound down.

"All bets are off, Cole."

"What do you mean?"

"I need to go." She squints up at him, into the sun. His face a silhouette.

He shoves hands into pockets, makes them into fists. "You can't."

The tracks stretch on a straight line to the horizon. In almost eight weeks, they have seen one train, a freight, seemingly empty. They have wondered what kind of schedule this reflects.

"What's going on, Jo?"

She scoops a handful of stones. She hears his question as if from a great distance.

"A few months ago, there was a bombing, at a golf course, in Oregon." She stares out at the horizon as she speaks, at the point where the tracks appear to come together. "Someone blew up a golf cart, and a couple people with it. Some big tournament."

Cole's legs begin to feel heavy, as if they are molds containing freshly poured cement.

"I saw it on the news. I don't know, I suspected." She stops. Shakes her head. "I had this feeling that it was Anthony."

It is as if a train is coming, and he can hear the whistle. Can feel the tracks rumble beneath his feet. But Cole's legs are too heavy to lift, and the train is in motion and Joanna cannot stop it and she lacks the will to move.

Joanna tosses stones at the creosote bush. "I thought I could lose it here. Put it behind me." Her throwing motion is all forearm and wrist. "And it was working." For the first time she looks at Cole.

"There's been another incident. Outside Seattle. People are dead, Cole. I have to find out if it's him."

The nature of a high-speed crash is that it shatters things.

She shields her eyes with her throwing hand. "I'll come back."

Cole is no longer sure of the horizon. He seems to be looking into nothing but sky. "But you have no reason," he hears his voice say. "It could be anyone. The odds." He wants to separate what's going on with Anthony. Her suspicions, and the logic of her thinking. He wants to talk about what they were supposed to be building here, what they have done to it. He wants to throw her words in her face, her fresh starts and no looking backs, her self-righteous push for full disclosure. He wants to describe the exact dimensions of the ache he feels. The number of boxcars. The gross tonnage.

"I have to find him."

Now Joanna looks at him, he at the distance. Unwilling to meet her eyes. Unable to find the horizon. "Where?"

"Seattle."

"It's a big place."

She shrugs. "I have to try."

He locates the railroad tracks in his vision. Wills them not to waver. "How long?"

She stands. Takes her hat. The sun has begun its languid dip toward the horizon. Her words a question. "Three weeks."

She straightens the star on her hat. Puts it on. Reaches to touch his arm, but he is no longer there.

SCREEN FIVE

June paces the living room, wringing her hands. The front door opens. Ward enters, briefcase in hand. Somewhere, a studio audience cheers.

"I'm so glad you're home, Ward."

He sets down the briefcase. Loosens the knot in his tie with one hand. "Honey, what's wrong?"

"It's the boys. I'm afraid..."

The doorbell rings.

June opens the door on a beaming Eddie. Rail-thin, body wound tight.

"What a lovely dress, Mrs. C. Every time I see you, you're looking lovelier and more radiant."

June blushes. "Why thank you, Eddie." There's tension in her face. Even so, all reassurance. "The boys aren't available right now. We're having a domestic crisis."

Offstage, Yvon pumps a fist in the air.

June closes the door in Eddie's unctuous face.

"Don't you think that's a little strong?" says Ward, seated on the edge of the sofa, ready to move into action once armed with information.

"No, Ward. I don't. We can't take this lightly. The boys need to be punished."

"What do you suggest, dear?"

June fusses with her hair. A bit flustered. "I've sent them to their room to think about what they've done. As far as I'm concerned, they're not welcome to join us for dinner."

Yvon throws his hands in the air. Papers fly.

"Cut!"

Cole straddles a wood chair, leans against the back rest. He sips Newman's Own Lemonade from a clear plastic tumbler and stares at a movie screen, oblivious to a grand sunset unfolding around him. Shades of lavender and purple. A box of Milk Duds in hand. Another, empty, at his feet.

Gene rides up on a piebald mare, swaying gently in the saddle. He stops a respectful distance behind Cole, dismounts, and leads the horse the rest of the way on foot. Gene wears a white shirt with red polka dots, crisp beige neckerchief, brown chaps that make his walk slightly bowed. His trademark hat. Traces of the landscape visible behind him, through him – his presence colors the terrain, as if he were another element in the sunset. He ties the horse to the post behind Cole, wraps the reins around the speaker holder.

"Howdy, Cole." He leans a forearm on the pole.

Cole turns, only now aware of his friend's arrival. "Hey." He has two speakers before him, each cord stretched as far as it will go. Voices broadcast in simulated stereo.

Gene reaches into a saddlebag, scoops a handful of oats and offers it to the horse, which nibbles from the holographic hand. He gestures toward the screen. "I miss much?"

Cole nods. "It's toward the end."

"Is this the part where he confronts the gal who sold him out?" Gene smiles in recognition. "The gutless producer who kisses up to her boss?" Behind them, the sky is majestic. "I love this part."

SCREEN TEN

A man stands at a water cooler, an office kitchen. Burgundy t-shirt, khakis, ponytail. White walls, white cupboards. Cardboard boxes filled with supplies. The man drains a paper cup. A woman walks past the entrance, short black hair. He spots her in his peripheral vision, sets out after. The music is subtle, soft piano. She turns into her office. He follows just before the door closes in his face.

"You weasel." He pushes the door closed. Tries to keep his voice steady. "Spineless wretch. Corporate tool."

She sits heavily at her desk. Silk suit. "Let me guess. You saw the press release."

"You traitor. You child. You neophyte."

She swivels in her chair. "Are we done? Can I get back to work?"

"You asshole," he says. "You've butchered the project, Hope. Killed it."

Hope stands at her desk. Holds her hands up, palms facing him, as if to shield her from the conversation, as if to end it. "Get over it, Cole. Do your job."

He paces the area in front of the desk. He can feel his blood heating.

Her eyes go to the window, to the flashing message light on her phone. "Look, Cole. It's a gesture toward discipline. An effort to be realistic about the market."

"Discipline," he sneers.

Hope moves to the edge of the desk. She's twenty-six. She's never produced a project of this scope. "What's wrong, Cole? Afraid of a little accountability?"

"*Fuck* you, Hope." The words explode from his mouth. His fist bangs against the door.

Cole flinches at the behavior. At the giant images onscreen. "Okay," he says to Gene. "That was a mistake."

The horse shakes off a fly. Gene shakes his head. "Sure, but you can see why he'd be angry. All that work. And the way she treats him." He fishes a Milk Dud from the box. Offers one to Cole.

SCREEN TEN

"I don't know how you've worked in the past," Hope says. One hand rests on the desk. "I don't know what you think you're owed. I do know that you can't scream obscenities, leave co-workers threatening voice mail."

He shakes his head from side to side, like a horse straining against a bridle. "It wasn't threatening."

"I run this project."

"You're a messenger, not a producer."

"I think you should leave." Hope takes a step back. "I think you should know how I'm seeing this. You're in an aggressive stance, you're blocking the way out of my office, your language is abusive." Hope takes a deep breath. Adjusts the jacket on her shoulders. "Turn around. Walk away. Don't make this worse."

"Wait," Cole says, arm outstretched toward the screen. "Hold it." He blinks, peels his face off the chair back. He can feel the indentation of the wood slat on his cheek. The movie screen is blank. At his feet, a lemonade carton, a Milk Duds box. A sound behind him. Gene dismounts a piebald mare. White shirt, brown neckerchief, brown chaps that slightly bow his walk. Undulating terrain visible behind him, through him. Cole rubs his eyes. It's as if the landscape has shifted a few degrees and things are not quite where they should be.

Cole points at the screen. "That's not the whole picture." His head foggy. "Yes, I made some mistakes. Lost control."

Gene ties the horse to the post behind Cole. "Slow down, son." Wraps the reins around the speaker holder. "What are you saying?"

"I admit, I said some things I shouldn't have." Cole furrows his brow, concentrating, trying to put the pieces together. "But at least I was communicating."

The land shines orange around them. The last throes of sunset.

"I'm afraid I missed something, Cole."

Cole scratches his head. The fingers of his right hand tingle with sleep. He laughs. "Never mind."

The night's first crickets.

The horse paws at the dirt.

Gene, head cocked, hand on hip, blushes.

"I can't thank you enough for Smiley."

A silence. The palpable absence of his friend. A pattern – people disappear because Cole's not available. "It was Jo's idea."

"I'll thank her, too. When she gets back."

Raised eyebrows. "Right."

Gene's face has a stoic confidence. "She'll be back. You'll see." He removes his hat, sets it on the pommel of his saddle. "What was all that you were saying a minute ago?"

Cole's eyes flick to the screen and back. "It's a long story."

"I've got time."

"Well, then." Cole pulls a second chair close beside him. Offers the carton. "Lemonade?"

"Nah. I'd take a Milk Dud, though."

SCREEN NINE

A woman, thirty, seated at a kitchen table. Wavy brown hair. Weary green eyes. Bandanna-as-headband, yellow with small blue flowers. Eyes narrowed. Mouth small.

"You want to know why I'm going."

A man, t-shirt, jeans, ponytail. "Yeah, Corinne. I'd like to know why you're going."

"You can't imagine. Why I might have had enough."

Sunlight streams through kitchen windows. Homemade curtains. Coffee maker. Spice rack.

The veins in the man's neck throb.

"You're not here," Corinne says. Hands over her head. "You haven't been here."

Hands thrust deep into pockets. The strength of denim. "I can come home earlier. I get caught up in it."

Corinne, fingers splayed over bandanna, hair that doesn't quite reach her shoulders. "How can you not get it."

He is bathed in sunlight. The window over the sink. The door leading out to the small yard.

The things people do to each other over time. The marks they leave.

"I never know when you're going to be here. For how long. You disappear – a week, ten days. You don't even answer your phone. Just traces of you left in the kitchen when I wake up. Artifacts – a coffee cup you might have drunk from."

Sunshine everywhere. Inescapable.

Silence. The hum of the refrigerator.

"All the things you were going to do with Rebecca. What do you think that says to her."

Corinne shakes her head. Eyes receding. "I'm not the one who's leaving," she says. "You left a long time ago."

Interior. Atomic Café. Day.

Cole pushes through the door. Victoria behind the counter. Wiping with a cloth.

"Honey, I'm home."

The place is deserted.

"And not a minute too soon. The children have been driving me batty."

"Batty. That's good." He slides into his booth. "What's the word, Vic?"

"Fighting off the crowds, as usual." She scoops ice into a tall glass. Fills it with cranberry juice.

On the stereo, John Lee Hooker sings the blues.

Outside, early morning low clouds give the day a dingy feel.

Victoria appears beside him. Sets down the glass. "Special delivery Vitamin C."

He looks up at her. "You're the best." Launches the soccer game.

She hasn't moved from his side.

"Boom, boom, boom, boom," sings John Lee Hooker.

"You okay, Juice?"

He scrunches up his face. "Okay as a guy can be after Portugal's trouncing at the hands of the French."

"No. I mean are you really okay?" Her eyes are small.

A sick feeling in his stomach. "Why?"

Her finger traces a line on the tabletop. Her eyes inquisitive. "Someone was here looking for you."

Cole's throat feels dry. He can't bring himself to reach for his glass.

Victoria fishes in the pocket of her jeans. Pulls out a business card. Sets it on the table before him. "He left this. Asked me to call him if I saw you."

His throat a desert. His juice a mile away. A mirage.

"Of course," Victoria says. "I've never seen you. I don't expect to." She leans on the computer monitor. "Tell me you're okay, Juice."

He looks down at the card. Simple black type. White stock.

William Saint Martin. Private Investigator. Scrawled underneath, a local phone number.

Victoria's voice, from far away. "Talk to me, Juice."

4.

Los Angeles has always been a haven. A place where no matter what you'd done, you could lose yourself. Reinvent yourself. This is the essence of Los Angeles. Its strength. The sprawl, the sheer distances, suggest that search is futile. Lost souls could disappear into the canyons of the Palisades. Erase themselves in the warehouses of San Pedro. Evaporate into the Hollywood hills, or merge with the haze that settles over the vast San Fernando Valley.

The promise of Los Angeles has always been based on illusion. The tantalizing intimation that you can have it both ways. Mountains and ocean. Rich city life and wide open space. A desert awash in orange groves. Focus on the exquisite fruit. Not on the stolen water that nurtured it. Or the pilfered land on which it grew.

William St. Martin wiped his brow with a linen handkerchief. His Saab parked on the dusty shoulder of Mulholland Drive. Top down. Lights slowly flickered on across the Valley as the sun burrowed behind the hills. All these intertwined lives. All this space in which to hide, this wind-haunted distance. It was astonishing how easily people could be found.

Interior. Day. St. Martin sips from a paper coffee cup, looks out through the tinted windshield of his Saab, across Alameda Avenue and through the window of the Atomic Café at Cole, who stands talking to the waitress, near the register. Through the layers of glass, St. Martin can make out no more than outlines. Sheer physical presence.

He marvels that Cole has come back here. That he has not only stayed in Los Angeles, but has continued to visit the place to which his sabotage can be traced. To which he would know it could be traced.

St. Martin drinks in small sips through the opening in the plastic lid. A notebook computer on the passenger seat beside him. Cellular phone. He has never liked stakeouts. While Cole has continued to visit the Atomic Café, he has not logged into the Z-Tech system in more than a week. St. Martin is intrigued by this combination of savvy and carelessness.

In the right, northbound lane of Alameda Avenue, a surveyor works, safety vest-clad, huddled over a tripod. St. Martin follows with his eyes to a point across the intersection, another man in another safety vest, holding a long stick.

"I can find him, but it could take time." St. Martin had leaned back in his Aeron chair. French doors open to the courtyard. The chirp of starlings in the jacaranda outside.

Warren had cleared his throat before speaking. "How much time?"

"A few weeks. A month."

Warren and Tolman, a study in contrasts in the visitor's chairs. The one impeccable – thick brown hair slicked straight back, manicured mustache, gym-sculpted body, the picture of restraint. The other balding, a fidgeter, gum-chewing, paper clip in hands, round face, round glasses – a turtle in shirt and tie. They looked uncomfortable out west.

Warren made a face. "Why not faster?"

"The police could move faster. Try for a warrant right away."

"No police." Warren moved his hands as he spoke, each word measured, his body back in the chair as if to create the greatest possible distance between himself and the person he addressed. "Not until we're sure."

St. Martin studied the long fingers he kept folded in his lap. "Bad for business."

Warren's face had flushed. Tolman's mouth sagged.

"We have a significant investment to protect," Tolman said. "Our reputation for security is what we sell on."

The distant beep of a truck backing up.

"You can't have people knowing how easy it is to hack your system." St. Martin smiled.

Warren's hands pressed together. Fingers extended. His voice thin. "We can't allow that perception."

"We'll work as fast as we can, but you'll need to be patient." St. Martin swiveled gently in his chair. "All these guys give in to the desire to show how clever they are. He'll try again, or go bragging to someone."

"What if he doesn't?"

"Then we put together what we have and go to the police. It'll be enough to assure a warrant. To seize his computer."

Tolman uncrossed his legs, crossed them again. "What if he's wiped the files?"

"He's arrogant," Warren said. "He wouldn't."

Tolman: "But what if he does?"

"Then we reconstruct the deleted files," St. Martin offered.

"What if we can't?"

St. Martin had leaned forward. His voice soft, hovering on the air. "If he's that good, you hire him back."

Now, St. Martin mulls the possibilities. That Cole wants to be caught. That he is oblivious enough to think they wouldn't suspect him. That he believes he is in the clear because Z-Tech would never risk the reputation damage in having him stopped publicly. There is something about the diffidence that St. Martin likes. He sips coffee. Watches through the car window.

He will follow Cole. Observe his actions. Set the trap.

SCREEN SIX

Heat shimmers in waves off the valley floor. The figures of the riders flicker in and out of focus, distant, not quite real. The pounding of hooves, insistent, relentless, seems close, and all that matters. They can feel the beat of it in their bodies, through the ground, as they lie pressed to the ridge top, watching. Breath growing short.

They look at the riders. At each other. The two fugitives. Male and female. They are tired. They want to rest. They've already exhausted one horse in the effort to shed pursuit.

"Who *are* those guys?" His voice indignant. Face perplexed.

This isn't the way it was supposed to work. They are supposed to escape. The posse half-hearted, operating out of duty, not conviction. The chase a token effort toward law and order. Sentiment on their side. That's the way it has always worked, in their favor, making them possible. This is different. The train had come up behind the Flyer, as if expecting them, as if someone knew they would be robbing it. The horses and riders exploding out the freight car door, a terrifying determination evident from the start.

But they knew the routine. They knew the land. They knew when to split from the gang, diffuse the posse, ride hard and long until they had worn down the resolve of their pursuers. It was a simple matter of their will to escape being greater than the combined will of those who would stop them.

Hooves pound, the force traveling through the ground, against their chests until he can't distinguish it from the pounding of his own heart. He has begun to see the ghosted images of these riders even when he closes his eyes. The distance between them never enough.

Six riders, flickering in and out of view. A cloud of dust kicked up behind them.

He is tired. Hungry. His body pleads for rest. But the pounding is inside his chest, inside both their chests, and compels them on. The growing sense that it will always be like this.

He looks at her. Her at him. For the first time, he sees fear in her eyes. A hunted look.

"Who *are* those guys?"

Cole, perched on his rock, the one at the crest of the hill that allows him to see both the refreshment stand and the entrance to the drive-in. Dog-eared copy of *Desert Flora and Fauna* in his lap, notepad at his side, he records characteristics of plants he likes, plants he intends to find for a desert garden.

"As Spring ends," he records, "the green leaves of brittlebush undergo a pronounced change in preparation for the heat and drought of summer."

He sips coffee out of a plastic mug. Hazy sunshine. The last wisps of low clouds. The heat – even in the morning – has begun to annoy him. The unrelenting light. Cole has emerged, intestines somehow intact, after a reign of terror on the toilet. A forty-eight hour flood. His supply of tissue dwindling until he could count the squares. Now he has flushed his fear and emerged with a new resolve, a cleaner colon. He survived the scare. He will call the bluff.

Lately, though, the work seems daunting. As if the key will never emerge, like an elaborate algebraic equation whose terms will never resolve, variables so enmeshed and interwoven they become a labyrinth of dead ends, of pathways so narrow and tortuous they defy navigation. For days, he has alternated between speed and security. Trading one to gain the other. Unable to break the impasse. The work tedious. Futile. Increase the complexity of the key by one digit. Comb the code, hours to implement a change which he knows by now will fail – will increase processing time. Then test to confirm his suspicion. The two elements – time and technology – locked in static relation. Each unwilling to yield. Find a way to alter the pattern. Change the dynamic. He knows it is possible. He just can't get there.

Most days he misses Victoria and the Atomic Café, the distractions of VR Soccer, the magic of unexplored possibility.

"A mat of thin, silver hairs grows over each leaf, gradually thickening until the leaf's surface is covered. The light gray hairs provide insulation, shade, a reflective surface, and a barrier to drying wind."

A white pickup truck slows to a stop along Winnetka Avenue. Cole watches a figure emerge, orange safety vest over a polo shirt. Creased pants.

"In this highly protected condition," Cole writes, "the plant's metabolism slows and it simply waits out the summer."

The figure removes a tripod from the bed of the truck, extends the legs, sets it in front of the vehicle, on the side of the road. A surveyor's glass.

On a list of plants he wants to find, Cole has ocotillo and yucca, woolly marigold and desert chicory, brittlebush and white burr sage. He will have a garden to surprise Joanna if – when – she returns. Thirteen days, give or take. He keeps watch on the figure in the periphery of his vision. Adjusting the sight line. Hands on hips gazing across at the drive-in. Cole has the creeping sense that the instrument is focused on him. He lets himself look up, to investigate trajectory, and it seems he stares right into the glass.

He fixes his gaze on the notebook. Feels eyes upon him. *Don't surveyors work in teams?* Someone holding a stick at the other end. A distant something against which to measure. Two possibilities enter Cole's mind. The less terrifying is that the land will be sold. They have never bothered to investigate ownership. As if they could simply claim squatter's rights. As if by ignoring the possible encroachment of their world, they could prevent it from happening.

Cole forces himself to read about streaked mariposa lilies, but it's only a series of phrases that pass before his eyes – "the bare-stemmed flower," "tufts of ascending white hairs," "an island of fertility." He is aware primarily of the instrument fixed on him, on his rock.

"Fuck." He sets down the notebook. Stares into the glass. The figure behind it immobile, bent to its task, part of the landscape.

A sip of coffee. The need to know. Cole sets off down the hill in the direction of the pickup, the tripod, the stooped figure behind it.

Cole's steps deliberate. Maybe two hundred yards separate them. At first, he's not even sure he's going to walk all the way over. It's a test, to see if the glass follows him. It doesn't.

Even when Cole reaches the road, the figure doesn't move. Cole thinks about back trouble. Pinched nerves. Slipped disks. His sandals slap the pavement. No acknowledgment of his approach. Across Winnetka Avenue. Past the pickup. Close enough to smell the man's cologne. Cole stands, hands on hips. It's as if he isn't there.

"Hey."

The man moves his eye away from the glass to look at Cole. Then back. "Hi." Linen pants. Manicured fingers.

Cole itches with annoyance. "Don't surveyors usually work in teams?"

The man stands straight. Looks at Cole. Wavy brown hair, thin-framed glasses, the inquisitive face of a child. "I guess they do."

Cole shifts his feet. A car zips past. "So where's your partner?"

"Don't have one."

The call of a bird in the distance. A tightness in Cole's chest. "Well how can you survey –"

"I'm not a surveyor." An economy of movement. This man doesn't seem to breathe. His eyes on Cole.

Cole's body tingles. Adrenaline surging. "Well what are you, then?"

A limousine glides past. Both their eyes follow it until it slips from view. "An observer."

The impulse to turn and ride fast and hard until the sounds of pursuit fade. "And what are you observing?"

"You."

The impulse to string barbed wire, to delineate an area of sanctuary, inviolate, lines which cannot be crossed. A twelve-foot stockade fence to keep out prying eyes ears bodies.

Cole woozy. He struggles to maintain the demeanor of a neighbor out for a chat about the condition of the lawn. Inside, racing screaming scurrying.

"And what do you hope to observe about me?"

A small shrug of shoulder. A raised eyebrow. "Behavior patterns. Habitat." Eyes not moving from Cole. "I'm a student of rare species."

Sun bores down on them. Cole scratches his head. The impulse to destroy, to release the petulance, to take the instrument, the tripod, and in a fury of arms legs motion strike out, raze it. The importance of an undisturbed surface. A rumbling in his bowels.

"I'm flattered," he says. He concentrates on controlling his body. *Stand still. Keep fear off your face. Prevent arms legs from striking out.* He wishes Joanna were here. "I don't suppose you'd go away if I asked you to."

St. Martin pushes out his lower lip a bit. A hint of a smile. Shakes his head. "Can't do that."

"Hmm," Cole says. Chews the inside of his cheek. An image in his mind – himself in handcuffs, a hand on his arm, guiding him along a dim hallway, hiding his face from a whir and flash of cameras. *Stop. Breathe. Plant the confident smile.* The one that says *I expected this. This is not a problem.* "You here to take me in?"

St. Martin smiles. "Only if I find a reason."

Cole considers pursuing this, but decides against it. A game has begun, the rules, even the objective of which he does not know. He turns slowly away, crosses Winnetka Avenue. A last look over his shoulder. St. Martin's eye rests against the glass.

"It's a problem, all right," says Gene. "No doubt about it." Red-and-white checked shirt, brown vest, fur-covered chaps. He leans against a speaker pole, hat in hand. The night's first stars emerge.

Cole paces back and forth in a dusty driving lane. His t-shirt bears the single word, *why?* A knotted muscle aches at the back of his neck. "I mean, if they had anything on me, they'd have sent the police." A hope that he is trying to make a conviction. "What does he hope to gain by watching me through that stupid glass?"

Santa Ana winds sweep warm air across the drive-in. Gene shimmers. His image vibrant.

"Unless he's come to steal my PC, or copy my files. But then why would he plant himself there, in plain sight?"

Gene shakes his head, sympathetic. With his square face and soft-seeming skin, he looks like the proverbial bachelor uncle, come to shower treats on nieces and nephews.

"The fact that he found me means he's traced my visits into the network. That's okay. I can deal with that." Cole's pacing a short, straight line. "But he can't trace it any further than the café. Even if he gets people to place me there. It's coincidence. And Z-Tech would never prosecute." The muscle in his neck throbs. "They'd lose all credibility. They'd have to acknowledge they launched with a second-rate system."

"What if it wasn't them that hired this guy?" Gene's voice has the scratchy quality of an old vinyl recording.

"Who else?" Cole tugs at his Suffolk University gym shorts.

Across two driving lanes, the Winnebago sits in a circle of soft light. Without the lamps Cole leaves on, without his holographic friend, the night would be pitch dark. "Maybe the more important question," Cole says, "is how do I get rid of him?"

Gene scratches the top of his head. "There are time-honored ways, son, but be sure you're ready to wear the black hat and a haunted look."

Cole shakes his head as if trying to dislodge something. "I want to know what he's up to. Isn't a lawman supposed to show his hand? Take care of business and go away." Fear snaking around his throat.

"Depends on the nature of the job, I reckon. Sometimes the best thing to do is get the outlaw to betray himself," says Gene. "To wait him out, make him crack." Gene fingers the brim of his hat. "But times have changed. I couldn't say how things work nowadays."

He pushes himself away from the speaker pole. "Does sound like he's waiting for you to make a move."

"He's waiting for me to try to sell the system. That's the best legal ground he's got."

"Son, I don't claim to understand computers, but I know a thing or two about showdowns, and it sounds to me like you have some decisions to make. Just how badly do you want to see this through."

Cole rubs the knot in his neck. Works his face out of a scowl. "I need to finish it."

A halo of clouds nuzzles the moon. Gene shifts his feet in the dust. "One word of advice." He hesitates. A breeze stirs the air.

"The reason the good guys usually win has less to do with the law being right than it does with the bad guys believing they're smarter'n everybody."

Cole kicks half-heartedly at the dirt, connects with a speaker pole. His big toe throbs, just out of sync with the muscle in his neck. Somewhere inside, he laughs at himself. Somewhere else inside, abject terror.

Gene stares down at his hat. Turns it slowly in his hands.

A disco beat begins to pulse through the speakers. The screen behind Cole flickers to life.

"Shit," Cole says. "Aerobics."

"Not me," Gene says. Puts his hat on. "You wouldn't have any of that lemonade, would you? I'm a bit parched."

"In the fridge. Help yourself."

Gene waves a hand in salute. "We'll catch up after."

SCREEN SIX

A health club. Exposed brick walls. Full-length mirrors. Treadmills, stair-masters, Nautilus equipment in a horseshoe around the room's perimeter. Rows of smiling men in plain white t-shirts and gray shorts, jogging in place. At the front of it all, facing not the class but the camera, the Harley guy, the Indian, the Hard Hat, the Cowboy, the Soldier. Brimming with energy. Pulsing beat accompanies their movements as they sing.

Body
Wanna feel my body body
Such a thrill my body

The Motorcycle Cop, in riot squad helmet, sunglasses and NYPD t-shirt, waves a nightstick in his right hand.

"Step lively," he says. "Let's get that blood flowing."

A score of men move in perfect synchronicity to the beat.
CUT TO

An overhead shot, all participants stretch their arms on the off-beat – sides, front, bend, stretch. Esther Williams would be proud.

The whole crew sings on the chorus.
Macho Macho man
I want to be a macho man
A roomful of men, their bodies as polished as the exercise equipment that waits in the background.
"Come on, stay with us," implores the Motorcycle Cop. "We're just warming up."

SCREEN TWO
A lone rider on a chestnut mare. A vast plain. Outcroppings of granite. Creosote. The rider in profile, at a distance. A single guitar plucks a chord.
Cut to a medium shot. The sheriff in black jeans. Black shirt. Black hat. A darkness under her eyes. A cheroot dangling from her lips. She has turned away her deputies. Sent them off, in other directions, on other routes. A vague promise to meet up with them in a few days. A vague suggestion that this way they can cover more ground. The truth is simpler and more harsh: She does not want to find him, and can't stop trying. It is a penance she plays out, a way of placating her sense of duty. She will do her job, and hope that the Kid has vanished, that he has had the sense to cross the border and be done with it. She would happily call this hot ride futile, would spend weeks uselessly combing the desert for a boy she knew was gone.
This way, the weight of it threatens to crush her.
She reaches back into a weathered saddlebag, for a canteen. Pours into her hand. Leans forward to let the horse drink. She ignores her own needs. She hopes to make herself dry and hard. So she won't feel, can't act.
The last time she'd seen him, they'd leaned against the wall, a wooden café table, a drink. He was jocular. They had roles in a scripted scene. They could call it off anytime.
She fingered her glass. Stared down into it. The watery brown of cheap whiskey. Could not bring herself to look at him, who

would not take this seriously. Who struggled to stay in character. He had become the outlaw. He wanted to remain the Kid. Free. Unaccountable. At play.

"They want you to leave the country," she said.

He smiled at her, and the smile was gutshot. "Are they askin' me, or are they tellin' me?" He would not acknowledge the fences that were every day more firmly in place.

The bartender watched a fly buzz the room. Caught it in his hand.

She pushed the hat back off her forehead. "*I'm* askin' you."

He leaned back. His pasted-on smile. His not-yet-dead body. She stood.

"Come on, sit down," he said. "We've still got time."

He would will himself to believe that there was room to run, that he was only being free.

She couldn't bear to watch. She turned and walked away.

Rain. Great sheets. Falling thick. Insistent. Joanna sits on a blonde-wood stool in the window of the Frontier Restaurant in Belltown, sipping coffee and wondering what she's doing here.

It has the quality of a guessing game. Would Anthony come here? If he came, would he stay? Is this the kind of place he would work? Hide and seek. But Joanna is not in the mood for games. The area is too vast, the time too short, her patience too thin.

Her fingers surround the coffee mug, seeking warmth. Half-eaten blueberry scone on a plate before her. A snapshot of Anthony, body moving away, head turned toward the camera, face bathed in sunlight. Even then, he was already leaving. Seeking shadows. She spins the photo on the counter so that Anthony rotates. Which direction will he point. She has shown the picture around town – *have you seen him? do you know where he might be?* A desperate notion. Who would have seen him, who would tell if they had?

A pair of elderly men – sixties, seventies – wearing cardigan sweaters and fedoras play checkers at a small table. Drink latté. Joanna likes to imagine that they carry the board with them for occasions such as this, seek shelter when the rain picks up. Raindrops bounce off First Avenue. Four days in Seattle, and she has found no trace of Anthony. Found a nice restaurant outside Pioneer Square. Bought an umbrella. Lost heart. She tries to tell herself that it's good news. That it means something, her failure to find him. That he is far from here. Working a shrimp boat in Biloxi. Washing dishes at a diner in Duluth.

It is as if there are two Joannas: the rational Jo who is here to prove to herself her son's innocence, to exonerate him of a crime only she suspects him of, by reassuring herself that he is not here; and the emotional Jo, who knows that her strength and encouragement should grow with each place that he is not, but who feels instead, in addition, the simple physical desire for mother and son to embrace.

A steady drip of rainwater from the blue awning outside.

Joanna leaves a five-dollar bill for her coffee and scone. Puts the photo into its Ziploc bag and into the inside pocket of her anorak. Drains the last of her coffee. She's had a chill since she stepped off the plane. She bundles up. Velcro flap across her throat. Resolve around her heart.

The rain has faded to a barely perceptible mist. A couple days of it, you don't even notice. Neon flickers on First Avenue. Reflects off the pavement. Queen City Grill Steaks Chops. A string of bars – the Virginia Inn, the Twenty-One Club. She tries to imagine Anthony here. To will him into being. Reminds herself it is absence she seeks to prove. Is there a number of days places whose accumulated evidence constitute proof?

A string of retail shops. The Gap. Kyoto Sushi. Keep moving. Cover ground. First Avenue Army-Navy. She stops only because it surprises her. The addresses were moving upscale. She's been thinking she'd like a pair of gloves. Pushes through the glass door. High ceilings. Camouflage clothing. Cardboard boxes filled with tiny products. A few random shoppers. Narrow aisles. Behind the counter, a man with a rust-colored toupee, a face weathered and deeply lined, like the underbelly of a whale.

Joanna locates a cardboard box filled with blue and gray gloves – $1.99 a pair. The thought of buying them depresses her. Neil Young sings from hidden speakers.

A glass case filled with hatchets, small axes. On a whim, Joanna approaches the counter. The toupee man leans on the faded wood.

She catches a glimpse of herself in a mirrored pillar. Haggard. "I ask you something?"

"No charge," the man says. Yellow corduroy shirt.

Water beads on Joanna's anorak. She removes the photo from its Ziploc bag. Lays it down carefully. "Any chance you've seen him?"

"Hang on a minute." The man looks at Joanna, then at the photo, then back at Joanna. Pulls a pair of black-framed half-glasses from a shirt pocket. "Can't see for shit," he says. Glasses in place, he holds the photo by the corners. He looks up, over the glasses, at Joanna, then back down. He nods.

Joanna fingers a jackknife in a cardboard box full of them. $1.39 in blue magic marker.

"I've seen this kid."

She looks up. Their eyes meet over the tops of his glasses.

"You sure?" She extends a finger toward the glasses. "You *sure?*"

"I'm not blind," he says. "I remember this kid."

"You *sure?*" A chill. A growing hope that makes her feel ashamed. Selfish. She checks herself. The likelihood of a mistake.

He taps at the photo. "Nice kid. Bought a watch cap and a hunting knife."

A picture of Anthony wandering the aisles, perusing weaponry. She hates to think of her son here. Gleaming steel. The undercurrent of disaffected rage. No. She has only her own lack of information, and Anthony's absence.

"You sure?" This time quiet, almost under her breath. Her heart racing. "I mean, a lot of people come through here."

"Nah. I remember this kid. Took a long time deciding about the knife. We talked."

She tries to place Anthony here, at the counter, weighing purchase decisions. Adrift in a new city. Amused by the man with the bad hair piece. A gray afternoon. A chill twilight. The warmth of the store. A moment of human connection.

"What about?"

"About the Huskies. About football. It was the weekend of the UCLA game."

A sinking. Joanna fights it. Maybe Anthony has begun to follow football. Maybe he made a passing comment – *guess they've gotta beat somebody* – to be polite. To stay engaged.

She nods her head. "I see."

A young woman – thin gray sweater, black t-shirt, thick metal ring in her nose that reminds Joanna of yoked oxen – moves to the register to ring up a sale.

"When was the UCLA game?" Joanna asks. "You remember?"

Joanna thinks she sees a smirk flash across the woman's face. She is an amusement to those she encounters.

The man folds his arms across his chest. "Three – no – four weeks ago. Said he was new in town. Looking for work. Did I know of anything?"

A rush of adrenaline. A flash of shame. "Did you know of anything?"

"Nah."

Urgency to form a question, as if an apparition has formed and only her words, their conversation, can give it substance.

"What'd you say he bought?"

"Watch cap. Hunting knife."

"Can you show me?"

"What do you mean?"

"Can you show me which ones he bought?"

He raises an eyebrow. "Course I can show you."

He leads her to a display case. Points down. "That one. Right there. Red handle. He was sure about that."

"I want one," she says. Riding the adrenaline wave. Improvising.

He shakes his head. Opens the case with a small key.

"What?" she says.

"Nothing." His hair piece seems made of something combustible. *Do not wear near open flame.* "You want the hat, too?"

She nods.

They walk to a folding table, a row of gray cardboard boxes, blue, black, burgundy knit caps. He hands her a black one. "This one okay?"

"You tell me," she says.

He leads her to the register. Enters the purchases. Her ears ring. Her brain buzzes. Three weeks. Maybe four.

"You're sure it was him?"

"You're his mother."

She hands him two twenties. "How'd you know?"

He looks over the glasses at her. A perfect expression of disdain. It occurs to her that this is the real reason he wears the glasses. He places the purchases in a white plastic bag. Hands it to her.

"Yeah. He mentioned the hunting with his father." The buzzing turns to a spinning in Joanna's head. He places her change on the counter. "How much he looks forward to it every year."

Reeling. Falling. Her knees rubbery. Is this what lost hope feels like?

"It's tough on the kids," the man says.

She looks down at the bag. Up at him.

He sees something on her face. Offers an explanation. "Divorce," he says. He folds the glasses back into his pocket. "Anyway. I wish you luck."

Cole stands amid plants and stones and bags of soil. Encircled. Things change quickly in this new life. He has marked out territory, a circle of stones within whose borders he will plant a garden. Three yucca. A half dozen desert chicory. Two ocotillo. The first fruits. "The marigold you may have a hard time finding for sale," the man at the nursery had told him. "You may just have to go out and grab you some." He did give Cole the name of another nursery, near San Diego, that specializes in desert plants.

Morning sun climbs deep into the sky. Cole practices deep breaths. *Look up. Look around. Let the sun warm your face.* Cole finds himself wishing for rock formations, a vast prairie that he could extend indefinitely, hidden outcroppings, quiet arroyos, dense stands of live oak and brittlebush.

He had a bad night. In front of the computer. Out among the stars. Unable to sleep. He imagined Joanna searching Seattle. Wandering wet streets, determined, directionless. Hyperkinetic. This whole story about Anthony something she constructed to get herself out of Winnetka. Away from him. An early morning, scanning the news on C-net. Cole's life ruled by numbers. Number of days since Joanna left: eleven. Number of days until she's due back: ten. Number of days Cole estimates until Z-Tech is due to deliver: 21. Number of ways he can drive himself crazy. So he has purchased plants. He will cultivate a garden. Make it part of his day. Like yoga, a way to nurture the new Cole. Balance. Conditioning.

To get his hands in the earth, to plant something and watch it take hold. To create something whose results he can see, to realize the fruits of his labor. Beauty. Revitalization.

The way even a moment with Joanna would change the shape of the day. He could swear the sunset is less colorful without her. The stars less vibrant.

One section of the circle. The first area to plant. Cole has marked it out with smaller stones. He will have a walkway, a bed of cedar chips that runs throughout, but first he wants simply to get something into the ground. His shovel has a green plastic handle, a green metal blade. He likes the obvious symbolism. He savors the impact of shovel against earth, makes a bucket-sized hole. Gently removes the first yucca from its pot. Cradles it in his hands. Eases it into the soil. He is cultivating a new aesthetic. Tapping into an old code.

A sound on the road behind him, distant. Different from the passing of a car. He stands to see the white pickup truck park. The muscle in the back of his neck begins to throb.

The door closes. The figure in the orange vest pulls tripod and stool from the truck bed. Cole's impulse is to close a curtain, draw a shade.

The glass trained on him. The figure seated, a folding stool. Orange vest, yellow stripes. Paradise lost. Cole pulls at the neck of his shirt for air. Bends to his yucca. Pats down the soil. He will not leave this place. There is nowhere to go. And how would Joanna find him? He works with his back to the road. To the glass. Hears the whoosh of a passing truck. But the awareness of eyes on him, the presence of the observer, drains oxygen from the atmosphere. He needs time needs Joanna. To weigh options. Construct fences. Consider possibilities.

Cole stands, hands on hips. Everything he had prepared for about such an encounter flummoxed. They would try to arrest him, or they would leave him alone. They would block his access to the system, and he would thwart them. Cole could imagine marshaling his energy for a showdown, a single climactic moment. He had not envisioned a protracted struggle, does not foresee having the strength. The unflinching nerves. What is the game? What are the rules?

"Fuck." Cole kicks at the dirt, makes his way down the hill.

Sun a white dot in the sky. Once again, Cole reaches the man's side with no acknowledgment of his presence.

"Hey!"

Again, the laconic movement away from the glass. He waits for Cole to speak.

"Enjoying the show?"

The man shrugs. "It's a job."

"Who *are* you?"

"I told you. An interested observer."

"No. Who *are* you?"

The man fishes into the pocket of a beige silk short-sleeve shirt, hands Cole a business card. His movements as deliberate as a chess player.

Cole has seen the card before. He barely glances at it. "No," he says. "I mean, who *are* you?"

St. Martin smiles. The orange safety vest creates vertical lines of sweat along his chest and back.

Cole nods. His stomach gurgles. *Drive fence posts into the ground. String barbed wire.* "Missed you yesterday."

St. Martin's smile is warm and confident. Disarming. "Thanks. I miss anything?"

Cole laughs. He juts his chin, trying to create a profile as tough as the land. "Nope."

The faux surveyor shrugs. St. Martin not playing fair. Not revealing his hand. "Here's what I figure," he says. "The encryption that launched on schedule for KBC was not your system."

Gurgle. *Must not run. Must not show fear.*

St. Martin waves a hand dismissively. "That part's simple. Here's where it gets interesting. The timing of your exit doesn't make sense. You gave up too easily. I don't see you leaving this project, even if you're disgusted with working for a guy who doesn't get it.

"So I'm thinking you knew Warren was freezing you out. I'm thinking maybe you had been protecting your backside for a while before your little incident – a few weeks, maybe even a couple months. Keeping a copy of your work."

St. Martin pauses for breath. Cole's palms moist. The pure physical urge to turn and run.

"I'm also thinking, and I know this is pretty far-fetched, that after you left you decided to have a little fun at Z-Tech's expense. Maybe hack into the launch system and mess with some transactions. Maybe you were visiting a place called the Atomic Café – which, for a month, had a number of dial-ins to the Z-Tech network server – doing a number on your former employer. Scheming to make sure their reputation was tarnished. To make sure their clients knew about the flaws."

Gurgle.

Cole's face feels hot. He concentrates on looking bemused. He envisions himself, Joanna, perched behind boulders, rifles in hand, warding off intruders. "You couldn't prove any of that," he says.

St. Martin's voice has an edge. "Want to talk about what I could prove?"

"Not especially." *Breathe. Remind yourself the law is unclear on issues of intellectual property. That Z-Tech would never – never – expose its vulnerability.*

St. Martin sits on his stool. Watching. Sun beats down on the day. There's no escape. "Is this key everything I hear it is?"

A flush of pride. "Not yet."

"But it could be."

Cole nods. "If I were working on it."

"Yes. If you were working on it."

Cole rubs the back of his neck. "You like wearing that getup every day?"

St. Martin fingers the orange vest. "Not especially."

"I don't suppose there's any alternative."

The detective shakes his head. "Can't think of one."

Cole nods slowly, his mouth in a frown. *A stone fence. The great wall of Winnetka, a vast edifice, running high and long. Unassailable.*

St. Martin smiles. "You'll get used to me."

SCREEN SIX

The bride, her dress and hat all lace and bows, stands at the window, looking down at the street. The sun-baked dirt, hitching posts on either side, the row of buildings eerily quiet. Somewhere down there, her new husband awaits the noon train, and the killer.

She has told him she'll be on that train, with or without him, headed for the new life they are supposed to begin together. She stands beside the window, stares down through the gap between lace curtain and window frame.

"I don't care who's right or who's wrong," she says. "There's got to be a better way for people to live."

The camera cuts to the empty street. The train tracks. The bride at the window.

A clock ticks in the background. It's three minutes to twelve.

*

Cole has lost the ability to sleep. It is becoming foreign to him. An experience he can only vaguely remember. He is amazed at how quickly this can happen – three, four nights and it feels as if you've never slept, as if the very idea of sleep is something you've heard about but can't imagine, a ritual of some exotic culture. He lies awake in his bunk. On his back. Wills himself to lose consciousness. Stares at the ceiling. Sometimes on the ceiling is an image of St. Martin, hunched over the tripod, eye fixed to the glass. That's when Cole heats milk on the stove. Then doubles back to bed. Other times it is emptiness. The yawning expanse of night. When this threatens to overwhelm him, he makes lists in his head. Favorite television shows from childhood. *Gunsmoke. The Three Stooges. Dick Van Dyke. The Rifleman.* Then favorite episodes. It goes on like this. Then the stretch just before sunrise, when the full realization dawns that in fact he will not sleep. If he cannot sleep, he cannot work. If he cannot work, he cannot finish. If he cannot finish, he will occupy this purgatory forever. Then Cole begins to sweat, because the only thing more terrifying than continuing the work is not continuing the work. Then the sun creeps above the horizon, fingers of light reach through the window and soon it will be time to face the code and search for an opening.

Sunlight through the window of the refreshment stand. The clack of fingers on a keyboard. Cole's legs asleep under his laptop. Back damp with sweat. Vision wavering. Ears ringing. He is oblivious to the dingy brown heat of the day. He is on to something.

```
if ((options.key_regeneration_time = convtime(optarg)) ==
-1) {
```

He has stumbled upon a way to expand the digital signature without increasing processing time. After days – how many? – of effort stymied; days – how many? – of no sleep; days – fourteen, scratched on the wall one by one in magic marker – of Joanna gone, the impasse has yielded. Time and technology somehow synchronized again. The digital key expanded – 238 characters – processing time actually reduced by half a second.

Or so he thinks. He cannot explain how it happened. Pressing keys changing parameters mechanically. In his perpetual semi-consciousness that is far from alertness, even farther from the satisfactions of sleep, he does not know what he has changed to break the gridlock, then he cannot understand why it works. Cannot get his brain around it. Has he merely introduced a change with superficial value which will unravel some meaningful function later in the chain. Is this a delusion of his altered state. *Walk through it. Work through the bugs.* Trace every line of this complex code. Weave in the new numbers, the new window parameters. Search for the logic of why it works. Test it.

If he can discover the logic, if the logic is right, if the tests confirm it, if he can eliminate the inevitable bugs, then he will be close. Then, how good is good enough. All this effort, it has to be a quantum leap from what has gone before. And yet, he could hold it back forever, shaving milliseconds from processing time. The pressure of commerce creates a balance. The will to win.

```
verbose("Generating %s%d bit RSA key.",
        sensitive_data.server_key ? "new " : "",
        options.server_key_bits);
```

How close is Z-Tech? How lucid is Cole, and how much can he trust his work? Cole takes some satisfaction in thinking of St. Martin outside, a slave to the tripod, on these September days, the worst air quality of the year. He thinks of Victoria telling him about children in southern California with days off from school due to smog alert, the reports on the radio of *limit outside activities today,* his own eyes burning, even indoors. But St. Martin will not always be a slave to the tripod.

Cole rubs his lids. Types code.

```
if (sensitive_data.server_key != NULL)
        key_free(sensitive_data.server_key);
```

He looks up from the screen. Remembers to breathe. To blink moisture back into his eyes. The walls seem fluid. Viscous.

Within each day, there are moments of lucidity where he feels as if he has slept, as if nothing is wrong. But they ebb and flow, and like the tide are full for only a short time before receding. In the absence of sleep, waking life takes on the quality of a dream.

And he needs wants long blocks of concentration in order to be
sure of what he has.

```
case 'o':
    if (process_server_config_line(&options, optarg,
    "command-line", 0) != 0)
        exit(1);
```

For more than twenty years, Joanna has been part of his life.
Long stretches of regular communication, their Tuesday talks,
then poof. No Jo. For weeks. Sometimes months. *The number
you have called is not in service at this time.* And Cole would shake
his head and speculate on where and when his friend would
surface. When this happens, he leaves messages with her father, in
New Jersey. *Just tell her I'd like to hear from her. To know that
everything is okay.* And always, eventually, she calls. *We got a
chance to spend a summer in Costa Rica. I baked bread in a
restaurant.* Or, *I stayed at Amy's cabin in Tahoe for a while.*
Joanna would laugh at him – *a couple of lapses in twenty years,*
she'd say, *otherwise you could count on me. How many people can
say that about a friend?* Maybe she's right. All Cole knows is that
he misses her. Fears a disappearing act.

Sunlight dimmed. The square of window shows brown light.
Vaguely brown air.

```
/* Saved arguments to main(). */
char **saved_argv;
```

How he will make it known if – when – he wins the race he
will deal with later. He only knows that he is unwilling – unable
– to set the work aside. There is nothing else. If Joanna were here,
she'd push him to stop. But Joanna is not here, and St. Martin is,
and certainty is near, so Cole gardens in the early morning, digs
in the dirt while the sun rises, meditates on the desert, on the
light, on the impossibility of leaving the world behind, and then
he burrows into his den and massages code.

```
/* Parse command-line arguments. */
    while ((opt = getopt(ac, av,
"f:p:b:k:h:g:V:u:o:dDeiqtQ46")) != -1) {
        case '4':
            IPv4or6 = AF_INET;
```

```
        break;
    case '6':
        IPv4or6 = AF_INET6;
        break;
```

Somehow, darkness. Cole has let his mind wander while the test has run, has let himself think about Rebecca. Maybe he has slept. Dreamed. Imagined his once-daughter dancing in a Christmas pageant at school, an angel, aged nine or ten, white dress halo and wings, him in the audience. They would go for ice cream afterward. The most natural thing in the world.

Enough. He shuts down the computer, stands and stretches. Pins and needles. Stars through the square of window. Find Gene. Invite him for lemonade.

Santa Ana winds blow warm across Winnetka, keep the air stuffy, stale. Corrugated fence rattles like a tin can on pavement and the giant screens yawn at Cole. Tonight they are holes in the universe, fissures in the time-space continuum from which the past leaks into the air around him. Playing kick-the-can on lazy summer nights with a horde of neighborhood kids, until parents would call them home, one then another until, within seconds, the game had scattered. Skipping European history his senior year in high school, a whole group of friends, a couple mornings a week, head for the donut shop, because they knew they could, because Mr. Ambrosino would fume but not punish. And then, somehow, forty-two years old, careening across the country in a Winnebago. When did choices begin to have such weight? When did actions solidify into a cast from which he could not see to depart? A voice leaks through the broken speakers. Stephen, a long-ago colleague at Z-Tech, who left to spend more time with his family, his girls. *I just don't see myself looking back in twenty years saying I wish I'd worked more.*

No sign of Gene. Just a sliver of moon and the too-dim stars and the stifling air. He wanders back past the refreshment stand, over the little hill, toward the boundaries of Winnetka, on the path down which he has seen Gene disappear but has never gone himself. What will happen? The pull of unanswerable questions almost irresistible. He walks the dark path. Trips over a rock. Twists his ankle in a chuck hole. Pain stops him. A breath. The

Santa Anas make him restless. Tingly. Scrub brush becomes more dense. The path disappears. Now favoring his right foot. He winds up at a cyclone fence topped with rusting barbed wire, a sign posted at eye level. *No Trespassing. Violators Will Be Prosecuted.*

Behind the fence, a building. Squat concrete rectangle, putty-colored, weeds flourishing in the dust – a faded sign, yellow and black, stuck to the side – *For Lease – McCutcheon and Associates.* Long rows of small square window panes, thick glass broken and cracked. He thinks of Rhonda Sparr, a would-be high school girlfriend he'd tried to impress by taking to an abandoned factory where you could wander in the darkness, bumping into worn-out machines. He thought she'd find it creepy-scary, something secret and cool.

This building may have been a warehouse, storing tires or fluorescent lighting. It may have been a factory, a tool and die shop. He imagines that this is where Gene originates. That there is a lab in the basement where a team of scientists experiment with free-standing holographs, where they have worked their way from mice to sheep to humans, where they wrestle with the bio-ethical implications of what they're doing. That they have released Gene into the world, a walking beta test. That in their basement laboratory, these devoted scientists monitor his progress, change his outfits, develop prototypes of other holographs – John Wayne, Marlene Dietrich. He imagines the scientists eating tuna salad sandwiches on thick white bread, green grapes, fluorescent bulbs buzzing overhead while they puzzle out ways to add dimension to the figures, the illusion of depth. Natural light does not penetrate there – a spiral staircase, black lacquered metal, connects them to life on the surface, the team remaining underground for days at a time.

Wind blows hot around him. Gene nowhere to be found.

Time for a drive.

The roads clear. His mind crowded. He rolls down the windows and presses the accelerator with a sense of urgency, as if he could leave it all behind.

Burbank.

"Juice. What's up?" Victoria silhouetted in the doorway in an oversized gray UCLA t-shirt. Her greeting carries little surprise, little indication that she finds the hour of his visit – twelve, one – strange.

He stands in shadow. In darkness. Crescent moon so distant it's nearly lost in the sky above them. "You said come by anytime."

She opens the door and he slips past her into the room. He had planned to sound casual – *I couldn't sleep, was in the neighborhood* – but her location makes that unlikely. His arrival could only be intentional. A small studio – converted garage – on a quiet street in Burbank. To reach it, you have to come back through the driveway, across a stone patio, past a barbecue console and a lemon tree whose overabundant fruit litters the ground.

He sits in the one chair, low-slung frame, green cushions. Victoria on a corner of the mattress that dominates the floor. Tired eyes. A small gooseneck lamp beside the bed lights the room. "I was reading," she says. "Learning about Hepatitis C." She rubs away fatigue. "We're all going to get eaten alive by viruses," she says. "They'll make us extinct. It's like a '50s horror movie."

He can think of nothing to say. Maybe it's the wind stirring up things everyone would rather not think about. "I was in the neighborhood," he grins. "Thought I'd drop in."

"How nice. Would you like a cup of tea?"

Wind chimes sing from somewhere. Branches scrape the side of the house.

He shakes his head. "No. Thanks."

"What's up?"

"Can't sleep. A little spooked."

"Yeah." Victoria sits, legs crossed, t-shirt stretched over her knees. "Everyone's got ghosts. I lay awake reading about germs."

He wonders what he is doing here. What he wants.

"I feel like I'm under house arrest."

"How do you mean?" The t-shirt slips off her knees. She pushes it down between her legs, rests her hands there.

188

He slouches deeper into the chair. This business of being vulnerable – being human – unsettling. "That detective." He frames a small rectangle with his hands. "The business card, remember?"

Victoria's eyes narrow. "I remember."

"He's watching me. He's there everyday."

She pulls her knees up. Hugs them to her chest. "How much trouble are you in?"

"It's like his full-time job. Waves to me in the morning when he gets there. Takes a lunch break. Packs up and heads home at the end of the day." Chimes again. "It's surreal."

"How serious is this?" Her eyes don't fully focus.

"As long as I don't do anything with the system, I can't believe Z-Tech will risk the showdown. If I tried to sell it, he'd move on me."

"What do you mean, *move on you?*"

He shrugs. "Arrest. Prosecution. The law's not clear."

Victoria shakes her head. "Walk away, Juice. It's not worth the money."

"It's not about money."

"What is it about?"

"Vindication, maybe. Accomplishment. Knowing you've achieved something."

A mockingbird calls outside.

Victoria springs to her feet. "*Shit.* Hang on." Sprints past him and out the door. The screen shuts behind her.

Cole hears the bird cry out again, louder. Curiosity moves him to follow. Outside, Victoria, arms loaded with lemons, runs deep into the long back yard. T-shirt flapping, leg muscles straining, she cocks an arm and hurls fruit skyward without breaking stride. Cole follows the citrus trajectory toward the top of a telephone pole. The bird's dark outline. Its taunting cry. The first fruit misses badly. Victoria plants her feet, hurls another. Five, six lemons pass in rapid-fire succession. A carnival shooting gallery gone mad. A smack of citrus against wood. A flap of wings. The mocking song fades as the bird flies to safety.

"Fucker," Victoria says. Hands on hips. Face flushed. Toes wiggling in the deep grass. "I'll step on it. Squash it like a bug."

Her right hand clutches a lemon. "I'm being taunted. Weeks. Every night around this time."

She looks at him, as if only now registering the hour of his visit. "Fucking insomnia," she says. Looks toward the stars, the slice of moon. "See what it does to me?" A score of lemons on the ground, at their feet. The scent strong in the air. "Some people take walks. Just makes me wired. What do you do?"

"I stare at the ceiling a lot. Drink warm milk, even though it doesn't help."

Stone barbecue beside them. Thick iron grate. It reminds Cole of smaller pits at a state park – Ashland, maybe – where he used to go as a child.

Victoria leans against the barbecue, arms folded in front of her. A sigh. "So what happens if you just sit on this thing?"

"Huh?"

"This encryption thing. What if you don't do anything with it?"

Cole considers a number of answers, all complicated. Boils it down. "Probably, he goes away."

"Probably?" Victoria rolls her eyes. Shakes her head. "I'm going to bed."

Inside, she flops onto the mattress. Slides over to make room. "I'm whipped. You can crash on the floor. Or you can be comfortable."

He lies next to her. A hand on her hip. She sprawls, arm across his chest.

SCREEN FOUR

Sunset on the open plain. Small figures in a vast landscape. Three horses drink greedily from tin pans, tethered to mesquite and scrub oak. Three men huddle around a campfire which grows brighter as the day dims. A bucket hangs over the fire on a makeshift spit, branches wound together with rawhide. The crackle of flame. The rattle of tin cups. The palpable exhaustion

190

of these men after a hard ride. Duke's horse, the bay, paws the ground with a foreleg.

The camera begins to track in toward the men, toward their pantomime.

A figure enters from the right. The camera stops, keeping him in the edge of the frame. White shirt. Ban-Lon slacks. Thin tie. Puzzled expression. A drained look in his washed-out cheeks. A downward cast to his eyes that says, *help me*.

"Cut," yells Yvon. He storms into view, a whirlwind of black and grey cotton. Swirls of dust at his feet. "Goddammit, Ward." He opens a saddlebag. Removes a steaming travel mug. Face red. Veins thick in his neck. A long drink. His head wags from side to side as he speaks. "What – the fuck – are you doing here?"

Ward scratches his head.

A horse whinnies behind him. Grumbling from Rock and Kirk by the campfire.

Ward looks at the horses. The fire. His feet have not moved. His brow furrows. His voice fragile. "I got a call for the next scene."

Duke's voice. "What's going on? We're losing light."

Yvon inserts himself into the space between Ward and the cowboys. An arm around Ward's shoulder. A word to the director of photography. "Two minutes. I promise we'll get this shot." To Duke and the others. "Sit tight. You're doing great."

He turns Ward away from the western scene. Begins walking him toward the camera. Speaks in a gentle voice. His face pinched.

"You're on the wrong set, Ward. That's all. We'll be shooting your scene in a few minutes. Soundstage five. Same as always." They walk slowly. Ward's face relaxes, comforted by the director's consoling arm. His soothing voice. "You probably noticed it looks a little different here," Yvon says. He strains to keep his voice level. "No June. No Wally and Beav." His face reddens. "No floral fucking living room." Yvon takes a deep breath. His grip around Ward's shoulder has tightened, so that Ward appears squeezed. Compressed.

The sun slips behind the mountains. A pink band of sky shades toward purple.

"Here's what I want you to do," Yvon says. "I want you to go to the trailer – the one for soundstage five. I want you to find Makeup. Tell them I said to make you extra pretty. In a few minutes I'll be over there, and we'll shoot the scene. Okay?"

Ward nods. Without his affable swagger, his familiar surroundings, he's a husk. He wanders off.

Yvon sucks at his coffee. Claps his hands. "Okay, people. Show's over. Places." He turns to the director of photography. "Chris, we've got five minutes. Let's get this."

Newton was good. St. Martin had no doubt of that. Too good to be easily traced, unless he wanted to be. Unless he didn't care.

The network logs had been an easy mark. It had taken St. Martin less than a day to identify the phone line Cole had used. A cyber café in downtown Los Angeles. Same location every time. Suddenly stopped on August 14. Which meant that either Cole was long gone from southern California, or wasn't afraid of being found there.

St. Martin kept the KBC shopping cart screen live on his monitor. Thought about the small alterations Newton had made, against the enormous chaos he could have caused. An altered quantity. A confusion of addresses. It was not about stealing. Newton could have diverted funds, stolen hundreds of thousands of dollars in a day, then vanished. But he stayed put. Small gestures. Taunts. Enough to get attention at KBC. Enough, St. Martin thought smiling, to cultivate doubt about their e-commerce partner.

It would be difficult, if not impossible, to tie Cole to the network sabotage. Cole would know that – it would be the source of his confidence.

Time to go to Los Angeles. Find a way to sweat Cole. Turn up the heat, and see how he responded.

*

Long shadows in the late afternoon. A brown film has hovered over the Valley all day, obscuring the mountains, creating a subtly altered landscape whose horizons are diminished. A ripple in the air suggests none of this is real. Cole on his rock. The race is over, for all practical purposes. Today, hours after Cole learned he had successfully shaved the encryption key to 14 seconds processing at 238 characters – putting him in the zone he was determined to reach – he read news of Z-Tech. The pending release of an upgrade to its much-anticipated, much-criticized key – early in Q4. Translation: they're delayed. Effect: Warren will be livid. Cole will win.

Joy. Relief. Diarrhea. The ever-present wooziness of the sleep-deprived.

And then, subtle but undeniable, disappointment. There will be no adrenaline rush. No exhilaration at a photo finish. No fist-in-the-air euphoria. Instead, it is as if the opponent has dropped out with a cramp. On his rock, Cole tries to remind convince himself that it was only ever about winning, about what he would prove to himself.

Brown-banded sky. The smog confines movement, defuses possibility. *Limit outdoor activities*, the radio says. He wonders if the smog limits Gene's outdoor activities. He hasn't seen his friend in days. He watches St. Martin watch him. Takes perverse satisfaction in the fact that the smog no longer seals shut one of his eyes, that the burning sensation has become something he hardly notices. St. Martin, for his part, keeps a container of eye drops handy. Periodically he dips into a pants pocket, removes his sunglasses, tips back his head and squeezes in drops.

If Cole could hack the KBC system, even for an hour. Post his key and let them experience error-free commerce. Then yank it back. If he could plant a rumor of a key for sale, demonstrate its possibilities then disappear. He could sweat Warren. Maybe destroy Z-Tech. But he is no longer invisible.

So Cole on his rock watches St. Martin. Contemplates the tests that lie ahead of him to confirm the key's effectiveness. To prove he hasn't hallucinated a solution. When St. Martin reaches for the eye drops for the third, the fourth time, Cole smiles. Cocky. Enjoying the idea that the detective's eyes burn. And St.

Martin – orange vest over polo shirt and black jeans – raises the container to his eye, slides sunglasses back in place, and resumes his vigil. Cole makes an elaborate gesture of rubbing his eye. St. Martin moves away from the glass, begins to walk in Cole's direction.

Let him come.

And St. Martin does, a calm steady pace, a not-fully-suppressed grin, a tilting of his head against the sun, until he stands before Cole.

"I hate LA," he says. "We don't have to deal with this shit up north." Hands on hips. "People tell me you get used to it, that your eyes develop a tolerance. But mine never do. Don't think I want them to." He moves his head slightly so his sunglasses look directly at Cole. "How about you?"

Cole stiff. He won't answer without certainty of context.

"Your eyes adjusted?"

"I'm afraid so."

St. Martin stares at Cole through sunglasses. That half-smile. "You look like the cat that swallowed the canary. I suppose you've heard the news."

Cole feels his face flush. "Don't know what you're talking about."

The detective nods. His shadow crosses Cole.

A hawk soars overhead. St. Martin follows it with his eyes. "Gets kind of dull down there," he says. "You pitch quarters?"

A laugh. Suspicion. A distant memory of idle teenage years as a counselor at YMCA day camp. Ways to kill free time. They'd play an I-dare-you version of baseball. Where it didn't matter whether you hit the ball. It mattered whether you stood in against the hardest, wildest pitches, and didn't flinch. Then they'd end their time together the same way, every day, quarters, the bonding of the fittest. "Not since I was a kid."

St. Martin's face inscrutable. "Well?"

Cole fishes in his pocket. Checks his change. *Fuck it. Stand in.* "Come on." Their shadows precede them, elastic in the late sun.

Outside the refreshment stand, side by side, coins in hand. Their silhouettes cross the dirt, bend onto the building.

"I'm developing a theory," St. Martin says. "Want to hear it?"

Wobbly. What he wouldn't give to drift into dreamland. "No."

"I've been thinking. Cole's a smart guy. Too smart to call attention to himself just for revenge." The detective touches a finger to his temple, then flicks it at the air. "That's how I put it together. I'm thinking anytime you work on a project like this, something as complicated as encryption, there are bound to be dead ends. Versions that have to be abandoned because they simply don't work." He draws an arc in the air with his hands. "Now we shift gears. I'm thinking maybe Warren is short-sighted enough to not have forced you to document your work. And I'm thinking one of these early encryption versions – one of these dead ends – ended up on the network at Z-Tech, and the real one, the one headed in the right direction, left with you. I figure maybe you're working on this encryption system on your own. Do it up right and take it to market. Show the fools back in Waltham they didn't know what a good thing they had."

He inhales. A long breath. A hand on Cole's arm.

The echo of hoofbeats, the sound growing in Cole's ears. No. Just his erratic intestine. *A guess. He's got nothing.*

"I'm almost done. What I haven't been able to figure – and I've got a pretty good imagination – is how you do this without getting busted."

Cole's mouth dry. Palms moist. "Quite a theory."

The detective shrugs. "I have time to think." He takes a practice toss, two, the coins rolling in circles toward, beside, then away from the wall before landing flat in the dust. "You'll never be able to sell it."

"Didn't say I wanted to."

"Then why pursue it?"

"Didn't say I was."

"Of course not." St. Martin looks at the ground. Shifts his feet. "I forgot myself."

A hot breeze stirs the air.

"A man of your talents. It would be a shame to see you end up in prison."

Cole holds a damp quarter in his left hand. A few others in his right. "I couldn't agree more."

*

Joanna at the corner of 2nd and Pike. Waiting for the light to change. *Don't Walk* flashes before her. She stands among a dozen people on the corner, hoping the fog will lift. Buildings fade after two stories. On the street, car horns; a work crew smooths concrete on a new sidewalk. Yellow caution tape flaps like confetti. Fingers cold. Legs tired. Across the street, Holy Ghost Revival, the Green Tortoise Youth Hostel.

Joanna, staying downtown at the Vance Hotel, near the bus station, had played a game of Let's Pretend with the bartender over a vodka tonic. "Say you're a teenager. You're new in town, you're on your own. Maybe a little scared. You need work. A place to sleep. You want to lose yourself in the life of the city. Breathe for a while."

Dark wood. Wine glasses hung from racks in the ceiling. Ed, the bartender, silver hair, smart red vest, munched peanuts from a bowl. Two kids in college – U of Washington. Moonlighting at the bar. He chewed and thought. The photo of Anthony in a Ziploc bag on the bar between them.

"I was a teenager new in town," he said. The television behind him showed some hockey game – a red team, a white team. "I'd go one of two places. University, if I was inclined that way."

Joanna shook her head. "He wouldn't be," she said. She'd already been there.

Ed held up a hand. A gesture of *let me finish*. "Pike, if I wasn't. Lots of kids end up at a youth hostel on Second Avenue, work hauling fish at the market. It's a good place to be invisible."

The light changes. Joanna moves forward with the pack, across Second Avenue toward the market. The press of humanity. Bodies in motion. Tourists with cameras. Office workers at lunch. The smell of souvlaki from a corner stand. A man sits on the ground, worn corduroy coat, grimy fingers splayed against the sidewalk. A woman in black heels red overcoat red lipstick nearly steps on his hand. Neither of them notice.

Joanna notices everything. Eyes alert. Ears tuned. Straining for a glimpse in the crowd. The impulse to follow someone every minute. Her body reacting to a posture, a voice, a way of holding a head. What will she do if she finds him. Ask? Would she know the truth, and what would she do with it. She walks.

The cluster of people in which Joanna finds herself slows, compresses. A boy and girl on the sidewalk who must be moved around. The boy, puffy down jacket, wispy mustache, slaps at the girl's arms, not like he means it. She pushes his hands away, her face indifferent.

Joanna catches a glimpse of hair, a way of standing in a doorway and her eyes follow to the entrance of a pawn shop, but the man whose appraising eyes meet hers is in his thirties, balding and gaunt.

Giant red neon on the roof greets her – PUBLIC MARKET. An enormous clock announces the hour – 1:30. Bodies push past, around her. The smells of fish, of bread, of impending rain. She remembers a book she used to read to Anthony as a baby – *Are You My Mother?* – a baby bird whose mother has flown to get food approaches all sorts of creatures – a pig, a cow, a tractor – with that simple, profound question. She wonders if it is ever possible to not recognize your own child.

She pushes past other idlers and under the market's long roof. There's no way to it but to plunge in. Her senses in overdrive. Neon announcements of fresh fish, a string of raw light bulbs along the ceiling. Bodies in motion in all directions. The cheerful sounds of commerce. A handful of tourists pause at a fish stand, salmon stacked in neat rows on glistening ice, king crab attractively arranged, men in white lab coats pulling in passers-by. How many of them must there be? Dozens. Interchangeable. "This one, you like this one?" Pulling a fish from the ice, tossing it to a wiry man behind the counter, who catches and wraps it in a single, swift motion. A polished act. The stand lit like a stage. A small man hauls a wooden crate, digs out shrimp, arranges them on a bed of ice. Joanna watches, in the background, tries to imagine that man as Anthony, Anthony as that man. Fish smell lingering on his hands. Arms aching, ears ringing at the end of each day. It is easy. But it is only imagining. She is bumped from behind, a stocky man who mutters an apology as he zips past. Then she is moving, not so much of her own accord as she is carried along in the crowd. A long row of fruit. Jams, jellies, honey. The timbre of a voice. Three boys with skateboards clustered in a corner. Leaning against a wall.

As a child, Anthony would draw elaborate pictures with sidewalk chalk, detailed scenarios of castles and knights, pirate ships laden with cargo. In the summers, in the hours after school, he'd squat on their cul-de-sac, an hour, two hours, lost in reverie, stopping only for the occasional car to pull in or out. Indifferent to the shouts of children playing hide-and-seek a block away.

Small signs sell product – *Fresh Whole Wild King Salmon* – *Jude Cove Oysters* – *Sweet, Big-Ass Grapes*. So many people. None of them Anthony. A stretch of crafts tables. Sweaters for sale. Wind chimes. T-shirts. Silver necklaces. An old jeweler, frog-shaped, enormous eyes in rectangular magnifying eyeglasses. The shouts of vendors. The press of bodies. Too much.

She seeks refuge outside, walks the narrow-but-less-crowded street, past restaurants and bakeries, a cigar shop. Steam rises from a manhole cover. Past a trio of ancient black men on the sidewalk, one strumming an acoustic guitar, the others clapping hands and singing.

> *Jesus walked this lonesome valley*
> *walked it by himself*
> *nobody else to walk it for him*

She stops in a brick and concrete park that overlooks the highway, Puget Sound. Pigeons. Speeding cars on wet pavement. Room to breathe. To gather herself. Across the highway, in the Sound, an enormous freighter docked, Cyrillic lettering on its side, blue and gray hull. How easy would it be to climb aboard such a ship, to stow away.

A seagull prowls the promenade, staring straight into the eyes of those who sit and eat on rough-hewn benches and plank tables. A woman, kinky curly hair blown back in wind, snaps a picture of the water, the freighter. The gull hovers in front of two men, one with hands cupped around a paper coffee cup, one eating from a foil wrapper. The coffee drinker pulls a newspaper from a green trash barrel.

Joanna watches the water. Grateful simply for the space to see. For the expanse of sky and ocean. She has walked the city until

198

she hurts. Until it seems to her that lost sons are everywhere, each one the direct result of some mother's failure – a missed hug, a curt reply, some unnoticeable human moment that tipped the balance and ended in a boy cut adrift, the leaving maybe not coming until years later, the mother maybe never knowing the moment that brought it.

The ocean. The sky. The possibility of breathing. She does not want to leave this spot. Does not want to enter more confined spaces, where she will have to fight off the realization that Anthony is not there.

In the past, when Cole has had trouble sleeping, he has channeled himself deeper into work. Here in the desert, there is work which cannot be done imperfectly. Which, once completed – two three days of concentration – will force new choices. Here in the desert, there is space for his life, his past, to unfold before him, for connections to reveal themselves. Cole lies awake on his bed, eyes fixed on the ceiling, waking dreams playing there like movies. The Cole Newton Film Festival. Tonight's theme: arrested development. He's 42 years old and he's had two significant relationships. Both failures. Both with the same assessment in the end: that Cole requires taking care of. The partner no longer willing. Until recently, Cole has not perceived himself as someone who requires rescue. Yet this is the picture that emerges as he lies in bed, as he alternately tries to sleep and gives up on the idea.

Close-up. A Federal Express package from Alison, an overnight-delivery goodbye after almost five years. *I love you but I can't live with you. Please don't call.* Alison, in college and beyond. Alison, who grounded him in the basics – eat, sleep, do laundry – he was clueless in the way common to men in their twenties. It was supposed to be endearing.

Six years with Corinne. Rebecca. Instant family. The stakes suddenly real. An opportunity he couldn't grasp. Couldn't reconcile. The familiar call of command strings, comfortingly abstract routines and sub-routines. Until he sat across a kitchen table from a worn-out wife, eyes deadened, telling him why she was leaving. He never saw himself as insensitive. Just preoccupied.

Cole and Corinne at the beach, the summer of the troubles. Her father and sister had died within months of each other. The nonprofit where she'd worked had collapsed. Time for her to lean on Cole. They took a day. Held hands. Side by side on a blanket in the sun. Atlantic Ocean sparkling. Sailboats. Swimmers. At water's edge, a girl and boy at play. Shoveling sea water into a bucket. The girl in sand-spattered diaper, the boy slightly older. Corinne wistful. "I want a baby." He should have listened and left it at that.

"I don't know," he said. "It's not a good time." How she took her hand away, and he tried to rephrase. "Let's love the one we've got."

He always intended to do right by Rebecca. They were playmates. Pals. Then somehow, a half-step away from the attentiveness he wanted to give. Winter Carnival at Bulloughs Pond. A town tradition. Skating. Songs. Ice sculptures. How he promised to take her. How something always came up. A project deadline that couldn't slide. *Next year, I promise.* He was out of town. He got the date wrong.

It is as if the desert has brought his failings into focus. As if echoes of Alison Corinne Rebecca are carried on the night winds. How could he know so little?

Victoria, at 24, seems to know so much. It seems to Cole that the universe should forbid such imbalance. These thoughts battle with command strings for attention in his brain. The work is what he has. What he has chosen. Yet, for all his devotion, what does he have to show? The culmination of his career a project he walks away from. Victoria is going to open a restaurant. Victoria has answers. Victoria has Eric.

Now, on the ceiling screen, the image is of St. Martin, eye to the glass. A hint of a smile plays on the detective's mouth. Now Cole closes his eyes, and the image lingers. Now Cole is dressed and on his way to the car.

He keeps the Squareback unlocked and is already in the driver's seat when he sees the note tucked under the windshield wiper. As he retrieves the paper, his eyes instinctively look toward the road. But it is the dead of night. No St. Martin. The note is on cream-colored stationery, the recycled kind with flecks in the paper.

Dear Jo,
I'm off to find what I find on my journey. Here's hoping you and Cole find what you're looking for on yours.
Love,
Emily

It troubles Cole to think that this space can be infiltrated. It troubles him that Emily is leaving and Joanna has not returned.

He points the car toward Burbank.

Victoria in her UCLA t-shirt.

"You eat anything today?" she asks.

"I don't remember. Possibly not."

Cole has tossed and turned, told himself he would not come here. For three nights. But he needs human contact. Grounding. Sleep.

"You always wear the same shirt to bed?"

"Not always." Dog-eared papers in her hand. Sleepless eyes. "You like tenderloin?"

"I love tenderloin."

"Follow me." She tosses the papers onto the mattress. The dim glow of the gooseneck lamp allows night to be night. He follows her to the fridge. She removes a long Tupperware container. "My mom gave this to me. It's supposed to be a loaf saver for Velveeta." She pops the top, grabs two forks from a drawer.

"Plates are up there." She points to a cabinet. Cole reaches in for two stoneware dishes. Victoria spears thick slices onto one.

"Nuke it for a minute and a half."

He punches in the numbers. The microwave hums.

Victoria sweeps hair back from her face. Scratches the shaved place at the base of her skull. "More than three million Americans are infected with Hepatitis C and don't know it. They're being attacked by something they can't detect. Passing it on to others."

"Lovely."

The whir of the machine. The smell of pork, and a spice Cole can't identify.

"It mutates its proteins to disguise itself from our immune systems. Each time our antibodies get to recognize and attack it, it changes form and escapes."

Cole leans his back against the kitchen counter. "It's no wonder you can't sleep."

"Most people who have it have no signs, no symptoms." The microwave beeps at them. "You feel fine. Ten years down the road, even twenty. Bam. Cirrhosis. And it's too late." She pulls out the one plate, slides half the meat onto the other. "Think about it."

"I don't want to think about it," he says. "Why do you read that stuff?"

"I want to know." She pushes a plate toward him.

The clatter of knives and forks. The sounds of chewing.

"This is delicious."

"Roasted pork tenderloin Tangiers," Victoria announces. "It's a simple rub – cinnamon, cardamom, kosher salt, freshly ground pepper." She pauses in her eating to put the lid back on the Tupperware and place the container in the refrigerator. "You bring your toothbrush?"

Cole speaks through a mouthful of food. "Don't know if I'm staying."

Victoria, hands on hips, head lowered so she can raise her eyes at him. "You sleep?"

"Nope. You?"

"Not lately."

"Course not." The sweet smell of cardamom. "That stuff you read."

"Yeah, and with you it's a mystery," she says. "Unexplainable." She licks spices from her fingers.

He scowls. Pushes the last piece of pork around on his plate. "I haven't figured out what I'm going to do with the system."

"Exactly." She scowls back. "Is it finished?"

"A couple days, if all goes well."

She shakes her head. "You're going to do it."

"Finish it? Yeah, I'm going to finish it."

"Don't be obtuse. That's not what I mean."

There is an inevitability to this that Cole could not have predicted. Like a magnetic field that, in the absence of focused resistance, exerts an inexorable pull. "I told you, I haven't decided yet."

"Right."

She turns out the light. Shoves papers aside. Falls onto the mattress. "Leave the dishes. I like the smell." Pulls the covers up around her.

He pushes away from the counter. Kicks off his shoes. Crawls into bed. The room feels small.

Moonlight through the windows. A row of short, wide panes high on the wall. Dawn not far away. The curve of Victoria's neck inches from his face. A jumble of thin braids on the pillow. Cole runs his finger along the stubble of the shaved place at the back of her head. She lies on her side, face buried in the pillow.

"Hey," he says. "How's the bird?"

"Hasn't been back." Her voice muffled by the pillow.

He takes deep breaths.

A smooth place under Cole's fingers draws his eyes to her head. On the left side, where his fingers expected to find stubble, they find soft skin. He props on an elbow, rubs the bald spot with an index finger. "This is interesting. What's this?"

Victoria's voice sleepy, like something drugged. "My parents were into foster kids. One of them was into matches." She props on her elbows. "One night when I was eight, I woke up and my head was on fire." She rubs the bald spot. "That part never did grow back." Cole lies on his back, tries to imagine Victoria as an eight-year-old. He would have been a senior in college. Cramming for a history exam while her hair was burning. "We were lucky," she says. "We only lost some curtains, and my hair. We found out later the last foster home he'd been in had burned down."

Cole massages the spot.

Victoria tucks her chin into her chest so his fingers have better access. "Don't be an idiot, okay?"

His fingers stop. "What?"

"You're going to finish it," she says. "And it's going to get bloody."

He starts to speak. How you don't create something just to stick it in a drawer.

"I know," she says. "You haven't decided yet."

How the game the race develops a momentum that carries you along. How achievement doesn't mean much unless it's recognized.

She curls into a ball, her back to him. "I hope you don't think this is courage."

He concentrates on the warmth of her sheets. He knows what it is: a failure of imagination – the simple fact that he cannot envision another way.

Sleep.

She wakes early. She's showered and dressed before he stirs. A shadow moving across the room. He has to remind himself where he is.

"Hey," he says.

"Hey." Her voice in the gray light of dawn. The smell of baby powder. She moves to the bed. Wet hair. Strawberry-scented shampoo. Her hand on his shoulder. "Go back to sleep."

He rubs his eyes. "Got work to do." Rolls onto his back. "You sleep?"

She nods. Cars on the street. Someone hauling trash cans to the curb. "You?"

"Mmm." A dog barks somewhere. "Tell me again, how would Eric feel about this."

Victoria withdraws her hand to her lap. "Eric would be fine with this. This has nothing to do with Eric. We help each other sleep."

He scratches his head. This morning like the last – the first – here. Awake in the gray light. The bliss of having slept.

"Listen," she says. "I gotta get to work, but you're welcome anytime you can't sleep."

Every night he can't sleep, but he has waited, because the boundaries are unfamiliar. Because he does not want to need anyone.

She pushes to her feet. "Lock the door, okay?"

204

Minutes later, Cole saunters down the driveway, hands deep in pockets, body stiff against the morning damp. How quickly he has grown to expect warmth. A thin layer of gray clouds that will burn off by noon. The feel of Victoria's hands in his hair.

A car moves along Buena Vista. Cole restless. He shudders, chilled. Digs out keys, starts across the road. Something up ahead – a glint of white – catches his eye. A white pickup truck parked, now with its lights on, now pulling away. A horn, a blue minivan moving toward Cole, driver gesturing. Cole hustles across the yellow dividing line. The van swerves behind him. The truck gone. Vanished. The chill remains. *What was St. Martin doing here?*

It is cold where Anthony wakes. There is dampness and dust, the smell of stale urine. He pulls the sleeping bag up over his shoulders, cinches it around his neck. It is the morning on which he has decided to leave Seattle, and he has slept atop the Fremont Troll, ending his stay in the city where he began it, nestled in the hollow of the sculpture under the Aurora Bridge.

He doesn't know if he will make it back here, to this city he has come to consider home. A few days handyman work at the Ajax Café in Port Hadlock, the end of a dirt road halfway up the Olympic Peninsula. A small miracle of a restaurant – dinners only – tucked in among boat launches, repair shops, fisherman's bungalows. Seagulls rested on pilings on the old wood dock. Permanent chill in the air. A place to sleep, meal money, and no advice.

"You could open for breakfast. I'd be your cook."

"Don't want to. Besides, look around you. Who'd come for breakfast."

He has lived on a houseboat whose renovation lay half-done, suspended in mid-construction, exposed studs beginning to divide the living space in two. He has begun to understand how you become connected to a place – the corn tortilla pie at Still

Life, the walk into Queen Anne, the view of the Sound from Gasworks Park.

He doesn't know if he will return to any of this, can't know if he will reclaim it, because he wants to see his mother and he can't know what will happen after that.

He sits on the back of the troll's hand. The sun is out, the air cold. He looks down Aurora Ave., the row of bridge supports to Lake Union.

Anthony has resistance to people, which they have to wear down, persevere through, to see the likable Anthony. Fremont has done that. People here have done that. A quiet friendliness and acceptance that feels real, not like the movie theater kind – *would you like butter flavoring with that.*

Anthony eats corn tortilla pie in the Still Life Café. The room half-full, mid-morning coffee drinkers who aren't in any hurry. Anthony thinks of this as his last meal, savors each bite. He has washed in the library rest room. Changed into clean clothes he bought at Goodwill. He has enough money for bus fare south, a few days food, a return ticket which he does not know if he will need. He knows that he wants something from his mother but he cannot say what it is.

A little blonde girl at the next table watches him eat. Up on her knees, leaning against the back of her chair.

"Hello," she says when he meets her eyes.

He waves to her, chews tortilla, melted cheddar, black beans.

"What's that?" she says. "Looks yucky." The girl is at the table alone, though there are two glasses of water and a cup of coffee.

"Tortilla pie," he says. He smiles at her. "It's one of my favorite things."

"I'm getting a scone." She sways from side to side against her chair back. Green eyes. Fair skin. "Scones are one of *my* favorite things."

He takes a sip of water. "I've always thought of scones as failed muffins."

The girl runs a finger along the wood at the top of the chair. "I like them. My mom says these are the best around."

Outside, clouds gather. Anthony has maybe a forty-minute walk to the Greyhound station. Where he is going, the sun shines all the time. Anthony scoops up the last bits of tortilla on his fork. "I'm going to visit my mom later today."

"Is she nice?"

The girl's mother arrives with two plates, two scones. A little blonde mother, with eyeglasses and a slightly wary expression.

Anthony nods to the mother. "Your little girl is sweet," he says. She smiles, sizing him up. Anthony has always marveled at the speed and agility with which parents construct and release fences. This mother looks nice. He has never thought about whether Joanna is nice. "I guess so," he says. "She's my mom."

The little girl nods. She leans against her mother, body touching body. She eyes her scone. She says to Anthony. "We're going to visit the troll." Dimples. "Do you know about the troll?"

He raises his eyebrows. Leans toward her. "I do," he whispers. "The troll and I are friends."

The mother watches the encounter.

"Sometimes people sleep there, you know."

Anthony pulls on his coat. Savors the flavors of the pie in his mouth. Wonders in what condition he will find his mother. "I know." He nods. "What do you think about that?"

The girl shrugs. "I dunno," she says. "Maybe the troll takes care of them."

Anthony smiles. "I like that idea."

The mother has been patient. Anthony senses it is time to go.

SCREEN TWO

Wooden wheels on a packed dirt road. The clatter of horses' hooves. Relentless sun. A dozen or so people in front of the General Store, across from the jail. Oddly quiet. There's little movement, even when the black buggy enters the frame, following a black horse, carrying its black-clad passenger. The men in the street move enough to accommodate the buggy, but they move grudgingly, as if voicing some objection. A trio of children kneel in the dust. A scattering of coins beside them.

She has had a hard ride. Her black suit, black hat gather the heat so that she feels dizzy. Everything flutters in her vision. She has come a long way in pursuit of this fugitive, on the promise that he has been detained. The travel, across dust-choked roads, through a country unclaimed, was the easy part. What has made the trip hard is the jagged uncertainty of her conviction. The knife blade in the fabric of her self. Cutting deeper at every rut in the road. A tattered sense of duty. His ways don't work. She has set her gaze toward this place, to do what must be done. Yet she feels deadened with every inch she moves closer to town, closer to the hanging. A part of her hoped she would arrive and find him gone.

Cicadas cut the air with an electric whine. The buggy stops just short of the jail. Alongside the crowd – a dozen men, a sprinkling of women. Eyes on her. Accusatory stares. The children who have not moved. Then she sees what holds their attention. The shotgun-shredded body of Hollomon, the man she'd deputized to hold the Kid. Sixteen holes where sixteen dimes had ripped through him, blood already fading to brown, mingling in the dust where he lay. The children exploring the body as if it were a relic.

Sweat on the back of her neck. The awful weight. "Will some of you people get him off the ground?" A few men move reluctantly. They drag the body across the street, thin trails of blood, swirls of dust. Only then does she see the other man, face down in the dirt, sprawled head first through the shattered jailhouse window. Shot twice in the back. The children watch her. Two boys, a girl. They saw. She can see it replay in their eyes. Picture exactly how it happened. Bell – *Walk toward me, Bell. Don't make me shoot you Bell.* – shot reluctantly, the gun planted for the Kid in the outhouse, Bell always too trusting. After the blast, the body almost floating, down the stairs, through the window. Glass everywhere. Hollomon had heard the commotion and started back from the saloon, sick in his stomach. By now the Kid had moved onto the porch, upstairs, fastened his gun belt, grabbed the shotgun loaded with dimes. Hollomon he'd shot almost greedily, with a smile. The one who'd pistol-whipped him, who'd confronted him with the coldness of his crimes and hounded him to get on his knees before Jesus. Hollomon virtually exploded in the sunlight. Boom and down. This was the blow that had silenced the street. That had frozen the townspeople into a crowd of mute witnesses. No one moved from that short stretch of road. So he had gathered what he wanted – the horse, the bedroll, a few dollars cash – and rode silently away. No one moved until she arrived and then the horror flowed into stares of hate at the blood on her hands, flowed until the body was dragged off and the crowd dispersed into isolated pockets of disgust and dread.

Every neighborhood in which she does not find him, every day in which the search proves futile, should be a victory. A reinforcement of the possibility that Anthony is not here. Every day she reminds herself of this, tries in vain to make herself experience this as reassurance.

She remembers a photograph. Three-year-old Anthony, on the front porch of their rented house in Delmar, arms stretched above his head, eyes squinting against the sun, naked and unashamed.

"You like the wine?"

Trattoria Micelli. Just off Pioneer Square. Potato gnocchi to fill her stomach. Red checked tablecloth. A waiter who's a little too friendly.

She nods. "It's nice."

"It's got just enough of the cabernet grape to keep it from being dry." Short, curly hair. A face eager to please. Hands clasped in front of him. He reminds her of a stand-up comic. Of a boy with whom Anthony used to play baseball, on Saturday mornings, in the parking lot of the NYNEX repair center. Aluminum bat, rubber ball. Peanut butter sandwiches she'd make them for lunch. He had advised her against the chianti. Steered her toward the syrah. She has already thanked him once.

"The chianti's fine, but I think this one's a great fit with pasta." He leans toward the table, his torso hovering, so that his head seems slightly larger than the rest of him.

Anthony at seven, on a stepstool in the kitchen. Electric mixer in hand. Joanna next to him. Flecks of cookie dough shooting in all directions. What was important was that they enjoy the time together. Anthony intent on his task. Eyes fixed on the glass bowl, the sand-colored dough. Joanna laughing. A speck of dough shot onto the bridge of his nose. Pulled him back from close-focus concentration. His eyes took in the spotted counter. His face began to worry. Then his ears took in his mother's laughter and he joined her, wide grin, both of them forgetting the cookies.

Somehow, the waiter has moved on. Left her to her half-eaten gnocchi. She stares out the window onto Yessler Way. At ten o'clock, the streets are quiet, the restaurant nearly empty. Seattle, the waiter has told her – Kevin Brian Tim? – is not a late-night town.

A few days in each neighborhood. As if this were sufficient to canvas its population. To check off each area and call it done. Union Square. Queen Anne. Belltown. She has searched the streets until dizzy. Shown the snapshot until disheartened. *He's my son. Have you seen him.* In her experience, children who run away have reason.

Fremont. Joanna sat cross-legged on a wooden dock, looking out across Lake Union. Bright sunshine. Wired on caffeine. Water lapped at the wood beneath her. In her hand she held a piece of paper which a week earlier she would have considered a clue.

Hi. My name is Chris and I'm looking for a boat to live on in exchange for maintenance. If you're interested, or know someone who might be, leave a message with Andrea at 536-2102.

A week earlier, Joanna would have believed that her ability to imagine Anthony here, to envision him writing such a note, photocopying it on bright green paper, and stapling it to the pilings at the docks at the marina was evidence that he had been here, had done that. She would have told herself that the open

210

door of the gray houseboat, through which she can see exposed studs, can hear the electric whine of a saw, was one of several such situations, and that Anthony had been, or maybe still was, part of one.

She would have found encouragement in it, would have considered the note something to investigate. Not anymore. Now it was merely evidence of her desperation, confirmation of a truth – that she was no closer to finding Anthony now, or proving his absence, than she was when she arrived. That she is capable of imagining him anywhere. When she does find someone who responds to the photograph – the man in the Army-Navy store, a waitress in a Fremont café – she doubts their information, suspects their recognition as a product of the intensity of her own desire and their eagerness to accommodate.

– *Do you know him? Have you seen him?*

The clatter of dishes. The silky sounds of a saxophone. The waitress, early twenties, blond hair pulled back in a bun, pencil tucked behind her ear. She'd looked at Joanna, searched her face as much as she searched the photo.

– *There was this kid who worked here for a couple weeks. Few months ago. How old is this picture?*

She grabbed the arm of a passing waiter.

– *Doesn't this look like that kid, remember, he washed dishes for us. Stayed a week or two.*

The man considered. A tray of coffee mugs in his hand.

– *I don't know. Could be.*

Joanna leaves cash on the table, moves for the door before her waiter returns. She walks up Yessler to First Avenue, where a cluster of young people linger at the triangle. The wrought iron pergola. A glass roof keeps out the rain. Lighted globes keep the square in perpetual twilight. A boy in front of Doc Maynard's argues that his passport should be considered valid ID. A spot of red on each cheek, passport clutched in his hand like a sacred tract. Inside the bar, a band belts out "Cool Jerk." She scans the faces of the young people around her. Cuts back down Yessler, a quiet block to the waterfront. Damp air seeps into her pores. Finds every unprotected surface. She burrows deeper into her

fleece. Wishes to avoid the press of people. The strain to find one
– the swipe of an arm, the sound of a voice.

Anthony's first flight. He was twelve. Divorce had been filed,
not finalized. Anthony spending every other weekend with his
father. It was not unusual for an outburst to cut their time short.
A Friday night. Anthony had walked to his Dad's after school.
Ben had rented a carriage house less than a mile from where
Joanna lived. Her idea. Keep it easy on the boy. He'd wanted to
move further south. Had found a place on the river, in Ravena, a
view to the water. But Joanna convinced him, Anthony had
enough trouble, and he took the place in Delmar. Where
Anthony walked after school. They had a blow-up before dinner.
Anthony left. Ben swore later that he didn't even know the boy
had gone. Thought he'd holed up in the den to watch TV.
Figured they could both use some time to cool off. Went in to
ask Anthony what he wanted on his pizza. Even then, when he
discovered that Anthony had left, he did not call Joanna. Told
her it never occurred to him that Anthony would go anywhere
other than back to her. That he didn't want to hear her gloat.
Midnight he called. A pang of conscience.

– *Just wanted to make sure he's okay.*
– *What are you talking about?*

She found him, two a.m., on the swings at Lincoln Park.

– *I was going to come home.*
– *When?*

It was the first time she felt she needed the hug more than he
did.

She's had premonitions. Moments where the sense of
Anthony's almost-presence was palpable. Where she could
imagine him so purely, so completely, that she half expected to
see him approach, or hear his voice behind her. Crossing
Fremont Avenue, walking into a news stand to buy cigarettes, so
convinced of his presence she turned, her heart racing. The
Fremont Troll, the sculpted figure beneath the Aurora Bridge.
She'd watched a girl and her mother – short, blonde, smiling –
looked down Aurora Avenue, past the bridge supports to the lake,
convinced that this was a place Anthony had been. The girl sat on
the troll's giant hand, a real Volkswagen beetle in its grip, stared

up at the creature's hubcap eye looming above her. Joanna had walked all around the sculpture, exploring every angle. In the end, she convinced herself only that she had become adept at conjuring. That her son was lost. That she would have just as much – or as little – luck in Pittsburgh. Or Poughkeepsie.

SCREEN NINE
Two riders silhouetted against a dying sun.
Single file along a dusty trail, pack mule strung between them. Five years they've ridden the western territories, Texas to Wyoming, Oklahoma to New Mexico. In dust and heat. In snow and rain. They have not eaten a satisfying meal. Have not slept a full night in a good bed. Worn horses. Worn saddlebags. Flimsy bedrolls. Chasing rumors. Tracking a memory of the child that was taken. They cannot be sure they would recognize her if they found her. They cannot be certain she is still alive. They cannot even know if the Comanche band they follow is the right one. But they are no longer capable of other activity. Cannot imagine any other life. Families killed. Friends estranged. Posted for the murder of a man they shot in self-defense. They've reduced themselves to a single, primal urge. The endless search as instinctual, as thoughtless, as drawing breath.
Sometimes, restless, in his sleep, he relives the funeral, the rock forming in him, the wild impatience. Mourners gathered on a hillside, knee-high crosses of unadorned wood, a handful of men, a few women. Voices carried on the wind.
Shall we gather at the river
the beautiful, beautiful river
gather with the saints at the river
that flows by the throne of God.
Stark stone cliff in the background, the now-empty wagon that carried caskets in the foreground. The preacher's words swallowed up almost before they were spoken. Blood rage boiling inside him, the rock gut of all he had seen, until he couldn't stand still.

Gathered the boys. Went for the horses.

Callused fingers strapped down rifles. Tightened saddlebags. The woman, full skirt, red shawl, plain brown hat, clutching a Bible to her breast, the mother of the one now long-since slain, pleading as he led the horse away, that first day, lifetimes ago. "Don't let the boys waste their lives in vengeance."

Here is Cole in this room, confining himself to this room, computer screen glowing, insistent. Sun through the small square of window near the ceiling means it is between ten and eleven o'clock. Shadows climbing above the counter mean somewhere between two and three. Seventeen magic-marker scratchings on his wall. He understands now how and why prisoners count the days, scratch their cell walls to fix in their minds the hope of release, to shape their concept of time toward some optimistic horizon.

In Cole's sleep-deprived fog, everything is slippery. That which should have substance not fully real. That which should be insubstantial altogether tangible.

St. Martin has stirred – why. Seeking to prove his theory. Ready to come after Cole. But without Cole's computer, or a clear move to sell the key, he can prove nothing. Can he? Now it is Cole's move, but he wants to be sure of the game, the stakes.

So he hides. He painstakingly cleans the refreshment stand, scrubs years of grease from walls and countertops. Empties and cleans cupboards, restocks shelves with his own supplies. Jars of dry roasted peanuts. Small bottles of Coca-Cola. Mallo Cups. Bananas and cheese sticks to close the intestinal floodgates.

St. Martin in Burbank is outside the boundaries. Against the rules. It could be that the detective is simply forestalling boredom. It could be something else.

Cole works at restoring the soda machine. He removes and cleans the plastic facings from each of the spouts. The cheerful colors and swirling typography. Coca-Cola. Sprite. Fanta Root

Beer. Detaches and removes the tubes that run down to the containers of syrup and carbonated water, thick with residue, clogged from neglect. He measures and cuts new lengths of tubing from a stash on a shelf. Labels with a black Sharpie marker on masking tape which tube will connect to which soda. The satisfying smell of virgin plastic. He is amazed at how long this process can take. Lack of sleep causes his motor to run faster. The sun's warmth a beckoning to give himself over.

Shadows creep above the counter. In four days, Joanna will be due home.

Darkness. The ghosted image of riders. Cole wakes curled on the counter top. He sits. Stretches. Shuts down his computer. Pushes his way outside. Warm wind. Clear, starlit sky. Deep breaths. He presses forward, not fully awake, through dust and tumbledown grass, across the undulating rows of his and Joanna's valley – *from this valley they say you are going* – no pleasure in the songs without her – up the hillock. Drops to his hands and knees. Face pressed close to the ground, he pulls himself with his forearms. Claws toward the crest, inches his way up until he can see the below. Heart hammering. The empty stretch of road where the white pickup would be. He breathes there for a minute. The smell of dirt. The cool ground.

He searches for Gene. Wonders if St. Martin has intervened, unplugged the projector, planned Joanna's leaving. To isolate Cole, take him down.

Three days of testing. To find out yes no, he has the key or he doesn't. It was supposed to be different. Cole in hiding. In control. His sudden emergence a spark. His work the powder keg. The whole thing blowing up in Z-Tech's face before they knew what happened.

The fading hope that St. Martin will lose interest, lose patience. The voice – Victoria's Joanna's his own? – that says *let it go*. Test it and bury it. Let St. Martin rot in the desert sun.

The tin fence rattles in the wind. Winnetka feels confining. Empty space, and not nearly large enough. Cole sings.

Out in the West Texas town of El Paso,
I fell in love with a Mexican girl.

Across the rows of speaker poles. Behind the refreshment stand. Along the path.

Gene, where are you? What have they done with you?

Hands on hips. Cole's mysterious building lurks in the distance. He tries to conjure the laboratory, the tuna-eating scientists, to imagine that Gene is in for repairs. Enhancements.

Big sky. Blanket of stars. Silence.

Might as well go to bed and practice not sleeping.

Toes stick out from under the blanket the way he likes. Computer safely tucked away on the shelf above his head. Security. A tumbleweed scrapes against the trailer. He wiggles his toes and sings.

Maybe tomorrow a bullet may find me
Tonight, nothing's worse than this pain in my heart.

A knock. Unmistakable. Cole short of breath. The pounding in his heart, his head. He tells himself it is Gene back from the lab. He crawls out of bed. Gym shorts. T-shirt. He cannot conceive a showdown in these clothes. He forces his feet toward the door. Hovers, his hand over the knob. Swallows. Swings open the door.

No one. The wind?

Always, he's more tired than he realizes.

Now a figure, in the shadows, moving away. Stopping.

"Cole?"

Not the detective's voice.

Cole starts to speak. Stops. Strains to see. Wiry black hair, frayed bell bottom jeans. A boy. Can't be. Cole finds his voice. "Anthony?"

"My Mom here?"

Cole leans into the night. Eyes slowly adjusting. "No." The boy – if there is a boy – seeks the shadows. Cole holds the screen door open. "Come on in."

The boy hesitates. In the darkness beside the Winnebago. "She's not here?"

"Far as I know, she's in Seattle. Looking for you."

The boy laughs. Dark cotton jacket. Guarded voice. "How'd she know?"

"She didn't."

He strains to see better. To confirm this sighting. "How'd you find us?"

"Sean."

"Come on in," Cole says. "Jo should be back soon." He flushes. The implication of hours, even minutes. If nothing else, he thinks, her son may be a magnet to draw her home.

"I'll check back."

Wind and sky. Light spills from the Winnebago, onto steps, a patch of ground.

Cole begins to call out – *stay* – but the boy disappears into darkness. Cole parks himself on the stair and lets the door swing shut behind him.

5.

St. Martin walks up the driveway at sunset, a smog-enhanced southern California special rich in oranges, purples and pinks. He has watched her arrive, park the car and carry in groceries. Given her time to get settled.

He has put Archer to work in Waltham. *Take the computer apart. Sift for wiped files. Any trace of a program smarter than what they had when he left.* He walks around back to the carriage house, past a neglected barbecue console. Lemons litter the yard. He wears a cardigan sweater over a silk t-shirt. Linen slacks. Shades of brown. Warren has turned up the heat. – *I want him for taking the key, not just for hacking.* – *It's a mistake, there's no solid case.* – *Just do it.* St. Martin pulls the sleeves of his sweater up over his wrists and knocks.

Victoria's face at the door; her swishing braids.

St. Martin watches her expression evolve, inquisitive to suspicious to guarded.

She nods her head. "I remember you."

"Yeah? I figured you must have forgotten. You said you'd let me know if you'd seen our friend." They are separated by a wood frame screen door.

"So maybe I haven't seen him."

St. Martin narrows his eyes at her.

She laughs. "Well, you shouldn't believe everything people tell you." There is a vitality in her face, an intensity in her gaze.

"I talk to you for a minute?"

"For a minute," she says. She leans against the door frame, arms folded. "Talk away."

"We talk inside?"

The hiss of traffic on Buena Vista. The Valley awakening.

She shakes her head slowly. "I don't think so."

He scratches the back of his neck. "You like Cole," he says. He runs a finger along the door frame. The scent of lemon on the air.

"That a question?"

"He's going down, one way or another."

"Do you have any idea how much you sound like a TV movie?"

Smile tickling St. Martin's face. He likes her. Likes them both. The game. "No," he says. "I don't usually work this way."

"How do you usually work?"

"Shoot first, ask questions later."

"Yeah," she says. "That looks like you."

"So help me out. What should I say next?"

"Something about how if I care about him I should convince him to turn himself in. How it'll be easier on him that way."

St. Martin nods. "That's not bad. I was thinking another direction." He leans against the door frame opposite Victoria. Bookends. "I can tie him to a crime scene," he says. "In a couple days, I'll tie him to a crime. You'll be an accessory."

"Oh," she says. "Intimidation."

"You play what you have."

"What do you want from me?"

"Tell me he was at the Atomic Café."

"You already know that."

"Tell me he used the computers. Tell me what he did on them."

"I don't know," she says. "He played soccer."

"Soccer?"

"The World Cup. What else you want to know?"

"Listen. You like Cole. I like Cole. He's a talented guy. But you don't pull shit like this and get away with it."

Dusk descends. Victoria a face a shadow in the darkening apartment.

"If he turns himself in, you won't be an accessory."

Victoria's face reddens. "He's got his own thing. He's not mine to control."

St. Martin steps back from the door. "You seem like a smart young woman. Just a piece of information I thought you should have."

Then he's off, back down the driveway, essence of lemon trailing him.

The sound of whistling. An unfamiliar tune. The clip-clop of hooves. Then singing. Cole looks toward the refreshment stand. Gene rides toward him on the piebald horse, blue bandanna flapping in a soft breeze.

Let my journey end
where the willows bend
'neath a blue Montana sky.

Both Gene and horse in full regalia. Midnight-blue shirt adorned with rhinestones and embroidered roses. White hat pushed back to expose a broad forehead. Holographic hair brushed neatly to the right, a jaunty wave at the front. Somehow, he's equipped the horse as well. Jeweled saddle blanket, a matching bridle which extends like a necklace up to the reins. Gene wears a gun belt to match. Rope coiled neatly beside pommel. Cole has never been happier to see anyone.

"Hey, stranger," Cole calls across the flat. "Good to see you."

Gene smiles. The horse ambles over to where Cole sits as the night claims the sky. "Good to be seen." Gene hops down from the saddle. Silver spurs gleam. Gene hooks his thumb inside his belt loops.

Cole wears a grin he can't shake. "You're all decked out. Got a date?"

Gene laughs. "My fortunes have taken a turn," he says.

A raised eyebrow. "Tell me."

The old cowboy strokes the horse's mane. The colt's tail swishes gently. "Cole, I had a good ride. Movies. Records. A radio show. Luckier than most. Then my time passed and the world moved on, and I made peace with that." The colt lifts a forepaw, then plops it down again. Nuzzles its face into Gene's neck. The cowboy star looks both at Cole and past him. "I did.

But I never lost the itch to entertain." He balls his fists in front of Cole, shakes his arms. "It gets in the blood."

Cole can't help picturing the warehouse, alight with secret activities, awash in mysterious experiments, manipulations to renew the King of the Cowboys. *If disco can make a comeback, why not Autry?* "What happened?"

"Some of the credit sits right with you. This place has made me feel young again. I've found myself picking up my guitar, plucking out a few songs I remembered. One thing led to another." An impish grin. Pronounced cheekbones give him the look of a cherub. And Cole understands something about why Gene was so popular – for all his hero status, he has a little boy's face. All his expressions convey emotional extremes – delight, sympathy, puzzlement, concern.

"What do you mean?"

The grin widens, deepening dimples. "I'm back in the saddle. Looks like I'll be making a record."

The horse twitches its head. Cole does the same. "Come again?"

Gene removes his hat, runs a translucent hand through his hair. "I've been working up a couple new songs, some old ones I'd always wanted to do. A little help from some new friends. Interest from a recording company." The first stars overhead. "It's happened so fast. Them fellers been a big help, and I do believe it's put more spring in my step."

A recording contract. Why not? If a holograph can eat pho, why can't a holograph release a CD?

"There's talk of doing one of those music videos that are so popular with the kids."

Cole looks from holograph to horse, and back again. Raises a hand to his mouth, and drops it. "That's great, Gene." The horse's tail thwacks against the rock. "We'll celebrate. Champagne. The whole nine yards."

Hands raised, a wall. "Can't touch champagne. Does nasty things to me. But I'd love to celebrate. Maybe get some of that noodle soup."

"You bet."

"You look like hell, son. You didn't go and shoot that feller, did you?"

Cole shakes his head. "No. Nothing like that."

"You steering clear of trouble?"

"I'm still here."

"Let's keep it that way." Gene hooks a thumb inside his belt loop. "I should go rehearse. But I'm glad to see you." He slaps at Cole's leg. "Joanna back yet?"

"No." A child's petulant tone. "Any day now."

Gene hoists himself into the saddle, and offers Cole a smart salute. "When she gets back, we'll have ourselves a party. I'll play you one of the new songs."

"I'd like that." Cole's voice calls out after Gene as he rides into darkness.

SCREEN ONE

A break on the set. Cast and crew surround the catering table, stretch out on the steps of the brownstone facade. The Cowboy. The Cop. The Construction Worker sprawls on pillows backstage. Biceps bulge from a denim vest. He nibbles from a plate of grapes and cheese. Yvon paces, pulls a mug of coffee from a metal trash can prop and muses to Chris, the cinematographer, a heavyset man in jeans and snakeskin boots. Heavy-lidded eyes.

"It feels stale," Yvon says. "We need to spice it up." An air of fatigue. He runs a hand through buzz-cut hair.

"How?" Chris says. "What do you have in mind?"

Yvon thinks. Sips coffee.

An engine revs. The Biker weaves his way through foot traffic, hands tall on handlebars, extended fork on his Harley stretching ahead of him. He wears black leather hat, vest and pants, and an expression of serious indifference. He swerves to avoid the red-haired assistant, who scurries off to find more grapes. Steers serpentine across the stage, mouthing "Blah, blah, blah" as he passes Yvon.

"I heard that," the director says. "Prima donnas."

The Biker turns his head to respond, decides against it. Has to swerve to avoid hitting someone new on the set. Hits the brake. Catches his balance with a foot on the ground.

"Shit," he says. "Watch where you're going."

The newcomer, dazed, white shirt, thin tie, Ban-Lon slacks, haunted eyes, steps back out of the way. Mutters an apology.

Yvon spots the interaction. The director's face flushes, then a smile appears. He touches the cinematographer's arm. "Chris," he says. "I've got an idea. Don't go away."

Cole stalks his garden. A green watering can festooned with a yellow daisy hangs on his arm. He walks the pebbled pathways looking for something to water. The problem with a desert garden is that it doesn't require tending. And Cole has already been out once this morning, to pat the soil around the plants, check the condition of the leaves, savor the crisp scent of chicory. Now, after an hour of computer work, he is back. No sleep. Inconvenienced by the self-sufficiency of his plants. He walks to the outer rim of the garden. Sick of sunshine and blue sky.

He begins to pour water around the perimeter, to inscribe a circle. He modulates his pouring speed so the water will complete the circumference. Steps inside it. Takes a series of deep breaths. Imagines himself engaged in ritual. Strengthening. Purification. A girding for the battle ahead. He sits in the center of his garden, the center of his circle, tries to center himself. Closes his eyes and breathes deeply, concentrates on the sun the space the quiet.

"So this is your desert hideaway."

Victoria stands at the crest of the rise that shields garden from road. She's smiling. Cole isn't.

"What are you doing here?"

Jeans. Ribbed knit shirt. Bandanna on her head. She ambles toward him. "Good morning. Nice to see you, too."

"Shouldn't you be at work?"

"It's my day off. Shouldn't you?"

Cole extends his arms toward the horizon. "My work is everywhere."

"How very Buddha." She hovers at the edge of the garden.

"So really," he says. "What are you doing here?"

"I need to talk to you."

"Something wrong?"

"Probably."

Cole on his feet. A touch of vertigo he's grown accustomed to.

"Nice place you've got here," she says. "Actual growing things."

He touches her elbow. "It isn't that I'm unhappy to see you," he says. "It's just problematic."

"This being a hideout and all," she says. She looks around her. The garden, the Winnebago, the surrounding screens. "It's smaller than I expected."

The twitter of sparrows.

"It's not the best idea for you to be here." Cole feels thirsty, but all the water has gone into the ground. "St. Martin was at your place. The other morning, when I left."

Victoria nods. Takes Cole by the hand. They step outside the garden. "He came by last night."

Cole's eyes narrow. Inside the refreshment stand, his computer cycles through code sequences.

"I like you, Cole. I'm willing to go a ways to protect you. But I won't go to jail for you."

"Whoa. What did he tell you?"

She digs her hands into the back pockets of her jeans. "That in a couple days he'll have you pinned to a crime. That I wouldn't be an accessory if you turn yourself in."

"Fuck," he says. The approach of riders. The pounding of hooves. "He's bluffing."

"You sure?"

"No."

The wet line of Cole's magic circle already fading. He's heading somewhere he's never been.

"It doesn't sound like he's waiting for you to move."

"No, it doesn't. But it doesn't matter now."

"You're being ominous. Explain."

"It's finished. Testing right now." Cole shifts his feet in the dirt. "One way or another, it's going to end."

"Walk away, Juice. You don't have to do this."

"Do what? I haven't *done* anything."

A sound on the road behind them. Victoria climbs to the crest of the rise.

"Don't –"

But she's at his rock. Sitting down. Looking now at the road, now at Cole.

He moves up beside her.

St. Martin, vest-clad, watches from the side of the road. Waves.

"Great," Cole says. He plants an exaggerated suburban-neighbor smile on his face and waves. Plants himself next to Victoria.

She shakes hair off her face. "What? Like he didn't see me come in? Like there's anything he doesn't know?"

Side by side on Cole's rock. They could be lovers having a quarrel. They could be putting together a grocery list.

"Hey," she says. "I've been meaning to ask. Who won the World Cup?"

Days when he was just a man doing his job. "It's been delayed. When this is over, it's Finland against Egypt for all the marbles."

"Tough choice. And which side will you be on?"

He squints at her. "The good guys."

St. Martin retrieves his practice throws. Rubs each coin between thumb and forefinger to erase the film of dust. Cole holds six quarters in his right hand. An ace up his sleeve.

"Hang on," St. Martin says. He pulls the eye drops from his pants pocket. Squeezes some in. Blinks away tears. "Southern California," he says. "You can have it." He offers the bottle to Cole.

"No thanks."

Inside the refreshment stand, not thirty feet away, Cole's computer runs test number two. There is an exhilarating sense of free fall. A man who can live without sleep is a man who can do anything.

St. Martin leans into the line they've drawn on the ground. Balances the coin on his thumb, cocked and ready.

"Why are you badgering her?"

The detective swings his arm. The quarter spins in the air, bounces off a tuft of grass and rolls a foot away from the wall. "We had a chat. She's a lovely young woman."

"You're squeezing her."

"She misunderstood."

Cole throws from more of a squat, a hunkered-down place. His coin flips high, catches the sun before landing flat, closer than St. Martin's. "Don't get her involved."

"She got herself involved." St. Martin tosses his second coin almost off-handedly. He doesn't even watch it swirl and land inches from the wall.

Cole fixes his eyes on the target and throws. He knows it is a winner as soon as he lets it go, but he watches anyway, follows its even flip and spin until it lands tucked against the wall. "I win."

"Don't be so sure."

Cole walks up to collect the coins. Puts them in his pocket. "More?"

St. Martin shakes his head. "Not today." He looks around the expanse of Winnetka. "There's a good living to be made in chip design," he says. "Spearhead development of the next celeron."

Cole rubs a toe in the dirt. "I suppose it might be, for some people."

The detective starts to speak, then doesn't. He ambles away, into the beginnings of a spectacular sunset. Purple and gold. Smog's contribution to beauty.

SCREEN EIGHT

Storm clouds dominate a late afternoon sky. The camera holds on the gunfighter, in the saddle, ready to ride. Horse impatient beneath her. The boy holding her with his words, with the pull he exerts, the question hovering in the air between them with the odor of sulfur.

"I gotta be going on," she says. Six-gun strapped to her side, barrel still warm.

The camera pulls back enough to reveal the child, tousled blond hair, soiled work shirt, suspenders – standing on the wood plank sidewalk in front of the saloon where three dead bodies lay. He wears a belt as a holster, into which he's stuck the barrel of his wooden toy gun. "Why?"

Her face weary. Aged beyond her years. "A person's gotta be what she is." Her road-worn buckskin shirt chafes at her neck. The horse moves beneath her, anxious, long white stripe on a dark brown face. "There's no living with a killing. There's no going back. Right or wrong, it's a brand, and the brand sticks."

The boy's eyes plead with her.

She reaches down, rubs the back of his head. "You go on home to your mother and father and grow up to be strong and straight."

Darkness descends on the afternoon. She pulls the reins, rides toward the hills, the boy calling after her, "Come back," his voice fading into the earth, into the eggplant-colored sky.

Cole keeps a stack of quarters on the kitchen table. Money he has won from St. Martin. He drains the dregs from a coffee cup and places the mug in the sink. Saturday morning sun floods the motor home. Cole is showered and dressed. His computer packed for travel. The encryption key has passed two tests. He will drive to San Diego in search of desert marigolds. He will keep his computer with him. See what the detective will do.

Still-wet hair makes a damp ring at the neck of Cole's t-shirt. He fishes car keys out of a ceramic dish and heads into the sunshine.

He lay awake all night, determined not to go to Victoria's. A matter of principle. Allow the detective no victory, however small.

His hand is on the car door handle when he hears someone behind him. A man, Armani jacket, t-shirt, jeans. A bottle of Evian locked in his grip. Cole tightens his grip on the computer bag.

"Good morning, friend. I'm looking for Gene Autry." The man is tall and thin, with curly hair in bunches. A long neck and mildly baffled expression, like a giraffe in sunglasses.

Cole stares at him.

The man pulls a business card from a breast pocket.

"Calvin Weller. A&R for A&M Records. Is Gene around?"

Car keys in his hand. Marigolds on his mind. *Is this St. Martin's move.* "I don't know. I haven't seen him."

Weller looks around. "Nice spread you got here. Kind of retro, the whole drive-in thing." He puts a hand out in front of him. "Don't get me wrong. I like it. A good shtick." He sips Evian. Moves toward the refreshment stand. "This where Gene bunks down?"

"No." Cole's arm blocks the way. "That's my office."

Weller nods, backs off. "I understand completely. You're his manager. I have no intention of squeezing –"

"Wait," Cole says.

But Weller has a hand up, a patrolman stopping traffic. "It's okay. Not to worry. Let me assure you –" he lowers his head to peer his green eyes over the tops of his sunglasses – "there's going to be plenty of pie for everyone." A conspiratorial smile. A sip of Evian. "Gene is going to be huge. I don't think he has any idea how huge." Weller touches Cole's elbow and then they are both in motion. "Walk with me. I have trouble standing still.

"There's very little new territory left. Everyone understands this. The trick is to dig into the past, find a way to present a thing. Gene has done that. It's brilliant. He's totally authentic."

Weller walks briskly. Cole has to concentrate in order to stay with him. He blinks his eyes several times. Weller doesn't waver. Cole casts a wary eye toward the detective, who backs away from the surveyor's glass, then leans in again. Cole can't resist the opportunity. He stays close. Conspiratorial.

"Look at the careers that have been resurrected, that no one would expect. Tony Bennett. Louis Prima. You could start and stop right there. They've caught the imagination of young people by going back to something these kids never knew. There's an integrity the kids recognize, a kind of cool they identify with. A ruggedness in the face of despair. Do I wax too philosophical? You've got thousands of kids swing dancing to music that was written before their *parents* were born. But," Weller says, pausing for a moment in his forward motion, "no one has successfully done the cowboy thing. Too macho. Too much swagger. That's the beauty of Gene. There's a vulnerability. Not an ironic bone in his body."

Not a bone in his body, Cole thinks.

"These kids are wary of kitsch. They're surrounded by it. But Gene's the real thing." Weller stops. Grabs Cole's elbow. They have traversed several rows of speaker poles. "So where we headed here? Where is he?"

"I told you," Cole says. "I haven't seen him."

Weller looks puzzled. His long head cocks to one side. "He does live here."

"Far as I know," Cole says. He holds the computer bag prominently before him. "He's not around much during the day."

"He's probably holed up, rehearsing."

"Could be," Cole says. "I know he's worked up some new songs." *Where do these people come from?* It's as if there's a man on a Hollywood street corner selling maps. "Just for the record, I'm not his manager. I'm his friend."

Weller is still for a moment, his attention fixed on Cole. Then, he is in motion, back toward the road, as if Cole no longer exists. "I'll try him tonight. We need to pounce on this." Weller's long strides. He stops abruptly. Hands on hips. Lawrence of Arabia. "This will be a great spot for a video." Back across the plateau, and he's gone.

SCREEN SIX

A long shot. Two riders approach a tall wooden gate. The camera tracks in as they dismount their horses. His a bay mare. Hers dappled. Hats pushed back off foreheads, muscles weary from the saddle. They've ridden for hours through land unclaimed, untended, untamed, to this temporary refuge, this ranch.

She unlatches the gate, and they walk their horses through.

The camera pans a stand of mesquite, a fence – barbed wire tied to wooden posts, rough-hewn, bark still clinging – ground which slopes gently down, away. Occasional patches of green interrupt the brown grass and dust. A house set down in the hollow. A corral where a half-dozen horses canter in circles. A well. A tin windmill set on rickety wooden poles. In the distance, a dozen or so cattle graze for sustenance.

"This is big," he says.

The windmill creaks in a hot breeze.

"This ain't so big," she says. "This used to all be open range." Her legs ache. A pain in her lower back. "The law of the land was that cattle could go anywhere."

They lead their horses by the reins, walk them toward the house. The animals plod forward, too thirsty, too tired to lift their heads. They bump each other. The horses. The humans.

"I grew up on an East Texas grub ranch not much different from this one," she says.

The house an anomaly in all this land. A tin roof. A wood plank porch. A spare wagon wheel leaning against the railing.

A short walk to food. Water.

There is an easy grace to their movement, a comfort in their companionship.

A line of fence posts stretches to the horizon. He catches her eye. A trace of smile.

"Folks say the West was conquered by the railroad," she says. The horse nuzzles her arm. "My daddy says the West was done in by barbed wire."

*

It's Cole's move.

Two tests have told him all he needs to know about the key. He'll run a third. But he knows what it will tell him. It's time. Have a little fun. See what he's worth.

What he'd give to watch Warren sweat.

He calls Berea, talks to Bo from a pay phone. His friend's voice reminds him there are people with houses, back yards, daughters. He wonders how his own voice sounds.

"No check yet, Cole."

"There won't be. That part's over."

A pause on the line.

"You okay out there?"

"I think so. I need a favor. I want to start a rumor about a key for sale. I want it to spread. Every contact you have. Anywhere they're willing to send it."

"That sounds like a bad idea, Cole."

"You're just passing along something you heard. Please."

He tends his San Diego marigolds on a Saturday morning. Checks for buds while the final test runs inside.

OneZero. Code Blue. The Hagen Group. Who to contact. How to word it. His connections at OneZero stretch back the farthest. Code Blue appealing because it's Z-Tech's arch-rival. But Cole is liking the idea of The Hagen Group. Young. Small. An operation that reminds Cole of Z-Tech's early days.

He pushes through the screen door to check the test status. The old Cole would have sat glued to the monitor. Instead, he has puttered in the garden.

Numbers flash past, a blur. There is an inevitability, a sense of wheels set in motion. There is impatience, an eagerness to see it complete.

Complete.

It is as if the word has popped from his head and emerged on the computer screen. It is as if today were any other day, a sunny smoggy September in southern California.

A deep flush of satisfaction.

Cole opens an e-mail window to Art Hagen.

Art.
Wondered if you'd have any interest in a 238-character
encryption key if one should become available.
Let me know.
-- Cole Newton

A simple mouse click. *Send now.*

Sunday morning. Somewhere in the world, people are going
to church. Cole digs his hands into dusty earth. Kneels on the
ground, feet tucked under him, the sleeves of his sweatshirt
pushed up his forearms. It is early enough that the sun
approaches the land at an extreme angle. Cole clears stones from
a path, scatters cedar mulch and sings.

Who cares about the clouds when we're together
just sing a song that tells of sunny weather

Winding cedar paths, yucca and ocotillo growing in areas
sprinkled with small stones. The refreshment stand restored, the
garden finished. Cole tries not to think about what comes next.

"You expect me to believe you've bonded with the earth while
I've been gone?"

Cole looks up in the direction of the voice, into the sun. A
silhouette. An apparition. "Any sane person would be in bed at
this hour."

The figure steps toward him, away from the sun's direct
backlight, and he can make out the features of Joanna's face, one
side of her mouth curled into a wry smile.

"Hey," she says. "Did you miss me?"

Cole stands. Brushes dirt off his jeans. "Miss you? No time to
miss you. I can barely get a moment's peace."

She moves toward him, tentative. He steps out of the garden
to meet her. They embrace, something inside him calm for the
first time in weeks.

"Welcome home."

They stand side-by-side, arms around shoulders, facing the
garden. Joanna's arm all bone.

"I like what you've done with the place. You make curtains for
the Winnebago yet?"

"Waiting for you to pick out fabric." Scrapes his sneaker in the
dirt. "How was the trip?"

She waves a hand in the air. Shakes her head. "Anything exciting happen while I was gone?"

It feels as if the whole world has changed. "I got a few things to tell you about." A reflection in the distance catches Cole's eye, he flinches his head away from it. "I'm sorry it didn't work."

Joanna shrugs. Her eyes have dark lines underneath. Her skin is pale. "We'll talk," she says. "It's early. Think I'll get some sleep."

Again, a reflection catches Cole's eye. Sunlight gleaming off something in the distance. He looks in the direction of Winnetka Boulevard. "You bring anyone with you?"

Joanna turns to follow his gaze.

A line of vehicles – cars and pickup trucks, boxes tied to roofs, chairs piled into truck beds – stretches as far as they can see.

The line leader, a weathered red pickup, turns into the driveway. The other vehicles slither in behind it.

"Fuck." Cole and Joanna, attached at the shoulder, a team, walk toward the fence break to investigate.

Cars and trucks – tiny old Hondas, Toyotas, Volkswagens – line the drive-in rows. People pile out. Folding tables emerge. Winnetka transformed. Cole finds it increasingly difficult to trust his eyes.

They approach the woman who has emerged from the red pickup that led the caravan.

"What is this?" Joanna's voice explodes.

The woman pulls wooden crates from the bed of her truck. Gray t-shirt over a washboard stomach. Muscles ripple in her forearms. She sizes them up. Smiles. "Flea market."

Cole and Joanna look at one another. At the woman.

"Opening day," the woman says. Crates filled with ceramics – mugs, bowls, candle holders. A few people have stopped to watch the interaction. Most continue unloading boxes from truck beds, back seats, roof racks.

"This is a problem," Cole says.

The woman lifts boxes from the truck, sets them on the ground. Cars continue to stream in. Four driving lanes filled.

"We sort of live here," Joanna says.

The woman pauses. A look at Cole. A long look at Joanna. "Interesting." An engine backfires. A car radio plays Indigo Girls. "I guess we'll be neighbors." She reaches into the truck bed for the last crate. It says Valencia oranges on the side. "Every year, first Sunday of the month, October to May," she says. "We've got a permit."

Winnetka a hotbed of activity. Joanna turns to Cole. "I can't deal. I need sleep."

Sun warms the air. Sky a clear blue. "We'll try not to set up too close," the woman says. "But I can't promise anything." A table of religious icons – the virgin Mary, porcelain Jesus with his heart in his hands – goes up beside them.

Joanna heads for the motor home.

The woman unwraps pottery, places it on a folding table.

Cole finds he needs to say something before he walks away. But his heart's not in it. "Don't fuck with the garden, okay?"

He falls into stride beside Joanna. "That woman has an attitude problem."

"No, she has a permit."

They walk around crates of record albums, a man making a magic-marker sign. Cole squints against the sun. "She was flirting with you."

"Was *not*."

SCREEN FOUR

A wide shot, three riders move across a valley floor. Distant hills dotted with vibrant evergreens, bald spots of blue-gray stone. A handful of bison graze in the dried grass, golden yellow, which looks as if it could stretch forever. A few puffy clouds, pure white, dangle in boundless blue. The camera tracks closer, covering ground as slowly as the riders, horses glowing with perspiration, the exertion of a long journey, rib bones beginning to show through skin. Their heads droop, eyes on the ground in front of them, hooves hasten westward.

Duke, Rock, Kirk. Faces lined by sun and wind. Eyes locked in permanent squint, as if the horizon were all that mattered.

They ride single file, sway gently in saddles, sores long since turned to callous. Air fresh with pine, water not far away.

"We must be into Montana by now." Rock, reins held loosely in his hand, body well back in the saddle.

Duke, hands on pommel, two days' growth of salt-and-pepper whiskers adding texture to his face. "I reckon we're a hundred miles from the nearest settlers."

The land keeps opening up before them. Out here, it is as if there were no such thing as a fence. A town. An impediment. The camera watches them from behind. Bedrolls strapped to saddles. Three riders. Staying a step ahead of civilization.

Rock's voice rings out. A chuckle. "Guess we're okay to stop for a while, then."

The day has turned overcast. Actual clouds gathered.

Joanna sits on the steel railroad track, tossing pebbles at a creosote bush. Cole beside her. The flea market crew gone, every trace removed. All that lingers is a feeling in the air, inside Cole, inside Joanna.

She tosses a stone. "It's not ours anymore."

Forearms on his knees. He wonders where the clouds came from. "You wouldn't believe it," he says. "It's like a parade."

"Flea market," she says. She has a handful of small stones. She throws methodically. "You'd think they could find somewhere else." Her arm moves forward, back. "Who would want to come out here?"

"You'd be amazed."

Smog and clouds make an ugly combination – dingy and grim.

She wears a thick cotton pullover the color of the soil. "Think we could bribe them away? Threaten them?"

A half-hearted smile.

In the distance, the canned music of an ice cream truck. It makes him think of root beer-flavored Italian ice. "Any luck?" he asks.

She pauses, left arm stalled at the top of her throwing arc. "Nope." Resumes her throws. "Zero."

"Sorry." There's a rustling sound each time a stone lands in the bush. The stones the color of the day – gray, brown.

"It was probably a dumb idea." She throws.

Cole starts to tell her about Anthony's visit, then stops. Although the sky looks dark enough to rain, he knows it's an illusion. When it comes, it will come hard and sudden.

"A lot has changed," he says.

She squints. "I like the garden."

"There's a detective here. He's kind of following me." The knot in Cole's neck throbs gently. "A couple days ago I finished the key."

She tosses stones into the bush.

He stares straight ahead.

"All hell's going to break loose," she says.

"Not necessarily."

She looks at him, an expression that says, *get real.*

"What's next, then?"

He smiles. "We could coach a soccer team," he says. "We'll find a field we like and volunteer."

"I don't think it works that way," she says.

"We could sell coffee and muffins. During flea market. Generate some income, now that the trust fund's cut off."

She gives him the look.

"We'll review our options."

"Great. Shoot it out with the lawman, or turn tail and run."

"You're cheery."

"It's shitty news to come home to," she says. "I don't like being boxed in."

"Well," he says. "What's your idea?"

She grins, caught. Raises her eyebrows.

"We need an idea," he says. "I may be a fugitive in two states."

She flashes her old smile. "We won't go to those states."

"Where will we go?"

236

She thinks a minute.

"Bolivia."

"Bolivia?"

"That's right. Bolivia."

"Bolivia doesn't exist."

"Does too. In South America. Or Central."

"Nope. It's called something else now."

"Well, whatever it's called, that's where we'll go."

"Why there?"

"Why not? It's warm, it's unfamiliar, and they've probably never heard of the Internet."

"Jo, it's the twenty-first century. Everyone's heard of the Internet."

"Not in Bolivia."

A rumbling grows at their feet. Cole thinks it is an earthquake, but then he catches Joanna's eye looking down the track.

"How about that," she says.

A freight train motors toward them. Four rust-colored boxcars and a coal-black engine.

They stand, move back a few steps. The blast of a horn. Joanna looks at Cole. Cole at Joanna. A gleam in his eye. The power of pure motion. Steel speed shakes the ground, the beat of it in their bodies. Rattling their teeth. The cars press toward them, headed vaguely east. Iron handles where people pull themselves up. They could leave it all behind again, ride the cool metal floor of a boxcar and watch the country roll past. Commit themselves to movement. Full force. Thunder. Around them. Inside them. They can touch it. Breathe it in. Cole closes his eyes, lets it wash over him.

The tracks hum as the train shrinks into the distance.

"Let's walk," he says. "There's something I need to tell you."

"There's more?" Joanna's ears ring.

They cross the undulating rows. The afternoon is gray, and perfectly still.

"Let me guess. I've got a rare form of cancer and I've got two months to live."

A bird calls. Shrill. Insistent.

"Anthony was here."

"*Where?*"

"Here."

"What do you mean, here?"

"Here." Cole points at the ground.

"When. How?"

"A few days ago. By the time I was sure it was him, he was gone."

"Explain." She's tired, as if a train has tunneled through her.

"It was late. I was trying to sleep. There was a knock. I thought it might have been the detective. He stood in the shadow of the Winnebago. I couldn't get him to stay."

"How did he look? What did he say?"

"He wanted to know if you were here. I told him you were in Seattle looking for him. He said he'd just come from there."

"*Shit.*"

"He also said he'd be back."

She swallows. Her mouth dry. Somehow they've arrived at her sculpture. Seeing it is a shock to her. Its garish angles, rough construction a surprise. It looks like a work created and abandoned years ago. She feels a drop on her cheek and wonders if she is crying. Then one on her forehead. Her arm.

"It's raining," she says.

They stand side by side, half turned to each other. The rain begins slowly, gradually. Drops thick enough to see, making moist circles in the dust around them.

Cole looks at the sky. A raindrop lands on his nose.

They walk toward the Winnebago. The rain picks up, dotting their clothes, the ground. She has the feeling it will rain for days. The sense that, when they emerge, it will be to a different world.

"I'm scared, Max." Joanna sips strong coffee, smokes her third cigarette of the morning in the cramped confines of Max's Airstream. Rain drums on the metal roof. An ancient porcelain-lined saucepan catches drips where a window leaks. Max sits opposite Joanna at the small kitchen table, slouched in his chair.

King lies on the bed, staring out the window as if he's never seen rain. With the windows closed against the weather, the small living space reeks of dog.

"We're going to lose Winnetka."

"Why?"

"I don't know what I was expecting when I got back." She flicks ash into a glass dish, watches the cigarette burn. "Cole says there's been a parade of people – and now a flea market. And Emily's gone and I'm glad, and I can't bear to look at that sculpture – it looks like some high school art project gone wrong." She drags on her cigarette, swallows the smoke. "I don't know."

Max turns his coffee cup in his hands. King barks at the rain.

"I mean, I've done what I can. Anthony wants to find me, he can find me. There's nothing else I can do."

The wind rattles the sides of the trailer.

"That's bullshit," Max says. A sour expression. Soft folds of skin landing in jowls. "You made a half-hearted effort so you could feel good about yourself."

Raindrops like bullets on the roof. King raises his snout and barks.

"King, shut up," Max spits. "Have a cookie." Pulls a dog biscuit from a Maxwell House coffee can on the shelf beside him, throws it at the animal.

Joanna's face feels hot. She looks at her coffee. At King.

A steady stream of water runs off the corner of the roof.

King chews at his cookie, held in his front paws, propped on the small window sill. His breath fogs the glass.

Joanna smokes. Her eyes small. "What should I do?"

"Oh, hell," Max says. "I hate advice. Giving and getting." He adjusts the knit cap on his head. "See if he did this thing and face up to it, the both of you, one way or another." He waves a hand, as if swatting a fly. "The rest – the hand-wringing, that cockamamie sculpture – is bullshit."

Joanna feels stung. Overwhelmed by the close space, the odor of moist dog.

"I like you, Jo, but you're a liar if you say you care about anyone more than yourself." Max's lips tight.

She watches her cigarette burn down to a stub in her fingers. Crushes it out in the dish. "You mean that?"

"Maybe I do." His chair creaks under him. "What do I know. Maybe I'm just mad 'cause you can't fix it all."

She has never before noticed the volume of skin on Max's face – folds deep under his eyes, his sagging cheeks. The air of an old bulldog.

"You don't look so good," she tells him. "You look worn out."

"I am worn out," he says.

King attempts a muffled bark. Max hurls a rawhide bone, which hits him in the side.

"The boy's not doing well," he says. "Spends the night in a plastic tent."

"I'm sorry."

"Yeah."

"What happened?"

Max shakes his head. "Nothing. He just gets weaker, more vulnerable. Used to be he couldn't eat butter, now it can't even be on the table. They've had furniture recovered, replaced. They have the house cleaned professionally, but he still can't breathe right for the dust. We keep hoping he'll get stronger, develop some resistance."

The light in the trailer is dim. Neither of them has bothered to turn on a lamp.

"Anything I can do?"

"Got a miracle up your sleeve?"

Joanna stares into her empty cup. Listens to the rain. King barks out the window.

"King," Max says. "Enough."

Cole is enveloped in the sound of rain. Cocooned in the refreshment stand, he sits cross-legged on the floor while water washes away dust outside. Peppers the roof. A modern-day Noah, he gathers his forces around him, two by two. Two sixteen-ounce Cokes (empty). Two Yodels. Two snack-size bags of barbecue potato chips. Two watermelon-flavored fruit roll-ups. Two messages on his computer screen, one incoming, one outgoing.

Cole –

I'm interested.

Let's talk details over lunch. I'll be in LA next week. Name the day.

– Art

Then,

Art –

How's Tuesday, 1:00. El Tepeyac, on Figueroa.

– Cole

What's the harm in a lunch. Discuss a hypothetical situation. Determine a dollar value.

He sends the message. He sips root beer from a plastic cup. Now that the soda fountain is fixed, he is thinking of tackling the ice machine. He shuts down the computer, sets it on the counter.

Wind blows rain against the walls. There's a wet spot on the linoleum, just inside the screen door. Cole refuses to close the storm door. He likes the sense that he is nestled safely in the midst of a tempest.

He knows St. Martin is out there, but he doesn't think about St. Martin. He thinks about Gene, about how a holograph might fare in the rain – does he seek shelter, would his transmission be interrupted, might he even suffer permanent damage. Or is he a new kind of being, immune from the elements. Impervious to trouble.

"Mighty pretty country," Gene says. He sits astride his piebald horse, reins in hand. He and Joanna look out across the Santa Susana foothills in the pale gray light of dusk. Joanna rides a silver mare, a hand taller than Smiley. Her hat, pulled low on her forehead, hides her eyes. They have ridden out past the borders of Winnetka, found a path into the foothills. Joanna has packed a picnic supper, cold fried chicken and tortilla chips and grapes, tucked into Gene's saddlebags, with a red-and-white checked tablecloth she bought for a dollar in Cheyenne.

"We could just keep riding," she says. "Not come back." Her horse shifts beneath her. Paws the ground. She is already sore from the saddle.

"Never works," Gene says. He looks fragile in the dusk.

"I'm beginning to get that," she says. "But I like it, the feeling you could go forever."

A half-moon hangs on the sky, as if left there from the night before.

"All we wanted was a chance to start over."

"Seems to me you got it. As clean as anyone."

They look out at hills dotted with scrub, with live oak and juniper and the occasional ocotillo, plants she could not have identified three months ago.

"Anthony will come back," she says. "What am I going to do?"

"I expect you may have to decide where you stand. What you can live with."

They goad the horses forward, side by side, a slow walk.

"We're all assuming he did this," she says. "Could be he didn't. Could be it's all my imagination."

"Could be," he says.

She sways in the saddle, yields to the rhythm of the horse.

"I used to take him to the movies a lot. We'd nosh popcorn and laugh together at the scary parts. He was almost never afraid – even when he was little, he could distance himself, remember it wasn't real."

In the moments after sunset, Gene becomes vibrant, as if he's captured the light so he might be projected on the world.

"I was wrong," she says. "I tried to stay out of it. To avoid knowing."

"It's understandable," Gene says. He brightens the path around them, like a flashlight, a human firefly. "The movies were easy. I had a set of rules—"

Joanna interjects. "Never shoot first, hit a smaller man, or take unfair advantage."

He laughs. "That's right. And everything worked as long as those weren't broken."

"Here, it's harder."

"Yeah. I'm still puzzlin' on that."

They climb a small rise. Her feet bounce in the stirrups. "You don't ever struggle with how you are?"

"Well," he says. "Sometimes. But I figure we're all broken one way or another. That's what connects us."

"And what do you do with that?"

"Hope that brokenness isn't where it ends."

A sky graphite blue under a bright moon. There will be a full complement of stars. "Hungry?" she asks.

"I could eat something."

Since the rain stopped, the air has been miraculously clear. Joanna gathers all her grit.

They turn the horses back toward Winnetka. They will ride inside the border and find a space to spread their picnic, Gene lighting the way.

SCREEN SEVEN

Two men in corduroy blazers, v-neck sweaters and open-collar Oxford shirts. Comfortable in their mock-movie theater set: royal blue backdrop, marquee lights, five rows of lavender seats. Plants tucked subtly into background sconces. The camera begins behind them, their figures looming in the distance, then sweeps around to discover them, Roger and Gene, in the front row, a seat apart.

"Cole Newton and his friend Joanna are starting over in an abandoned drive-in movie theater in southern California. They've each run away from their lives, careened across the country in a Winnebago stuffed with snack foods in the belief that they can escape what haunts them." Roger speaks with raised eyebrows. He leans toward the camera, punctuates his words with his hands. "Cole has stolen an Internet encryption system from his employer, though he'd say that because he created it, it belongs to him. Joanna suspects her runaway 16-year-old son of terrorist acts and can't stand still in the face of her own powerlessness."

Roger's small eyes gleam behind thick glasses. Short silver hair, owl's chin. On a movie screen behind him, Cole and Joanna move west. "Skilled as they are at avoidance and self-centeredness, hard as they try to outrun their troubles, trouble inevitably finds them. Their frontier hideout is challenged from all sides, resulting in the showdown that only they manage not to see coming."

The shot widens to include Roger's smiling, holographic cohort. "Joining me tonight is Gene Autry, the legendary king of the singing cowboys. Welcome, Gene."

"Thanks, Roger." Gene's chair has been draped in canvas to lend his image more depth and substance. "I'm pleased as punch to be here." He is noticeably stiff in unfamiliar clothing. He gestures back toward the frozen faces of his friends. "But you're being a little hard on them."

A bemused grin. "I'm not even reviewing yet. I'm summarizing. And I think it's fair to say they've each made some questionable choices."

"They're doin' the best they know how."

Roger's brow furrows. He's torn between admiration for his guest and the desire to do his show.

Offstage, Yvon reaches for a mug that isn't there. "Fuck me." He bites his lip. "Didn't anyone tell him dead cowboys should be seen and not heard?" Beside him, the red-haired assistant director opens a bottle, hands him a pill. He gestures at Roger, his finger making a circle in the air. *Move it along.*

Roger's furrows fade. His face reasserts its tolerant smile. "As soon as these two sad sacks reach California, their troubles begin."

"Now wait," Gene says. "That Cole's a smart feller. And Joanna, she's got gumption."

Yvon searches in vain for a coffee cup.

"That's not the question. The question is does it make a good story. Do we care. And that's —"

"I care. *They* sure as shootin' care."

244

Yvon's fingers drum on the tabletop. The AD pats his hand. Bites her nails.

A crash. A door closing. Roger's eyes move toward the sound at the back of the set.

A man, white shirt, thin tie, Ban-Lon slacks, slightly gaunt of cheek, pushes past plants, wanders in behind Roger and Gene, squinting into the marquee lights, a tub of popcorn cradled under his arm.

"Fuck." The vein in Yvon's forehead pulsates.

The red-haired AD calls, "Cut."

"What is this?" Roger looks at Ward, at Gene, at Yvon.

Ward looks at the floor. "I've done it again."

Yvon has moved onto the set. Hyperventilating. The red-haired assistant hurries toward him. Eyes darting between actors and director. A hand on Yvon's back. "Slow, deep breaths," she coos. Behind her, rhododendron. Boston fern. "You are an island of calm."

Ward munches popcorn. "I didn't know you were shooting."

"Is this a joke?" Roger's face red. It's not clear if he's addressing Yvon, Ward or the cosmos.

Gene's face wears a puzzled smile.

Yvon pushes the assistant away. He reaches for the rhododendron pot, pushes the greens aside and drinks. He sputters, spits out mud, water. "*God damn it!* Who on this set is trying to poison me?" He flings the pot to the floor.

The AD stands before him, exasperated. "*What* did you think you were doing?"

The director spits dirt. Vein pulsing wildly. "You told me there'd be coffee in the planter."

"No. I told you we were *adding* planters. I said there'd be coffee in the false back of a front-row seat." She gives no ground. She flips open a hidden compartment on the chair back, removes a steaming travel mug. Holds it out to him. "*Coffee.*"

Director and assistant, toe to toe.

Yvon grabs the mug. "Fine. You deal with this." He stalks off. "She's trying to kill me."

Roger frowns. "Can we do a show here." No one acknowledges him.

Ward's face has a deer-caught-in-the-headlights look. Gene gives him a tentative thumbs up.

The AD puts a hand on Ward's shoulder. "Everybody take ten," she calls. Turns to Roger and Gene. "Deep breaths, kemosabes. I'll be back." She gently leads Ward offstage.

Anthony returns under cover of night. He squats in the dirt in the dark, watchful. Stealthy. A single dim light wafts from the Winnebago. Stars glow overhead. Anthony is jangly from too much caffeine, not enough sleep. He scratches at the back of one hand with the fingers of the other, digs hard until he numbs the itch. No moon. He steadies himself, fingers splayed against the dirt. His mother is inside. He can feel it.

Cole and Joanna sleepless on their beds. Staring at the ceiling.

"So what's with this record deal?" Joanna, hands tucked behind her head, knees up.

Cole shakes his head. His feet stick out off the end of the bed. "He's cryptic about it. I'm not sure how much to believe."

"It's plausible," Joanna says. "It could happen."

"Anything's plausible anymore," Cole says. "I mean, after all."

A knock at the Winnebago door. Joanna there in an instant.

He is as tall as she is. Round shoulders, a thick build, and shaggy black hair give him the look of a bear. A flannel shirt, unbuttoned, t-shirt, jeans.

"Hey, Mom."

Joanna wraps her arms around him, holds him in the doorway. He as much allows the embrace as melts into it.

She pulls away to look at him. Holds him again.

"I've been waiting for you."

Joanna has hold of his elbow. Pulls him inside.

"Hey, Cole." Anthony slouches a little. As if he's trying to tuck his head into his shoulders, as if he could retract his neck.

"Hi. Welcome back." Cole up, at the edge of his bed.

246

"God. I can't believe you." Joanna holds her son's arms, grips at the bicep. "Where have you been?"

"Same place you were, from what I hear."

"Seattle."

He nods. "Seattle."

Joanna runs a hand through her hair. Grips Anthony's bicep with the other. "I can't believe you're here. I gave up." She wants to talk and listen and move and be still, all at once. "How did you find us? Never mind." Looks at her friend, on his bed. "Cole, he's here."

Cole pushes tentatively to his feet. "Want some lemonade? Tea?"

A stray black curl droops over one eye. "Tea," Anthony says. "Mom, you're hurting my arm."

Joanna loosens her grip. She bounces on the balls of her feet.

Cole opens the cabinet door. "Peppermint. Earl Grey. Irish breakfast." He turns on the heat under the kettle.

"Peppermint, please." Anthony digs his hands into his pockets, works them, as if fishing for something.

"Where were you?" Joanna says. "I looked. Three weeks."

"All over," he says. "How did you know?"

"A hunch." She flushes at the half-truth, not ready to ask the hard questions. He notices her blush and looks at the floor.

"Tea, Jo?" Cole at the stove.

"Yeah. Thanks. Whatever."

He puts tea bags in two mugs. Kitchen sounds make conversation easier.

"So where were you?"

Although Anthony dwarfs her physically, there is an authority to her bearing, acknowledged in his, that any careful observer would note. Mother and son.

"Around," he says. "Where did you look?"

She lists the names. She wants to fill the air with words. Create a cushion of talk. "Fremont. Belltown. Queen Anne." Her son has grown since she last saw him. He seems categorically older. But still – always – a mother, she sees the child as well. Every moment of him alive in his face his body. He is the baby in her arms and the teen cooking breakfast and this bear before her.

"I was in Fremont. The houseboats."

She slaps her hands together. "I knew it," she says. "Pike Market?"

The kettle hisses.

He shakes his head. "Thought about it. Too crowded." He offers a name to her. "Port Hadlock, on the peninsula."

"Never heard of it."

His face relaxes into a smile. "I loved it. I could have stayed forever. There was a restaurant, tucked in among boatwrights. Tried to talk my way in as a cook."

"Good idea," Joanna says. "You could do it."

"I know. I told the guy."

The kettle whistles. Cole turns off the burner. Pours steaming water into two mugs.

"I felt at home there," Anthony says. "The whole area. This café in Fremont. The view from Gasworks Park."

"What made you leave?"

Anthony shrugs. His words half question. "Needed to find you."

Cole sets mugs on the table. Pulls on jeans. "It's a nice night," he says. "Think I'll go for a walk." He slips out the door. Tea steams on the table.

The space smaller with just the two of them. Crowded with history.

"Anthony, I need to know something." Her stomach tightens and she hears her own words as if from inside a tunnel.

The trailer is silent. Just blood beating in her ears. And he looks at her and then at the floor and a rock lands in her stomach to stay, and nothing will ever be fully right again.

"Why? How?" Stone striking stone.

Still looking at the floor. A mop of black hair. "I did the first, not the second. I never meant to hurt anyone."

There is a scream inside her, a prolonged animal moan. How did they get here. What road led to this Winnebago, this wave of words. The sound of her son's voice would carry her to where Anthony is twelve nine six, to a swing set or a suburban street, delivering newspapers in the rain. She could lose herself there, but she forces herself to focus. To stay with the one thing she is sure of. "You need help."

"I'm not proud of what I did." Anthony pulls his hands from his pockets. Scratches. "But I did it and it's done and I'm not going to jail."

"You might not have to. They're going to live. We can talk to people."

Joanna paces in small circles. Anthony sips tea. The smell of peppermint.

"No, Mom," he says. "It's too late."

"Don't say that," she says.

News images flash in her mind. The Bellevue bombing. Bodies strapped to stretchers. Blood-stained sheets in the harsh light of television cameras. She tells herself that Anthony didn't do this one, that those *he* hurt will recover.

Anthony hunched in the Winnebago. Scratching the back of his hand. The skin cracked at the knuckles. Raw.

"What happened?"

"Some kind of rash. Comes and goes."

"You need to see a doctor. Get something for it."

"Right, mom."

He sips tea.

Water drips in the faucet.

"I don't know what happened. I was angry."

"With me?"

"With everything. With being outside."

"You need help."

"I've had help."

"Maybe it wasn't the right kind. You can't keep running."

"Why not?"

He scratches. Traces of blood on his knuckles. A raw band of skin on a wrist which holds a faded friendship bracelet, red, yellow, white thread. "For the first time in a long time, I felt here was a place I could live. But I couldn't."

Joanna hasn't touched her tea. "It bothered you too much?"

"It bothered me that it didn't bother me. That most of the time I could just look at it and say it happened, like it was someone else."

"What about the other times?"

"The other times, I feel like I'm going to drown."

You need help, Anthony. The words on her lips. She swallows them before they come out this time. Gestures at the bracelet. "Your wrist might get better if you took that off."

"Can't," he says. "A gift."

She fingers her mug. "Stay a few days," she says. "Think it over."

Eyes closed, he wags his head side to side.

"This isn't like skipping school."

Anthony scratches. "Right, Mom. Thanks."

A plane flies overhead.

"Where will you go?"

He shrugs. His eyes move around the room. "Not far. I want to figure things out."

"Stay here. We'll figure it out together."

The head wag, eyes open this time.

So many confrontations. The boy never defiant, simply immovable. Joanna feels ancient. Exhausted. "It can't go on like this, Anthony." She closes her eyes. Opens them. "You need help."

Anthony shoves his hands in his pockets, pulls them out again. "I gotta go, Mom. We'll talk."

Joanna grabs at his arm, holds him in the doorway. "No," she says. "I can't do this." Her eyes wet. Vision blurred. Grip tight at his elbow.

"Can't do what?"

"Turn yourself in." Her voice soft. "If you don't, I will."

Body turned toward the door, head turned toward her, Anthony hesitates. His lips start to form words, then stop in a small, straight line. He pushes out into the night.

Crickets.

Cole had thought about going to Burbank. Thought about taking a sleeping bag and camping under the stars. But he had too much nervous energy to sleep, too much curiosity to leave. Whichever way it went, Joanna might need him.

So he wandered along Gene's path, heard a lone guitar, and followed the sound through some low-lying scrub and a stand of live oak. Beyond the trees, in a clearing, the virtual cowboy strummed a holographic guitar and sang. Horse tethered to a tree. Stars twinkling overhead. Cole squatted in the cover of a live oak and listened, Gene's voice peaceful, reassuring, miraculous.

> *Let my journey end*
> *where the willows bend*
> *'neath a blue Winnetka sky.*

SCREEN SEVEN

The Sheriff stands on the front porch, shrouded in night. Her trail coat heavy with dust. A rifle hangs from her hand. She has followed him here, carried the weight of wishing he would leave and knowing he wouldn't. She looks in through the window. Through the chintz curtains. The Kid and the woman on the bed. Sounds of love.

A porch swing groans. She sits, legs crossed, rifle across her lap.

The last time she'd seen him, she'd tried again to get him to listen. The Kid at the café table, that playful grin. She, the Sheriff, poised to go, rifle in hand, already tired.

"You could leave," she'd said. "You could go to Mexico."

He drank whiskey from a small glass. One hand on the table. "They're sure pushing on me to go somewhere."

"Mexico might not be bad for a couple months."

The eyes met hers. The grin. "Depends on who you are."

Now, the Kid's voice, through the bedroom window. "I'm hungry. I'll see what Pete's got in the cooler."

Bed springs creak. Bare feet on wood.

She pushes herself up. She knows the side entrance to the kitchen. She enters with the rifle pointed before her. No one there. He has taken a detour. She sits. Listens. Maybe he decided to leave. Maybe, even now, he is mounting up out back, ready to ride south.

Then she hears his laugh, and the door pushes open, and his voice calls, "Hey Pete," and he crosses the threshold, dressed only in jeans and a holster, and his hairless chest reminds her how young he is, how skinny – all bone and sinew – and he sees her and there's the grin, even as his hand reaches for the gun. And she raises the rifle and pulls the trigger and there's an explosion in his chest and he falls.

In the space where the Kid stood, behind the now-closed door, is a mirror. In the mirror is the Sheriff, or some haggard, crag-faced, impossibly aged version of her. Hollow eyes. Gun raised, pointed now at her reflection. She fires. Shards of glass shoot across the room, envelop her. She looks down at him. On his face, a confused smile. A smile that says, *Why'd you do that?* That says, *I'm just a kid.* She steps over the fallen body, out to the front porch, to the swing, where she will wait silently for dawn.

Los Angeles always looks brightest after a long rain. Clean air, cool breeze, mountains in stark relief against a perfect sky.

Cole and Art Hagen at an outdoor table, a Mexican café on Figueroa. Chips and salsa. Cold beer. Cole has spruced up – a trim and a barber's shave, a shirt with a collar. Hagen wears a sport coat over a polo shirt, and slacks. Thin blond hair. They've driven from the airport, stopped at the County Museum of Art. Strolled the beach in Santa Monica. It's time to talk business.

Hagen turns a water glass in his hand. Beads of condensation sparkle in the sun. "What would you be looking to get from this?"

Cole moves rice and beans around on his plate with a fork. He smiles. "Hypothetically?"

"Sure. Fine."

"A retirement fund."

The waitress sizzles past them, a plate of fajitas smoking in her hands.

"Specifics," says Hagen.

"Let's say half a million."

A tortilla chip held between thumb and forefinger, Hagen cocks his head. Black sunglasses. "If it's everything you say, it would be worth that. But we'd have to overcome certain obstacles."

"What do you mean?"

Hagen crunches the chip. "The non-compete that you're under. The fact that the code is stolen."

Cole's ears burn.

Hagen raises a pre-emptive hand. "In the eyes of the law, at least."

It's a game. An experiment. This is the part – negotiations – where Cole has historically turned things over to the business types. Where he's already off looking for a new problem to solve. "I'm not even saying it exists. We're talking about what it would be worth if it did exist."

Hagen spreads his hands on the table. "Relax. I just want to be sure we're protected."

The waitress skirts their table, registers the gravity and moves on. A slow day. Only three tables occupied. *Fuck it. Commit.*

"Okay. Let's say I did this. Let's say you're interested. The question then is where to start?"

"Obviously, this lunch never happened."

"You and I have never met," Cole says. "Contact through dummy email."

"We'd need files showing the early stages of the work."

"Done."

"We'd create a trail of internal memos. A project history on our end."

"Yes. Good."

"It's a lot of work, Cole. A big risk. Why would I do it?"

A sunny day. A clandestine conversation. It's just like the movies.

"Because you could win. Put yourself on the map." A stucco wall shields them from the road. The buzz of traffic. "If we've never met, how do I get paid?"

Hagen smiles. "Easy. It's called international private banking. We set up an offshore account for you – Tonga, the Cayman Islands. Anonymous. Free from the prying eyes of governments."

Free fall. The exhilaration of not knowing where you'll land. "Sounds like we have a deal."

Hagen crunches a chip. "Slow down. How do I see this program?"

Cole scribbles on a napkin. "Check this URL at three o'clock eastern time tomorrow. Run some transactions."

Hagen pockets the napkin. "I'll be in touch."

Cole approaches the Winnebago. The meeting with Hagen still zinging his brain. Joanna sits on the steps.

"Hey," he calls. "What's going on?" Sits beside her. Heart mind racing.

"Just another quiet night in Winnetka."

The first stars appear in a clear sky.

Cole tries to still himself. Yoga breathing.

A match creates a halo of light. Joanna inhales smoke.

"How you holding up?"

She smokes. "Okay, I guess."

This thing with Hagen could work. If everyone stays cool. "Can you actually go through with it? Turn Anthony in?"

She shakes her head. "But I wish I could. He can't keep running."

"He'll need our help. We can write letters. Talk to people. Set up counseling. That might sway a judge."

Joanna looks out at the darkness. Distant. Just she and Cole and the night sky.

A harmonica plays softly. They look at each other, puzzled. Then, over behind the refreshment stand, footsteps. Voices.

Weller, the record company man, huddles close to Gene, Evian bottle in hand. "Think about it." Weller's voice. "Tony Bennett. Louis Prima."

They pass the building, Gene struggling to keep up. Resplendent in a tall white hat, pale blue shirt with pearl buttons. Harmonica in hand. He glows, vibrant as fresh paint.

"It's there for the taking," Weller tells Gene.

Gene sees Cole and Joanna. Stops and waves. Says to Weller, "Hang on a minute," and walks over to them.

"Quite a show, ain't he?" Gene says.

"He's something," Cole says.

"You having fun?" Joanna asks.

"Surely am." Gene reaches back into Smiley's saddlebag, hands them each a card. "The record company's rented me a little bungalow near the studio. They'd like me close by while we make the record. I'll be going in a few days."

A sadness passes through Cole. Its depth takes him by surprise.

"You okay, son?"

"Yeah. I just didn't expect you'd be leaving."

"It's not forever. Besides, you'll come see me."

"You bet."

"Hey," Weller calls out. "Didn't I tell you?" A wide grin, as if he's given birth to the night.

"That you did," Cole says.

A warm breeze. A sky awash in stars.

Gene nods toward the A&R man. "He's on me to make a music video."

"I could see that," Joanna says. "What do you think?"

"Not my style. A man's got to know his limitations."

A hundred feet away, Weller paces. His impatience palpable.

Gene tips his hat. "I'd best be going. Take care of each other." He waves and moves on, dimples flashing.

"Well," Joanna says. "Who would've thought?"

Cole nods. He could fight Z-Tech in court. Worst case, he could head for Mexico. South America. Anything is possible.

St. Martin has vanished. It is as if the rain has washed him away, without a trace. Two days now, no sign of him in Winnetka, no sign in Burbank. He has packed it in. Quit, or been called off.

"The coast is clear," Victoria told him.

Cole sits on the floor of the refreshment stand, the air already stifling. The linoleum has lost its morning cool. He stares at the monitor, re-reads a message from Hagen.

Cole –
I'm impressed. It may be all you say it is. I'll need another look. And I'll need to think about the other factors. Give me a few days.
– Art

He chews dry roasted peanuts. Sips root beer. The freedom of not being observed. The absence of intrigue. With the detective gone, and Hagen ready to deal, it's beginning to feel like business.

Only Joanna had a different perspective.

"You're nuts," she told him. "You've gone loopy." She sat on the counter in the refreshment stand. Nothing to do now with her days but wait and think. "I'll tell you what it means. It means he's coiled, ready to strike. He's marshaling his forces." She was cynical. Who could blame her?

"You told me you'd walk away," she said. "You promised."

It was true. There was nothing he could say.

Now he shuts down the computer and walks out, the sun already blinding.

Joanna on the steps of the motor home, smoking. T-shirt. Khakis. Gray wraparound sunglasses.

"Hey," she calls. "I'll buy you breakfast."

Seeing her across the drive-in rows, her voice in all this space, makes Winnetka home.

"I ate breakfast."

"Brunch, then."

They walk toward each other, toward the Squareback. She gets there first. Sunlight gleams off the chrome bumpers, the mirrors. There's a note on the windshield, tucked under the wiper. She reads it.

Mom –
Maybe you were right.
Maybe I'm ready.
Can you meet me?
Johnny D's on Ventura, 11 am

She looks up from the note. Urgency in her eyes. "What time is it?"

"Ten forty-five."

She reaches for the door handle.

"Come on," she says. "We've got no time."

SCREEN FIVE

They dive back to the safety of the doorway. Bullets pop around them like fireworks, a Fourth of July finale. The one is gutshot, the other hit in the thigh and wrist. They lie on the stone floor as the shooting stops, the only sound their heaving breath in the heat and dust.

Bolivia.

He props himself on his elbows; winces at the wound in his stomach. "For a minute there, I thought we were in trouble."

She rolls onto her back and smiles. Sunlight through the glass-less window is brilliant on the stucco wall. Light has never seemed so beautiful.

Deep breaths. Sweat on both faces. They grab for gun belts and reload. Pain staggers their breathing. Two pistols each.

They are attending their own wake. A moment of silence in honor of their own legend, their unlikely, across-two-continents ride, while half the Bolivian army climbs into position, lines rooftops and parapets, rifles at the ready. There is no indication that they recognize the futility, where either betrays even an instant of doubt or despair. It is as if they have survived so many unlikely situations that, despite the wounds, despite the dogged pursuit, despite the presence of half the Bolivian army, they cannot conceive their downfall.

She snaps shut the chamber of her last pistol. Then he. A little nod toward one another. A bright rectangle of sunlight on the wall behind them. They push themselves to their feet.

"When we get outside," she says, "when we get to the horses, just remember one thing –"

And he leads the way, her voice a reassuring echo in his ears, through the entry, out into blinding sunshine.

"It's possible they didn't die."
Evening in Winnetka.
They sat side by side – Cole, Joanna, Gene – three bodies straddled the backs of three chairs, three glasses of lemonade on the ground before them, the image of the two gunfighters, Butch and Sundance, frozen on the screen.
Joanna looked at Cole with disdain. "Four hundred Bolivian soldiers," she said.
Gene's expression half-amused, half-thoughtful.
Cole folded his arms across the chair back. "You never actually see them get killed."
"Half the Bolivian army," Joanna said. "They all miss."
The credits rolled. The piano played a nostalgic tune.
"I'm just saying."

An excruciating Tuesday in the San Fernando Valley. Heat shimmers in thick waves off the pavement, distorts everything. Air so smog-choked it hurts to breathe.
Cole parks the Squareback at a meter on Van Nuys Boulevard a block away from Ventura. Joanna pumps in four quarters, the metal handle scalding. A digital display outside the Wells Fargo Bank branch reads 113 degrees.
They walk slowly. The heat discourages movement, unnecessary gestures. Joanna silent. Cole hums a snatch of song – "Don't Fence Me In."
A handful of browsers at the news stand on Ventura and Van Nuys. A boy on a skateboard slides past, using the curb cut-out to gain momentum across the street.
They turn onto Ventura, gain the shade of the bank building. Cole flashes her a smile. "It's gonna be okay, Jo." But a shadow has crossed her face.

"I've got a bad feeling," she says.

Because she's looking farther up the block and she sees police cars double-parked, lights flashing, an ambulance, back doors flung open, a crowd gathered on the sidewalk.

Cole mouths words, but the words get swallowed up in the heat before she can hear them.

She quickens her pace. Cole hastens to stay with her. They are four, then three storefronts away from the diner, from whatever has happened. Her heart pounds – she can feel it in her ears, can taste the blood that moves through her veins, the heat and the smog and the mingled sweat of the crowd. Her knees wobble. She takes Cole's hand. Past a travel agency, where a plastic doll in a grass skirt dances in the window and a garish cardboard sign implores *Do Hawaii for Less.* Blue light spins, reflects off sidewalks walls cars.

A dozen people hover at the diner entrance. Two police officers in blockade stance. A man in a dark suit, jacket on despite the heat. Yellow tape – POLICE LINE DO NOT CROSS – outlines the entrance, blocks the sidewalk. It dangles, loose, hasty. She pushes through it, Cole behind her. Blue light bounces off the diner's plate glass window, flashes of red, the reflection of an orange stripe, the word AMBULANCE.

And then they are through the door and in the diner and three heads turn and one of them is on a man who's speaking to the other two, his voice firm, cadences measured, and he's pointing at something on the floor and it's eerie quiet in here and with the lights bouncing crazy everywhere it's like the juke box is playing on a busy Friday night but there are no customers no sound. And then Joanna's eyes Cole's eyes follow along the man's arm and beyond to where it points, to where a body lies face down and even before she sees the curly black hair and the faded friendship bracelet on his right wrist and even before she knows the extent of the injuries, before she sees his now-silenced face and even before the Federal agent comes over to tell her, she knows that the body is Anthony and that it is dead.

The lights spin around her and for a moment she is back in the bar with the sculptures whose gloved hands reach elegantly for the ceiling, and the hip-hop beat vibrates through the floor where she stands waiting for Emily and everything is new and anything is possible and then a rough hand is pulling at her shoulder, and a voice.

"How did you get in here?"

The face doesn't match the voice – it's a younger face, a thinner face, long and meticulously shaved and under a fringe of closely cropped light hair. The face reminds her of a marathon runner, a track coach. The man is slight, no bigger than she, but he moves her with his arm and she feels it is powerful and it jolts her alert.

"Get them out of here," the voice says, and the men, the other two men – no, one is a woman and they are police officers in pale blue uniforms with sweat stains under their arms, have hold of her, of Cole, and she feels herself moving backward and she says

"That's my son"

and the movement stops, but the hands still have hold of her and the backward motion could resume at any moment and for a second Joanna is out of her head and thinks *Cole, this is about Cole, this is the end of Cole*, and she sees the hands, the police arms holding her friend and thinks *you can't, I need him* and thinks *I told you* and the lights flash blue and red and she thinks about why she needs him and then she remembers it is not Cole being arrested it's the body on the floor that used to be her son and there are tears in her eyes which make the light dance even crazier and she needs to talk to the man.

"That's my son," she says again and she is amazed at how there is no blood because she can smell blood and even taste it mixed with the stale grease in the air and the perspiration and the heat.

The man – blue suit, white shirt, dark tie – is scratching the back of his neck. His face pinched. A siren chirps outside. "Ma'am," he says.

"That's my son," she says, and now she feels Cole's hand on her shoulder, and she realizes the other hands have let her go, have let them both go and the lights bounce off the long mirror over the counter and begin to hurt her head.

And then Cole is beside the body, walking around it, and his face is red and he is crying.

And then she is beside the body and squatting down and
looking into the face that used to be her son's and touching the
back and then she pulls her hand away and brings it to her mouth
and that's when she sees the blood.

"Ma'am," the voice says.

And someone helps her up.

"Get her some water."

And bodies move – two more officers have arrived, and the
man in the suit from out front – and then there is a glass of water
in her one hand and she's leaning on a table with the other, and
Cole is beside her holding her arm and the man is speaking to
her.

"Ma'am," he says through a small mouth. "How did you
know he was –"

"He asked me to meet him here."

And there is the crackle of a police radio and the officers
talking behind her and she hears the words *shooting* and
terminated.

"I'm sorry, ma'am," says the man in the blue suit. "But we
believe your son was responsible for two bombings recently in the
Pacific Northwest." The man removes a wallet from his coat
pocket, flashes identification. "Agent Stephen North. Bureau of
Alcohol, Tobacco and Firearms."

Behind her, an officer bumps into the counter, mutters,
"Shit."

"Would you like to sit down, ma'am. There are some things I
need to tell you."

She shakes her head no, and the tears make the lights dance in
her eyes. Someone hands her a handkerchief but she doesn't
think to use it. "He told me he did the first, but not the second."

"Ma'am, we can talk about that later. There are some things
about this that you need to know."

Her head aches from the quiet, from the smell of the blood on
her hand, from the lights.

"We believe your son provoked us into shooting him," the
agent says, "that he arranged it so that we would find him and
kill him." The agent scratches the back of his neck. "The officers

came in to make the arrest. He drew a gun. Moved toward them. It turned out to be a water pistol."

Two attendants wheel in a stretcher. Move toward the body.

"Not now," the agent calls. "I've got the mother." The squeak of rubber casters on linoleum. "Give me five minutes."

"Are you okay, ma'am?" he asks and she nods and he keeps talking, but right now she's not hearing.

Anthony pushing through the door, unbuttoned flannel shirt, black t-shirt, the thick mop of black curls wet with perspiration. The heat inside would have taken him by surprise, nearly matching the heat outside. The grill cook, wiping his forehead with a white cloth, Anthony knowing the heat of that work, empathizing. Straddling a stool, seeing his face in the long mirror, preparing the words – *I'm ready, Mom.* Pushing hair out of his eyes. *What do we do.*

"He sent us a letter, with a sort of clue. We believe he wanted to lead us to him."

Joanna looks at the blood, already dry, on the back of her hand.

"A groundskeeper at the golf course where the first bombing took place. He remembered – he described – a vagrant teenage boy he'd found sleeping in the caddy shack early one morning. ATM usage in Klamath, in Seattle, at the Greyhound station, in L.A. A name to connect with a face. It wasn't difficult."

She nods to acknowledge what the agent is telling her. "A letter?"

"Words clipped from magazines. An anonymous confession." She must look puzzled because the agent says, "It's not as unusual as you might think. There were fingerprints."

She is aware of tears on her cheeks. She is hungry for potato chips and a beer. She wishes that someone would turn the body over, so that Anthony's face wouldn't be pressed against the linoleum, but she lacks the energy to ask.

He wouldn't have noticed the door opening. Maybe already sipping a glass of ice water. Maybe thinking about leaving – escape to someplace air-conditioned – except that she was meeting him here. He would have heard his name called behind him in a voice not hers, not Cole's. Puzzled and relieved and

alarmed – how to undo it, how to say *I've changed my mind* –
then spinning on the stool, away from the door, away from the
voice, and seeing the faces the uniforms reflected in the mirror
and reaching inside his shirt his belt and imagining himself a
doomed outlaw hero, seeing himself move gracefully in slow
motion, the gun drawn, the pop of bullets that sting, that spin
him around still further, then the silence, the awful endless
silence as he feels himself fall.

One of the officers calls out and the agent says excuse me a
moment and moves away and then the body is in Joanna's vision
and it looks like it couldn't possibly be Anthony. And then Cole's
hand is on her shoulder and she realizes that some part of her has
been expecting this – not the blood, maybe, but the body – that
there is an inevitability here that makes her feel less devastated
than overcome.

And she looks at him, at Cole, and the lights dance around
him and again for a moment in her head it is Cole they are after,
Cole they are taking away or taking down.

The diner's air conditioner must have broken. The heat is
oppressive. Cole keeps his hand on her shoulder. The officers and
the agent talk behind them, and she's looking into his eyes,
through tears, a strange expression on her face. And he feels cold
inside, and he too is crying and he can't stop, and he wonders
how they ever let things get this far, and he wonders if the air
conditioner, when it's working, moves the smell of stale grease
out of the diner. And then Joanna's cold hand is on his chest.

"It should have been you," she says.

SCREEN SIX

Main Street, Hadleyville. Deserted. Just a broad swath of dust,
hitching posts on either side. A row of buildings gone eerily
silent. A clock ticks.

CUT TO

Train tracks stretch to the horizon. A prairie that seems to extend forever. Beside the rails, three brothers await the arrival of the fourth. The killer. The ticking grows louder.

CUT TO

A grandfather clock, ornate hands, roman numerals on a gilded face. The camera pans in, the minute hand advances: high noon.

CUT TO

The marshal, tin star pinned to his chest, duty weighing heavy on his heart, determination a rock in his belly, sits in his office, beads of sweat on his temple, his cheekbone. Face lined with disgust – with those who would not stay, with himself, who could not leave. Takes paper and pen, writes the words "Last Will and Testament."

The marshal scribbles quickly. Thoughts of his bride, the hurt on her face, the angry words between them.

He checks the chambers of his gun. His hands shake.

A train whistle pierces the air.

A series of faces – the bride, the brothers, the marshal – react.

The train tracks. A puff of smoke distant on the horizon.

The marshal folds his will into an envelope, checks his gun one last time, and pulls open the door.

CUT TO

A steam engine at the depot. The killer joins his brothers.

CUT TO

The marshal alone in the deserted street. Church bells toll the hour. The camera pulls back until the figure is small, until the buildings and the empty street dominate the shot. And then the marshal slowly walks toward the depot.

A close-up of his face, etched with apprehension, with the determination that will not let him stop. A bruise high on his cheekbone. The camera cuts back and forth, from the marshal to the brothers, as they close in on each other, until the brothers reach town.

The marshal pauses in the shadow of the General Store, lets them walk past him, to give him some slight advantage. Then he calls out the name.

He shoots one in the street, then ducks out of sight into a barn. Climbs to the loft. The opening where the bales are loaded. He shoots the second brother from there. Then slips away. Hugs walls, shadows. Fear gone from his eyes, replaced by the cold look of a hunter.

The bride has heard the gunshot and left the train. Runs toward town. Into his office. Grabs a gun. She shoots the third brother – saves the marshal, really, from a danger he didn't see. They had him cornered in the saddle shop. She sees it through the window and shoots this one, the last brother, in the back.

But the killer sees her, and then has her. A hostage. He calls to the marshal. "Come on out."

"I'll come. Let her go."

And he does come out, into the dust of Main Street. And as the killer watches and waits, the bride squirms free and the marshal shoots his nemesis dead. For a moment, all is still. His expression has not softened. The townspeople trickle onto the street. The marshal looks into each face. Then he helps his bride into their wagon, and just before he climbs in beside her to leave for their new life, he tears the star from his vest and throws it in the dirt.

Whether or not you believe in magic, in the possibility of transformation, of life growing from parched starved land, the desert would have you believe in miracles. Would speak softly that, despite all evidence to the contrary, there is life here.

He has put Joanna to bed. Has thought about driving to Burbank. Has worn erratic lines in the dust around the Winnebago.

Hours with the police. Questions. Forms. The logistics of death. The formal identification of the body. Joanna distant through it all. Vacant. Cole walked them through what needed to be done. *Birthplace. Social Security Number.* His hand on her arm. "Come on, Jo. They need to know this stuff." Moving toward the moment when he could take her home. She would not make arrangements for the body. *Do you know of a funeral home you'd like to use.* Stone silence. *Would you like us to recommend one?* She shook her head. She left the room.

They drove north in silence. Black vinyl interior of the Squareback stifling. Cole impatient with freeway traffic – there should be a bereavement lane. Joanna sat eyes closed head back the entire ride. Cole wondered if she were asleep, or cocooning. Either way, he thought. It was late afternoon when they pulled into Winnetka. Cole parked the car. No air movement, despite open windows.

"Jo. We're home."

Eyes closed. Body still. "I know."

Fifty yards away, the Winnebago baked in the afternoon sun.

"You want me to help you in?" Cole thought about Mallo Cups and sixteen ounce bottles of Coca-Cola, the rush of road under their wheels, the simple joy of searching supermarket aisles for snack foods.

"I want to sit here a while."

He sat, too. Hands on the steering wheel. He closed his eyes and saw blue lights flash inside his lids. The body sapphired, unreal. He opened his eyes. Got out of the car. Closed the door gently behind him. He walked around behind the Winnebago, to where Joanna couldn't see him. Leaned his back against it. He thought he'd let tears come, but there were none. Just an awful stillness. So he puttered, pretended to have things to do, and when he came back in an hour and found her asleep on the hot seat, he carried her inside and put her to bed.

SCREEN THREE

The girl appears, hair in Comanche braids, wild-animal look in her eyes. She has come early to their camp across the river. For what – to see the boy, to watch them, to kill them. After ten years, she is not the girl they had known. Lived longer among Comanche than among her own. The older man hates her for what she has become, the concubine of the one who massacred his brother's family. His hand goes to his gun. He has made no secret of his hatred to the boy, now a man, who somehow clings to the idea that she is still the girl of eight who was taken.

His fingers curl around the handle of his pistol. Her body leans forward, eyes aflame with hatred or simply acquired wildness, and in the moment he allows himself to hesitate, to consider that somehow once this was his brother's child, she turns and runs.

His battle-battered body lumbers after her, a bear to her doe. And then the boy-man is up, calling to him – *Stop*. Calling to her.

Down one hill. Up another. A wake of dust behind them. A slippery slope. Near the crest, she falls, and he is on her. Over her. Then she's up. She wrestles to escape, arms flailing. He throws her down. Draws his gun.

The boy's voice, a single word like thunder. "No –"

Again he hesitates, the three of them frozen in some crazy family portrait, bloodlines beating between them. And then his gaze softens, surrenders, and he picks her up. A way to subdue her, a way to cradle her in his arms.

The three figures approach the small farmhouse. Camera low to the ground. Grass waves in the breeze. The neighbors, the homesteaders who've waited these years for their return, emerge on the porch. As they near the house, the boy and girl walk faster, then break into a trot. They are all embraces when he – the searcher – arrives moments later.

Interior. The camera looks out through the darkened doorway as this hybrid family, this reunion, enters the house to celebrate. One by one they cross the threshold and disappear. Only he – the searcher – stops outside. No one turns to wonder after him. Perhaps they expect him to follow. Instead, he hovers there, framed through the doorway, half-turned toward the house, half toward the road that leads nowhere, anywhere. The camera lingers on him, the ambivalence of his stance. Neck bent, torso listing slightly to one side. You can almost feel his determination to stand tall, out of nothing more than habit.

*

Cole sits on the Winnebago steps. A skyful of stars. Inside, all is still, and he hopes imagines that Joanna sleeps while he keeps vigil. He shivers despite a warm breeze. She has not left the Winnebago in thirty-six hours, except a short visit – at his insistence – to the funeral home.

"Jo. They have to do something with the body."

"You go."

"It has to be you. You have to sign things."

"Cremate." She would not look at him. When he moved in front of her, she lowered her head.

"What do you want to do with the ashes?"

"I don't care."

"Jo, you have to —"

"He's gone. What difference does it make."

Now Cole waits for her to want something. He stares across at the refreshment stand, thinking he should walk over and check email. Five minutes, and he'd know if there was news from Hagen. Not tonight. Tonight he'll sit, ready, in case she needs him.

Joanna wakes from a dream. Anthony calling to her across a crowded train platform. Two sets of submerged tracks divided them. She searched the landing, trying to find stairs, a bridge, a way across. No one would help. Men women rushed past.

For two nights she has slept fitfully, an hour or two at a time. At first, she did not go outside, because Cole lurked on the steps, paced in the dirt. She'd wake to dull headaches and a dead weight. Finally, she pushed past his concerned face, his quiet questions. *are you alright? do you need anything?* She has walked Winnetka. She has stood beside her sculpture with a sledgehammer, intending to smash it. Stopped in mid-swing, struck only air.

Now, in the other bunk, Cole sleeps, his face peaceful as a child. She resists the urge to slap away that peace. She hates the abyss that has opened inside her. On the table are daisies from Gene. The smell anchors her. She pulls on gym shorts, tucks in her t-shirt and runs.

She runs hard and she runs south, runs with her teeth gritted until she can shake the feeling that her legs are coated in concrete. She runs through Woodland Hills, crosses Mulholland and leaves streetlights behind. No moon. A handful of stars. She winds through Topanga Canyon, the road so dark in places she can hardly see two strides in front of her.

There is an ache in her side. Whenever the pain eases, she picks up her pace. She runs through the urge to smash Cole, to smash his computer. She runs through a canyon of grief to find a rhythm. She runs not to escape pain, but to encode it in her body.

A dog barks, runs out of a driveway at her. A mongrel, teeth flashing. Blood beats against her temples. A surge of adrenaline. She slows, crosses the street, but the dog snaps beside her, at her heels.

She stops. Turns. Her breath coming fast.

The dog, forepaws planted, snarls.

Come on, she thinks. *To the death.*

She stares hard into the dog's brown eyes, her own feet planted, torso leaning forward. Locks her gaze until the dog shies, quiets and backs slowly away.

She runs the dark streets. Houses with no lights. Aches in her side, her legs, her head. She picks up the pace. She runs through Topanga until she can taste the ocean, feel the moist air on her arms. Then she gives in to the hurt, walks on blistering feet, sits on the sand and licks at the salt that runs freely down her face.

SCREEN NINE

Storm clouds in a late afternoon sky. Gunfighter in the saddle, ready to ride. Six-gun strapped to his side, barrel still warm. Sulfur hovers in the air. The boy's face is weary. Road-worn buckskin chafes at his wrists. He scratches there, and the backs of his hands.

"There's no going back from a killing," he says.

The camera pulls back to reveal the mother – tousled black hair, soiled work shirt, suspenders – standing on the wood plank sidewalk in front of the saloon where the dead bodies lay.

"Wait," she says. "This is wrong."

She looks for the director, the cinematographer. For someone to yell *Cut.*

A shot rings out. The boy puts a hand to his chest. There is blood.

She yells, "Wait."

She yells, "Cut!"

Another shot. She scans the scene for the director, but he is nowhere in sight.

Side by side with Max on his bench in his trailer. He has wrapped her in a wool blanket, his arm tight around her shoulders.

"Thanks for the flowers, Max."

His face strained. His bald skull like some drought-scourged landscape. "Glad you liked them. I grew them myself."

"You did not."

"Alright."

King lies at their feet. Max has made coffee, but neither of them has moved to pour any.

Joanna rocks slightly, and Max rocks with her.

"Max?"

"Yeah."

"I'm hot. Can I take the blanket off?"

270

"No."

Bright blue sky through the window.

"Everybody's being so accommodating. I can't breathe." The dog is so still, Joanna wonders if he's sick. "Really, Max. I'm sweating."

"Okay." He helps her shed the blanket. It falls to the floor, where King paws at it half-heartedly. She pulls Max's arm back around her.

"What am I gonna do, Max?"

"Same as ever, I suppose. The best you can."

Although it's a warm day, the dog has crawled onto the blanket. She finds it's good to be with someone. She finds that numbness is a blessing, a cushion against the chasm that opens inside.

A handful of letters arrived somehow. A few bunches of flowers. Anonymous sympathy that materialized at their doorstep. Joanna had no idea how it got there. She just wanted it to go away.

"You take care of it," she asked Cole.

She kept to herself. Spent her time in the Winnebago, or took the car and returned hours later. She kept their interactions mundane – *do we need anything? do you want the car?* Sometimes, he'd try to inch deeper.

"Jo, I'm sorry."

She poured herself a glass of juice. "Yeah. Me too."

"There's nothing you could –"

"Leave it." She turned her back to him.

"We've got time, Jo. We'll take it slow."

"I'm thinking about going to Mexico." She stood at the small sink. Stared out the window.

"We could do that," Cole said.

"I'm thinking alone." She didn't move. Just stood there until Cole got uncomfortable and went outside.

A few days later. Cole walks the garden path with Victoria, holding a spray of black-eyed susans she has brought.

"I've always liked these. They're like mini-sunflowers."

"I'm glad." Underneath all the silver hoops in her right ear is a tiny angel. She wears black shorts. Leather sandals. "Eric says to tell you he's thinking of you both."

They walk past a pile Cole has made of flowers and letters. A quartz stone as paperweight.

They leave the garden, walk in the shadow of the refreshment stand.

"How long you been wearing that shirt?" she says. "We're talking days, not hours, right?"

It's a nice shirt. A shirt with a collar. "I don't know."

"Maybe you should get out of here for a bit. Wanna go bowling? Get some food?"

"I can't."

They circle the building. Victoria's braids flop back and forth.

"What are you going to do, Cole?"

"I'm going to help Jo get through this."

"That's not what I mean."

"I know what you mean. "

They sit on the dirt in the shade. Sun has burned through morning haze. "Don't you think it's a little scary that St. Martin has disappeared?" She has perfect toes.

"Only if I think about it." But he hasn't. Nor has he thought about Hagen. He should check email. Push the deal through and disappear himself.

"Cole, I won't do this."

"Do what?"

Victoria stops. Car keys in hand. The angel in her ear catches the sun. "This whole gunslinger showdown you seem determined to play out. It can't end well."

He knows he should say something, but what. It's complicated, and he doesn't feel like explaining himself. Or know if he could. She watches her fingers trace the outline of the key. Then she's moving toward her car. "Don't be an asshole," she calls over her shoulder.

Sun everywhere. He watches her feet recede. Just once, he'd like to be the one to walk away.

"I'm so sorry."

The girl stands at the Winnebago's screen door. Straight brown hair flat against her head. Brown eyeglasses. Inquisitive face.

Joanna looks out at her. "Go away."

"You're Joanna?"

"Yeah."

"I'm March. Like the month."

"Congratulations."

"Anthony didn't tell you about me."

A catch in Joanna's throat. She rests a hand on the door frame. Looks more closely at this girl. Eager eyes. Thin lips. How she'd be beautiful when she smiled. "The friendship bracelet."

"That's me."

"I didn't get details. We didn't have time."

The girl lowers her head. "Can I sit?"

Curiosity battles the desire to stay numb. "Help yourself."

She does. The girl's face has the swollen, red-rimmed eyes that come from prolonged crying. It hadn't occurred to Joanna that anyone else might be missing Anthony.

She pushes through the door, parks herself beside the girl.

The girl picks at frayed threads on her jeans. "I left flowers. A poem."

"I've been a little preoccupied," Joanna says. She tries to focus on the furthest row of speaker poles.

The girl wraps her arms around her knees. Scooches into a ball. "Wild place you got here."

The whoosh of cars somewhere. Dust and scrub. The way plants cling to life.

Her eyes study Joanna. "I can't believe he's gone."

"Yeah, well." Joanna has no sense of day or time beyond what she can see. It is light. The sun is out. That this girl would show up here, think she has any claim on Joanna. Any claim on grief. "Do you squint because you can't see well, or is it some affected teenage thing?"

The girl keeps looking at her. Deep brown eyes.

"We met in Boulder," the girl says. "Hooked up pretty much right away. We'd meet at the mall, a coffee shop. Somewhere every day." She smiles, and she *is* beautiful. A spot of red on each cheek.

Anthony's best friend for a time had been a neighborhood girl named Bridget. When he was ten. Joanna would try to picture them together at fifteen, sixteen.

The girl's voice. "I wanted so much to meet you. Now I'm not sure why. You're not like he said. He said you were nice."

A trace of smile crosses Joanna's face. She had often imagined the moment when she would first meet an Anthony girlfriend. How they'd get along. What they'd talk about.

"He could have been a botanist. He was great with plants. Or like a park ranger, riding a horse around some urban nature preserve. Kids asking him questions, him knowing the answers. *'This one? Right here? Long-leaf pine.'*" The inflection is pure Anthony.

Joanna wishes she had a cigarette. A full-body pillow. "So what do you want to be?"

"How do I know. I'm seventeen. I want Anthony back."

She tries to imagine this girl with him. Eating breakfast. Holding hands.

Joanna can't remember seventeen, but she's sure it must be tough enough without big brown glasses. "You ever think about contacts?"

March puffs her cheeks. Lets the air out. "You ever think about easing up?" She pushes the glasses higher on her nose.

How they would sit together. Lives intertwining. Sleepy-eyed stories over early-morning coffee. A sense of family, extended.

"He'd get into political arguments with my Dad. Dad kept trying to tell him he had too much compassion to be an anarchist."

Joanna raises her fingers to her lips, intending to smoke, but there's no cigarette. "Your parents know you're here?"

"My dad. Yes."

Hazy sun bakes the hard ground. It will be a dry year.

"Look. You're a nice girl and all, but —"

"We went hiking one time. Me and Dad and Anthony. At the end, looping back near the trail head, we skirted this farmer's land, across a field to get to the car. There was a goat in a pen, a wood rail fence. We start across the field, the goat's bleating, next thing we know, this goat falls into step beside Anthony. Like it was his lost pet. Three times we got it back inside the fence, three times it busted out and came to him. We finally had to pull the car to the edge of the field, Dad and I, then have Anthony make a run for it before the goat got loose again."

Joanna can see it happening. How Anthony would have reveled. Claimed he had this magical effect on animals. She finds herself covering the girl's hand with her own. Surprised at how old her fingers look. She looks out at the rows of speaker poles. If she could turn a knob. Hear his voice. "Somehow I imagined meeting his girlfriend under different circumstances."

March laughs. Her cheeks flush. "I know what you mean." She bites her lip. Threads her fingers in between Joanna's. "It's cool here. Can I come back sometime when we're not so sad?"

Joanna reaches an arm out, catches the girl in a hug. She is falling and cushioned at the same time.

The sun sinks into purple-tinged clouds as Cole walks from the refreshment stand. The air is humid. His mind clouded. He has just checked email.

Cole –
Let's do it.
I need a few days to build a history
and set up your account.
— Art

He stared at the words on the screen. Waited to feel the thrill of victory.

Joanna is on the Winnebago steps. A cigarette burns in her hand. "It's time," she says.

He stops before her. Nods vaguely. "Yeah?"

Her eyes shadowed. Hair askew. She looks out on Winnetka and smokes. "Don't you just wish it would rain?" She stares into the distance. Haze, but no clouds. Dirt hills and brown grass stretch to a horizon not far enough away. "She's a good kid. I want to do this while she's here."

The ashes. He sits beside her on the steps. Wonders if the girl will be part of whatever comes next for Joanna.

Smoke curls in the air. "I'm going to need you."

"I'm here."

She puffs her cigarette. Blows smoke.

They drive to Pacific Palisades, to a spot on PCH where the road looms high above the sea, near the place where Joanna and Cole first reached the country's edge.

Joanna holds the urn, a simple ceramic affair. They get out of the Squareback, a ragtag quartet in sunglasses and jeans. Walk the narrow dirt path to the edge, a steep slope to the water.

Cole. March. Max.

Joanna supports the urn with one hand underneath. Faces her companions, her back to the water. A daisy tucked behind her ear. "Don't know what to say." It feels like a show they are performing without an audience. Without a script. Max stares at the ground. Cole's hand on Joanna's shoulder.

A breeze ruffles the grass. She looks at the girl. "You have anything you want to say?"

The wind blows brown hair in swirls around her face. "No way."

She touches the girl's shoulder. She wants to tell her everything she is feeling – how the world is irretrievably broken, how she is grateful that Anthony lived, how it's okay to hurt, just as it's okay to be happy, even there right then, to enjoy the sun the air the people even if you don't understand how you came to be on this precipice holding a jar of ashes that used to be your son.

She closes her eyes. Listens to the sound of the waves. "He was never at home in this life. Couldn't – wasn't willing to – make himself fit. I loved him." She remembers something she heard somewhere about the human heart: how it only grows strong when you let it be broken. She takes the lid off the urn, scoops handfuls of ash, waves them into the air as if they are magic dust that could right the world's wrongs.

Anthony drawing elaborate castles with sidewalk chalk. Anthony running zigzag across the street in the early morning mist, in and out of her rearview mirror, flinging newspapers onto lawns.

Ash swirls in the air. Drifts toward the ocean. North and south along the coast. Dusts back toward them, so that as they walk to the car, she has the sense that they each carry a trace of Anthony, that he will linger in their midst.

They take March to the airport. Joanna walks her to the gate.

"Well," the girl says. She fiddles with the strap on her backpack. "Nice meeting you and all."

Joanna puts an arm around her. "Come visit," she says. "Soon."

Cole and Joanna sit under a blue Winnetka sky.

High noon.

Cole in a lawn chair beside the Winnebago. Joanna in the dirt, leaning against the front wheel well. Inertia the order of the day, and the day before.

Midday heat. All dust and sunshine. Cole can taste it. He's restless. "I'm thinking road trip," he says. "The In 'n' Out Burger in Simi Valley, the A&W in Fillmore."

Joanna shakes her head. "Not me."

"Come on, Jo. It'll do you good." To get her doing something. Anything. "My treat."

But she's not listening. His eyes follow hers out toward the rise, toward the road.

A black hat appears, disappears, reappears. Then a body. St. Martin. Black polo shirt. Black linen pants. Black fedora.

"Shit," Cole says.

Joanna stares into the distance.

St. Martin clears his throat. Removes his hat. Holds it over his chest. The sun a distant spotlight in an azure sky. He looks from Cole to Joanna. "I'm sorry for your loss."

Cole paralyzed. Yoga breathing. *He came to pay his respects. To say goodbye.*

The sun has baked Joanna dry. She nods. "You'll excuse me," she says. "I need to puke." She wipes dust from her jeans. Goes inside.

St. Martin lowers his head, raises it. Squints at Cole.

"It's over, Cole." His fingers play with his hat brim. "I've got witnesses who'll place you at the Atomic Café. Records of the time you logged on the computer. Reconstructed files from your Z-Tech machine."

"You can't."

"It's not perfect, but it's enough."

Fuck. Not now. Cole scoots to the edge of his seat. The chair creaks.

A distant hum of traffic. The call of a whippoorwill.

"Warren really has a bug up his ass about you."

Ten movie screens focus all the light in the world on this patch of ground. He hasn't come all this way just to be undone.

Cole pushes to his feet. "Listen." He stares at the detective. "I've got an idea." Not really. More of a glimmer. Something just starting to take shape.

Cole and St. Martin face each other in the dust.

St. Martin's voice quiet, clear. "Yeah? What's that?"

He hears St. Martin, but he's seeing Joanna, at the Palisades. How she stared at him in a way that unnerved him. How he watched blame – hatred – flare then fade in her eyes. How her voice, when she spoke, came quiet. Kind. Her hand on his chest. *Enough.*

"How about you let me go?" Okay, a little blunt, but he's improvising. "No one's better off with me in prison."

A hint of a smile. "Just let you walk."

"Yeah. Something like that."

"Now why would I do that?"

Because you like me. Because she needs me. "Because you believe in second chances. Because you want to do some real good in the world, and there aren't many opportunities." *Because there's been enough blood shed.* "Because you're interested in justice more than punishment, and while I would argue there's more than one take on justice in this situation, I know you'd agree justice would be done if Z-Tech got the completed program. *My* program." Cole's mouth dry. He studies St. Martin through Tombstone sunglasses. In the harsh light, with everything exposed, he's beginning to see. "So take it. Take the computer. Take the disks and the passwords and the server codes and files. Take it all. Give it to them. Tell them you got the machine and the work, but that I slipped out the back door. Then let me do it."

Now St. Martin's face wears a broad grin. He shakes his head. "I'll disappear."

The sun is blinding. St. Martin puts the fedora back on. Adjusts the fit. "Let's assume for the moment I play along. Why?"

"Because it doesn't matter anymore." It's only as Cole says it – only in hearing his own words – that he realizes it's true. That Joanna was right. It should have been him. But it wasn't, and he can't change that.

"It's great work," he tells the detective. "Beautiful. Far better than what they'll have." There are challenges here. Help Joanna. Figure out how to build a life. It doesn't have to be too late. His history, his choices now staring him in the face, what he can finally see, while there is maybe still a chance to keep from pissing everything away: the work is just ash in the wind, and what matters is – *oy, fuck* – human relationship. Friendship. Love. He laughs. He can't help himself.

St. Martin's grin has been replaced by something that might be a smirk, or might not. "You're a piece of work."

It doesn't seem to be a question, so Cole doesn't respond. He wonders if Joanna is really inside retching.

St. Martin's voice. "You ever make this kind of choice before, Cole?"

"Which kind?"

"The kind that shows character."

He purses his lips. Ponders. "I don't believe so, no."

"Why should I trust you now?"

Cole thinks, *I could have sealed the deal two days ago and been in Mexico.* And while that's true, it's not the point. He shakes his head. "No reason."

Relentless sun. No shadows.

St. Martin might be looking at Cole, or he might be studying the dun-colored hills in the distance.

The air is still.

"No one in this business hears from you again. Ever."

Cole squirms inside, nods slowly.

"If you fuck with me, you know I'll find you."

Cole slides the sunglasses down the bridge of his nose. The light blinds him. "I understand."

"Get the computer, Cole."

Late afternoon. Long shadows. A ring of haze surrounds the hills.

Joanna sits shaded beside the Winnebago wheel well. Knees tucked toward her chest. She speaks without looking up. "I know this quiet spot in Mexico. I can rent a house. Take it easy."

"Take the Squareback," Cole says. "I'll help you pack. Pick up anything you might need." Fisted hands in jeans pockets, he concentrates on what he can feel. Feet touching ground. A caring bigger than his own need.

She nods. "I might be gone a while."

Swallow. "It's okay. I'm not going anywhere." He's eager to try himself, to find out what he's capable of. Buy a car. Visit Max. Make things right again with Victoria. In the garden, she'd encouraged him. *Send me postcards from a foreign land. Bring me back something.*

"You should take a trip. Go to Canada. Vancouver."

"Maybe. I wanna work on the garden. Expand it."

"You have any idea how lucky you are?" She extends her legs, reaching her feet out of shadow into sunlight. "And how utterly undeserving?"

"I do." A hint of breeze. "Mexico, huh?" His voice soft. "You'll need supplies. Cokes. Tortilla chips. Tapioca pudding."

They have the car packed within the hour. Sleeping bag. Books. Food. Clothing. Joanna shuts the Winnebago door. They walk side by side to the Squareback. The sun hovers atop the foothills.

Three hours with St. Martin. Showing him files and passwords. Waiting while he had Archer validate the code.

"If you're fucking with me," St. Martin repeating.

"*I know.*"

Now a bright band of orange light glows at the horizon. Joanna climbs into the car. Rolls down the windows. Cole leans down to her. Rests his forearms against the door frame.

"Tell me again what you're gonna do," she says. Brown t-shirt. Tombstone sunglasses.

"Visit. Read. Think." A hint of breeze. "Probably get a car. Maybe one that needs work. Tinker with it."

"You're scaring me."

"Shut up."

She turns the ignition. The motor hums. "I wasn't sure you had it in you."

"I'm still not sure I do." His arms vibrate to the pulse of the engine.

"I'm proud of you, Cole."

"Don't say that. It sounds final."

"Don't worry." She looks out the windshield, then back at him. "Ride with me to the gate?"

They make a loop around the grounds, move slowly along the rows, past speaker poles and behind the refreshment stand, where Cole first met Gene.

"You think he'll come back?"

Joanna looks at him over the tops of her sunglasses. "Gene? Like he's going to live in some bungalow in Studio City."

"Things change. He's got a record contract."

She shakes her head. "He'll be back."

"I figured we'd have heard from him."

"We did," she says. "He left flowers. A note."

"You didn't tell me."

"Didn't want to. I was mad."

Joanna guides the Squareback across a drive-in row and points the car toward the entrance. Stops.

Cole climbs out. Shuts his door. Walks slowly around to her side. "I've got an idea. When you get back, we see what it would take to buy this place."

"No promises, Cole, No guarantees."

"I'm just saying. Pool our resources. Gene will have all that record company money – what's he going to do with it?"

She grins.

"Don't say anything now," he says. "Just think on it."

"Okay."

They clasp hands. Fingers interlaced.

"Hey," Cole says. "You know how to get there and all?"

She takes her hand back. Slides the sunglasses on top of her head. "South, right?"

"Right."

Joanna puts the car in gear, rolls slowly toward the entrance. Cracked pavement and weeds. The ticket booth. The car rocks and bounces. Dust rises behind it.

Orange-purple light haloes the hills. Happiness, Cole thinks, is a fickle thing.

Somewhere a guitar plays softly, and a familiar voice sings:

Move along, blue shadows, move along
soon the dawn will come, and you'll be on your way.

But until the darkness sheds its veil,
there'll be blue shadows on the trail.

Behind Cole, heat shimmers in the distance as the sun fades below the foothills.

ACKNOWLEDGEMENTS

I couldn't have written this without the love, support, hazing, and laughter of friends. You know who you are. Thanks for believing.

Special thanks to the Boys, and to the members of the Supper Club. Your encouragement is sustenance.

Finally, this is for Barb and Megan, who make everything brighter, more alive, more satisfying.

Many thanks for the inspiration gained from the following sources:

Songs:
"Back in the Saddle Again," words and music by Gene Autry and Ray Whitley © 1940 (renewed) Western Music Publishing Co. (ASCAP).

"Blue Shadows on the Trail," music by Eliot Daniel, lyrics by Johnny Lange © 1946 Walt Disney Music Co. (renewed).

"Cowboy's Lament," traditional.

"Don't Fence Me In," words and music by Cole Porter © 1952 Warner Brothers Inc.

"El Paso," words and music by Marty Robbins © 1959 (renewed), Mariposa Music.

"Happy Trails," words and music by Dale Evans © 1951, 1952 Paramount-Roy Rogers Music Co. Inc. (ASCAP) Copyright renewed 1979, 80 and assigned to Paramount-Roy Rogers Music Co. Inc.

"High Noon," words by Ned Washington, music by Dimitri Tiomkin © 1952 Leo Feist, Inc. (ASCAP), copyright renewed 1980 Volta Music Corp./Mrs. Ned Washington/Mrs. Catherine Hinen (ASCAP).